USA TODAY BESTSELLING AUTHOR

DALE MAYER

DESIGNS TRILOGY

BOOKS 1-3 OF THE DESIGN TRILOGY

DESIGN TRILOGY
Beverly Dale Mayer
Valley Publishing Ltd.
Copyright © 2013

ISBN: 978-1-988315-77-5
Print Edition

About This Boxed Set

Dangerous Designs

Drawing is her world...but when her new pencil comes alive, it's his world too.

Her... Storey Dalton is seventeen and now boyfriendless after being dumped via Facebook. Drawing is her escape. It's like as soon as she gets down one image, a dozen more are pressing in on her. Then she realizes her pictures are almost drawing themselves...or is it that her new pencil is alive?

Him... Eric Jordan is a new Ranger and the only son of the Councilman to his world. He's crossed the veil between dimensions to retrieve a lost stylus. But Storey is already experimenting with her new pencil and what her drawings can do – like open portals.

It... The stylus is a soul-bound intelligence from Eric's dimension on Earth and uses Storey's unsuspecting mind to seek its way home, giving her an unbelievable power. She unwittingly opens a third dimension, one that held a dangerous predatory species banished from Eric's world centuries ago, releasing these animals into both dimensions.

Them... Once in Eric's homeland, Storey is blamed for the calamity sentenced to death. When she escapes, Eric is ordered to bring her back or face that same death penalty. With nothing to lose, can they work together across dimensions to save both their worlds?

Deadly Designs

Drawing is her world…but when she's banished to a deadly new world and needs help, it's his world too.

Her… Storey Dalton wants to go home – but something goes terrifyingly wrong and she ends up in her worst nightmare. There's no escape…not without Eric or her stylus. Then she finds someone who needs rescuing even more than she does…

Him… Eric Jordan races to save Storey, only to realize a close family member has betrayed them both. Now the enemy is closing in on him. When he meets up with Storey, he knows her plans are a bad idea, but she won't be dissuaded…and it could be their only way of staying alive.

It… The stylus, now bonded to Storey's artistic soul, is determined to survive this new chaos – against all odds. But damaged from a prolonged separation, he can't help Story or Eric – without making things worse.

Them… Storey is determined to make things right. Eric is determined to help her. Neither counts the personal cost, until their very lives are in danger.

Darkest Designs

Drawing is her world…but when she's pushed into the In-Between and thought lost forever, it's his world too.

Her… Storey doesn't want to become a living dead lost In-between. She thought she'd known the worst that could happen…but she wasn't even close. ey Dalton wants her life back. Her home back. Her world back. The way they were before she messed with time. She does not want.

Him… Eric thought he'd seen the worst that his father could do…but he hadn't…unfortunately. Heartbroken and panicked, Eric tracks Storey to the misty dead space – and follows her in. There is a way out – but not a way that anyone would willingly choose.

It… The stylus has no way to help with Storey's latest predicament. But survival is paramount. Only this time it can't do it alone. There might be help available…if they can save someone else…first.

Them… Storey wants to save her world. Eric wants to save Storey. The stylus wants them to save someone else. But can anyone save them all?

Sign up to be notified of all Dale's releases here!
https://geni.us/DaleNews

Dangerous Designs

(Book 1 of Design Series)

Dale Mayer

Dedication

This book is dedicated to my daughter Kara, who asked me to write books for her. Dangerous Designs is the third young adult series I have started for her.

Enjoy!

Acknowledgments

Dangerous Designs wouldn't have been possible without the support of my friends and family. Many hands helped with proofreading, editing, and beta reading to make this book come together. I had a vision, but it took many people to make that vision real.

I thank you all

CHAPTER 1

SOME DAYS JUST sucked. Then there was today – with a whole new level of bad. Storey Dalton, sixteen, was now boyfriendless.

Jeff had moved away from Bankhead six months ago, but in her mind, they were still a couple – until his Facebook message this morning. Like what was she supposed to do with that? He had a new girlfriend and wanted her to be happy for him. She stomped a hapless weed in front of her. The girl's name was Pam. Who called their kid Pam? Sounded like her mother's cooking spray.

The sun shone down so brightly its reflection off the creek blinded her. And of course she'd forgotten her sunglasses. Swearing, she headed to the shady side of the path through the woods where the poplars grew tall and straight. Halfway to school meant halfway to nowhere today.

Jeff had been her best friend first, and then finally her boyfriend. But only for the last couple of months. They'd no sooner made that magical development in their relationship when she found out his family was moving. So what if they were apart? Wasn't true love supposed to survive everything? Even she couldn't hold back a snicker at that thought. *True love my ass.* The only truth here was that Jeff was no longer hers. She could spit she was so mad.

She kicked at a rock in her way, then kicked it again when her first attempt failed to make it move. Just like her life. The town of Bankhead was dying. The mine had closed, and everyone cute or interesting had moved away. The place was a ghost town. There were less than a couple of hundred kids in school now. And that covered all twelve grades.

Her prospects weren't looking too bright at finding a replacement boyfriend. Tall and slim to the point of being almost skinny, she wasn't exactly a raving beauty – all elbows and knees. Jeff had called her unique, an artist with an interesting perspective on life.

She pulled her leg back and lashed out at a bigger rock – hard. *Damn, that felt good.* Grinning, she went a little wild and kicked the shit out of a good half dozen stones. Reveling in the solid slap against her foot and the hefty force she could apply, Storey struck out at life, her lack of friends, and most of all at her current boyfriendless state.

The last kick did it. A pressure gauge in her chest released and she laughed as the weight slid off her shoulders. "He's found someone else, fine. So will I. So it may not be today or tomorrow, but I'll find someone too."

As she passed another big rock she seriously thought about giving it a good whack, when a glint beside it caught her eye.

A pencil. She grinned in delight. She loved pencils. Had a shoebox full in her bedroom. Picking it up, she brushed some loose dirt off. Unusually flat with a well-loved look to it, the bare nub of lead showing spoke to the artist in her. "Cool. We're a well-matched pair. Both tossed away by those we love." With a sense of kinship, she zipped it safely into the side pocket of her backpack and headed off to school.

THREE DAYS LATER Storey had had it with Bankhead High School, her supposed friends, and especially her teachers. They weren't horrible. They were worse – at least today when any and all distractions were unacceptable.

Couldn't they see she was busy?

Her artwork demanded her attention.

"Storey, please stay after school so we can talk, again," said Mr. Madison, the history teacher.

A twitter rippled through the room. Storey ignored him, flicking a look of disgust to the room in general; she refocused on the design she had to get down. She called them doodles. Other people called them freaky. Not that she cared. She'd been drawing since she could hold a pencil. She wasn't about to stop now.

She couldn't. In a small corner of her mind, she knew that wasn't normal. That same corner of her mind knew this drive, this insane need to draw above all else was seriously wrong.

But it didn't matter.

With a toss of her shoulder-length hair, she bent her head to deepen the inside edge of a curlicue.

She heard the teacher's heavy, long suffering sigh. "All right, everyone. Read over the next chapter and do the first ten questions for practice. We'll go over the answers tomorrow. Class dismissed. Except for Storey."

Damn. She glanced up quickly, caught the smirks of the kids walking by. She needed just a few more moments. The pencil warmed in her hand. She quickly readjusted her grip and sketched faster. The amused looks in her direction didn't deserve acknowledgement.

The room emptied in a crush of movement and excited chatter until only silence filled the room – and the scratch of her pencil.

Mr. Madison strode down the aisle of desks until he stood before her. His hands burrowed deep in his pockets as he rocked on his heels. "Storey," he snapped. "Put down that pencil and talk to me."

Disgusted, Storey tossed the pencil down and slouched back so she could see him. Tall, almost droopy, his normally placid face had pulled in on itself as if a lemon had been shoved inside. Wrinkles furrowed his brow as he glowered down at her behind his seriously thick glasses.

"You've been in my class for six weeks. You hand in all your assignments and you did well on your test. You're often distracted, but these last few days…I just don't get it. It's like you're off in your own little world." Frustration twisted his face tighter. Storey watched in fascination as the skin folds expanded then folded back up as he spoke again. "Why can't you pay attention?"

This again. She shook her head. "I can't. That's why I draw." Irritation took over. "I've already told you that. I have trouble focusing." Closing her book with a snap, she stood up only then seeing she'd already picked the pencil up again and was doodling on her fingers. Weird. The pencil marks shouldn't show up on her skin. She glanced up at her teacher. "It's not just your class. It's all my classes."

His shoulders slumped and some of the anger drained from his voice. "Have you spoken to a doctor about this?"

"I've been on every kind of drug there is since first grade. Nothing has worked. Now I don't take anything. What's the point? I have two years to go, then it won't be a problem anymore." She bent down, grabbed her backpack and put away her sketchbook and homework. Straightening, she stood up and waited to see if he had anything to add.

"You have a future. You're smart, a hard worker, at least in the short term, but don't you want to do more – be more?"

His words haunted her long after she'd walked out of the building.

"Of course, I want more, damn it. Who doesn't?" she said to the empty sidewalk. But who could think about the future when the present was such a mess? Sure, she had her mother, somewhat. She had no siblings, for which she was both sad and grateful at the same time. They would have been company, except then they'd be in her same situation, and she wouldn't wish that on anyone. Who'd want to be the kid of the poor single mom despised by the rest of the community? It's not that she thought there was anything wrong with her mother's choices, but being a practicing Wiccan and owning and running a small candle shop in a redneck town like this one, well…not fun.

She kinda liked the emptiness of the skeleton community left at Bankhead. Except for the limited options in friends and boyfriends, of course. The traffic was calm, there were no lines at any of the stores, and nothing bad ever happened. Of course, nothing good ever happened, either.

She picked up her pace and managed to cut her trip home by half. Her latest doodle had its claws into her. True, that was an odd way to describe this gnawing inside to draw, but it felt right. After finishing a picture, she usually experienced an incredible sense of satisfaction and release. That part felt good, the actual creation part – not so much. These last few days, there'd been no satisfaction. In fact, the process had been so much worse. Past driven. Tormented might be a better term.

Her mother believed she'd outgrow her weird doodles and become a real artist eventually. A large rock went flying into the creek at her side as she contemplated that concept. How did you outgrow something that was a major part of yourself? It's not like she could outgrow a leg, or her hands. They were just as much an integral part of who she was as this compulsion to draw. An urge that had gotten much worse lately. A fact that was starting to make her seriously uneasy. Being an artist was fine with her, being obsessive about it – not so much.

"Hey, Storey?"

Storey spun around but continued to walk backwards. A tall man in black was walking up behind her. She frowned and reassessed her first impression. Not a man, a teen on the brink of adulthood. And one oddly familiar. Right. He was the new kid at school, a rare enough event that it caught even her attention. She'd caught a glimpse of him in the morning, navigating through the hallways. Tall and slim, dressed in black from top to toe, even his short hair matched, giving his white skin a bleached look in contrast. He'd make a perfect vampire.

She couldn't help but smile. "Hi." For the life of her she couldn't remember his name. Her eyes locked on his square jaw, deep forehead and blazing blue eyes. His face would be hard to forget.

A lopsided grin slipped out, fascinating her.

"I'm Eric. You probably don't remember me. I just started at school today." He fell into step as she continued on her way.

"This is your first day and you know *my* name."

"I recognized a fellow artist in the first class we shared and…" His smile deepened. "Your name would be hard *not* to know after the number of times I heard a teacher call it out today."

"Oh." Heat crawled up her face. Her stride stretched out, making him increase his pace to keep up.

"Sorry. Didn't mean to upset you."

Surprised, she shot him a quick sideways glance. "You didn't. Everyone knows I spend most of my time caught up in my art. Getting yelled at is no big deal."

The same grin flowed in her direction. She watched, captivated at how his face changed with his moods. Her fingers itched for pencil and paper. His voice was striking too, gravelly with a sense of humor lurking just beneath the surface.

"What? Am I wearing my lunch on my face or something?" He swiped his chin self-consciously.

Her eyes widened. "Sorry. I didn't mean to stare," she muttered and walked even faster.

"Hey slow down, we're not racing anywhere. And you're tall, but I'm taller."

Confused, she slowed down, sliding a sideways glance his way. "What does height have to do with it?"

"That I can walk as fast as you, I just don't want to."

Yeah, he was weird. "You don't have to walk with me at all." She couldn't help but point that out. Give him a chance to beg off and go his own way. It was kind of hard to believe he was still there in the first place.

"I know. I want to."

She snorted. "And why would you want to do that?"

"Because I like your artwork. It's unique, dark."

This time there was no holding back the look of disbelief. "And you like dark art?"

"Yup. It's cool." They came to a corner. "This is where I turn off. I live just down there." In spite of herself, Storey looked in the direction he pointed. He lived close to the old mine. Not the most affluent area of town. Still, it wasn't loser city like where she lived.

"See you tomorrow." He waved and walked away.

Storey crossed the road, watching as his lanky frame disappeared in the distance.

What was that all about?

A horn blasted her. She jumped and spun around. Crap. She'd stopped in the middle of the intersection like a love-struck idiot. With an apologetic smile, she moved out of the way and finished the trip home in irate confusion. What the hell was going on with her these days?

Once inside, she stormed up to her room. Flinging her backpack onto her bed, she pulled out her sketchbook and her new pencil and threw herself down on her purple coverlet to stare at her latest drawing.

Cool. Dark. Unique. His words. There was nothing cool about it. Terrifying. Crazy. Disturbing. Any and all of those worked and so much more besides. She stuffed her newest pencil behind her ear and tried to see something that was good in the picture. Coiling, snake-like lines and lattice intertwined, showing an entrance of some kind, broken and abused, as if someone had pounded on it for a long time – and had given up.

Tucking the pencil into her fingers, she started shading the broken slat on the top corner. It didn't look quite right, yet. But how could she know? She'd never seen this place before.

Her subconscious spawned this stuff. Was she crazy? She felt like it most of the time. Lord knows, everyone else agreed. Except her mom. And Jeff had never appeared to notice. At least he'd never said anything about it to her.

Since he'd moved, she'd buried herself deeper into her sketches to help deal with the pain of his leaving and the loneliness she'd been left with. Only in these last few days had she'd realized just how deep she'd gone.

Her pencil shifted to shade the edges of the lattice on the right. Thickening it, darkening it, smoothing the top piece and dropping the bottom down lower. Time ceased to exist as she fine-lined and perfected the image.

"Storey? Are you in there?"

Storey reared back with a jerk, looking around to see her mother poke her head around the door.

"Hi, honey." Her mom pushed the door back and walked in, her long, metallic-orange dress swirling around her legs, her brown hair bouncing off her hips. "What are you doing?"

Draw. Storey. Draw.

"Nothing," her standard response to her mom's standard question.

"Oh, that's a nice picture."

Storey raised an eyebrow. Nice? That's the last thing it was. Typical of her mom though. "No Mom, it's not nice. It's not anything."

"Oh, honey. Don't be so hard on yourself. You'll work your way through all this. Soon you'll draw nice pictures."

Come, finish it. Draw, Storey, draw.

Storey closed her eyes and let her mother drone on. She would no matter what. Finally, she interrupted the flow by asking, "Did you want something?"

Her mom stopped, her mouth open, and cleared her throat. "Oh, yes – dinner's ready."

Opening her eyes again, Storey wrinkled up her face. "I'm not hungry."

"That's not fair." Her mother's voice changed, cajoled. "You don't even know what's for dinner."

"It doesn't matter." Storey rolled over to her belly and continued with her drawing. Her mother gave one of those heavy sighs she was so good at before withdrawing.

Come play with me, Storey.

Storey glared down at the artwork. "I'm here. I'm here. What do you want from me?"

Draw. Just draw.

Storey fell back under the creative spell.

CHAPTER 2

DURING SCHOOL THE next day, Storey struggled against exhaustion. She'd slept badly, having awakened over a dozen times. Her eyelids drooped. The teacher spoke, startling her awake. She straightened, blinking several times, her gaze instinctively dropping to her backpack on the floor and the sketchbook tucked inside. With a slight shudder, she returned her attention to the blackboard and the lesson of the day. She could survive this class. It shouldn't be that hard. She dropped her head backwards and groaned. The next two years stretched before her in dismal eternity.

"What are you drawing?"

Surprised, she twisted around to find Eric grinning at her from the seat behind hers.

"You're awake, I see."

She flushed and faced the front of the class. He wouldn't stop.

"I asked what you're drawing?"

"I'm not drawing anything," she muttered.

"Then what's that?" He nudged her right shoulder and pointed to the open page of the red binder in front of her.

Straightening in shock, she realized every inch of space on the paper crawled with pencil lines. She'd deliberately kept her sketchbook stuffed deep inside her backpack and still she'd found a way to keep at it – by filling up her notebook.

Ice settled in her belly.

Did this drive…this need to draw have such a strong hold on her that she couldn't *not* draw? That she did it when not realizing? Even on her skin, like on her fingers yesterday when there'd been no paper near? Was she that obsessed? If so, how had it happened? When? Had there been a specific point of no return?

"I like it. What is it?"

She had no idea. Storey studied the familiar looking scribbles. The markings had the same style, yet in no way resembled the full page drawing she'd done last night. Or did they? Frowning, she realized this picture could represent an enlargement of one corner of that other picture, incorporating her geography class notes into the design. She slammed her book shut.

"Hey? Why'd you do that?"

The teacher ended class at that moment. Storey jumped to her feet, snagging her backpack in one hand and notebook in the other before racing out of the room.

"Wait up!"

Eric's voice became lost in the crowd. Good. She hadn't planned on listening to it anyway.

THIS WAS AN easy job?

A simple job, Paxton had said to him and his father. "Go find the girl. Become friends with her, and if she has the stylus – retrieve it. Preferably, without her knowing. You're close to her age, so it should be easy to gain her confidence. The important thing is to bring the stylus home. Before the girl causes irreparable harm through her ignorance."

Eric Jordan had jumped at the opportunity, not giving his father, the Councilman, a chance to argue. Not that he would have. Eric had studied all he could, become the best Ranger he could be. Even more, he'd become an expert on the alternate dimension. Yet in all that time, he'd never been allowed to cross the veil that separated the two worlds. This was a great first assignment. How hard could it be?

Harder than he'd thought. Storey was turning out to be an interesting female. He'd been watching her for a couple of days now. He got along well with girls. They considered him friendly, caring, comfortable to talk to. What wasn't there to like? But if that were all true, why was this one so prickly? Then again, she was an otherworlder. That could account for the difference.

And he suspected she *did* have the lost instrument, making his mentor Paxton's guess correct. If her drawings were anything to go by, the stylus had started bonding already. Not good. The tool had been lost when a scientist had fallen ill on a rare research trip across the veil that divided the two dimensions. Soulbound items were special in his world. Important, coveted, and passed from one person to another only through death. They were also incredibly powerful. Not something to be left in the hands of a sixteen-year-old otherworld girl.

He watched as Storey bolted from the classroom as if demons were chasing her. Had that been fear tightening her fine-boned features as she'd studied at her artwork?

Why? She'd created it.

Or had she?

STOREY RAN STRAIGHT home. She burst through the front door and came to a skittering stop. Her mother's Wiccan friends were meeting in the living room. Great.

On the other hand, their presence gave her an excuse to hide away in her room and sort through these odd drawings. See if there was a connection in them. A message.

And that was just stupid.

"Storey. How nice to see you home early." Her mother, decked out in her ceremonial robes and her face covered in heavy paint, walked over. "Why don't you join us, sweetie?" She motioned toward her friends, all in full Wiccan gear. "We're going over the weekend's events."

It was all Storey could do not to wince. Giving the others a quick smile, she brushed past her mom. "No time. I have homework."

She raced up the stairs and into her room, slamming the door behind her. No wonder everyone thought she was odd. Look at her mother. She'd been shunned and taunted when younger. Now most of the other kids just crossed the road to avoid her. Then there were the whispers and sidelong looks. Odd how her relationship with Jeff had brought acceptance. Until he'd left.

Life had been normal until her father had walked out a decade ago, leaving her homemaker mom struggling to make a living. Her mother had been 'finding herself' ever since. The store and a new religion had been her answer. As much as Storey hated what it had done to her life, she understood that the candle shop had put food on the table all these years. The Wiccan part, not so much. Her mother held some rank on the Council and, of course, she dressed the part, even danced outside on full moons. Storey did not want to know if the group did it naked.

Some things were just too much information.

She pulled her sketchbook out of her backpack, then grabbed her red binder from class. She plunked down on her bed and flipped through the pages in both books. And stopped. Yes.

Leaning close, she studied the images. The newer one *was* an enlargement of the lower right hand corner of the bigger drawing, where she'd run out of paper. Odd how ancient the doorway in her pictures looked. She rarely drew anything medieval or historical looking and had no idea why she would have now. What did it mean?

Tracing the picture with her fingertips, she tried to understand why it was so important to sketch such detail. Her fingers moved slower and slower in a repetitive and oddly mesmerizing motion. She lost herself in the movement, feeling soothed and comforted by the knowledge that, if nothing else, she'd created this.

A tapping on the window drew her attention. The sun had gone behind a cloud. Even as she watched, rain pelted the glass, giving everything an oddly distorted look. Kind of matched her life right now. With a sigh she refocused on the large sketch.

She stopped. Then frowned. Had the picture changed? Shifted? Bending her head, she studied it closer, then shook her head. No. It was the same. At least she thought so. Anything else was so not possible. As she went to close her books, she paused again.

There. A new line. She studied the picture. She hadn't drawn it – or had she? Stupid, that's what this was. If she hadn't, who had? She had to have put it there. Tilting her head to look at it from another angle, she realized the line still wasn't quite right. She snatched up her pencil and thickened the left side of it, widening it on the bottom.

There, that was much better. It felt right.

Silly maybe, but the change made her happy.

She switched to staring at the weird enlarged picture she'd made in class today. With the geography notes underneath, it was irritating to look at. Within minutes, she had redrawn the picture into her sketchbook properly.

Now that she could see it more clearly, she realized it *was* an actual door of some kind. Not just a vague entrance-way. Now it had defined edges. Without a latch or knob, yet the right size and shape. She laughed at her imagination. So there was a door. Now wouldn't it be great if that meant she could just open the door and walk right through?

The last thing she did was add a flat, metal looking door handle to the right side.

Snick.

Storey glanced at her bedroom door. "Mom, is that you?" Her door was closed and stayed that way. More unnerved by her reaction than at the noise, Storey hopped up and checked to see if someone stood outside her room.

The hallway was empty. Laminate floors and red and gold painted walls stared back at her, remnants of the previous owners.

Closing her door on the horrible colors, Storey surveyed her own lemon and lavender room. So much easier on her eyes. The rain continued to hit the window, filling the room with a steady pounding. With everything as it should be, she sat back down on the bed and picked up her drawing.

And caught her breath. She'd put the handle in as a joke.

It was no joke now. The freaking door was open. She peered closer. At least she thought it was open. The edge of the door was now a thick black line hinting at a darkness on the other side.

She dropped the book on her bed and bolted to the far side of the room. She chewed her nails, not taking her eyes off her picture. The open door stared back at her.

An open door she hadn't drawn. She knew that. Still, she couldn't stop a quick glance at the pencil in her hand. Just in case. There was no way. Really? How could those couple of lines give off such an ominous vibe? With so much power? Chills rippled across her shoulders.

Inviting her? Warning her? Freaking her out – *hell yeah!*

Storey knew she wasn't that good an artist.

Could she be having blackouts? Momentary relief bloomed at the idea. Then she reached up and touched her temple. She didn't suffer from headaches. She hadn't been injured. As far as she knew, she was healthy.

How could the picture have changed without her or someone else changing it? And why? She studied the lines of the door. Flat, thick lined, almost needing something from her. Waiting for her to do something. But what?

It's not like she could walk through the thing. And even if she could, it's not like she would. Who knew what lay on the other side? A half chuckle escaped. Right. Now she *was* losing it.

Storey grimaced as she shoved the drawing deep inside her bag, then closed and tied up the outside straps as a deterrent. Determined, she grabbed her English reading assignment and focused on finishing her homework. When she couldn't keep her eyes open any longer, she dropped the book to the floor beside her, clicked off the light and fell into a deep sleep – a sleep full of weird dreams and strange voices calling to her.

Storey, come and get me.

Storey come.

We need you, Storey.

Disturbed, she bolted upright, gasping for breath. She stared wildly around the room. Who said that? No one. She was alone – and clearly losing it. Her heart banged in her chest. A film of sweat covered her skin. She took several deep breaths and tried to calm down. Talk about nightmares. She shuddered and lay back down. It took several minutes to get her breathing under control and when she did, she started to get pissed.

"What the hell do you want with me?" she snapped in the direction of her backpack and the drawing safely secured inside. "Crap. This is too freaky, even for me."

"Storey, is that you, honey?"

Her mother knocked on the door and pushed it open, the light from the hallway lighting the few silver strands in her otherwise brown hair. "Can't you sleep?"

"Sorry if I woke you." Storey sat up, brushing her own jet black hair back off her face. "Just a bad dream."

"That's because you didn't have any dinner. I checked up on you after the meeting finished. You'd fallen asleep." Her mother's fingers twisted around a dangling lock of hair as she stepped into the room. She bit her lip. "Storey, you have to eat. You're already skinny enough."

Bone rack is what a jock had called her last month. Looking down, Storey realized they could be right. Her hip bones stuck out to match her big elbows. And her body had developed to the point where she barely missed the skinny scarecrow look. Too bad. She might have been able to make that work.

"I'm eating, Mom. They had pizza in class today, so I didn't need my lunch. Ate that on the way home." That was a lie. Still, she had more important things to worry about than food.

Relief washed over her mom's pretty face. "Oh, I'm so glad to hear that. Sometimes I worry about you."

Sometimes? Didn't she mean all the time? Was that normal for moms? Then again, there was a world of difference between normal and her mother.

"What time is it?" Storey looked out the window. Blackness stared back.

"It's just a little after midnight. Please get into your pajamas. You don't want to be sleeping in those jeans." She backed up to the open door. "If you're all right, I'll say good night. It is witching hour, after all." With a carefree grin, her mom closed the door.

Witching hour. Right. Only in her house. Sighing at her mother's antics, Storey collapsed down on her covers and fell into a light, troubled sleep.

"Storey."

She sighed. "What now, Mom?"

No answer. She sat up and glanced at the closed door. Weird. She could've sworn she'd heard someone calling her. Lying down again, she pulled her blankets over top, not bothering to get changed into her nightclothes.

"Storey."

She bolted upright. *That's it.* Who the hell was playing games with her?

"Storey."

Throwing back the blankets, Storey knelt on her bed. "Who said that?" she hissed into the early morning air. Not trusting the gloomy light, she flicked her bedside lamp on, quickly scanning the room. Empty. "I am so losing it. This is nuts."

Her gaze landed on the backpack on her floor. Her eyes widened. *Oh no.*

"No, no. Hell, no." She shook her head, slowly at first then more wildly. "This can't be happening. It's a picture. Nothing more. Nothing less. I created you. I can destroy you."

That's exactly what she was going to do. She dragged the backpack onto her bed and opened it. The knot defied her first and second attempts, before she managed to pull the laces apart and yank out her sketchpad. "I don't know what's going on here, but enough is enough."

She flipped to the last page she'd been working on and grabbed it at the top left and pulled. It wouldn't tear off. She tightened her grip and tried again. It refused to budge. Scared now, she threw it on the floor and in a fit of defiance, she jumped on it.

And fell through the picture, through the floor even.

She went right through the doorway in her picture.

CHAPTER 3

AND LANDED IN complete nothingness.

Storey's knees buckled. She pitched forward, barely catching her balance, and froze. What just happened? Suffocating blackness surrounded her. No bed, no lamp, no floor even. No glimpse of the moon or the rising sun peeked through in any direction. Looking up, she searched for the broken planks of her floor or ceiling tiles from the basement. Something to prove she'd fallen through the bedroom floor.

There was nothing.

"Hello?" Silence. The first stirrings of panic slipped down her spine. Taking a deep breath, she struggled to stay calm, to understand. There was no easing of the unrelenting darkness in any direction. Somehow, she'd ended up in a pitch black, empty hole.

Her bedroom had disappeared. And this space had appeared. Her stomach threatened to spill its contents, bile climbing her throat. Her imagination couldn't help jumping from one wild scenario to the next, each worse than the one before. From thinking she'd fallen through the basement, to the idea of being caught between the floors – like, could you go in-between? She even considered that she might have tripped and fallen into a hidden store room.

She wasn't even going to consider that she might have been abducted by aliens.

This couldn't be happening.

Yet it had.

She swallowed. Then swallowed again. Closing her eyes for a moment, she struggled to remember what she'd done. The last thing she remembered was throwing that damned picture on the floor and jumping on it. On it? On the opening? Therefore on the doorway. And through it?

Her eyelids popped open.

Could she have jumped through a picture of a door as if it were a real exit? She shook her head as her mind stretched and reached the impossible conclusion.

And if she had…where was she now? Where did that strange passageway lead?

Wherever the hell she was, she'd damned well better find a way out. Once she realized her eyes couldn't adjust to the all-encompassing darkness, she reached out, her arms wide, hoping to find something solid. Her fingers twitched as her mind filled with thoughts of the many unpleasant things she could encounter. Spiders being the number one yucky critter in her world.

Nothing. She'd entered a space where she alone existed. Panic brought the acid in her stomach bubbling back up. This had to be a dream. A nightmare. She brightened. Maybe when she jumped on the sketchbook, she'd fallen and hit her head. Maybe she had a concussion? That had to be it. Eagerly she checked her head for blood, at minimum some tenderness.

Her skull was as thick-headed as she was. Storey groaned. "Please, someone," she cried out. "Is anyone out there?"

Eerie echoes went on forever.

She shuddered, the blackness threatening to suffocate her. She bent over and breathed once, twice, three times until the rapids in her stomach calmed down. As she stared down where her feet should be, it hit her. The floor was solid. Stomping to prove it, she crouched down to touch the surface. Hard, cold wood or maybe even tile supported her. It gave her hope.

Someone had built it. That meant people. Somewhere.

She had to have fallen into a storage space or something, a closet even. Okay, that would mean one huge-ass closet, but it was possible. She took one deliberate step. She stretched her arms forward. Still nothing. Bending down, she touched the ground and crabbed forward, her hands making sure there was something for her to stand on before taking the next step.

She continued for another ten steps. And stood up.

Was the darkness less cloying? She sniffed the air. Still bad, musty. She put out her hands again – still nothing. Fisting her hands on her hips, she stood and contemplated the situation. *What a piss off.* Where the hell was she? And as much as she'd like to understand how she'd gotten here, the priority was getting out.

And fast.

"WHAT IS SHE doing?" Eric tilted his head to study Storey's sideways crab imitation on the monitor in front of him, a frown crinkling his forehead. He'd rushed into the lab at Paxton's panicked call, only to come to a halt in front of the wall sized screen that showed Storey inside a crossing.

"I have no idea," Paxton retorted. "She wouldn't be doing even that, if you'd kept an eye on her."

"Hey," Eric protested. "That's not fair. You didn't even think she could *do* something like this. How was I to know?"

An irritated "Harrumph," from beside him was his only answer.

"So now what?"

"We watch."

Shooting a sideways glance at Paxton, Eric struggled not to scrunch up his face in disgust. "Uhm, isn't that a little mean?"

Paxton beetled his brows. "Mean? How are we going to know what she can do if we don't watch her and find out?"

"I don't think she has any idea of what she can do. Look at her. She's afraid she's going to run out of floor and fall off."

"And she might. If she'd created that."

The younger man gave him an incredulous look. "You can't possibly think she did this on purpose?"

"Right." Paxton shook his head in his far too familiar *I taught you better than that* way.

"Honest. I've spent days watching her. She's a good artist, yes, but she creates mindlessly"

"Then how did she create a portal?"

Eric paused and chose his next words carefully. "I think it's the stylus."

"What are you talking about?"

"I think it's bonding with her."

Complete shock rendered the old man silent. "Oh my. How is that possible? Do you know for sure that she has it? You've actually seen it in her hand?" He spun around to study Storey's movements in the tunnel. "It *can't* become soulbound to her. She's not one of us."

"I think I saw it. She wouldn't let me take a close look. This," Eric waved at the monitor, "proves it. It's the only way she could open a portal."

The older man shuddered. "This is not good."

"I'm assuming the stylus is trying to come home?"

At his mentor's gasping cough, Eric turned to stare at

the red splotches appearing on Paxton's face. "Are you okay?"

"No. No, I'm not," he snapped. "This is terrible. Something has to be done. She can't come here. She's one of *them*." He almost spat the last word.

And? Eric didn't see that they had a choice. The stylus had latched onto Storey and appeared to be coming home whether Paxton approved or not. In fact, according to the monitor, the two of them had almost made it.

Eric watched as Storey bent once more to the floor and crabbed her way forward. "We have to do something. This is painful to watch."

The older man pivoted. "This can't happen. That the stylus was lost in the first place is unacceptable. That one of those otherworlders should have picked it up is worse…that the stylus is accepting…even strengthening the bond is…" Paxton stopped talking, overcome by emotion. He pressed his trembling fingers against his temples.

"It might change things if we assist her, you know." Eric gestured at Storey. "Chances are, she'd appreciate the help."

A calculating look brightened Paxton's slate blue eyes. He rubbed his hands together. "Yes. Yes, that might work. She already knows you. You could cross over and let her out on *her* side of the veil."

Eric considered the logistics. "She hasn't exactly welcomed me so far. A rescue could do a lot to help that."

Paxton nodded. "She can't be allowed to find out the power of the stylus. Get it away from her."

"It might already be too late. If she's soulbound already, we can't separate them. You know that," he countered.

The old man wrung his hands as he considered the problem. "Certainly we can. We have to. The stylus is too powerful. Too dangerous. But first things first. Get her out of the crossing and retrieve the stylus."

Eric shook his head. "I'm not going to participate in anything that will cause her death."

Paxton straightened to his full height and stared down his long nose at Eric. "Then go. The longer the two are together, the harder it will be to separate them. Get the stylus now and she lives. Don't get it and she dies. Either way that stylus has to come home."

With that order, Eric adjusted his soulkey, tapped into his codex and shifted dimensions.

STOREY WAS BEYOND pissed and had jumped completely into terror. Something had gone majorly wrong in her world. And she didn't know how to reverse it. Initially anger had held the fear in check, but now it clogged her throat and clouded her vision. She'd gone from being warm and cozy on top of her bed to lost in this dark hole, a chill settling into her bones. The thought of being stuck in this blackness forever kept shudders creeping up and down her spine. Please, let this not be the end of her world.

The world had to be out there somewhere. No direction appeared to be a better bet than any other. She couldn't just stand still forever.

"Hello? Is someone there?"

Storey spun around, excited relief blasting through her. "Help! Hello? Can someone hear me?"

"Hang on. I'm coming."

Oh thank God. She was saved! Storey couldn't believe it. Someone must have heard her screams. She glanced down at her jeans, relieved that she wasn't in her usual sleepwear – a camisole and matching shorts. To think she'd almost changed for bed. Then again, she might not have been found at all.

The darkness in front of her lightened. Storey pivoted to see a slice of sunlight opening up behind her. The strip widened, highlighting the old worn plank floor at her feet. Weird. She dashed to the doorway, open enough just enough for her to slip through, and blinked in the bright light. The sun crested the familiar shape of her mountain top. It was morning? How long had she been in there?

She turned to look at her rescuer.

Eric.

His grin flashed, that killer look of pure bad boy. Like he'd just come off a hot night. She gulped. The goose bumps on her arms had to be from the cool mountain air.

"Hey, Storey. What the hell were you doing in there?"

"In where?"

Storey spun around and studied the door she'd just exited. It didn't look like the one in her picture. In fact, it looked like an ordinary plain old door. Wood, some kind of cut molding running around the edge and a standard issue round door knob. The door attached to a large front wall of some kind. No sign identified the purpose or location. Stripped of paint and worn, the whole thing had an abandoned look to it.

"Where am I?" Puzzled, she backed up to get a wider view of the building. "What is this place?"

"It's an abandoned mine entrance."

She spun around. "It's what?"

Eric pointed out the landmarks. "This is the trailer entrance to the old Bankhead mine. Remember, it closed down a few years back?"

"How do you know? I thought you were new?" she murmured with a sidelong glance. Way off topic, but the fact that she could actually keep a conversation going right now was a freakin' miracle. So what if it was a mine entrance? What she really wanted to know was how the hell she'd managed to get inside.

"If you didn't know what the place was, how did you get inside?"

Trying for an air of nonchalance she didn't feel, Storey went for simplicity. "I fell down a hole, ended up in the mine."

A long slow whistle escaped his lips, his eyes widened in shock. "Wow. Good thing I found you when I did. You could have been stuck in there forever."

Oh, God. He was right. A shudder worked up her legs, reducing them to the consistency of wet noodles. But as much as she wanted to bolt from the place, she knew she had to have answers. Otherwise, what would stop her from ending up there again? She needed to go back in – with the door open for light.

"Come on, let's go home." Eric faced the wide, gravel road overgrown by bushes and weeds.

Storey glanced from the door to the road then back to the door. She had to know. "Just a second."

A few quick steps and she had her hand on the door-knob before she could talk herself out of it. It wouldn't open. She frowned and spun back to Eric. "Did you lock it again?"

"Lock what?" He walked back and tested the door himself. It wouldn't open. "No. I didn't. At least, I don't think so."

"Freaky," she murmured. The door *was* old and rusty. Eric stood off to one side, hands on his hips, glaring at her. Had he locked it to stop her from going back inside? Then why not just say so? Or maybe he'd locked it accidentally.

"Are you coming?"

"Yeah," she said with one long last look at the door.

She'd explore later. When Eric wasn't around. And when she had a flashlight.

Something beyond weird was going on and she needed to know what it was.

CHAPTER 4

SCHOOL SLOGGED BY. Storey was desperate to get home, yet every time she checked her watch, it appeared to have stopped, forcing her to check the clock on the back wall.

"Yes, Storey, it's at least two minutes since you last checked the time. What's the matter? Do you have a hot date or something?"

Snickers raced around the classroom, gaining momentum until they became an outright laugh.

"She's probably heading to the coven for her initiation." That comment came from somewhere off to the left. Storey didn't bother looking for the culprit. Could be any one of a dozen people hitting at her because of her mother.

Laughter swelled.

Stone-faced, she slouched lower in her seat. To hell with them.

"So if we have everyone's attention again," Mr. Morrison continued with a smirk, "there's going to be a quiz on chapters eleven and twelve tomorrow. Study and do well. Don't study, don't care and maybe fail. Everyone is dismissed." He waved good-bye before wiping off the blackboard.

Letting the class empty ahead of her, Storey took her time to collect her stuff. The last thing she wanted was to attract any more attention.

"Nice pencil. Can I see it?" Eric's long, black, jean-clad legs showed up beside her desk as she crouched to repack her overstuffed backpack.

Storey snatched the pencil off her seat where she'd set it and slipped it into the side pocket of her bag before zipping it shut. "It's a pencil. Nothing special."

Eric studied her face. "An art pencil?"

"Nope. Just a pencil."

He raised his left eyebrow. "Then why won't you let me take a look at it?" He waited another moment. "Where did you get it? I'd kinda like one for myself."

"Check the stores. I'm sure someone will carry it." Storey turned and walked out of the classroom.

Paying attention during school had been impossible with memories of her crazy, late-night outing running through her brain. She'd made it home from the mine that morning and raced to her bedroom, only to discover the undamaged sketchbook still lying where she'd thrown it on the floor. She'd stood stunned in her open doorway. No gaping hole in the floor, no damage even.

Of course there wasn't. It couldn't be any other way. Still she couldn't reconcile what had actually happened in her mind. Finding escape in running away, she'd grabbed a change of clothes, a bite to eat and had left for school without waking up her mother. She'd needed time to think. Time to assess what the hell had happened. And why.

All the while, she'd questioned Eric's opportune arrival at the mine entrance. It's not like he'd offered an explanation for his presence there at that hour. Then again, neither had she. Still, as much as she appreciated the rescue, his arrival outside the mine entrance had unlikely coincidence written all over it. She didn't believe in those. Ever.

He was up to something.

Shaking her head, Storey glanced behind her to make sure she was truly alone before racing the last leg home.

Her mother might be a little odd in the eyes of the town folk, but she'd done one thing right – she'd taught Storey common sense. Storey's instincts screamed at her about Eric. He was too good-looking, too interesting and too interested in her to be normal. He was…*different*. Good different or bad different? Too early to tell.

She knew one thing – she wanted to go back into the mine.

Apprehension wafted through her. Okay, so maybe she didn't *want* to go back into the mine. It was more like she *had* to go back in.

Home loomed in front of her. With it came a sense of awe. A sense of joy. A grin split her face. She, Storey Dupont, had a door into a mine shaft through her bedroom floor. She didn't know how and she sure as hell didn't know why, but there it was. And she was going to go through it again – soon.

Well, after a snack and picking up a few supplies.

In the kitchen, she threw back a tall glass of water and opened the cupboard. There were fruit snacks in there somewhere.

"Storey?" Her mom wandered into the room, dressed in lounging pants and a camisole, rubbing sleep from her eyes. Jesus. It was three in the afternoon. Her assistant must be watching the store.

"There you are. Are you all right?"

"Of course, I'm fine, Mom. Why?"

"Well, Gina called this morning and mentioned that she saw you walking very early this morning with a boy."

Storey glanced over at her mom and caught her deep blue gaze – not accusing Storey, exactly. At least not yet.

"And I know you were in bed last night because we spoke."

Storey turned back to the cupboard without responding. Great. Someone had spotted her and had tattled already. About Eric no less.

After a moment, her mother continued, her voice forced into light casualness. "She was pretty sure she'd recognized you." She cleared her throat. "Did you leave the house early? Without saying anything?" She hesitated. "And with a boy?"

Distracted, Storey struggled to find an answer.

"Storey?"

Storey had to give herself a shake. "Yes, I woke up early and thought I'd go out for a walk. You were asleep when I got back, so I got ready for school and left."

"Oh. Uhm. You're not trying to exercise at that hour, are you?" Her mother moved closer, reaching out a hand to Storey's arm. She peered up into Storey's eyes. "I know you've had a tough couple of months since Jeff moved away, and I know you want to be like the other girls and all, but you're getting so skinny. I'm worried. You're almost anorexic."

"What? No, I'm not. Look, I couldn't sleep so I went down to the creek to watch the sunrise." She reached out and gave her mom a quick hug. "I'm fine. I eat. Honest." Storey hoped the conversation would die a natural death at this point. Her mom had spent most of Storey's preteen years trying to make her 'see the light' in one matter or another.

Storey had always preferred the dark, which might account for her need to get back into that blackness.

She still hadn't figured that trip out. She wanted to try it again, but to enter from the mine side so she could have her exit ready and have the benefit of daylight inside. If Eric had been able to open the door, she should be able to as well. What was the chance of the mine having power and working lights? And then, after checking it out thoroughly from that side, she'd try going through the floor again.

"I have to go out for a bit. What time is dinner? I promise, I'll be home and I'll eat."

"Around six. Where are you going?"

"Just downtown. Maybe buy a new pair of jeans." Like hell. She hated shopping. Still, she had to find some excuse.

"Do you need money?" Her mother brightened at the mention of such a normal, girlie activity. She reached for her purse and pulled out a couple of twenty dollar bills. "Here. I can't think of the last time you asked me for some. You're such a good kid."

Storey knew better than to answer that statement. Pocketing the money, she thanked her mom and headed back outside. She started walking in the direction of the mall. Once out of sight of her home, she changed course and retraced the route she'd taken home with Eric that morning. She knew the area vaguely. When she came to the gravel road, she knew she was on the right track. In her mind, she'd half doubted that the door would even be there. Rounding the bend, she stopped in relief. There it was. She ran the last few yards. At the entrance, she looked around and frowned. This was too accessible. Shouldn't they have made this entrance more secure? To stop kids from going inside.

She tried the door knob. Locked.

No surprise. She opened her backpack and pulled out a thin metal tool she'd gotten from Jeff months ago. They'd watched this cool video that had demonstrated how to pick locks. She'd tried it on her own house and had managed it with both a bobby pin and a credit card. This wire thingy was the best.

Bending down, she studied the side of the knob. This door had a different locking mechanism than the one at home. She frowned. This might not work. She played with the steel pick for several moments, then switched to using her bank card. Still, it wouldn't open. Frustration mounted. She wanted in. Damn it. She studied the surrounding area.

Eric had gotten in. If he could get in, then so could she. Ten minutes later, she had to give it up. The damn thing wouldn't budge.

Hands fisted on her hips, she considered her options. Should she go home and try to enter from her room again? With a flashlight, she should be able to find the door from inside the mine.

This method certainly wasn't getting her anywhere.

The return trip home was fast. She slipped onto the back porch and into the kitchen without letting her mom know. She hurried to her room. Gathering up a piece of chalk and a bottle of water, she searched for her flashlight, finally locating it under the bed. At the last minute, she snatched up her hoodie and checked that she had her cell phone…just in case. Turning her attention to the sketchbook on her floor, she hooked her backpack on her shoulder. Taking a deep breath, Storey hopped onto the bed, stared down at the picture in front of her…and jumped.

She landed on the floor. "Damn it." Scrambling back up onto her bed, she tried again. Nothing. What was wrong? And if it worked once it would work twice. So what was different this time? She considered this issue while standing on her bed, looking down. She'd been scared and angry last time, could that have made the difference? If so, she was getting pretty damned pissed just thinking about it now. She jumped. Nothing. Feeling like an idiot, she climbed up and said, "Open sesame." Then jumped.

Nothing.

Shit.

This was ridiculous. "Why is it not working?" She sat on the edge of her bed, picked up the book and studied the sketch. She bolted upright. "What the hell?"

The door in her sketch was no longer open. Somehow, though her hand hadn't touched a pencil to paper, the door in her drawing now appeared closed.

She hadn't done it herself. Whatever had opened the door – had closed the door. That's why she couldn't get in anymore. The damned door was closed.

Reaching into the backpack, she grabbed up her pencil and tried to make the door in her sketch look open. The pencil wouldn't touch the paper. She flipped to a new page, and tried to copy the sketch onto the fresh paper, only this time with the door open. Except the pencil had a mind of its own and drew the door closed.

Storey sat back.

What was going on here?

Magic?

Satanism?

Surely not. Her mother dabbled in Wiccanism…could she have done something dangerous? Not likely. The religion was all about good not evil – no matter what people thought. The sunlight shone through her bedroom window, brightening the room, making it hard to think on dark and supernatural factors in the face of so much light. She glanced back down at her book. The light shone on the picture, giving it an odd look. Twisting the sketchbook around, she flicked it up and down in the sunbeam. Nothing changed. Her pencil flashed.

She held it up in the weird light. Though it was old and kind of ratty, the kinship she'd felt with it had only strengthened with time. It flashed again. What was that? She bent closer, trying to see what was inscribed on the side. She hadn't even noticed it before. She twisted it slowly in the light. There.

It was some kind of script.

Storey tried to read it. She twisted it around and around. The writing faded when not in the sunlight. In the light, the writing etched itself in as if by some unseen hand.

"So cool," she murmured. "What does it mean?"

And how could she find out? Grabbing a different pencil, she tried to copy the script down on a piece of scrap paper. It took several tries at holding it in the light to get it just right. The inscribed lines didn't appear to be words, per say, or at least not in any language she'd seen before. Numbers? Dates? She didn't know. Taking the scrap of paper downstairs to her mom's computer, she scanned it in, then dragged the image to her flash drive. Back upstairs, she searched the Internet for ancient fonts and languages.

By late afternoon, she'd found nothing. *Damn it.* For the millionth time, she glanced at her floor and wondered if she should try again. She decided against it. The time had disappeared on her and she didn't want to spend the night in that mine. Still…maybe she should. It wasn't *that* late. She hopped off her computer chair and walked closer.

"Storey? Dinner time."

So much for a quick trip into a tunnel, at least for the moment. "Coming." She put away her stuff and tucked the scrap of paper with the copied script under her keyboard. She couldn't explain why she felt the need to hide it. For the same reason, she'd renamed the scan as Chemistry Paper. That should keep people in the dark. Not that anyone would see it. Still…

She headed downstairs to dinner and dishes. That was another thing that sucked about being an only child – no one to share the chores with.

It took another hour before she could return to her room, telling her mom and her mom's arriving Wiccan friends that she had a lot of homework to do. She rolled her eyes at that lame excuse. When did she ever do homework?

Closing her bedroom door behind her, her gaze caught and held on her sketchbook. Should she try again? The phone rang. Storey ignored it. It was never for her. She had a cell phone like everyone else.

"Storey, answer the phone, please. It's for you."

Storey stilled. Who'd be calling her? On the house phone?

"Storey, did you hear me?"

"Yes. Thanks." She walked to the little stand in the middle of the hallway and picked up the cordless phone, then headed back to her room. "Hello?"

"Storey?"

"Yes." Her frown deepened. She didn't recognize the voice. "Who is this?"

"Eric."

"Eric." She winced. Was that breathy squeaky voice hers? Yikes. "Why are you calling? And why this number?"

He laughed. A deep sound that sent the butterflies in her stomach into flight. *Damn.* That was so not a good thing. What could he possibly want?

"I wanted to make sure you were all right after being locked in that tunnel. And you didn't give me your cell number."

She flopped on the bed. "What? Oh. Here it is." She rattled off the number of her cell. Although she rarely used it, she'd rather her phone calls were private and off her mother's radar. "And yeah. I'm fine. I wasn't really locked in."

"So what do you call it then? I'd planned on asking you about it today, except you left so quickly, I didn't get a chance."

"Sorry about that. Not to worry, I'm fine," she said lightly. Silence stretched between them. She took a deep breath. She shouldn't say anything. She should keep her mouth shut. "I might go back there."

"What!"

She winced. "You don't have to shriek. God, you sound like a girl."

"Great. Thanks for that." She could almost feel his glare through the phone.

She rolled her eyes and sat up. "There's something weird going on. I want to check it out."

"And get locked in permanently next time?"

"Yeah, now that's one of those weird parts I don't understand. How could you have been passing by at exactly the right moment? Not to mention how could you have opened that door? When I tried, it was locked up tight."

The ensuing silence was ominous. The tone of his voice dropped, giving it a dangerous edge. "You tried to open the door? When?"

"Right after you got me out, remember Then again after school. I wanted to explore the entrance, only I couldn't open the door. It had a weird lock on it."

"I'd imagine that's to keep people out. Did you ever consider how dangerous it might be to go back to that place?"

"Uhm." She grinned. "Not really."

"Are you always this impulsive?"

She shrugged. "Yeah, maybe."

"I can't believe it. You need a keeper." Outrage shimmered through the phone.

"Like that's going to happen," she scoffed. "And if

you don't have any other reason for calling, I'll say good-bye now." She didn't feel like getting chewed out by him any more than she did by one of her teachers.

"Wait. Look, please don't go back into the mine. It's dangerous. I don't want you to get hurt or lost."

Storey lifted an eyebrow and stared down at the phone. He didn't? How'd that happen? "I won't. I'm used to doing things alone."

"I don't care." Exasperation slipped into his voice. "Please don't go alone."

"I have to. There's no one to go with me."

"I will. I'll go with you."

HE HADN'T SAID that, had he? That way? Damn. Yes, he was supposed to get close to her, only he hadn't wanted to get *close* to her. The night sky had deepened, darkened to obsidian. What he really wanted was to protect her from doing something foolish that could impact both their dimensions. But what that could be, he didn't know. Humans had an insatiable curiosity and a self-destructiveness that horrified his people. If they killed themselves off, it wouldn't impact his people. If they killed the planet though, both sides would die.

For that reason, his government had worked hard at not letting Storey's people know they existed. His home had to be protected from the uncontrolled humans. A veil separated their worlds and all access to crossover points had to go through a major vetting process. Only the best of the scientists were allowed over and only with a strict security detail. In this way they could keep watch over the Earth in the human's dimension.

Their shared planet had to be protected. They just didn't know how at this point. The population of his world was less than one percent of Storey's yet still spread across the same area, so hidden surveillance was the only way.

Everything had been in happy harmony for ages, until this. No treachery was involved. Just a simple accident and a scientist had lost something that could put both worlds at risk. A team had been dispatched immediately. They'd followed the inherent energy of the ancient tool to its location only to watch as one of the otherworlders picked it up in front of them.

Storey.

"Eric?"

Eric gave himself a mental shake. He was being an idiot. Storey was his assignment. Any way that made it work, made it right.

"Sorry, I was distracted by something else."

"Yeah, duh."

"I meant it. I'll go with you. We can try to open the door from this side. If that doesn't work, then I don't know what else to try. It worked last time though," he added helpfully.

"Right. I might have another way in. I'm just not sure."

Eric frowned, all his senses on high alert. "How?" His voice sharpened as he realized what she implied. The only other method to enter that tunnel was through a portal.

"There are other entrances. Most old mines have abandoned shafts."

"Hence all those warning signs saying danger. Remember those?"

Her voice deepened, slowed. And she should have. Talk about focus. "You know, I'm not so sure I do."

Great. Now she had selective vision too. "Well, they were there."

"No need to snap at me." She sniffed.

He grinned into the phone. She was starting to grow on him. That defiant streak of hers baffled him. He couldn't help but be intrigued.

"I'm going to try again."

"Try what? The door? Not tonight?" He tried to sound horrified. From what he'd observed, most people on this side of the veil avoided going out in the darkness. His side was the opposite. The sun shone hotly so much of the time that many people preferred to go about in the dark. The geography of both sides was the same, with one sun and one moon, an atmosphere necessary for life and various animals and plant life dotting the countryside. The two peoples resembled each other physically. There the similarities appeared to end.

Storey's people appeared to be less developed. They relied heavily on what they called technology. They appeared to choose their futures by the type of work they liked or the type of work that found them. Giving away their power instead of corralling it and fine-tuning it. He didn't know if they had the same abilities of his kind. Maybe they had died off over the years. In his world, everyone had some special skill, which developed throughout childhood. Once an adult, they were already in their field. They knew what they were meant to do because they'd already been doing it.

He didn't get it.

These people had so much to give. So much more they could do.

Yet, they did nothing. They watched an object called TV all day or played games on another box called a computer or a video game. His world had similar machines, but not for games. Never for games.

"Hello? Are you there?"

Sheesh. "Sorry."

"Look, you called me. Not the other way around. I'm

going. You can come or not come. I don't care. I'm going to bed now. See you tomorrow."

"Wait."

She was gone. Damn it. He stared down at the phone in his hand, something else these people appeared to be permanently attached to. Now what had she said? He'd missed part of it. Something about going back and he could come or not. So, she *wasn't* planning on going anywhere tonight?

He understood only so much of the weird innuendos and body language of these people.

Was she going back tonight?

CHAPTER 5

S TOREY WOKE ENERGIZED the next morning. It was
Saturday. She planned on going to the mine. By way
of her floor – as soon as she figured it out. As much as
she'd told Eric he could come, she wasn't planning on
telling him about her private entrance.

She grabbed up her favorite pencil and sketchbook.
Opening to the right page, she laid it down on the floor.
As it hit, something caught her eye. Her heart sped up
and she crouched down for a better look. The door in her
picture had unlocked itself. She might just be able to get
through.

First she had to get dressed. She didn't want to end
up in some strange place dressed in nightclothes. After
donning jeans, t-shirt and sneakers and brushing her hair,
she stood on her bed and considered if she'd forgotten
anything. Her backpack was still packed with water and a
flashlight along with chalk to mark her locations. She'd
get it right this time.

After a few moments pondering the contents, she
added her pencil and a smaller sketchbook. And felt like
an idiot. If anyone saw her preparing for a trip through
her bedroom floor, they'd have her committed.

She stood up, took one deep breath for courage, and
jumped.

And went right though the floor.

She came to an abrupt halt in the darkness. Her knees

buckled, sending her to one side. Instead of being afraid, she laughed, joy and relief mixing with a sense of exultation. She wasn't crazy. This wasn't her imagination. She'd really jumped through her floor. No damage. No broken beams or flooring or ceiling.

Just a doorway in her sketch. How amazing was that?

Standing up, Storey searched the darkness, listening for identifiable sounds. She'd thought long and hard about what she'd do once she made it back here. Cocking her head to one side, she realized she could hear…nothing. No sounds of water running down the walls, or mice scrabbling against the ground. Not even a bit of breeze whistling down the tunnels. Nothing.

She clicked on her flashlight sending light slicing through unforgiving darkness. "How could anything be so absent of light and sound?" She frowned. Her voice didn't even echo. Had it last time? Sure it had. Still it was different now? She didn't remember much of her science lessons on light and noise, but thought emptiness helped create the echo effect.

So weird. Standing still, she sent light out as far as it could reach in all directions. Then she checked out the space behind her.

Nothing. No walls shone back on her. Turning the light onto the floor, she studied the flooring and wondered at the smooth look of the planks. So perfect, they didn't appear real. It wasn't what she'd expected.

Then she checked out the ceiling. The light went into endless darkness. If there was a ceiling, it was so high as to be untouchable. She knew she hadn't jumped more than eight feet. Her knees hadn't hurt on landing.

So, if she'd jumped through the same hole and landed in the same black nothingness, where was the damn door?

Taking out her chalk, she drew a large circle with an X in the middle of it. She wanted to mark her position so she didn't get lost. At least this way if she were to jump again, she'd be able to check that she landed at the same place. She didn't want to consider that she might have ended up somewhere new.

First things first, she needed to find the door. Last time it had been behind her. With her flashlight showing the way, she turned, searching behind her for the door. Last time that first slice of light had appeared to be a long way away. In truth, it hadn't been more than thirty or fifty feet.

She paced off thirty paces and stopped. She couldn't see anything anywhere. Looking behind her, relief swept through her at the X on the floor in the bright beam of light. Good. She just needed to do this systematically. Taking a deep breath, she moved forward another thirty paces. Still nothing showed in her light. Uneasiness squirmed in her stomach. Keep going forward or try a new direction? Deciding to move another thirty steps, she paced again, and then stopped and drew another big X, labeling it number two. Then she backtracked to her original spot and paced ninety paces in the opposite direction. By the time she finished, she'd created a square with four Xs at the corners and a big X in the middle. Not much help, considering she had yet to find a perimeter wall.

She stood in the middle of her markings and puzzled over it. What kind of tunnel could have no walls? Not possible. She tried to visualize the space. It had to be a natural cave to require no support beams or walls. Damn. Why hadn't she brought a bigger flashlight? Annoyance flooded through her. Oh wait, maybe because she didn't have one!

Her cell phone rang. Such an ordinary thing, and so normal in the midst of so much abnormal, its very mundaneness surprised her. How could she get reception in here? "Hello?"

Static filled her ear. Figured. "Hello?"

She tried answering several more times, then clicked it off, returning it to her pocket. A moment later, the musical notes on her phone sounded again. A text. Hmmm. She clicked on it to read the incoming message.

Where the hell are you?

Eric. And pissed.

She answered. *I'm in the mine. I told you to come if you wanted.* After she hit send, she waited, a half grin on her face. He wouldn't take it quietly. Her instinct proved right as a text came right back. *I'm on my way. WAIT.*

"Like I have a choice." She sniffed at his autocratic response. Speaking to the empty space around her she snapped at the missing Eric, "Then hurry up. Where the hell is that door?"

She passed the time by walking out to each of her circles and spent several minutes studying the darkness around her. There appeared to be nothing there. Walking back to the middle, she sat down to wait. Within minutes another text came through. She hopped to her feet. Eric said he was approaching the door. She waited for the welcoming sliver of light. It never came. Nerves bunched as she waited and worried. What if he couldn't open the door? He'd done it once. The wait seemed interminable. She chewed her fingernails as she waited and waited.

Damn it. She sent him another text, reading aloud as her fingers whipped across the keyboard. "What's wrong?"

"*I've opened the door. Where are you?*"

Shit. She hopped to her feet and spun around looking for the doorway. He wasn't there. Shakes and shivers wracked her slight frame as she realized the enormity of her situation.

She'd landed in a different place.

Eric had come to the rescue. He was at the door to

the mine. He'd actually managed to open the locked door again, clearing one of the hurdles she'd worried about, but she wasn't there.

So, where the hell was she?

ERIC STOOD IN the doorway. "Storey? Storey, are you here? Where are you?"

Leaving the door wide open, Eric stepped inside and took a long look around. He could see the back wall. There was no sign of her. "Shit." Where had she gone?

A horrible thought surfaced. She couldn't have jumped elsewhere. She didn't know how. At least he didn't think she did. No, she'd said she was here. So, this is where she *thought* she was.

"Storey?"

No answer. Could she have gotten out? He pulled out his phone. Her incoming text asked where he was. Double shit.

Where was she? And how could he find her?

Paxton. Using his codex, he coded in the notes that would allow him to cross the veil where he stood. In seconds he breathed the air of his own world. After a quick glance around, he headed for Paxton's office.

"Finally." Buried in books, eyeglasses perched on the bridge of his nose, Paxton snorted at him. "Your father has been asking about you. I do hope you have the stylus with you."

"We've got a problem." Eric raced to the holograph screens. "Storey jumped again. Only she's gone somewhere else this time and I can't find her."

Paxton came running, his long midnight blue robes flapping in the wind. "Oh dear! This is exactly what we were trying to avoid. We can't just have a human running loose on our side. There's no knowing what kind of chaos she could create."

"She's not trying to cause any trouble." Storey was curious, not a terrorist. Eric was compelled to defend her. "She thinks she's in the same place as last time, but I just checked and she's not there."

"That's because she's here. She's jumped to Stanshor mine!" Paxton tapped one of the screens on the left.

Eric peered closer. Sure enough Storey stood in the middle of a different portal. "What? How could she have made it there?"

"The stylus. It's trying to go home. That's the closest jump to the science hall."

"How would the stylus know that?"

"Through its ancient memories. It's taking her where it wants to go. You have to get her back to Bankhead Mine."

Eric snorted. "And how do you expect me to do that? She's a thousand miles in the wrong direction." He fisted his hands on his hips and snorted at the monitor. How the hell had she done that?

"Jump with her."

"She'll know," Eric warned.

"Not if you do it right. Jump at the doorway. From one to the other. If you catch it right, she won't even know what the world outside of Stanshor looks like."

Crap. "That's a lot of 'ifs.'" He rubbed his temple, trying to work through the process.

"Too bad. If you can't keep her under control then you have to clean up her messes." Paxton motioned behind him. "Use the doorway in my office. You can dial up Stanshor, then let her out like she's expecting you to."

"Right. Good luck with that," he muttered the last under his breath, loving the new expressions he'd been picking up on the other side. And they were so apt. Storey wasn't stupid. She'd know something was up.

Eric walked into Paxton's office, wondering what he was going to say to her. If he let her know what she'd done was illegal in his world he could kiss his career goodbye. Keeping her in the dark was going to be even harder.

He set the coordinates for Stanshor and walked through Paxton's doorway to the entrance of Stanshor Mine. The development here was at least ten times bigger than the one in Bankhead. If she'd gotten lost in here, it could take days to find her. And that's if he knew where to start.

The door was locked as per standard practice. Using his soulkey, honored with the highest security, he unlocked the mine door. Taking a deep breath, he pushed it open. He could only hope she was there.

He stepped inside, careful to keep the door partially closed so she couldn't see out.

"There you are. What took so long?"

Her voice, sharp and stressed, snapped out at him. Temper? Or something else. Bemused, Eric could only watch as she strode toward him, backpack in hand. He partially closed the door behind him. He couldn't have her escaping until he'd made the changes. "Well, hi. How are you? Nice of you to come and rescue me. Sorry for being such an idiot and jumping into a cave again without anyone knowing."

Good. The sarcasm in his voice garnered him a disgusted look as she went to brush past him. Past him? Shit. He spun to close the door.

Her hand wrapped around his arm, a last grasp from a dying person. "I have to get out." A shudder rippled down her and she sucked air through her clenched teeth. Her eyes stared toward the crack of light. Eric studied her finely etched features and narrowed his gaze.

She was headed for a panic attack. He had to get her out of here and fast. Shit. The timing had to be perfect. "Let me go first." Not giving her a chance to argue, he stepped in front of her and strode the short distance to the door. Using his codex, Eric shifted the locations until the entrance to Bankhead Mine stood outside and not the entrance to Stanshor Mine. He'd never done this type of shift before. How long would his luck hold?

"I have to get outside." Storey burst past him, her voice tight, flat.

Crap. He grabbed her arm and tugged her back. She spun around and ended up in his arms. Huge chocolate eyes, so close to his own, widened in confusion. It's not what he'd planned but…he couldn't help himself. He lowered his head and swallowed her startled response with a quick kiss at the same time as he pushed down on the transporter button.

At least it was supposed to be quick. And he hadn't meant it to be hot. At least not that hot. He'd aimed for warmer than friends and cooler than lovers. Instead, sparks flew as flames licked across his skin, burning, searing the taste of her, the feel of her in his arms, forever in his mind.

He shuddered. *Step back. Danger.* It wasn't supposed to be like this. Eric pulled back, struggling for air. Storey stared up at him, her eyes the color of molten chocolate, confusion swirling in their depths.

"Hey." His voice wavered, just a bit. He recognized it. Thought she might have too. He cleared this throat. "That was an *I'm just glad to see you alive* kiss. Sorry it got a little out of hand. I was afraid you'd be lost in there forever." Turning her gently, he nudged her out into her world. She was dangerous. She'd wreak havoc if left on her own in his dimension. She was already wreaking havoc. With his heart.

CHAPTER 6

S TOREY WANTED TO look back on this moment and
be proud that she'd acted like Eric's kiss hadn't just
blown every other kiss out the water. In fact, she now
knew she hadn't been kissed before. At least not properly.

Yeah, Eric knew how to kiss.

*Come on, Storey, you can do this. Act natural and, for
heaven's sake, close your mouth and quit gawking.*

She forced a smile and lifted her face to the sky. Surely, he couldn't know about the tumultuous flutter of her
heart or stomach. And the shudders wracking her spine
were on the inside and not something he could see. She
stole a glance his way, grateful he was checking out the
entrance to Bankhead Mine and thankful she was outside
and not still locked inside. She took several gulps of fresh
air and closed her eyes, waiting for her senses to return to
normal.

Why had he kissed her? And why like that? Or had
the second part been a surprise for him, too? God, she
hoped so. To think her reaction had been one-sided
would be one of life's nastiest jokes.

Sensing his gaze, she opened her eyes. His blue eyes
studied her. With a nonchalance she didn't feel, she said,
"I didn't realize how wonderful fresh air smells and how
warming, how healing, the sun is."

Pursing his lips, he gave her an understanding nod.
"After being locked in a mine twice, that's understanda-

ble. The real question is — was the experience bad enough to stop you from repeating it?" He waggled his eyebrows and hooked his arm through hers. "Come on. I have to get home."

"Oh?" She shrugged. Trying to put more distance between her and that dynamite kiss she added, "I thought I'd stay and explore some more."

He grunted. "Damn good thing I closed the door then, isn't it? Does the law matter to you at all?" His voice rose in exasperation.

He grabbed her shoulders, spinning her around until she couldn't miss the sign in front of them. "Can you read that? No Trespassing." He snorted at her. "Is that simple enough? This is private property. You can't just wander around here. It's dangerous."

She stood toe-to-toe against him and glared.

"I got it. Except I'm not a kid anymore and I can make my own decisions. Something weird is going on and I'm going to figure out what it is. You don't like it. Fine. You don't have to get involved." That he was right wasn't enough to make her stop. She had to sort this out. She could hardly forget the whole thing happened, could she? "Thanks for helping me. Go on and enjoy your don't-rock-the-boat existence."

She stepped back and took a look around. "I wish you'd tell me how to open the damn door." At his look, she added, "Not going to happen, huh? Fine." She threw her backpack over her shoulder. "Thanks. I can manage on my own."

She strode off in the direction of home, her head and heart a mess. Then she came to a sudden stop. Spinning back around, she asked, "Where were you earlier? When you texted to say you had the door open and where was I?"

He shrugged, a sheepish look on his face. "I wasn't

here yet. I thought the scare might stop you from playing these dangerous games."

She gasped. "That's so mean." She strode off, almost running to get away from him. How could he have done something like that? And then there was that damn kiss. Why did he mess with her feelings so badly? Whatever. She didn't intend to spend time with him anyway.

The sun shone bright and warm, helping to chase away the last of the uneasiness lingering in her mind. The panic had subsided and the anger had burned through the rest of her nervousness. She took a deep breath and sighed.

Strong arms grabbed from behind.

Eric spun her around until she stood facing him. A very pissed off Eric. So why did she have to notice how anger lit the deep blue in his eyes and hollowed out his face, highlighting the strength of his jaw bones? She did so love the dimple in his chin.

"Are you always so disagreeable?"

She raised one eyebrow and refused to back down.

"I guess that means yes, huh?" His jaw clenched as he glared down at her.

Odd how nice it was to look up at a guy. "That's not fair. You don't know everything that's gone on. You're judging me without having all the information."

"Then talk. Explain it to me." He stepped back and crossed his arms, waiting.

She snorted then shifted to look up at the sky. She shouldn't have brought it up. What to tell him? How much would he believe? No one would believe everything. "I don't know how much to tell you."

"Everything." There it was again, that dominant, implacable wall.

She sighed and tucked her hair behind her ear. "You won't believe me."

"Try me."

There just wasn't any give in him. "This might take some time."

"I have all the time we need."

"Really?" she challenged. "I thought you had to go home."

"I'll make my excuses later."

She grimaced. Of course he would. "Fine. But I want to sit down somewhere first."

"Over there."

She checked out where he pointed. Several large rocks sat under the boughs of a blue spruce. "Okay. But don't blame me if this all sounds a little farfetched," she warned.

He sat down, crossed those long legs of his and waited.

She frowned. "I don't know where to start."

"At the beginning."

Well, duh. She sat back and took a deep breath. "Several days ago, well maybe a week now. I don't know. The days have whipped by so fast." She chewed her bottom lip, trying to understand how that had happened.

"And," he prompted.

"I found a pencil. That weird one you asked about."

"Where?"

He said it so abruptly she paused, thrown off track. It took her a moment. "On the way to school, I walked through the park and saw it by a rock at the side of the creek. Just lying there."

There'd been a sense that she'd been destined to find it. That she had a connection with it. Not that she was going to tell him that. "Anyways, I've always done artwork of some kind, only…after getting that pencil, it's like I've been obsessed." She slid a sidelong glance his way. "I mean really obsessed. I don't notice when I'm drawing, but it's like I go into a trance or something. I cover every available space on any page. Sometimes, it's just doodles and other times it's really cool stuff. One of the drawings was a door."

Eric leaned closer, his eyes narrowing at her words. "What kind of door?"

She shrugged. "It was scrunched up, so I redrew it on a clean sheet."

She paused.

"And?" Impatience prodded him up off the rocks to pace around before coming back to crouch down in front of her. "What happened next?"

Storey puzzled over his attitude. But she'd started so she might as well carry on. "I got mad one day because the drawings wouldn't leave me alone. They wanted me to draw, draw and draw some more. I felt like I was losing it. Or that they were controlling me." She took a deep breath. "I threw the book down on the floor in my room. I had been on my bed and I was so frustrated, so angry…I don't know…anyways I stomped on it…and that's when things got even weirder."

"Weirder?" His gaze caught hers and held on. She couldn't break the link, it was so intense. "How?"

She took a deep breath. "When I jumped onto my book, I went through my bedroom floor. One simple hop off my bed and I ended up inside Bankhead Mine."

SO, THAT WAS it. Eric sat back, stunned at the sheer simplicity of the steps that led to her crossing the veil and entering his world. At the same time, it scared the hell out of him. If it happened once, or twice in this case, it could happen anytime with anyone. Not good. If anyone else had picked the stylus up, the stylus probably would have remained dormant. However, with Storey being an artist, an open young mind, the stylus had a perfect tool to get it home.

He studied Storey's face. She'd dropped her gaze to the rocks at her feet. Ashamed? She appeared to be over her panic attack and now sat looking curiously embarrassed. He still had trouble reading her facial expressions.

"So, now that I've told you, I'm heading home." She sent him a quick uncertain glance before hopping off the big rock.

"Wait."

Hesitating, she stalled, her back to him. "What now?"

"I believe you." He walked around to stand in front of her.

The impatience drained from her face as hope filled her eyes. "You do? Really?"

"Yes."

They stood and looked at each other for a long moment, the beginning of acceptance sparking between them.

"Don't suppose you'd care to demonstrate, would you?" Eric asked.

A half frown crossed her face. She glanced at the sky and then back at him. "Only if you know how to unlock the damn door from the inside."

Right. That's how she'd gotten out both times – he'd helped her. He looked back the way they'd come, his mind spinning with possibilities. "Maybe."

"Maybe, isn't good enough. I don't relish the idea of being stuck in there any longer than I was today." She continued in a barely audible voice, "And preferably not that long."

"Can I see the book and the pencil, if you don't mind?"

She studied his face. "I suppose that's okay. We have to go to my house then."

He motioned toward the path and grinned. "After you."

STOREY DIDN'T KNOW how she'd ended up so involved with Eric. Every time she turned around – there he was. If only the other girls could see her now. Not that they'd believe their eyes. They'd barely believed it when she dated Jeff. Still, her heart lurched at the thought of her old boyfriend. He'd wanted her to move on. *He* certainly had. The corner of her mouth drooped.

"Tell me what happened today."

Presuming he meant the jump to the mine, she explained the series of events that led up to getting lost again. "I thought I could find the door on my own this time." She took several more steps, before continuing. "I paced off specific distances and marked the floor with chalk to stop me from getting lost." She shrugged carelessly. "Somehow, it didn't work out that way."

"Plans rarely do." The cryptic tone of his voice confused her. Studying his face didn't give her a clue to his thoughts.

At her front door, she stopped. Who was home? It was Saturday, so her mom would be home. Annalea, her assistant, would be minding the store again today. "My mom is here."

"Is that a problem?"

She groaned. "All the time, just not for the reason you might think."

"Oh?"

Refusing to answer, Storey opened the front door.

"Storey? Where have you been? I thought I'd let you sleep in only to find you weren't even in bed—" Her mom, dressed in her typical lounging pant set, stopped her all-out flight down the stairs as her gaze landed on Eric. Flustered, she finished descending and fluffed her hair.

Storey rolled her eyes.

"Hi. I'm Storey's mother. Nice to meet you."

Eric smiled down at her. "I'm Eric. A friend of Storey's."

Stepping back, Storey watched the two interact. No surprise registered in Eric's voice or face as he looked at her Wiccan mother. But then he might not know about her religious beliefs. Wasn't this an important weekend for her, too? In the back of her mind, nearly forgotten under the weird mine stuff, the memory of her mom mentioning a special ceremony poked at her.

"How nice. Please come in. Storey, where were you this morning?"

Storey stiffened slightly. "Same as yesterday. I woke up early and walked through the park with my sketch-book. I met Eric there."

"I wish you'd told me or left me a message. I don't like waking up to find you gone."

"Sorry, Mom. You were still asleep, and I didn't want to wake you." Storey brushed past her and headed up the stairs. "I'm just going to show Eric some of my art. We don't have much time – he's expected back at his house."

"Oh." Her mother smiled at Eric. "In that case. She's very talented, you know."

"I've noticed."

Storey watched from the landing as Eric smiled at her mom, then she took the stairs two at a time. He followed her up. At the top landing, he glanced at her, a question-ing look in his eyes. "Problems?"

"No." She led the way to her room.

At her doorway, she paused. Had she put her under-wear away? How humiliating if she hadn't. With a grimace and a deep breath for courage, she flung the door wide and stepped inside. Her sketchbook lay on the floor, just as she'd left it. Pointing it out, she stood back and watched him approach it. One thing was for sure, from the care he took with the sketch, he might actually believe her.

She couldn't help leaning back against the wall, a little stunned at the realization that she had a guy in her bedroom. Wow. Kind of cool. Then again, she was behind the times. Many girls at school were already having sex. Of course, there were those with parents who would freak if they saw a guy in their daughter's bedroom, too. Her mom had let Eric waltz right in.

"So where's the stylus?"

"Stylus? You mean the pencil?" Why would he call it that?

"Right. Where is it?"

"In my bag." She slid the bag off her shoulder and pulled the ties open. Rummaging through, she remembered that she'd stuffed the pencil in her pocket. Pulling it out, she handed it to him.

He snatched it up, then dropped it immediately. "Ouch." It landed on the floor and rolled several feet.

"What is your problem?" She scrambled to pick it up. "It's a pencil, not a knife or a bomb." Straightening, she sat down and held it out for him again. His response was tentative at best. Narrowing her eyes, she watched him grasp it as if the stupid thing was going to bite him. She had to admit seeing it in his hand made her nervous, like she was in danger of losing something precious. After a tense moment, she said, "Hand it over."

"What?" He stared, mesmerized. "Awesome pencil. I'd love to have one myself."

Something about the way he said it made her uneasy. Yeah, he'd like to have one, but not a different one, he wanted hers.

"Now."

He looked up at her, his jaw line firming, squaring as if fighting himself over her demand. For a moment she wasn't sure he was going to give the pencil back, then he tossed it her way. As her fingers closed around it, relief coursed through her. Now she knew how that old hobbit had felt in the Lord of the Rings movie when he got back the ring. She frowned at the whimsical thought. Except this wasn't a magical pencil.

A light bulb went off in her head.

She was an idiot…because that's exactly what it was. The pencil had to be magic. How else could she walk through a sketch? She couldn't, unless she'd used something special to make it.

"Where's the blow up picture you did?"

Startled, Storey tried to focus on Eric now standing in front of her.

Storey pointed out the book off to the left on her computer desk. He picked it up and made a weird sound.

"You're acting really strange, you know that?"

"Am not." He turned the pages, studying each intently, his face filled with conflicting emotions. Something about his demeanor made her uneasy. His stare struck her as too intense, his spine too stiff, his attention too focused. She kept her eyes trained on him as he meticulously checked out her book.

He sucked in his breath, the color draining from his cheeks. After a long moment he spun to stare at her, his eyes gone the color of obsidian. "When did you draw this one?"

"Last night. After we talked. I actually haven't taken a look at it since." She leaned forward, but was at the wrong angle to see it clearly.

Eric stared at her in horror and started whispering

some kind of weird chant. She'd heard plenty of spells being cast over the last few years, yet she'd never heard anything like what he was speaking. "Are you a Wiccan?" she asked curiously, when he took a breath.

Pale and shaking, he shook his head. His voice hoarse, he said, "You have no idea what you've done."

"*I've done?* I haven't done anything." So much for his understanding. He didn't look well. As a matter of fact, he looked closer to passing out than anyone she'd ever seen before. "Are you okay? You look like you're going to faint."

"Faint?" he cried out in horror.

"Hey, chill. I don't want my mom running up here."

He sank down on the bed beside her, shaking his head. "I'm trying to keep my voice down. You're a little tough on my ego."

Storey closed her eyes and prayed for patience. "Ego? You are one weird guy, you know that?" Opening her eyes, she stared at his stunned, almost devastated eyes. "Okay, please explain. What is going on? Why are you upset and what do you think I've done?"

In a hushed, thick voice, he said, "Unleashed thousands of demons from the world in between."

Storey stared at him. *Figures.* She'd finally met a guy who seemed to like her, was a dynamite kisser and sure enough he had looney tunes playing away inside his head. "Huh? What did you say?" She shook her head. "No wait. Never mind. Look…" She stood up and walked to the door, opening it. "It's gotta be time for your medicine or something. It's definitely time for you to go home."

He stared at her with empty eyes. She started to freak a little. "Did you hear me? You need to go home. You said you were supposed to earlier and I understand now. No problem. I won't tell anyone. Just…please go."

With a shake of his head, he stood up. "I can't do

that. I need you to meet someone."

Storey shook her head. "No way. I'm *so* not going to meet any of the people in your life."

"Look I'm not sick. I don't need medicine. I need you to understand that this pencil, this stylus is special. It creates doorways – as you've found out. Somehow, you've opened a door that has remained sealed for hundreds of years. Even I don't understand the repercussions here. But," he emphasized, "we have to fix this."

"Fix what? I don't understand. You aren't making any sense."

"Like what you told me earlier down by the mine made sense?" He closed his eyes briefly. "You trusted me to listen to you and now I'm asking you to listen to me. The stylus enhances your abilities. In your hand it can create doorways." His blue eyes opened to blaze down at her. "Please. It won't take long. We could be there and back in an hour. I need you to show these drawings to someone."

Peering into his eyes, Storey wondered how to tell if someone was late for his dose of anti-psychotics. "Where?"

"Not far."

"Not far doesn't mean much."

"This is important. Vitally important. Please. What harm could it do to talk to him?"

He reached out and grasped her hand. Staring deep into her eyes, he pleaded, "Please. We have to go show him this." He flipped the sketchbook around so she could see the picture. A picture on a different page.

"Show him what? That's just something I drew before falling asleep last night. I was doodling on the door."

"Look at it closer," he ordered.

Playing along, she took another look. The markings looked different. She realized the doorway stood slightly ajar. Just then Eric shifted his fingers and she could see the picture clearer.

There, wrapped around the wood, as if trying to force it wider open, were eight long, knobby fingers.

THE MOMENT HE felt the shift in her attitude, his panic eased. At least most of it. "Thank you." He stepped back, rotating his neck and shoulders as the tension eased.

"I didn't say I'd go."

"Yes, you did." He closed her sketchbook. "Let's go. Now." As much as he wanted to take the stylus from her, it was clear that it had already bonded, and the person who'd tried to take it from her had better watch out.

"Wait. What's the rush? Besides, what am I going to tell my mother?"

"We'll explain that you forgot your homework and that I have the assignment that you're missing."

"That's great for you. I don't do homework."

He shot her a look of disgust. "Then you should. Do you really just want to work at the corner store all your life?"

"I *don't* work at a corner store," she snapped.

"No, but that's all you're going to be good for with your education level, isn't it." Thank heavens for the comprehensive database they kept on the humans. His studies had allowed for a unique insight to Storey and the society she lived in.

"Arrgh. Who are you to talk?"

She stormed downstairs. The chanting reached them first. Right, preparations for the ceremony. Rather than disturbing them, Storey and Eric made a quick exit out the back door. Eric's pace picked up outside. He practically ran – back in the direction of the damn mine. When they reached the edge of Lewis Park and where she'd told him about the portal, she'd had enough.

"What the hell are we doing back here?" She glared at him and backed up several feet. "We're almost back to where we started."

"We're probably close enough." He dug into his pocket and grabbed a weird silver bracelet that he clasped around his wrist. He tapped a series of buttons on it, filling the air with a musical set of notes.

Story narrowed her eyes at him. "What's that?" she asked suspiciously. "I've never seen anything like it."

"No, it's not common over here."

"Over here?" She surveyed the deserted park and the overgrown path that led to the mine entrance. How come in all the years she'd lived here, she'd never once gone down the path to the mine?

"Yes, over here." He grinned, reached out and grabbed her hand. "Just a few more steps. Here."

Spluttering her protests, she snapped, "I don't want to go with you anymore. I've decided I don't like you. You're beyond irritating, you know that."

A strange voice interjected. "No, he doesn't, but the rest of us do."

CHAPTER 7

STOREY SPUN AROUND. Her jaw dropped. "Where'd you come from?" she demanded, her eyes locked on the costume-clad man now before her. "You weren't here a second ago."

Her voice rose to a loud gasp and her eyes widened as the wall behind him came into focus. She gulped and spun in a circle. The sky had disappeared. Leaves no longer crunched under her feet and the fresh woodsy scent no longer drifted her way. Her stomach wiggled, then wiggled some more as she gulped for air. Where was she? And how had she gotten here?

They'd been standing beside the creek then…a shudder snapped from her toes to her head with realization. Swallowing hard, she shifted closer to Eric.

The wizened old man with a huge beard and tufts of hair decorating his bald head glared at her. His gaze switched to Eric. "What have you done? Do you know how many rules you've broken?" His voice rose to a high pitched squeak at the end. His hands, fisted on his hips, all but disappeared into the folds of his robes.

Storey studied the angry character in front of her. The angle of his chin, that aristocratic nose tilt, that demanding voice – yeah, he was used to giving orders. And expecting them to be carried out. He was a little out of her experience. She couldn't help asking, "Who are you?"

A piercing blue gaze landed on her and narrowed.

"I'm Paxton. And you're Storey Dalton." The gaze shifted to Eric. "Explain."

Eric opened his mouth. No words came out.

"Now." The bright blue gaze hardened to steel. When Eric didn't immediately jump in with an explanation, he added, "You're done. You know that, don't you?"

"I had to," Eric protested. "You don't understand."

"No. I don't." Paxton spread his arms wide. "I can't until you explain."

Eric glanced over at Storey. "Let me have the sketch-book, please."

She gazed at him for a long moment, not fully under-standing yet knowing it was important. She handed it over. Her stomach knotted as Eric flipped through the pages, searching for what he wanted. He went too far and had to go back a few pages, letting out a small hiss as he did so.

"Here." He twisted the book and placed it under Pax-ton's nose.

Paxton's eyes widened. Glancing from Storey to Eric then back again at the picture, he asked, "How?"

"Show him," Eric said to her.

Reaching into her pocket, Storey pulled out her pen-cil or stylus, as Eric called it, and held it up.

The color leached from Paxton's face and he took a small step back. "No. Oh, no."

"Oh, yes."

"What?" Storey was beyond confused and she had no explanation for the coldness in her stomach. Ice had spread out to her limbs. Wrapping her arms around her belly, she wished she knew what the hell was going on. "Look, I don't understand. What's wrong with that picture? It's just a sketch. It's not real or anything."

"Did you draw this picture?" At Storey's nod, Paxton continued, "With...that?" He pointed to the pencil.

Again she nodded. He closed his eyes and started speaking in some weird language. The same one Eric had used earlier.

"Do you guys belong to the some religious group where you speak in tongues or something? I've never heard a language quite like that."

"You mock us?" shrieked Paxton, stiffening in outrage. "Do you realize what you have done?"

"Obviously not," she snapped. "Since no one will tell me what the hell is going on."

Eric's eyes widened. He stared at her wordlessly.

She glared at Eric, catching his wince before he covered it up. "Now what?"

"We don't swear here. It's considered rude," Eric whispered. "Paxton doesn't know that word but anyone who's studied your language might."

"Rude? I'm supposed to worry about my manners now? What the hell are you talking about? Over where?"

He spluttered. "Please, show some respect. Don't swear."

"All right, geeze." His look didn't improve. "Oh, for crying out loud. Geeze is *not* a swear word." She glowered at him. What was his problem, anyway? And since when had he become such a prude?

Paxton's cheeks sucked in like small craters.

"Whatever." She held out her hand. "I'll take my sketchbook now, thanks." Hand outstretched, she snapped her fingers when Eric didn't pass it over. "I don't know what game you're playing, and I don't care. I want no part of it. So, I'm going home."

"No, you're not." Paxton drew up to his full height. Storey's gaze widened as he stretched above her. How tall was he?

"You'll stay in our world until we get to the bottom of this."

"Your world," she snapped. "What are you talking about?"

"You are…" Eric paused…took a deep breath…then rushed to get the rest of the sentence out. "You are in another dimension."

"Oh, for the love of God." Storey threw up her hands at the stony looks shooting her way. "Look, I've had enough. You zip me to another dimension, whatever that means, without asking my permission, tell me I can't go home, give no explanation as to what is going on and then expect me to be calm about it!"

Eric reached out a reassuring hand. She stumbled back out of range. "No." She pointed at Paxton and said, "Hell, no."

This time, Eric grabbed her shoulder and gave her a good shake. Glaring down at her, he said, "Stop. I know you don't understand. Just, please, calm down. I *will* explain." He glanced over at the steaming Paxton. "I promise."

Storey stepped back, glaring up at him. "You'd better. And for your information, I swear when I'm pissed off, so don't piss me off. That includes shaking me."

He closed his eyes briefly, dropped his hand and stepped away. "You'd make a saint crazy," he muttered.

Paxton gasped in outrage. "Which you aren't," he roared. "You should be able to control this…this female."

"Control," she gasped in shock. For some reason the whole mess slid from bad into ludicrous. "I must be having a bad dream. Eric? Control me? I don't think so." She started to giggle.

"Oh, thank you very much. See how she treats me?" He scowled at Paxton. "Why did you have to go and say that?"

"That's enough from both of you. This is no laughing matter. We have a crisis on our hands and need to find a solution." He glanced down at the sketchbook now in his hands. "Quickly. Wait in my office while I call an emergency Council meeting."

Storey was still giggling as they took several more steps, then she stopped. This wasn't just a room. This was some kind of laboratory. Stunned, she could only stare at the pristine white counters, walls, ceilings, even the huge monitors were white with a black trim. "Eric?"

"You're in my world now. It's very similar to yours." He hooked his arm through hers. "Don't panic. Everything is fine. I walked you across a veil that exists between the two worlds."

"Veil?" Easy for him to say. Getting her head wrapped around the concept, not so easy. Still, there was no arguing that she walked on tiles and under some kind of weird fluorescent lights instead of grass and sky. "You're not from my world?"

"Nope." As she stopped in front of a large series of monitors, Eric added by way of an explanation. "It's Paxton's communications center. He controls the crossings."

"There's more than one?" She slid him a sideways look. "Does my side know about your side?"

He pursed his lips and shook his head. "We don't think so, but it's possible. There are several crossings; we keep most of them shut down. We travel to your side when we have specific research to complete. To the best of our knowledge, there aren't any crossings from your side to ours – at least not regulated ones."

"So, I'm the first to visit?" For some reason that concept tickled her. She'd always wanted to get away from her life. Now she was in the most bizarre, abnormal situation imaginable and didn't know what to think. Contrary was her name. She should be scared, but it was as if the jumps into the mine had prepared her for this eventuality. Well, not quite *this* reality. Then his words penetrated. They'd been coming to her world whenever they wanted to – yet no one at home knew.

"Come this way." Eric tugged her arm, leading her toward a closed door. She followed, trying to take in everything. So similar and yet...different.

Eric looked normal enough. Paxton didn't. He was a little on the odd side. Then again, what if a monk, Goth or a Muslim person came here? Eric's people would consider him representative of her world, too. "This isn't fair. You know how to do all this and we don't."

"Fair?" Paxton ran up behind them. "Look what happens when you do know a little bit." He brushed past and through the door ahead of them.

"Really." She exhaled heavily. "Let's not forget who left a stylus in my world in the first place. I wouldn't have found it if you'd stayed where you belong." She wasn't going to take the blame for this – whatever *this* was. They shouldn't have sneaked over to her side. Having perpetrated one wrong, they shouldn't have compounded it by leaving something dangerous behind.

"I know."

"Come, come. Don't dawdle. We don't have time. Everyone is almost here." Paxton hurried ahead of them, tossing an urgent look back their way.

Storey didn't get it. "How did everyone manage to get here in the time it took me to walk the length of the floor?"

"Things are a bit different here." He grinned down at her. "You'll see."

"That's what I'm afraid of," she muttered. "Some info would be helpful. Does everyone look like you and Paxton, for a start? I don't want to walk into that room and find talking alligators or some such thing."

He laughed. "No, we all look like you. Although, we

call ourselves Torans. And Paxton is a little more unique than the rest of us."

"Is that what you call it?"

Eric stopped at the doorway, twisting to look down on her. "You're stalling. You can do this. Heck, I even went to school and attended classes with you. How bad can this be?"

Glaring at him, she stormed through the doorway and came to a sudden halt on the other side. "No one ever smiles in your world, do they?"

The normal looking room was full. Crowding around a large oval table in the middle of the room were dozens of people and even more stood in the back. Everyone stared, frowning at her. Too bad. Her dreams of a magical world spiriting her away went up in smoke. They all looked depressingly normal.

"They aren't that bad." Eric stepped forward. Staring ahead, his back straight, he addressed the room formally. "Greetings, Council. May I present Storey Dalton. She's from the other side of the veil."

Storey couldn't help stiffening at the multitude of curious and judgmental looks zeroing in on her.

"So I understand," answered a rotund looking man at the head of the table. So round and short, he took up almost two chairs yet could barely rest his arms on the table. And his face…she shuddered. Beady eyes stared out from between the fat rolls with a power that defied description. "And apparently you are responsible for bringing her here?"

Eric's voice deepened. "That's right, father. I felt it best."

Father? Storey glanced between the two men, but didn't recognize any family resemblance. One height challenged and the other height gifted. The change in Eric's voice, however, yeah, there was that whole parent relationship mess between them.

"And just how do you think breaking our rules, rules which have held for centuries, I might add, as now being for the 'best?'"

Eric opened his mouth to explain, when Paxton stepped in. "We don't have time to sort out his punishment right now. We have something much bigger to deal with."

"Punishment? You're going to punish him for bringing me here?" Storey couldn't contain her outrage. Whether she wanted to be here or not, she knew Eric believed he'd done the right thing. "In that case, you can send me home. I'm not going to help if he's in trouble over this." It was all she could do to refrain from swearing. If they pissed her off more, then all bets were off.

"Shh. It's all right. I won't be punished."

His father grunted. "We'll make that decision without any input from you. Breaking the law is a very serious offense. It's not like in your world, young lady. We care about doing the right thing here."

"It's hardly admirable that you sit here and criticize my world when you've been sneaking in and out, taking whatever you want, for centuries. That's called stealing in my world. We'll have this discussion after my people's scientists come over here for several hundred years and steal what they want from you," she snapped in outrage. She strode several steps forward and stood with her hands on her hips, anger vibrating up her back. How dare they?

"Uh, oh," murmured Eric. He stepped up beside her as if bracing for a mortal blow.

The temperature in the room dropped.

Paxton rose and came running over to stand in front of her. "That's enough. She doesn't understand our ways. In this case, I believe Eric was right to do what he did."

A murmur rustled throughout the room. To have

stood beside her, siding with her…had to be big. Storey didn't care how big. She hadn't been a conformist in her world, she wasn't about to start now.

The breath wooshed out of Eric and his shoulders relaxed.

"Eric, take her over to the seats so we can get started."

Storey noticed the two empty chairs only when Eric motioned toward them. Paxton waited until they'd sat down before addressing the swelling crowd. "Now. This problem is one for both our worlds. Several weeks ago a research team, Denby's team, I believe, crossed over. They were there for less than an hour when Sarcov, the head scientist, became sick. We think at this point he might have been allergic to some of the plants he was studying."

Eric shifted. Storey shot him a questioning look. He never took his gaze off Paxton.

"…in the panic to treat him and get him home, the team missed packing up some equipment. As a result, his stylus was lost."

The murmur in the room swelled. Paxton held up his hand. "I know. I know. We weren't made aware of this until Sarcov woke up in the hospital and asked for it." He looked around the room. "We sent a team back immediately. And they were almost upon it when they saw a young girl stoop to pick it up. They followed her, hoping to recover the instrument, only they lost her in the school." He nodded toward Storey. "This is the girl."

He stopped to pin the seated members with a cutting glare, before saying, "What's important to understand is that she picked it up with her bare hands and had no problem in doing so."

Over the growing murmur of excited voices, Paxton glanced over at Storey. "I'll explain in a minute."

"Storey didn't know what she'd found. As an artist, she was happy with her find, thinking it was only a writing instrument. Except she soon found herself driven to draw on every surface from her textbooks, homework, even her own arms."

Storey pulled her sleeves down over her wrists. Her fingers clenched in her lap. She hadn't thought he'd noticed. She'd tried to wash it off, but no go.

Eric interjected. "Sorry, Storey. I didn't say anything to you because I didn't want to make you uncomfortable." He turned back to address the elders. "She was listening to the stylus. It's been trying to come back home."

His father shook his head. "That's not possible. She's not capable of hearing the stylus. They speak only to their owners."

Paxton shook his head. "It *shouldn't* be possible. However, as we've never lost anything over there, we don't *know* what's possible and what's not. Especially with something soulbound."

Eric's father's gaze narrowed, sharpened. "Doesn't that defy the term?"

Another seated elder spoke. "Exactly. If the stylus was soulbound, how did she manage to pick it up?"

"We're not sure of anything in this case. It's possible," Paxton suggested, "that due to Sarcov's illness, the bond between him and the stylus weakened. It's also possible that crossing the veil changed something that contributed to the bond weakening. The stylus might have been able to detach." Paxton shrugged. "We just don't know."

Murmurs rose through the crowd.

Paxton straightened and raised his right hand, commanding silence from the audience. "We don't have all the answers here. There are much more important issues to focus on. We know that Storey picked up the stylus and used it for her artwork. However, without knowing what she was doing, she drew a doorway and actually managed to go through it, thus entering our world."

The crowd cried out in shock. "What? She came here? Without us knowing?"

"Yes, that's correct. Except the monitoring system tracked her movements."

Storey leaned toward Eric, her eyes widening in shock. "I have?"

"Yes. The mine is partially on our side."

She blinked. Then blinked again. "So, when I went through the floor in my bedroom and ended up in the mine, that was the same as crossing the veil?"

He studied her face then grinned, that same lopsided smile. Damn, he shouldn't be allowed to do that.

"Something like that. The stylus actually took you to a formal crossing zone in the mine. You couldn't get out because it wasn't active on our side. It's only because the crossing notified Paxton of your activity that you were found at all."

Dismay crossed her face. "Are you saying I might have never gotten out?"

"If we didn't monitor the veil then yes. It's quite likely you'd have died there and no one would have known." He reached across to cover her clenched hands with his. "However, Paxton *did* find you. He told me and I opened the door on your side of the world to let you out."

"And the second time I went in?" Storey struggled to understand.

Eric grimaced. "The stylus took you to a different gate entirely, presumably because the first attempt didn't work. I had to make it look like Bankhead mine when you walked out." He tilted his head, this time a glint of amusement in his eyes. "I also have a soulkey that unlocks almost anything. It has a few other functions that are dangerous to use if you are untrained."

The mine door. Storey shook her head and laughed.

"No way. That's not possible. How could I not notice?"

He flushed then mumbled, "I did it while you were…distracted."

She blinked. Memories flooded in. That kiss. That hot, wonderful, mind-blowing kiss. "That's why you kissed me?" she hissed. "Oh, my God."

Eric's face slipped from the color of a sun-kissed peach color to a fat ripe tomato. Storey glanced around, noting multiple disapproving frowns deepened as they understood, too. "Oh crap. Sorry everyone. Swearing is common in my world. It's not an insult against humanity over there."

"It's not over here either; however, it is a sign of disrespect," said another older male, this one just as disapproving as the others at the table.

"Right." She grimaced. "I'll try to remember that."

Paxton took control of the conversation again, lowering the noise level in the room instantly. "The real problem is that Storey drew something else." Paxton reached for Storey's sketchbook sitting in front of him on the table. "This."

He flipped through the book until he found the right page, then held it up to show everyone.

The crowd erupted into an outcry of shock. Storey grimaced as she looked at it. That hand was beyond creepy. "I don't know if it matters or not, but I don't remember much about drawing that picture."

Eric's father groaned and smacked his hand down on the table. "That just makes it worse. How could you?"

"How could I what? Draw? I've always drawn. It's never created portals into another dimension. Keep in mind, I wouldn't have done anything if you people hadn't left that instrument behind on your invasion."

"Invasion? Did she just say invasion?"

"What invasion? What is she talking about?"

Paxton once again held up his hand to bring the conversation back under control. "We're not pointing fingers here. A series of accidents has brought us to this spot. We have to focus. We are in a crisis, let's deal with that."

Arguments and shouting broke out across the room. Storey slunk low in her chair. Who could get used to all this fighting?

"Stop," roared Paxton. "We have to find out what this drawing represents. And if it is what I think it is, we have to find a solution – fast."

Eric's father shot a disgusted look at Storey. "This is just a drawing. She can't possibly wield the power of the stylus."

Another elder seated at the table spoke up. "Just what are you thinking the problem is here?"

Paxton addressed the room, his voice deep and deadly serious. "I'm afraid it's the Louers."

Dead silence. Then absolute chaos erupted.

Louers? Storey wracked her brain. Nope, the name meant nothing to her. Obviously, it did to everyone else as questions flew at Paxton too fast for him to answer.

"The Louers. Oh my. I thought they'd been wiped out."

"Are they real?"

"We got rid of them, didn't we?"

The questions rose and fell all around her. As she caught the gist of the conversation, the puzzle pieces fell into place. Storey thought she finally understood. "Are you saying this hand belongs to one of those Louers? And that by drawing a doorway, I actually created a door they could open too?"

"Exactly." Paxton nodded like she was some favorite student. She'd love to be, except her next question would drop her right down to a failing grade.

"So who and what are the Louers?"

CHAPTER 8

H ER HISTORY LESSON wouldn't start until later. By that time, Storey expected to be comatose. It didn't seem to matter which side of the veil she was on. Neither side could get an agreement out of a group of people – decision by committee was a waste of time. The bickering had been going on for hours. At least it felt that way to Storey.

"We should set up a committee to study the problem. We'll appoint an overseer who can pick his team and set out steps as to how to proceed."

"Oh, not this again." Storey groaned as the same idea was hashed over and over again.

"What?" asked a skinny, bald-headed guy dressed similarly to Paxton. "Have you got a better idea?"

"Hell, yes." The same hush fell over the room as she once again lost her cool. "Oh, right, I swore again. Well, I've got to tell you – it's a little hard to have any respect for a group of people who are so busy trying to get someone else to make a decision that nothing gets done." She stood up, ignoring Eric's restraining hand on her forearm. "I know I don't understand how things work over here, but maybe someone could answer a couple of questions. Such as, can I draw the door closed? Can I rip up the paper and have it no longer exist? How about I draw a group of people taking these Louers and forcing them back to the other side?"

"Will someone shut this girl up. She's wasting our time and has caused us nothing but trouble. Someone get her out of here." Eric's father, the arrogant asshole, appeared to be some kind of leader here.

"Why? Because I'm trying to understand what we can and can't do. It seems logical that if the stylus opened the door, it could close it, too." She strove to keep her voice reasonable.

"I don't think it works like that," Eric whispered.

"That's the problem. None of you know how this works." She spread her hands out on the table. "You're all so used to doing something one way that you can't see there might be another way to approach the problem."

"It's not that. There are rules on our side. The Louers were our enemies. Since they've been gone we've had peace."

"Yeah? Did you go on secret research missions and steal from them, too?" she scoffed. "You guys need to work on your communication skills."

"And you need to stop insulting us."

"Why?" she challenged. "What are you going to do?" She stood, reached across the table for her sketchbook, and then walked to the doorway. "You don't want me here. I'm obviously of no value, so pardon me if I leave." She strode out, letting her sarcasm fill the room.

"Don't let her leave. Eric, stop her," the Councilman shouted.

Eric stood up and snorted as Storey walked away. "What do you want me to do?"

"Well, she can't just run loose over here. Who knows what kind of damage she could cause?"

Eric snorted again. "Like we do in her world. It's not like we registered with her any of her governments and sign in and out on our visits. Neither are we under guard at any time."

The Councilman's icy voice sliced through the room. "Lock her up. She's the enemy."

Storey gasped and spun around. Seeing the vindictive look on his fat face, she headed for the doorway.

"No, wait." Eric raced behind her.

His father called back. "Eric. She's not one of us. Remember your place."

Shooting his father a disgusted look, Eric left the conference room. He caught up with her in the lab. "What are you doing?"

"Going home. I came here at your request. I can't help you. Therefore, I'm going home."

"You can't just leave. Don't you understand? This is a different dimension. You can't just walk home." Eric ran his hand through his hair. "I know this is tough, and I'm sorry. I'd forgotten what it's like when this group gets together.

"It's called bureaucracy on my side."

"Yeah. Same thing here."

"And yes, I can just leave." Storey waved the stylus and sketchbook at him.

"What, you're just going to draw the other side? And expect to walk right into it?"

"Or something that's even easier." She sat down cross-legged on the floor and sketched madly for a couple of minutes while Eric watched over her shoulder.

"There's no way that's going to work," he scoffed.

"Maybe and maybe not," she answered him without raising her gaze from her picture. "Then again, you're so used to the rules of your world that you don't even know if the rules can be broken. And sometimes you don't need to break anything. You need to find a way around things."

He squatted down beside her. "True. I'd think you might need to know the rules before you can break them."

"Apparently not or we wouldn't be in this mess now."

She shot him a grin before refocusing. "Wait and see. If it doesn't work, no problem, then you can use your decoder and take me home." She finished her drawing, painfully aware of his lack of response. She stood up and waited until he'd straightened and looked at her. "They won't let you take me home, will they?"

He grimaced, dropping his gaze to the ground and kicked out as if at an invisible rock. "No."

"Well, you're going to have to if this doesn't work," she said coolly. "You brought me here, so it's up to you to do the right thing and take me home. Especially as you brought me here without my permission in the first place. You said you wanted to show someone my work. You didn't say I'd be going to another dimension to make that happen. And you didn't say I wouldn't be going home."

"Let's hope this works, so I'm not put into that position."

Studying her sketch, Storey added, "Seems like parental control, discrimination and assholes are all the same no matter which side of the veil you're on. Too bad. I was hoping your society was more advanced and my people could learn something from you. Not going to happen, though."

"We *are* more advanced," he protested.

She walked over to the wall she'd been staring at. Nodding once, she ripped off the paper and looked around. "Do you oh-so-much-more-superior people have such things as pins or tape?"

He snorted, walked over to the closest bench and pulled off a piece of something gray. Returning to her side, he said, "It's neither and won't cause any damage like those two will."

She sniffed disdainfully. "We have sticky stuff like that at home too." Flipping her hair, she stuck the gray ball onto the back of the sketch and hung it on the wall.

Taking a few steps back, she studied the picture in relationship to the rest of the room, grabbed her pencil and drew a couple of quick horizontal and then vertical lines on the wall outside of the picture. She nodded. "Okay. See you around – maybe."

She walked purposefully toward the picture that she'd incorporated the wall into.

"Eric, what are you two doing?" Paxton ran into the room. "We need you back in there. Bring Storey so we can keep track of her."

Storey shook her head. Not going to happen. She was going home. With a small wave of her fingers, she walked into the wall – and through her picture.

"No. Oh, no. She can't do—"

Storey grinned as she stood in the middle of her own bedroom.

Apparently, she could.

ERIC'S JAW DROPPED.

Paxton stood in place, wringing his hands. "Oh dear. Not good. This is not good."

Eric blinked, then blinked again. She'd done it. Even after he'd said she couldn't. How stupid could he be? And not just him. His people were just as guilty. She'd been right. They'd been locked into the surety of knowing what worked and what didn't. Therefore, they'd never questioned the boundaries of that knowledge.

Storey hadn't had the same restrictions. She'd taken the steps to find out just what she could do.

Unbelievable. Shocking really. He pulled himself out of the dangerous bout of admiration to study the doorway Storey had opened, then backed up several feet. She'd drawn a hallway, as if the picture on the wall was a portion of the wall itself. Using the doorway to her bedroom as the vanishing point in the distance, she'd created a long hallway to her room. A perspective drawing with her room as the single point in the center.

Brilliant, really.

Eric turned to face his mentor and received another shock.

Paxton was terrified.

He'd never thought to see fear on Paxton's face. Consternation, even worry, anger, but fear, now that was a new one. One he didn't like.

"Oh, dear. What are we going to do?" Paxton held his hands together and stared at the wall.

"What's going on here? Where's the girl?" His father bellowed from the doorway.

Eric stiffened. Maybe it was Storey's influence, or maybe, he was just seeing the light for the first time. He pulled the sketch off the wall and folded it.

"The girl? *Storey* has gone home."

Eric braced for the storm to hit.

"What? You took her home? How dare you? You will be punished for this."

Years of being educated in a strict school, where obedience and respect for his father, their leader, was all that held Eric back from letting the words spill over. He could only stare in disgust at his father, a father who'd been absent from most of his life. "I didn't take her back."

"Not directly, but you let her leave," Paxton cried out in anguish. "Oh, dear. This is terrible."

"She was never a prisoner, Paxton. She came at my request. To show you her picture. Realizing that no one here would listen to her or wanted her help, she decided to go home."

"She was supposed to have been your prisoner. It's your fault," snapped his father.

"Why? I was told to retrieve the stylus. Nothing about trying to keep Story captive. Not that I could have," he added thoughtfully, staring at the wall.

"You could have used chains and the dungeon. At least they'd have gotten the job done."

Cold settled into Eric's chest. The dungeons were for the worst of the worst. Dark, wet and miles underground where prisoners went insane or, more often than not, died of neglect. Originally built for a different purpose, the only prisoners ever sent there were traitors. People who went against the Council. If they'd planned that for Storey, he was glad she'd escaped. Since when had his people been so harsh, so unforgiving? Being on the inside, he'd never questioned his way of life or those in power. No one did. Everyone had what they needed. At least as far as he knew. Why worry? For the first time in his life he questioned the morality of his government. "Our dungeons have never been for anyone but slaves, when we had them, and the worst criminals in our society. There's so few of them the dungeons aren't worth maintaining. I hardly think Storey's actions warrant such a punishment."

"Well, possibly not the dungeons." His father backed down on that point. "But we can't just have her running around loose on the other side. Who knows who'd she'll tell? What damage she'll do?"

Eric shook his head in disbelief. "She's just a kid."

"She's already caused damage." Paxton came to Eric, as if willing him to understand. "You have to see the truth here. She can't be left to do as she pleases."

Eric cocked his head, fear for Storey and a deep-seated anger slowly building, twisting into a fury he'd never known. "What is it you're planning to do?"

"You must bring her back, of course. Even a dimwit like you should be able to see the sense of that." The sneer on his father's face sharpened.

The fury boiling behind his self control was going to
kill him. He swallowed hard. "Really. *I'm* to bring her
back so she can be your prisoner? So you can take away
her memories, force her to be a lab rat for you to study?"

Paxton suddenly rose to his full height. "Don't use
that tone with me. Of course she must come back. She
still has the stylus."

"Which is soulbound to her. They can't be separated
anymore."

"We don't know that. Sarcov has almost recovered.
He might be able to bond with it again."

"It can only bond with one person at a time."

"Right. So now you see how important it is to get it
back," his father snapped.

Eric stared at the two men, his anger being quietly
drowned by fear. "You can't take it away from her unless
she dies or, as in Sarcov's case, it appears as if death is
imminent. Storey is neither of those."

"Oh, don't be naive. She's dangerous. Of course, she's
going to have to die – eventually."

No. No, surely that's not what he was hearing. Eric
shook his head slowly like a bull with a red flag being
waved in his face. "You want me to bring her back so you
can kill her?"

"Well, I wouldn't put it that way." Paxton tried to
smooth the harshness of the conversation over. "We
might need her."

"Her name is Storey. The least you can do is call her
by her proper name."

"What are you talking about? She's one of them." His
father's outrage boiled over. "They don't deserve our
respect. They're animals. Mindless in their actions, eating
and killing their way through life with no consequence for
their future."

Eric reared back. "And what's so different about what

you're suggesting? Didn't you just tell me to go and get her, so you could kill her?" He sneered. "How dare you put yourself on a pedestal above her and her kind? Is this what you've raised me for? To view myself as better than the others just because they live on the other side of the veil?"

"We are more advanced than they are. Our technology is superior, so are our energy capabilities. We must protect our way of life." Paxton tried to appease him. "These humans would overrun us with sheer numbers, strip us of our knowledge, our resources. You can see that, right?"

"We don't have any information on what they can or cannot do. Storey said something else that's true. We've gone over to her world time and time again, bringing back anything we wanted or needed to develop our technology. That's the *only* reason we've developed beyond them. We've never once shared what we've learned, including the new medicines and healing lasers that have wiped out illness here. No. She's right – we've stolen everything from them."

"Nonsense. We're doing what we've always done. We've lived like this for centuries. How can you start to judge our ways now? That girl is dangerous. Look at how you are speaking to me. You've never talked back before." His father snorted at him.

Eric frowned at the truth of his father's words. When his father had said to do something, he'd done it – blindly. Regardless of right or wrong. There'd been a time or two when he'd wondered at the wisdom of the orders, but had followed them regardless.

How horrible was that? Shame filled him for his past actions, or lack thereof, and for his own treatment of Storey. She deserved better. He'd tricked her into coming over here and hadn't even taken her home again.

"Now, I want you to go there and bring her back." His father drew himself up to his full height which, being more than a foot shorter than Paxton at his side, made him look ridiculous. "And I want you to go now."

Eric tilted his head and studied him. Paxton waited, holding his breath. Eric ignored him. "And if I don't? Then what?"

His father's face turned beet red and absolute rage shone from his eyes. He gritted his teeth and stuck his jaw out. "What did you say to me?"

"I asked you what the penalty would be if I refuse to commit murder." Eric raised his eyebrows. "That is what you are asking of me, isn't it? If I bring her back, you will kill her. That makes me an accomplice in the eyes of the law."

"No. I am not going to argue about this. This person, this girl, has threatened national security. She doesn't get a trial and there won't be any charge of murder. She is a danger to us all."

"Says you."

His father went seriously quiet. When he spoke again, his voice was flat and dark. "I am going to make myself clear right now and we will never speak of this again." Steel shone from his eyes. "I am ordering you to go to the other side of the veil, retrieve the girl, and bring her back here. Should you fail to do so, you are guilty of the same crime of which she is accused. And then…" he paused for effect, "a team will go over there and do what you weren't willing to do yourself – by force if necessary."

Paxton closed his eyes and bowed his head as if the worst had happened.

A chill swept over Eric. This was his father. The father he'd idolized growing up. The father he'd respected all through his brief years. The father he'd done everything to impress was ordering him to bring Storey back to be killed – or be killed himself.

"STOREY? IS THAT you?" Her mother burst into her bedroom. "There you are. I swear I seem to spend half my time looking for you lately."

"I'm here, Mom. What's up?" Storey hated the coolness in her own tone. Her day hadn't been the best to begin with. She warmed her smile.

"Oh, Eric didn't come back with you, did he?" Her mother peered around the corner of her room as if looking for signs of him hidden in the closet.

"No, Mom. He had to go home."

"Oh." She smiled brightly. "He seems like such a nice boy."

"Yes, he seems nice." Then, looks could be deceiving, as she'd found out.

"Is he…special?" Her mother's hopeful expression fell as Storey shook her head. "You two looked so great together."

"Maybe. Unlikely. I don't know. I wouldn't get my hopes up, if I were you." Storey knew her Mom had watched her social life with a wary eye during her relationship with Jeff and immediately afterwards.

"Well, if it's meant to be and all that." She smiled. "Why don't you come down and have a cup of tea with me?"

"Who's here?"

The smile dropped from her mom's face fast. She hesitated. "Do you resent all the company? I never thought." She nibbled on her bottom lip. "We do have a lot of company though, don't we? I'm sorry. It's your home, too."

Oh, brother. "Mom. Stop. I'm fine with the company. I'm glad you have so many friends. That you're happy with your life and your beliefs." Mostly, anyways, but she wasn't going to open up that discussion. Not now.

A smile peeped out. "I wish you'd consider joining…"

"I know. At the moment, I'm not feeling it." Although after what she'd seen today, Wiccan didn't seem as odd or farfetched as it had yesterday. "I'll make my own decision. I just need some time."

"Then time you shall have." She smiled. "And there's no one downstairs right now. Let's go have a cup of tea and some fresh poppy seed cake."

"Best offer I've had all day." In a rare moment of concord, the two linked arms and headed for the kitchen.

Storey could only hope her bedroom would still be empty when she returned. She'd forgotten to consider one tiny problem – how to close the portal she'd created from her side.

Chapter 9

G ETTING ALONG WITH your mother beat trying to avoid her. Two hours later, Storey headed to her bedroom door, yawning. She had homework to finish but no energy to care about such minor details. Pushing her door open, she came to a sudden halt.

She gasped, checked behind her to make sure she was alone before stepping in a shutting the door behind her. "Oh my God," she hissed. "What are you doing here?" Leaning against the door, she stared at Eric, who lay half asleep on her bed. Damn, he looked good there. As if he belonged.

Not.

"About time you got here. I've been waiting forever."

"Why? What do you want from me?" Pulling out her computer chair, she sat down facing him, before her knees gave out on her. "And how did you get in?"

"Same way you did, only I removed the paper as I went through so we couldn't be followed."

She raised an eyebrow. "Cool. Too bad I didn't think of that. Then again, I wasn't sure if it would work in the first place."

"Well, it's not there anymore."

"Thank God. It's a little creepy to have people entering my bedroom from another dimension. Maybe the kitchen or living room, but not my bedroom, thanks."

He just stared at her.

"Okay, I'm babbling. Sorry. It's just a little unnerving to have you here out of the blue like that." She stared out the window.

"They want me to bring you back."

She tilted her head and studied the look on his face. Odd wording. Hmmm. "And what do you want to do?"

"I don't want you to go over there again."

She raised an eyebrow. So much for seeing where the relationship with Eric might go. Long distance didn't quite cut it, as she already knew. Look what had happened to her and Jeff.

"Good, then I won't. The last visit was enough for me, anyway."

"They'll send someone else if I don't bring you back."

The shadows lengthened in the early evening light. "They again." She watched him carefully, sensing more to the story. "How much force will 'they' use to make me go back?"

His face paled.

Her stomach twisted. "That much, huh?" She didn't want to dwell on it. They didn't look like the kind of group that lived and let live. "Did they come to an agreement about the Louers yet?"

Eric shook his head. "I think they're more concerned about you being a loose end."

Her eyes widened. "They're afraid of me? Of what I might say? Do?" At each successive nod, the knots in her stomach tightened. She closed her eyes. Think, damn it. There had to be a way out of this mess. "What are my options?"

"I don't know. I've been lying here and going over them. None are great."

"List those you've considered."

He appeared to choose his words carefully as he listed off choices that included him never going back, going back and helping his people after negotiating her return, hiding by moving to another part of the planet so the people coming behind him wouldn't be able to find her.

As he rambled on, she had a distinct sense that something was wrong. "Okay, out with it. Something else happened. What?"

He sat up and swung his feet over the bed. "They'll kill you if you go back."

She swallowed. Hard. "As a conversationalist, you suck."

His lopsided grin slipped out. "Sorry. Not used to this kind of conversation."

The grin did it, easing the weight on her chest threatening to suffocate her. She grinned back. "Yeah, it shows. So they don't want to leave any witnesses behind, huh?"

"Something like that."

Silence fell.

"You're serious, aren't you?" How had everything gone so wrong? A few days ago life had been normal. She'd been wishing for something new and different to come into her life. A death squad from another dimension wasn't what she'd had in mind. "So, if I go with you they will kill me. If I don't go with you they'll send a team over to retrieve me then kill me anyway? Where's the option that lets me live?"

"I think that's the run part, so they can't find you."

"Except you have technology that allows your people to track me, while I don't have anything to help me evade your people. So that's hardly an option." She studied the fatigue in his eyes. He looked like he'd been to hell and back. "What happens to you if I don't go back with you? Anything? Or just a slap on the wrist because you didn't follow orders?"

He stood up straight, his face lean and ravaged. "Death. The Council says I will face a death sentence if you don't go back with me."

Storey couldn't believe it. Studying his face in disbelief, she found the truth in his pain. Eric's father was head of the Council. If he'd ordered his son's death over this…he was a monster. "Why would your father do that?"

"According to him, you're a threat to national security and that outweighs his parental concern."

"Bullshit."

He winced.

She laughed bitterly. "Sorry, but that's a load of crap. There's no way I'm a security issue. He's power tripping."

"Maybe, but it's effective. He issued the order in front of witnesses. It has to be carried out. There is no rescinding that kind of order."

She stood and stared up at his face. Nothing like parents to remind you of your humanity. "I'm sorry. It has to hurt to hear your life has so little value."

He snorted. "You think?"

"I'm not going back there. Not so they can use me as a lab rat and then kill me out of their own fear."

His eyes stared down at her, closed briefly then opened, bright blue lights shining deep. "I know and I wouldn't want you to."

"Except that means your death."

"I know," he said, his face seriously grim, his decision clearly made.

She respected him in that moment.

"Okay, this is ridiculous. Now that we've settled that, let's come up with a way to make this right for both of us."

"Do you think that's possible?"

It was that faint hope peering from deep inside his eyes that settled her determination to find a solution. One where they both got to live.

ERIC STOMPED ON the hope trickling through him. It wouldn't do to put too much credence in Storey's skills. What she'd achieved so far was phenomenal. But he had to face reality. Paxton hadn't helped after his father had stormed off. "You shouldn't have pushed him like that."

"I pushed him?" Astonished, Eric could only stare at his beloved mentor.

"Yes, you forced him to declare his intentions with the girl. He can't back down now. We might have found a way around this mess but for that."

"Like what?" he scoffed. "She's right, you know. We're all about us. Not about them. Everything is our way. The mistake was ours in the first place."

"She didn't have to pick up the stylus," Paxton said fretfully.

"She hardly had a choice – it called to her. You said yourself that it wanted to go home. No one is looking at that. People need to realize she's a victim here. The stylus targeted *her*. She didn't mean to do this. She had no idea that she could do any of this."

"Regardless of how this started, she's in the middle of it now. We have no solution to the Louers either."

"She'd have been happy to help."

Paxton snuck a glance around the room, then leaned forward to whisper, "Do you think so?" At Eric's nod, he said, "Then go bring her back. Please. Our very existence is at stake here."

Eric studied the older man. Did he believe that? Or was it just another attempt to get Eric to do his bidding? "I can't deliver her to her death."

"Don't think of it that way. It would be a state sentence being carried out."

"It's murder." Eric said. "I'd be bringing her back

under false pretences."

"No. Not at all. Tell her we need her help."

"And what?" Eric threw up his hands. "And don't tell her that as thanks, we're going to brand her as a traitor to the state and have her killed? Are you insane?"

Paxton reared back. "No. But if you don't bring her back, then a retrieval team will go after her anyway and you'll both be killed."

Eric had contemplated the two horrible options. He didn't want to die. Neither could he let Storey be killed. "Even when the orders are wrong?" Fatigue slid through his voice. He was more tired than he could believe, and none of it was related to how he felt physically. The emotional stress of the last few hours had leeched everything from his system.

He glanced around the lab where he'd enjoyed so many comfortable hours with Paxton. Paxton had been more of a father to him than his own flesh and blood version. "Tell me, would you bring her back, knowing you were bringing her to her death?"

"If I had to, as much as I don't like the idea, yes."

"Why is it a 'had to?' Why is death the only option? She's not going to hurt us – particularly once she understands the problem."

"You don't know that. We have to get the stylus back. That she should be bound to it is intolerable."

"Why? Maybe they have soulbound objects over there."

"We've seen no sign of such a thing."

"Again that arrogance. We haven't seen them, therefore, they don't exist? Why do you insist we're better than they are?"

"That's not what I said. Don't go putting words in my mouth." Paxton's voice turned testy. "Get ready. It shouldn't take you long to find her."

"It won't be easy to persuade her to return," warned Eric. Already he was calculating how long they had to make their getaway.

"Don't take too long. Your father will give you a few hours, overnight probably. If you're not back by noon tomorrow, a retrieval team will be sent over."

"Is anyone else over there now?"

"No. There aren't any planned missions in the next year."

"Hmmm. Just wondered if we had spies living on the other side of the veil."

Paxton stared at him in shock. "Of course not. We've never done that. What for? They've never been a threat to us before."

"And they still aren't."

"It's time for you to do what you need to do." Paxton gave him a hard look.

Eric frowned, studying Paxton's face. Had there been a weird inflection in Paxton's voice? The wording had been interesting. *Do what you need to do.*

Now, lying here in Storey's room, that's the phrase he focused on.

"Hey, are you there? Felt like I lost you somewhere, just now."

"I'm here."

He stared at her, his gaze flat and concerned, for a long moment. Long enough for her sunny smile to fall away and be replaced by a worried frown.

"Run away with me."

"WHAT DID YOU say?" she squeaked. Was that horrible, high-pitched girlie voice really hers? *Oh God.*

"It's the only option. I can teach you how to evade

my people, and you can teach me to live over here."

"Why run, then?" she asked cautiously.

He stared at her again in that deep, intense way, as if he could see to the center of her soul. Maybe he could. His people seemed to have untold skills and technology, she thought resentfully.

"The retrieval team won't be polite. I'm afraid of the lengths they might go to get the information they want from your family."

"Oh my God. Are you saying they might hurt my mother?" At his slow nod, she collapsed beside him on the bed. "This is so not happening. I didn't care until you mentioned my mom getting hurt." She buried her face in her hands. "I've been so stupid."

A warm hand squeezed her shoulder. She dropped her hands to find him leaning over her.

"You haven't been stupid. That you managed to do what you did, took a remarkable amount of resourcefulness and ingenuity."

"Really?" She raised an eyebrow at him, inordinately pleased when he nodded. So he thought she was smart. Well good. She was no dummy. She knew that. "Running away isn't the answer."

"Why not?" He sat down beside her and held her hand. "We can't fight. There are too many of them."

"Maybe. Once we start there'll be no end to our running. No, we have to find a way to remove the 'kill order' from my head."

"My father won't back down. He believes you're a threat and that's that."

She studied his face. "For a society that talks and doesn't act, it seems odd that he'd make one statement and then stand by it."

"That's why they talk so much first. Once they embark on a course of action, they stand by it."

"What if we kidnap him – until he changes his mind?" Eric looked so horrified, she had to laugh. "Kidding! But we need to do something offensive instead of defensive. Once you're on the defensive, it's hard to get off of it."

"What, did you take Spy 101?"

Tossing her hair over her shoulder, she grinned. "Football."

His shock had her laughing out loud.

"Then we kidnap someone other than my father. The security surrounding him is impressive."

"What about your security?" she asked curiously. Did no one care about Eric?

"Don't have any."

Nice father, worried more about protecting himself than his son, but she refrained from pointing that out. "Could we negotiate?"

He frowned. "I don't understand."

"What if I offer to help, providing the death sentence is rescinded?" she chewed her bottom lip, worried by one big issue. "And can we trust them to keep their part of the agreement afterward?" She wasn't sure they could. "Hmmm. Why are the Louers so feared?"

"It has to do with the kind of people they are. They're more like a pestilence that feeds on others. Literally."

"Gross. Are you saying they're cannibals?"

"Supposedly. At least according to the archives they're human-like, but more animal in behavior."

"Like a dog? Horse? A monkey kind of thing?" She couldn't quite reconcile the long boney fingers pushing the door open in her drawing with any kind of animal.

"I don't know."

"Or are they just 'lesser people' like your kind consider me to be?"

"I'm not sure." He frowned. "I hope not. Everything

I've learned has come from the archives."

"Written by your unbiased ancestors, no doubt." Storey snickered. "Why were they locked away in this third dimension anyway? And don't forget that outside of that hand in my drawing, there's been no sign of Louers in either dimension."

"As far as the archives report," he admitted at her knowing look, "they hunted my people. They had stealth and skills that gave them the upper hand in wars. We were a peaceful people. They made us slaves. It's said that they ate our kind, as well."

"Well, the slave thing certainly isn't new and neither is the war. Your people were the weaker of the two and lost the fight. Maybe your people did something to bring the battle on their heads, and they rose up against you."

His gaze widened. "No."

Storey wasn't so sure. It might have happened that way. If Eric's people were in any way like her own, war was almost second nature. And Eric might not know all the facts. After seeing his people in action, she doubted they were as innocent as he'd like to believe. His wouldn't be the first society to wipe their history, and therefore their record, clean. She'd learned that much in history class. "How long do we have?"

"Until early tomorrow, I'd say."

"Does Paxton monitor all the screens all the time?"

"Yes. He or someone on his staff."

"Then why don't we go back to your world? They can see that you did your job and…" she held up her hand to forestall his words from flying out, "and then you can help me escape again."

He rose and stormed around the small room. "Because I can't guarantee your safety."

She nodded. "That's why we're going to have to be crafty."

"I don't understand."

"Come on, I'll show you." She snatched up her sketchbook and sat down beside him.

"Storey, are you in there?" Her mother knocked on her door. Panic-stricken, Storey turned to face the door as Eric tried to squeeze his length into her closet, scrunching beneath her hanging clothes. Grabbing her mp3 player, Storey walked to the door and opened it, a quizzical smile on her face. "Of course I am. What's up?" Music blasted from the cheap earbud in her hand, the other one sat in her ear.

"I thought I heard you talking to someone."

Storey snorted. "Yeah, right. As if. I don't have any-one to talk to, remember?"

"Well, Eric would talk to you. He seemed like such nice boy."

Uh oh. She so didn't want her mother talking about this, especially not when Eric could hear. She shook her head. "We're not going there, Mom."

"I just wanted to tell you I'm heading over to Sandra and Daren's place, if you don't mind, that is?" She appeared anxious, as if waiting for Storey's approval.

Storey sighed. "Mom, that's great. Go have fun. No, I don't want to join you, and yes, it's totally fine that you're going."

Her mom gave her a worried look. "Are you sure?"

Maybe it was the imminent threat of death or the thought of her mom waking up to find her gone – maybe forever – that prompted Storey. Regardless, she leaned forward and kissed her mom on the cheek. "I'm sure. Go have fun."

Relieved, her mom turned away. "There's some snack food downstairs if you get hungry later."

"We just ate, Mom. I'm fine."

"You didn't eat much. I could…"

"No. You couldn't. Stop. I'm old enough to know when I need to eat. I'm not hungry. If that changes, I promise I'll go and find something."

"Okay then. I might be late, so I'll see you in the morning."

"G'night, Mom."

Storey closed the door and turned to lean against it with a heavy sigh. Her mother would be devastated if something happened to her only child.

"You okay?"

"Yeah. Let's get started." Story crossed over to the bed and opened her sketchbook to a clean page. "Where are they likely to take me, once we get to your side?"

"The worst case would be the dungeons."

She gave him a horrified look. "What? That sounds bad."

"It is. Nasty place. Most prisoners sicken and die." He pondered the idea. "I don't think they would start with that punishment."

"Good," she muttered. "I'm looking to draw exits from your world to mine."

"That's risky," he warned. "I can't guarantee where they might take you."

"True. However, if you hand me over and I have some exits on me already, then I could get home if I don't happen to care for the accommodations. And I need to take spare paper for my stylus, just in case."

He shook his head. "You're going to have to be so careful. If they catch you, they'll take the stylus away from you and you won't be able to use it."

"This is why I want to draw the exits now. While I have the stylus." She twisted the pencil in her hand. "Do you think I could draw a weapon? An assistant? A new happy world for your people? Like what are the limits of this thing?" She stared down at the pencil, wondering just what was possible. "Have you used one yourself?"

"No. There are very few of them in existence, and they bond to the death, so a new bonding can only happen when the owner dies."

"And mine belonged to a scientist? Weird." She studied the pencil, trying to read the writing trying to not think about what might happen to her if the Torans took it back. "So no one really knows what they can do."

"No."

"If I draw a cupcake with it, will it create one?"

"I don't think so. Whatever you draw has to be contained in the paper."

Scrunching up her face, she struggled with what he was saying. "So I drew a door and the paper became the door. If I draw a window and hold it up, can I see what's on the other side?"

Confusion filled his gaze and then he blinked hard. "It's not like the picture is going to change and show you what's there. Maybe you can put your face through the paper or something. I don't know. Honestly, I think you're going to have to try it out."

"Except I don't want a window unless I could see something useful. Like into the dungeon so I could see the walls and then draw them as a way to create a door out again.

"Hmm. Not going to work."

A weird sound rumbled through her room. She bolted upright. "What the hell is that?"

Eric got his feet more slowly. "I'm not sure. It can't be good."

The noise sounded again, under her feet. She bolted upright. "I'm going to look."

With Eric on her heels, she raced downstairs to the living room. Her mother had gone, leaving the house empty. She dashed into the den, which sat right below her bedroom. The far wall had splintered and cracked. As they stood and watched, several strangely long, bony fingers crept through the crack, breaking pieces of plaster as they slid further out. Dirty and rough, with short, cracked fingernails, the fingers scrabbled for a hold on the wall.

"Oh shit. Oh shit."

Eric gulped audibly. Running his hand through his hair, he stared at those fingers in horror. A quick glance at his face confirmed Storey's suspicions.

"The Louers?" she whispered in dread. At his nod, her heart pounded inside her chest and her mind screamed at her. How could this have happened? Why were they *here* and not on Eric's side? She'd never considered this. She looked around for something, anything, to make this all go away. She glanced down at her hand, still holding the sketchbook and stylus.

Crouching down, she balanced the book on her knee and slapped down a sketch of the wall in front of her, without the crack. Then she added a door and placed a deadbolt on the side, separating the two worlds. She could have done it in half the time, but her fingers were trembling so badly, she kept messing up.

With one clean stroke of the stylus, she locked the deadbolt in place. And sat back to stare up at wall, her chest heaving from the effort. Her breath caught in her throat. Did it work?

No. Maybe? The hand was still there. It tried to wiggle as if struggling to move but incapable.

Eric gasped.

"Oh shit," She sketched faster, drawing in the crack to resemble, as close as possible, the damage to the wall in front of her. There was a hard snap, and the fingers disappeared. Then she drew a paint brush in the act of painting the entire wall in plaster. Her breath labored as she struggled to keep her panic under control.

Using a stick hand, she quickly sketched the brush moving across the wall covering up the hand and the crack. As soon as she finished, she looked over the top of the book. The hand was gone and the cracks in her wall were gone – at least where the paint brush had stroked. On a hunch, she turned to a clean page and drew another paint brush, wrote 'eraser' on it then ripped it crudely off the page. With Eric watching her in astonishment, she folded the paper such that only the brush shape showed. Walking to the damaged wall, she stroked, erasing the mess there. Unbelievably, one stroke at a time, everything disappeared. Panicked still, she couldn't stop until the last of it was gone and the wall looked as it had before. Even then, her hand continued to rub the eraser over the wall.

Eric grabbed her hand and pulled her gently into his arms. "It's done, stop!"

Shuddering, she gasped for breath. "Oh, my God."

"You can say that again."

"So much for not being able to create tools."

Holding her tight, he rested his chin on her head. "I can't believe you just did that."

"I didn't do anything. It was the stylus." She took a deep shuddering breath and let it out. "Do you think they're gone?" Pulling back, she peered up at him. "Like really gone?"

"I don't know. What about the outside of the house? Did that fix the problem or just hide this side?"

She shot him a horrified glance and bolted toward the front door. The screen door banged behind her as she ran outside and around to the back of the house. Eric raced around the corner as she was backing up to take a wider look. There were no cracks, no broken siding. Nothing to say anything odd had occurred at all.

Her breath gusted out. Hands on hips, she surveyed

the back wall in amazement. "That thing was coming through the wall – as in *between* the inside and outside walls."

"No." Eric reached out a hand to touch the wooden siding. "That's the part that still confuses you. He was coming between the dimensions. Good thing it was the living room. He could have just as easily come through your bedroom." He glanced at her. "I gotta tell you, that was incredibly quick thinking on your part."

She flushed, grateful for the darkness, and wiped her hands on her jeans. "Thanks. I didn't think at all about it. I just reacted."

The evening air was cool. She shivered as she walked back around to the front of her house. "I wonder if it was the stylus telling me what to do?" His quick frown had her adding, "Or don't you think it can communicate?"

They walked up the three steps to the front porch and Eric opened the door for her. "You tell me. By now you know more than I do. Keep in mind the stylus probably doesn't know or care about the Louers. It seems to just want to get home."

Still the idea had come at the right time, and she couldn't help wonder at the intelligence level of the stylus. She studied it as she had so many times already. It looked like a thick art pencil. Remarkably unremarkable. And it was anything but.

Back inside, she returned to the once damaged wall, looking for proof of the event. Her fingers tentatively stroked the painted drywall. Sure enough, a tiny spider network of cracks dotted the wall and left the paint cracking. It didn't look bad, just old and unloved. She rubbed her temple. "Wonder how long before my mother notices."

"Hopefully forever."

Storey snorted. "Oh, she'll see it. All of a sudden she's going to realize how weary and old the room looks and will want to repaint."

Now that the crisis had passed, she had to admit she felt a little shaky. Or maybe shocky was a better word.

"I think we should leave."

"Yeah? Your world or mine?" She studied the worry etched in his wrinkled forehead.

"It's possible the Louers made it into my world." The frown rippled across his features. "If they did, my people are particularly vulnerable to them."

Storey glanced back at the wall. "In what way?"

"They're terrified of them, for one. We were raised knowing our people were once enslaved until they couldn't work anymore and ended up as food. Plus, my people aren't fighters. We don't have wars."

"Ever? Amazing. Kinda cool, too. Who'd have thought an entire species of people could survive without trying to kill each other off?" She searched his face wondering if he was telling the truth. Or the truth as he understood it.

"Never," he said firmly.

"Only with the Louers?"

"Yes."

"Not even with my people?"

"No. We fell across your world in our attempt to banish the Louers."

"So then there could be many other dimensions out there?"

He paused, as if considering this for the first time. "I don't know that there aren't. We've never come across any, though."

"And you've never gone looking." Interesting. As long as something didn't cross their path they didn't go out of their way to learn more. Not a curious people. But rigid, in keeping to what they knew. Not liking change, or progress, or criticism, apparently. Good to know. Could she turn their traits against them in her bid for freedom?

CHAPTER 10

"ARE YOU SURE you want to do this?"

Straightening up, Storey winced at her backache. She'd collapsed to the floor an hour ago when they'd finally retreated to her bedroom from the family room. Her last drawing was finished. She stared at the stack for a long moment. There were a million events she couldn't plan for. A thousand more she might not be able to handle. There was no way to plan for every contingency.

For what had to be the twelfth time, Storey nodded at him as she slouched onto her bed. There was no point in trying to get Eric on board with the plan. He belonged to a society of talkers. She couldn't expect more than that from him. A teeny bit of her was disappointed. She could have used an action man right now. Sex appeal was great, but could she count on Eric when things went wrong?

She didn't know. She could only hope so. Someone needed to watch her back.

She wanted, no needed, to have paper and the stylus with her at all times. She wondered if there was a way to duplicate or split the stylus. To have two, a dummy one they might believe was real and confiscate so she could keep hers. In fact, she probably had something similar in her art kit. And that was something worth checking out. How would they know?

Scrunching up her face, she considered the problem

of duplicating the stylus. There was only one way to find out. She picked up the pencil and drew a picture of it on the page in front of her. Her fingers raced to keep up as the pencil took on a life of its own.

Eric finally noticed her actions. He crouched down beside her. The bedroom had taken on a cozy feel with the two of them working so closely together for the past few hours. He was studying her sketchbook, a frown wrinkling his brow.

He glanced up at her, his frown deepening. "You don't need to look at your creation while you're drawing anymore?"

"What?" Storey glanced down at the page and gasped. "Oh good Lord."

Her hand moved across the page at a mad pace, but she wasn't the one controlling it. At least she didn't think she was drawing right now. Her hand and even her forearm felt separate, unhinged at the elbow from the rest of her. Sketching so fast, she couldn't track the lines as they formed. "Wow," she whispered.

"Double wow." They both stared in awe as the picture became a photographic image of the stylus. "Have you ever done this before?"

"Never."

In silence, they watched and waited for her hand to stop. Her arm dropped to her side and she could now see the whole picture. Her eyes widened. "The stylus has colored ink?"

He snorted. "The stylus doesn't have any ink."

Storey gulped. "Holy crap." She stretched her fingers. They weren't even sore.

"And now what?"

She stared at him and gulped louder. "I'm not sure." Her eyes were drawn back down to the picture. She reached out with her left hand to touch the incredible likeness, only to back off at the last minute, laughing nervously. "I'm scared to try."

Eric stood up and strode over to the window. "We're going to be hunted down and captured, locked away and maybe killed. We should be running to the other side of the planet. Instead, you're drawing pictures that scare you." He shook his head. "I don't understand you."

"But do you get this?" Jubilation rang in her voice.

He spun around to stare at her in complete exasperation. "What? Do I get what?" His gaze landed on the object in her hand. His jaw dropped open. "What the hell?"

Storey stared in shock then gave him a fat grin, almost bouncing on the bed in joy. "You swore. *Finally.* Good for you."

He stared at her uncomprehending. "What are you talking about?"

"You. You swore."

"Swore?" His eyes widened as he shifted his stance and fisted his hands on his hips. "I did not. I couldn't have."

Her grin warped into a smirk as she watched his reaction. "Oh yes, you did. You said, 'What the hell.'"

His face froze. She laughed in delight.

Glaring at her, he said, "That's hardly the issue right now. We have something more important at stake here."

Smirking, she held up the second pencil. "I think this is beyond cool."

"Do you think it works?"

"That it comes off the paper at all is a blooming miracle. I highly doubt that it's a stylus. I wasn't even thinking of creating a usable one, only a fake one for your people to take off of me, allowing me to keep the real one."

His gaze switched from her left hand to her right hand and back again. "They're identical."

"In appearance," she cautioned, twisting the new pencil around and around. "This isn't even flat like the paper. It's 3D. Unbelievable."

She reached over to hold the new pencil under the light from the lamp at her night table. Sure enough the wording lit up under the warm glow. "Wow. They're perfect copies."

"How did you do that?"

She shrugged. "I'm not sure. I thought about creating a copy of the stylus. The stylus took over and created it for me."

"Can we test it?"

"Why not?" She reached for the sketchbook and tried to draw a line. Nothing. She sat back, disappointed despite her expectations. Pursing her lips, she said, "I didn't really think it would work. The real stylus has a power of some kind. This is a flat carbon copy."

"This just might work…with two styluses you have a chance." He ran his fingers through his hair. Poor Eric. For the first time, real hope glimmered in his eyes. His world had flipped these last few hours. That his father was bent on having her killed was one thing, almost understandable given his people's fears, but to have a kill order on his own head if he didn't comply…now that had to hurt. How would she feel if her father sentenced her to death?

"And you'd care?" She couldn't help asking. What did he really feel? Guilty, because he'd taken her over there in the first place? Or did he feel that same connectedness she felt?

"Huh?" Confused exasperation slid through his voice. "I wouldn't be here otherwise."

She stared at the floor, a giddy ripple snaking through her body. Maybe he did care. Not that she'd let him know it mattered. "So, we're good to go?"

He stared at her. "I still don't like it, but yes, let's get moving. The sooner we get there, the sooner we can find a solution to this mess."

Storey couldn't stop her biggest worry from dominating her thoughts. *What if the solution was one that didn't allow either of them to live?*

STOREY AND ERIC used her drawings to cross the veil to Eric's world. With his guidance, they crossed via Stanshor mine.

"You're sure this is the best entrance?"

"Yes. It used to be a central meeting point for various city members. They'd travel here via codex," he said, holding up his wrist. A long metal band covered his skin from elbow to wrist, "and then come to the hall as a group." He strode into the murky depths of the cavern she'd been happy to forget. He stopped ahead of her and pointed at the ground. "Why did you do this?"

Storey paused to stare at the crosses she'd marked on that fateful day. Had it only been yesterday? Or the day before? She shook her head. Her sense of time had warped. For the first time, she wondered at the long-term side effects and health problems of crossing the veil multiple times. "I was trying to mark out distances, so I'd be able to find my way back again."

"Smart."

There it went again. That little wiggle inside. Damned if she knew why she should care about what he thought of her. She followed him through the darkness to a destination only Eric appeared to know. Storey peered through the blackness, yet saw nothing. He glanced from time to time at his codes. "Is that like a GPS or something?"

"GPS? I don't understand."

"Hmmm." Rather than try to explain something she didn't perfectly understand, she asked, "How does the codex work?"

"It's a digital map, I guess you could say. You can punch in coordinates or places and it can tell you where you are and direct you to a specific place."

"So you just dial up Earth 2.0 and it sends you to a doorway?" She bumped into his back. He held the flashlight in front of him, lighting the immediate space. Everything else appeared to be absolute darkness. "Oomph."

He reached around and grabbed her hand, pulling her up beside him without slowing his pace. Keeping her hand in his, he answered, "Kinda. But a lot more complicated than that. With it I can also create a doorway if I need to in an emergency, and it can send me across my world instantly."

"Perfect way to evade capture."

"Not really. It leaves a signature that is automatically tracked by Paxton's computers. Wherever I go, they'll know."

She frowned. "Okay, not so great."

"We're here." Eric stopped on the spot, showing her the flashing colors on his codex.

She stared at it in disbelief then looked around, "That's it? Just because the colors are different, you're willing to trust that little piece of technology. Look around you. We're nowhere." Her voice rose at the end and it was all she could do to stop herself from yelling. "That's a whole lot of trust in nothing." Her voice echoed on for a long time. She shivered, staring out into black soup that thickened and darkened even as she watched.

"It's all right. Everything's going to be fine." He wrapped one arm around her shoulder and pulled her closer. She didn't protest. In fact, she couldn't resist snuggling up to his comforting warmth. The place gave her the creeps.

"Right," she muttered. "So now what?"

"What do you mean?"

She shuddered again. "Why is it so cold all of a sudden? And what do you mean, what do I mean?" she said in exasperation. "Honestly, sometimes I think you're from another world."

"Well technically…"

With a look of disgust she tried to search her surroundings. The soup had blanketed out everything but Eric, and that's only because she was right beside him.

She shivered. "How do we leave then? I'd like to get out of this."

"That should happen in about five, four, three…"

She reared back. "What the–"

Blue sky beamed down on her.

ERIC REALIZED HE hadn't considered what the transit must have seemed like for her. Everything in her world was so visual. Billboards, television, trains. And everything took so much time. Look at the long hours he'd been forced to attend her school. What a joke. School on his side of the veil was mornings only. And still they finished in half the time that her school system did. Plus, from what he could see, his schooling system taught the youngsters so much more.

That's not to say there weren't some good things over there, he admitted to himself.

"We're here? Just like that?"

"Yes. That's why the darkness thickened and swirled around us. You felt the cold because you haven't had a chance to adapt. I'm used to traveling that way and no longer notice the temperature change."

She sniffed the fresh air while he watched. Did it smell the same to her? Cleaner? Fresher? Foreign? Her features shifted and she seemed to take gulping breaths – almost tasting the air. Curious, he watched the expressions flit across her face. What was she thinking?

"Do you have any pollution here?" She spun around studying the terrain. "Do you have cars? Trains?" She tilted her head back and stared up at the sky. "Airplanes?" With a funny sound that was a cross between a laugh and snort, she added, "Do you even have clouds here? The blue sky looks painted on, it's so perfect."

Spinning around, she tried to take it all in. Her hair flew out in all directions, her t-shirt twisting snugly around her body. Tall compared to the girls he knew, she had an unconscious beauty she made no attempt to capitalize on. Odd, yet endearing. He grinned. Such inquisitiveness. "We don't need those kinds of transportation because everyone has variations of the codex."

"Everything is so different but so much the same."

"Exactly. We as a people developed separately, biologically, environmentally, and socially. Our government structure is completely unique. We don't even have bicycles."

"Don't need them either, do you. Everyone has a codex?"

He watched the unformed queries blaze in her dark chocolate eyes as they darted from one thing to another. "No," he corrected patiently. "They have different units, called taprins, that can take them to any of the many transit points we use. Then everyone walks from there. But those units are only good for local travel."

"Cool. I like the sound of that."

He grinned at her, loving the innocence mingled with

eagerness. She had something he hadn't recognized before. What he'd taken as aggressiveness, or maybe *stubbornness* was a better word, was actually spirit. So unlike the girls in his world, who were quiet, graceful, yet contained. They didn't need to be high-spirited. Their lives were easy, peaceful, ordered. But they lacked the spontaneity he'd come to appreciate from Storey.

Another difference between the girls he knew and Storey was her mind. Hers raced and bounced off different things, stopping to question anything of interest before zipping forward. He admired her. He also liked her. That she was seemingly unaware of her physical appeal made her even more unusual. His brief stint at her school showed the females of her age wore tight clothing, bright colored paint on their faces and decorations in their ears, nose, even eyebrows. Storey wore nothing like that. Through confidence or disdain, he didn't know. It set her apart. She made no attempt to attract males. In fact, she ignored them all equally.

Except maybe…him. That he enjoyed her, respected her…and dare he say…cared for her, was a big surprise he hadn't considered prior to taking this job. He didn't see how she could be part of his future, yet he already knew there'd be a gaping hole in his life if she wasn't.

"Which way?" Storey waved her arms at the multiple paths stretching out before them.

Eric studied the bright green and yellow bushes adding a cheerful look to the early morning. Given the number of choices, he quickly picked one of the least traveled paths. They needed to stay under cover as long as they could.

He glanced around, realizing they could be pounced on by guards at any time. "This way."

CHAPTER 11

S TOREY FOLLOWED AS Eric hurried toward the trees ahead. He'd gone from standing around to full speed. Weird.

She made it seconds after him. Still gasping at the unexpected pace, she grabbed his arm, barely slowing him down. "What's the panic?"

He twisted to look down at her, that sideways grin sliding her way. "I just remembered that people could be looking for us. Here we are, standing around like ducks in hunting season."

A horrible comparison. She shuddered. At least she now knew they had ducks and a hunting season.

Brushing back the green overgrowth, Eric trotted ahead. "We'll enter the city by the back gates."

"Aren't they guarded?" She hurried to catch him. His long legs ate up the miles, leaving her sputtering in shock. Normally, she let other people eat *her* dirt.

"Not by people," he said.

Wincing, she decided not to ask. She'd find out soon enough. "How much further?"

"Half an hour, give or take." He headed off again at a quick clip. "Or less, if you'd move a little faster."

After that comment, she jogged to keep up. Focused on trying to maintain his grueling pace, she slammed into him when he came to a sudden stop.

"What's wrong," she gasped, staggering back several

steps to bend over and catch her breath. She closed her eyes briefly. Damn, she'd developed a stitch in her side. Eric wasn't even out of breath.

"We're here."

Thank heavens for that. Straightening, she surveyed the immediate area. Where was here? What could he see that she didn't? Thick evergreens clogged her view on one side. Not big fat trunks of an old growth forest, but thousands of skinny trees so crowded together she could barely see through them. Everywhere else appeared to be open field. No building. No fence. And certainly no gate. "What am I looking at?"

"A forest?" Again that superior amusement. It was really starting to piss her off. Glad he thought her ignorance was so funny. Not.

She shot him a disgusted look. "Yeah. I can see that. What about your gate?"

"It's on the other side of this group over there." He pointed out the trees in question.

"Is your codex telling you that again?" She shielded her eyes from the bright light to stare where he pointed. It didn't help.

"And the fact that I've been here before." He walked toward the invisible gate, a happy bounce to his step.

She wished she had the same endurance. This last leg of the trip had tired her. The stitch in her side still irritated. Several steps later, she slowed as the blinding sun darkened. The air had taken on a static emptiness, a weird sense of something missing. Shivers slid down her back. "Hey, Eric. What's with the change in light?"

"It's a standard gate warning for anyone approaching. It means we're here."

"Warning? I don't like the sound of that."

"Normal for here and not a big deal if you follow the safeguards."

"Whoa. What safeguards? What are you talking about?" She cast a quick look behind her. She couldn't shake the feeling of being watched. "Hey, wait up."

"I'm here."

"Not here enough." The blackness swirled around her, making her choke with the thickness of it. She reached out for Eric. He pulled her closer. She gasped and pressed tight against his side. "Don't you dare let go. I hate this."

He chuckled, his warmth breath tickling her cheek. She had to smile. "No worries. Stay close."

She snorted. "You think?" She twisted around, that eerie sensation crawling up her back again. Tugging, she tried to get him to move. He planted his feet and resisted.

"What is your problem?" he burst out in exasperation.

"Something is watching us."

He stilled. "What are you talking about?"

Peering up at him through the deepening mist, she tried to understand the odd flatness in his voice. "Don't you feel it?"

"What? Feel eyes on us?"

"Yes." She searched the suffocating blackness. "As long as I can't see them, they can't see me. Right?" she joked.

"In theory. Besides we're in the gate. Nothing can get us in here." He wrapped his arms around her to pull her close. She huddled in his arms, her eyes darting in all directions.

Her stomach was in knots. So were her nerves. "What kind of animals do you have over here?"

"All kinds of them." His grin flashed in the dark.

"That's not helping. Animal predators?"

His warm chuckle lifted the hair at her temple, sending a different sensation down her spine. "Of course. You're really spooked, aren't you?"

Lifting her head, she stared up at his laughing blue eyes. Here heart tumbled. She sighed. "Am I overreacting?"

His chest rumbled against her. "No, not when it's all new to you."

She dropped her forehead against him for a moment, then she asked, "Is the gate like the one in the mine?"

"Sort of."

"Why can't you give me something other than half an answer?" She'd barely finished when a scream sounded next to her. She half climbed Eric's tall frame. "What the hell was that?"

Clasping her tightly to his chest, he whispered into her ear, "Shhhh. An animal hunting. That's all. Quiet."

She stilled. Her heart in her throat, her nerves quietly shattered while her eyes stared into the damn soup. Her nose quivered.

"Just another minute more." This time the warmth of his voice wafted against her neck. She shuddered. Eric almost made her forget her surroundings. He squeezed her tighter. Going on instinct, she snuggled closer.

This was his world. She had no way of defending herself. She didn't even know what dangers existed. She'd never felt so helpless in her life.

"Hmmm."

Regret nudged her when she realized Eric's arms were loosening. She lifted her head and looked around, hoping for the blue sky again. Not happening. Black, cloying night surrounded them. She swallowed loudly. "Didn't it work? Is this where we're supposed to be?"

Eric stared down at his codex. "I'm not sure. The codex is flashing that we've arrived."

"Arrived where? It doesn't look any different from before." She waited for the dense fog to clear. It didn't. "Is your codex broken?"

"Not likely. It worked fine up until now."

She didn't like the confusion on his face. The silence around them had a muffled sensation to it. Not a clear air type of silence, more of a padded chamber type of thing. "Did it though? You said you'd been here before. Have you physically been at this gate before?"

He didn't answer.

"You haven't, have you?" She couldn't believe it. He'd duped her. "So how do you know if any of this is right?" she exclaimed, frustration stiffening her backbone. She pulled back slightly to stare up at him.

"I've seen pictures of this place. I've studied the area and the gate itself." He tried to pull her closer. She resisted, wanting to read the truth in his eyes. "This should have passed by now. But then, all gates take a different amount of time. This one could be slower."

"It's not slower." She knew it, and again had no idea how or why. "Something is wrong."

"Not yet it isn't."

"If… something has gone wrong, where would this wrong be?"

"Huh?"

"Where would we be if the gate didn't work?"

He frowned. "I don't know. It's never happened before."

She disengaged from his grasp, turning to look around at the heavy charcoal colored mist. Better than cloying blackness, but not by much. She wafted the mist around, hoping to clear some of it. "Never? Or never to you?"

"Never that I know of."

"What are the probable things that could go wrong with your codex?"

"Like dialing the wrong number you mean? Nothing like that. Each is a preset code." His eyes widened.

Reaching out, he grabbed her hand. "Stay close."

"Could the numbers have been changed? Like by Paxton?"

He frowned. "I don't know. The codes are old. Well before his time."

"But it's possible. And, I'm just thinking aloud here, is it possible that we're in some kind of middle zone? No man's land? A different dimension again?"

"I really don't know." He spun around to look behind him, then turned back to face her. "We could be at a different gate. Lost between gates even. Like I said, it's never happened before."

"Well," she suggested, "why don't you dial your codex and take us back to Stanshor Mine and we'll try a different, more traveled route."

Understanding brightened his eyes. He lifted his wrist. No lights flashed. Nothing glowed. Grim-faced, he tapped several buttons. "Now it's not working at all, apparently."

Her stomach sank. Of course it wasn't. They weren't meant to go back. "Could Paxton have done this on purpose or could something else have gone wrong that would change the codes?"

"What could go wrong? Nothing goes wrong in my home." He winced. "Although my people might say losing the stylus was wrong. But only that." He rushed to say.

They stared at each other, puzzled. Then it hit them.

"The Louers!" they cried.

Storey's mind went blank, just for a moment, then raced ahead. The possibility that they'd arrived in the middle of a war was too much to contemplate.

Cautiously, Eric spoke as the voice of reason. "Let's not jump to conclusions. That's only one possibility."

"True." She nodded at his codex. "First things first.

Do you have a way to get us out of here?"

Glaring down at the codex, Eric's frown deepened. "I don't know. Outside of trying to walk out of this."

"Which may or may not work. So…" She pulled out her sketchbook and stylus. "Where should we go? To my world or deeper into yours? Are we thinking Louers have invaded? Or are we thinking Paxton did this to stop you from going home?" She stared up at him. He stared back, an odd look on his face. "Hey, are you in there?" she snapped her fingers in front of his face. "Pull it together. We're in trouble here, in case you didn't notice."

"Let me reset my codex. Could be just a glitch?" He tapped a series of buttons again while Storey watched. Frowning, he studied his codex and the unchanging mist around them. "What's the chance it needs another minute? A reboot so to speak."

She snorted. "Get a grip. The gate is either not functioning or this *is* the destination. Either way, I'm not impressed." She plopped cross-legged on the ground. It didn't look like dirt or tile, more like black compressed nothing. Refusing to dwell on it, she opened her sketchbook and flipped to a new page. Her mind raced, searching for possibilities. After her one horrible encounter with the Louers, she'd hate for the same nightmare to take over Eric's world. Just because his father was an asshole, that didn't mean everyone else was.

"What are you doing?" He squatted down beside her.

"I'm trying to figure out where we should go. What if the Louers have entered your world? Do you want to help your people? Haven't you imagined them tearing into your friends' homes and attacking your family?" She stared down at the sketch forming under her fingers. The stylus had warmed, heating with an urgency all its own.

"I don't have any friends." His voice held a cool indifference.

She looked up, startled. "What?"

"I said I don't have any friends. I have teammates, coworkers, associates. No friends. Everyone in my world is part of my work."

"Girlfriends?"

"Not really." Short and curt. Hmmm. Some history there, but not her place to ask. And she didn't think she wanted to know. "Didn't you make any friends through work?" Most people made friends with their coworkers. After all, that's where most people spent the bulk of their waking hours. It only made sense that strong friendships would form during this time.

He shrugged. "My father."

"Yeah, I can see how he'd put a damper on things. I have to admit my mother and her little candle shop have certainly brought me grief." She returned to her drawing, her mind a muddle of remembered grievances with the townsfolk. Her poor mom was harmless. So what if her store was new-agey and her religion was different. *He* had no friends? Yeah, well, she could relate.

"He's not all bad."

"No one is." She could feel his stare and ignored it as the picture emerged from the sketchpad. Paxton's lab. She sighed. Talk about walking back into a lion's den.

Eric studied the picture taking shape. "Paxton is a good man. He's a government man who cares about my people. About me. He's trained me for the last decade, longer even."

"Decade?" She shot him a questioning glance before returning to her picture. "Sounds like he's been more of a father to you than your own father."

"That's true." He reached across and tapped the paper. "You're thinking to go back to Paxton's lab? Did you forget there's a death sentence on your head?"

She sighed. "No, I haven't forgotten that. I hate to

say it, but I'm thinking they may have more important things to worry about now."

"If they do, they might consider you responsible."

She stared at him in dismay. "See, that's the problem with you guys. You just don't want to accept responsibility for your own actions. This isn't all about me. This is about you and your people. Remember, I didn't sneak into your world and leave you an innocent-looking bomb to play with."

He grinned and shook his head. "I can see your point. However, just because *I* might understand, doesn't mean the others are going to be so open."

She snorted. "Well, they damn well better be. This is a result of their actions. The buck stops with them." Her hand stopped. She studied the finished picture with a critical eye. "I suppose that's close enough. I suggest we do a second picture. I don't know. Possibly of the same mine again, so that we can step into Paxton's lab and check out the climate, then if the Louers are trying to take the place over, we can use the second picture as an escape route. This way we'll have enough for both of us to carry – in case we get separated."

He nodded, apparently content to just watch. "That was the original plan anyway, right?"

"Kinda." She sketched quickly, her hand a blur, until she was satisfied with the second drawing. She had to admit that the stylus had improved her artistic ability tenfold. "That should do it. Now let's go."

He stood up and held out a hand for her. "You first."

"No, I think we'd better go together."

"We won't fit. You made complete doors, not partial ones that suggest bigger ones."

"True, but, as I'm learning I'm finding it's more about what you're thinking than the actual size of the drawing.

He stared at her, dumfounded. "Huh?"

"Don't worry about it. Come on."

She ripped off the first page. "How can I go through and take the paper with me?"

"Like I did in the lab. Just grab it on the way through."

She placed the sketch on the ground and motioned for him to step onto it. Casually, like it was every day event, Eric stepped through and disappeared from sight. She shook her head. There's no way she was *ever* going to get used to that.

Taking a deep breath, she knelt on the paper keeping a firm grip on the corner with her hand. She fell through.

Tumbling into Paxton's lab, she groaned as she smacked into the hard white tile. Kneeling wasn't a good idea. Then again, as she surveyed the paper in her hand with satisfaction, it allowed her to bring the gate with her.

"That wasn't very graceful." Eric's voice was a little fuzzy.

Struggling to her feet, Storey turned to face him. "It also gave me a hell of a headache."

Eric stood, legs straddled, hands on his hips, staring at her. "You've crossed through a lot of doors recently, some damage is possible."

She shot him a worried look. "What kind of damage?" Shaking her head, she added, "Never mind. Don't tell me. I can't do anything about it now." She spun around, realizing that the room was empty. "Is this Paxton's lab? If so, then where is he?"

Eric walked around, opening doors then closing them after checking the rooms on the other side. "He's always here. We'll have to go looking for him."

"Where does he live? He must eat and sleep somewhere else?"

"Yes, but he lives here most of the time." Eric fisted

his hands on his hips. "He should be here."

Storey understood. War, and all that it entailed, wasn't part of Eric's thought process. He'd never encountered it. Didn't live with the possibility every day, like her people did. He had no idea of what was going on here.

There was no point explaining things to him. He'd have to sort through this on his own, eventually.

It wasn't for her to tell him that his peaceful world was under attack.

CHAPTER 12

S TOREY HEADED FOR the last door.

Eric reached it ahead of her and opened it. "There should be lights on." He scanned the room before crossing past the big oval table and to the door on the far end. Storey followed.

The meeting chamber didn't appear to have been used since she'd been here last. Cups and bottles littered the table and the chairs sat everywhere, as if pushed back in a hurry. It was consistent with an emergency meeting having been called or everyone having left at a run.

Eric disappeared into the next room. Only it wasn't a room at all, but a long hallway with doors set off each other in military precision for as far as Storey could see. The floor gleamed in white tile. The walls and ceiling sparkled in winter white, almost blinding her. Nothing but black hardware marred the pristine color.

"What's with all the white?"

"White is a power color here." He came to a stop at the third door on the left. He knocked.

The doors reached from floor to ceiling. Storey couldn't help comparing the building to an institution of locked cells. There was a real creepiness to the emptiness. "If there were people walking around, the place wouldn't be quite so off-putting."

He turned to give her a curious glance, then pushed open the door, calling out, "Paxton, are you in here?"

No answer. He poked his head around the corner of the door and called out louder, "Paxton?"

The stillness of a place that should have been teeming with activity gave her the willies. "It's not Sunday, is it?"

Eric pushed the door fully open, then paused to look back at her. "You ask the darnedest questions. What does Sunday have to do with it?"

"I don't know. I just thought that if it were Sunday, then it would make sense that no one was here. If you have church, that is? Or if it were night time? Could everyone be asleep? Are we even on the same clock?" She couldn't stop asking questions. Besides it would help take his mind off things.

His lips quirked. "Remember, we're still on the same planet. Same solar system. If it's daytime on one side of the veil, it's daytime on the other. It is Sunday, although we call it something slightly different here." His face became serious again. "But even on Council days, this building is always manned."

He walked through what appeared to be a small apartment, heading for the far side of the room. There was a weird set of cushions on the floor. Furniture of some kind. As she passed it, her leg accidentally brushed the edge and it moved. She jumped back, shrieking, her hand slamming against her chest. The pillows rose and adjusted, almost as if it were fitting to her size.

Eric snickered. "No church. No religion as you know it. The Council sets the rules for everything." His grin widened. "And we don't have time to play with the chairs."

Giving the piece a wide berth, she glared at him. "I don't consider a cushion that looks like it's going to eat me as funny, thank you."

"That's a polo chair." At her blank look, he added, "One size fits all."

She gave the cushion one last assessing look, realizing it had shrunk back down to its original size. Handy. The next room appeared to be a bedroom. She wandered around. What else was different over here? The bed looked normal, although higher than she was used to, with a small set of stairs on the side. No headboard, but a control panel of some kind had been mounted on the wall above some more weird looking pillows. She stayed well away from it, just in case it moved, too.

Everything was white.

Glancing down at her black jeans, black boots and her charcoal t-shirt, she realized she looked and felt like a dandelion among the roses.

Eric checked out the room and stood in the doorway of another room. She could only surmise that it was a bathroom of some kind. Not that she'd seen anything along those lines since she'd been here. As soon as the thought crossed her mind, she realized she needed to pee. *Damn.*

She headed in the same direction Eric had disappeared. It wasn't a bathroom. It appeared to be another workroom. "What on earth? Why would he have another lab here?"

"This is his private space. And the one other place I expected to find him." He ran his fingers through his hair in frustration. "Paxton doesn't *go* anywhere else. He can't. Where the hell can he be?"

"He *can't* go anywhere? Ever?" She studied the all white and silver room, so painfully clean she had to resist the urge to toss a cabinet to make it look normal.

"No. You don't understand. He doesn't do well in the outside – something to do with his extreme age."

"How old is he?"

"No one really knows. He won't talk about it. Somewhere between one-fifty and two hundred."

Storey choked. "Two hundred. What is the life expectancy of your people?"

He frowned. "Same as your people, I imagine. Although, we've stopped disease and slowed aging, so maybe not."

She blinked. "Did you say stopped? You mean you wiped those two things out? We could sure use that technology. We live to seventy or eighty and anyone who makes it over one hundred is considered ancient."

A weird crack sounded in the other room.

Pushing her behind him, Eric held his finger to his lips and motioned her back to the main living room. He snuck up to the doorway and peered inside. Something crashed to the floor in the other room.

"Crap. What was that?" she whispered, racing to his side.

"Get down." He yanked her behind the wall. "Are you nuts?" He stood up and peered around the corner. "Whoever it was is gone." Racing to the window on the far wall, he searched the outside grounds.

"A window?" She laughed and ran to his side. "That's the first one I've seen here. I wondered if you had them."

He shot another strange look in her direction. "You're really odd, you know. Come on. We have to continue searching." His voice had chilled. "Someone has to be left around here."

Storey followed in silence as Eric strode from door to door, opening each and every one, calling out constantly. No one answered. The place, the whole huge mausoleum, was empty.

"Do you guys have an underground bunker, a safe room, or something?"

"Not if you mean like a place to hide when under attack. Remember, we don't have wars. This is extremely unusual."

That's not the word she'd have used. But if this problem sidelined the death sentence on her head, she was all for it. She stood in the hallway and waited as he finished checking each door. Nothing. "Now what?"

"We're going to my place."

She perked up. "How far away?"

"Only a couple of minutes."

"Oh good. Do you have bathrooms here?"

He winced. "Of course. You are so weird."

"I'm weird. Look at the way you're acting. I'd have contacted the people I care about to make sure they were safe then I would check the media for updates. The Internet would be teeming with news. Look at you. You don't even know where to look. Do you have media here? Computers? Internet? Phones? How much research did you have to do to blend into my world?"

She was almost shouting by the time she finished, struggling to keep up with him as he followed a series of twists and turns. He came to standstill in front of yet another white door. It opened on its own.

"How'd you do that?"

"It's my apartment." He shot her a puzzled look. "Why wouldn't it open for me?"

"Gee, I don't know, maybe because you didn't open it with your hand."

"I don't need to, it's tuned to my vibration."

She nodded. "Yup. I can see how that might work. Not."

She walked into another sparse, almost utilitarian type of apartment. Eric's had even less furniture than Paxton's rooms, and it was equally as nondescript. There was no personality here. Nothing on the walls to liven things up. If she lived here, the first thing she'd do is get out her paint brush and color the world.

"How long have you lived here?"

"Again with the questions. Since I was old enough to live on my own."

Sensing this might answer a lot of questions, she asked, "How long ago was that and how old were you?"

"The same age as everyone else. Fourteen."

She sucked in her cheeks. The same as everyone else. So at fourteen, everyone in his world was independent. She kind of liked that. "How old are you?"

"A couple of years older than you. I think Paxton said you were what, sixteen, seventeen?"

"Yes, just turning seventeen." A loud buzzer sounded. Relief washed over his face. He raced to the far wall and placed his hand on a circle looking thing. A large screen materialized, taking up most of the wall at his head height.

"Greetings, Eric."

"What's going on? Where is everyone?" Eric stared into the blue screen. Standing beside him, Storey couldn't see anything but a blue snow. She had no idea who he was speaking with.

"We're under attack. Central is on lockdown." A computerized voice gave a general status report. Understanding filled Eric's face. "Who's attacking? We've never even had enemies before."

Storey winced at the shock in his voice. She already knew the answer.

"The Louers are attacking."

THE BLUE SCREEN died. Eric yelled, shoving his face right up to the monitor. "No, wait! I need more information. Where are you?"

The reception blinked off and on, then a cracked voice said, "Mansfield gate has been reopened."

Eric blinked. "Mansfield?" he whispered. Fear settled at his feet. It couldn't be. He raised his voice. "That's not a real place – is it?"

The static on the screen increased, drowning out the computerized transmission.

"Now that's a weird phone."

He spun, having forgotten she was standing beside him. "It's not a telephone. The visual is broken, that's all."

"So how do we get to Mansfield?"

No way. She couldn't go with him. She shouldn't be here now. The whole game had changed. This was no longer about saving the two of them; it was about saving his people and their way of life. "Not we, me. My country is at war. You shouldn't be here. Go home and stay there. Look for a place to hide over there, just in case. You might be lucky and the Louers will be too busy here to worry about attacking your world."

She made that cute little sound again. The one that was a cross between disbelief and thinking he was an ass. It had grown on him. Like she had. And that was dangerous. He had to help his people. He couldn't afford to be distracted.

"They already have, remember?"

"Not like this." He spun around, wondering if he needed anything before he left to find the rest of his countrymen. Distracted, he said, "Look I can't worry about that right now. I have to find the others. I wish Paxton was here. He'd know what to do."

"You need to go wherever you're supposed to go during lockdown."

He stared at her in confusion.

"He said Central was under lockdown," she said.

His confusion cleared. Right. Lockdown procedures. He'd been so caught up with the Mansfield gate news.

"There's a second base in the basement. It's just never been used."

"Let's go."

"No, you should go home." He hesitated. It wasn't fair, but now that the worst had come to pass she needed to know. "They're going to blame you for this. There's no way they aren't."

"I'm not going there again. I'm not to blame. I contributed, yes. Because I didn't know what I was doing, but now that I do, I might be able to help."

He shook his head vigorously. "They are going to shoot you on sight. You won't get a chance to explain or help. They're going to look for someone to blame. You."

"All right already. Go." She pushed him out the door. "I can get home myself."

"I'll wait until you cross." There's no way he would leave her here alone. Not now. Anything could happen to her. He narrowed his gaze. He couldn't afford to back down on this one.

Storey stood eye-to-eye with him, then weary, she ran a hand through her black hair and eased back. He really wanted to snatch her up into a tight hug at that moment. He didn't dare.

Dropping her backpack to the floor, she pulled out the one sketch from Paxton's lab. "The same architecture has been used on the hallway. I should be able to get home from here."

She placed the picture on the floor and hesitated. Taking a deep breath, she looked at him one last time. "Take care of yourself."

He swallowed hard. The reality that this could be their last meeting settled into his gut. "Wait." He snatched her into his arms and kissed her. Hard. Just like last time, fire licked at his hardening muscles. Lust filled his groin, and the pain of parting filled his heart. He might never see her again.

He tore his lips away before he devoured her on the spot. "Please go home." He stepped back, afraid his legs wouldn't hold him. "I need to know you'll be safe," he said hoarsely.

With a crooked smile and without a sound, she jumped on the picture and through the floor.

She was gone. Just like that.

Bewildered, Eric realized she'd managed to take the picture portal with her again. Unbelievable. How she'd managed to learn so much without training amazed him. Time for her later, at least he hoped so. But not now. He couldn't afford the distraction. Not when his whole world was under attack. He had to find the basement, a place he'd never been.

IT WAS A relief to step into her own bedroom once again. To know that she could get back. Having the portal in here was downright convenient, just not conducive to getting a good night's sleep. Who knew what or who else might crawl through? If only she'd known then what she knew now, she'd have created the portal somewhere else but still close by. Who knew that once opened, the portal was available to anyone from the other side. She needed her picture, but they had codexes and who knew what all else. It would be all too easy to end up trapped in her room. Or worse – wake up with a stranger coming through in the dead of night.

Her fingers stroked her swollen lips. Eric. She hadn't wanted to leave, to leave him. For all the comfort of being home and seeing the same old furniture and purple walls she'd lived with for years, there was no satisfaction to being here.

Dumping her backpack on her bed, she headed for the washroom. At the doorway she stopped, a niggling sensation reminding her she'd yet to be separated from the stylus since this mess had begun. Being apart didn't feel right even now. She ran back, did a quick change of clothes, snagged up her bag, and then headed to the washroom. Downstairs, the evening air had cooled the house. Darkness added to the clamminess, the empty feeling chilling her further. She'd thought her mom would be home by now, but apparently not. She'd traveled to another dimension and back and her mom was still out with her friends. Weird.

Heading to the den, she checked on the wall. And couldn't stifle the sigh of relief that there was no evidence the Louers had tried to break through again. There had to be a way to stop them from coming here permanently. The last thing she wanted was to have to keep an eye on the wall every time she came home.

She only had Eric's word that the Louers were horrible. She needed to stop them from coming into her home, but she didn't want to kill them all off. She didn't even kill spiders. But there had to be a happy solution for everyone here. If only she could find it.

Could she draw a lock on the original door? Or draw another dimension between her world and theirs? Then if they did cross they'd end up in the new place and not know there were more dimensions. Did just drawing something like that make it so? That brought her back full circle; just what capabilities did the stylus have?

Retrieving her sketchbook from her room, she decided to find out.

She pulled up the old rocker, turned on the pole lamp and sat facing the repaired wall. Figuring out a solution could take some time. Would the stylus figure it out for her? She held the thought of a permanent solution, of a locking system and a dimension between her world and theirs, then let the stylus work.

If the Louers found a better world than hers, they might be happy there and look no further. Her world *was* lovely. So, theoretically theirs would be too. They might find it like a holiday resort, compared to their current living standard. Something she knew nothing about. Again, she had only Eric's word that the Louers were the bad guys – but if they *were* like locusts, destroying everything in their path, then she wanted to make sure they stayed a long ways away from her world.

Not realizing what she was doing on a conscious level, she rocked gently in the chair as her hand flashed and dipped, crossed and slashed through its creation process.

She closed her eyes and leaned her head back. How she could do this without looking she didn't know. Still, she was so tired…and she let the room slip away.

The front door opened a little later. Storey recognized the familiar sound of her mom's return. Damn. She rubbed her eyes with her left hand. Moonlight poured into the dark room, lighting her sketchbook. The stylus was still busy creating. She didn't want to stop. This was too important.

Her mom walked through to the kitchen. "The power is out, Anton."

It was? The power had gone out and she hadn't noticed? Had she actually slept? Then the rest of her mother's words registered. Storey stiffened, her eyes widened even as bile rose up the back of her throat. *Anton?* Her father? No way.

The deep male voice made her heart beat a jungle roll in her chest.

"Probably just a breaker. There could have been a power outage, I suppose. I'll go check."

Jesus, it almost sounded like him. At least, as her imagination remembered him. Her dad had left ten years ago. What was he doing here and why would her mother act so…so normal about it all? And how the hell would he know where the breakers were located?

Swallowing heavily, Storey glanced at the clock. She'd been in here for an hour plus. In the dark. "Hi. I'm in the den," she called out.

"What are you doing sitting here all alone with just that little bit of light? Are you okay? And why aren't you in bed asleep?" Her mother entered the room, worry evident in her voice. Storey was sorry for that. She hadn't meant to be such a constant concern.

And there was more to come. She needed a cover story for the cracks in the wall, too. "I'm just sitting here. I couldn't sleep, so I came down to draw, but it's too dark without lights. Weird. Then there was that even weirder tremor, earlier."

"What? An earthquake? We didn't feel a thing." Storey's mom hurried to her side, placing a hand on her shoulder. "Are you okay? You weren't hurt by it, were you?"

An odd rose perfume wafted over Storey. Strange, she didn't recognize it. "No. Just restless afterwards."

"Oh, dear. You should have called. We'd have come home." Her mother looked around the small room. "I hope there's no damage."

"I couldn't see much with the power outage. Maybe a little cracked paint." Storey grinned in the dark. What a great cover story. And dreamt up in mere seconds.

"As long as you weren't hurt, the rest is nothing. It's probably time to throw up another coat of paint anyway."

Storey smiled.

"What's with your bag?"

That worried note had entered her mother's voice again. Storey glanced down at her backpack, thinking quickly. "It has my art stuff in it."

"Oh." And there, that predictable relief again. Storey didn't think she wanted children if it meant a roller coaster ride of emotions like that. A man walked into the room. Storey stiffened, searching the gloom to see his features.

Her father.

Her heart and mind took an immediate hit. No contact in ten years and now he just walked in like he owned the place. Her eyes locked on him and wouldn't let go. How many times in the last ten years had she wanted, needed to see him again? She gulped softly. Not trusting herself to either slug him or hug him, she chose to stay where she was.

"The tremors must have knocked the power out. There's no phone either. I can go to a neighbor's house to check and see if they have at least a cell phone working or wait until morning. They might have it fixed by then anyway," he said.

Storey's gaze widened. He was acting as if he lived here – the nerve. And how did he know about the neighbors?

"Considering the time, we might as well go to bed. The power will be back on in the morning, I'm sure."

Storey wasn't. Her world had been rocked several times tonight. Her hand still sketched at a mad pace under the cover of darkness. She needed to finish. Soon. At some point, exhaustion would take over. Mental chaos had begun to move in. At least there was no room for the nagging doubt about leaving Eric and his people alone to fight this war.

"Storey, are you going to bed now? You have school tomorrow."

"It's a school day tomorrow?" It felt like Saturday. But then Eric had said it was Sunday. Crap. She was twisted up time-wise, as well. *Damn.*

"No, Sarah. Remember, she has the day off."

Storey stared at him in the dark. She did? She didn't remember that. Good thing the lighting hid her expression. Besides, how would he know?

"Oh that's right," Her mother turned back to face Storey. "She was supposed to go on that religion field trip. Like we would want you learning about other religions. We're Roman Catholics all the way."

Religion field trip? Roman Catholic? Uh oh! Who'd stolen her mom and put these fakes in her place? Storey didn't know what to say. Something major had happened. Not to her, but to her family.

"Are you two feeling all right?"

"I'm not too sure." Her mother rubbed her forehead. "In fact, I'm starting to feel slightly woozy. I think I'd better go to bed." She traipsed out of the room. Storey couldn't believe what she saw briefly in the ray of moonlight. Her mother wore a dress, like a regular dress and high heels. That so didn't happen. Where were the floor length hippy dresses and bangles that jangled with her movements?

"Where were you guys? You mentioned it earlier, but I forgot."

Her father spoke from the doorway. "At church, of course. We understood you needed to stay home and do your homework. That's always been your priority and we're so proud of you for it. Now don't stay up too late." He walked out, leaving her stunned and gasping for air.

What had just happened? If these were her parents, then they weren't in her normal world. Had she returned to her world or had she gone to a different one?

She glanced down at her drawing. Could she have done this? Could she possibly have created another dimension? Another reality? A parallel reality? She got up, still holding the stylus and sketchbook, to check the wall where the Louer had tried to come through earlier. Relief washed through her. The cracked paint was still there. Evidence she was in the right dimension.

Unless that had copied over too…

Oh God.

Please not. And if she had copied an entire world, which one was she in now?

CHAPTER 13

ERIC TRIED TO remember the emergency instructions drilled into him during his first years of training. Like so much of his early learning, his training had been mindless rote instructions, ignored the minute the tests were over. There'd never been a conflict or a war in their immediate history and no one had considered the possibility of a fight in their future.

They'd been so wrong.

He had yet to see any Louers, and his images of war, gleaned from the archives, had all focused on screaming crowds and bloodshed everywhere, fighting and chaos erupting on every corner. This deathly silence didn't fit the image.

Making it to the ground floor, he wasted more precious minutes looking for the entrance to the basement. The steel door stood implacable in front of him. It wouldn't be automatically keyed for him and he couldn't remember the codes to get in.

Damn it.

Shocked at the swearing, even silent curses, he stepped back. Storey's bad habit was rubbing off on him. Not good.

He massaged his temples and tried several combinations in his head. As soon as the right one showed up the door should click open. Numbers flitted in and out in a steady stream as he reviewed the various codes he'd been forced to memorize throughout his life.

The massive door made a series of clicking noises and unlocked itself. Relief washed over him. He pulled the door open. With a final glance around at the deserted hallway, he entered the darkness.

STOREY SAT FROZEN, ever nastier possibilities filling her mind. All thoughts about returning to Eric's world fled as she realized she had to put her own reality back to rights. How? She had no frickin' idea.

Lost in thought, she didn't recognize for a long moment that her hand had stopped moving. The stylus was done. She gathered up her bag and slipped up the stairs to her room. Not wanting to attract her parent's attention she quietly shut the door and slipped into her bed. Under the covers she used her flashlight to study her drawing. She didn't quite understand what she was looking at. The picture appeared to be earth displayed as an onion with multiple layers wrapped on top of each other. Were the layers dimensions? Had she created a layer here? She'd wondered about it but...

She grabbed her school eraser and scrubbed at the center layer. It wouldn't erase. Changing tactics, she worked on a smaller mark on one of the outer layers. Again, she couldn't. Were these creations permanent?

Sick awareness settled into her gut. What had she been thinking about while drawing? So many things. Most recently her parents. Before that, wishing her mom would conform a little more and Eric, well all she'd had on her mind was how she'd hated to leave Eric's arms. After that, her thoughts were consumed with trying to find another dimension for the Louers.

She gulped. Could the power of thought, when paired

with a stylus, change a person's belief system? Change their history, too? And those around them? Dear God.

It didn't make sense that she could, without training, change something so drastic, so major in life so easily. And if the changes had happened to her parents, had they also happened to other people? Did her mom still have the candle shop? Did the townsfolk still look down on them? And what about Jeff? Was he or had he ever been her boyfriend? Or had they never met?

Storey gulped. Was she still Storey? She didn't feel any different. But apparently she acted differently in this place. Homework? Caring about her schooling? Nuts. Did she even live in Bankhead anymore?

She ran to the window. The same overgrown oak tree scraped along the sill. Her familiar backyard shimmered in the moonlight. Relief washed over her. So that much was still good. More had to have changed though to have her father in her life, not to mention a change in her mother's religious beliefs. And if her mom's clothing tastes had changed, that meant the alterations were old and very deep.

The power of what she'd done scared the crap out of her. For the first time she understood Paxton's fear. And what was the chance he knew the stylus could change reality like this?

Laying the stylus down on the bed, she sat a little away from it. It had taken a long-held wish and brought her Dad home. It was her fault, she fully accepted that. Now she needed to understand how she'd done this, so she could fix it. Then she'd be more than happy to stop playing God with laws and tools she didn't understand.

Studying the stylus, she had to consider giving it back. "If you're so dangerous, you shouldn't be running around my planet loose like this."

So how did she become one of those in the know?

Then it hit her. If the pencil could change her parents' belief system, then surely it could give her more information – like an instruction manual on using the stylus and information on Eric's world. For that matter, it might be able to tell her how to defeat the Louers.

How could she get the stylus to release the information? Through a drawing? Storey grabbed a granola bar from her bag and munched. She was hesitant to draw herself; who knew if her poor rendition would create that face on her bone and tissue. She could put her name down.

Wincing, she realized that knowing more of the potential disasters she could create made her hesitant to do *anything*. A little information went a long way, and she was terrified of making things worse.

But she had to fix this.

"Stylus, how do I make this all better?" She picked up her pencil and grabbed her sketchbook.

ERIC WALKED THROUGH the darkness, waiting for his eyes to adjust – except they weren't adjusting. Of course, he hadn't thought to bring a light with him. Who'd have thought the basement wouldn't have the same control system as the rest of the building where the lights came on automatically? "Hello? Anyone here?"

Silence.

What if no one had come here? This area appeared to have been closed for decades. Centuries. He stopped, recognizing a wall in the gloom in front of him. He placed a hand on the wall. Relief overwhelmed him when he realized he'd reached another doorway. He searched for the number sequence and managed to retrieve it in half the time. The door opened, light spilling his way.

Thank heavens for that. He stepped around and into the glow.

And stopped in shock.

AS A TEST, she sat crossed-legged on the bed and asked the stylus to give her information on Eric's people in a safe manner. A curious lightness washed over her as her hand moved across the paper. She gave it a moment to do what needed to be done without her mind filling in the pieces, which might or might not affect the picture, she then opened her eyes and looked. The picture appeared to be a large filing cabinet. One drawer was open. The label on the slightly raised file said Eric Stodd's Memories.

Way cool.

She blinked several times and looked around her room. Everything else appeared the same. Placing the tip of the stylus on Eric's file, she closed her eyes and thought about him. Instantly, she could see him running as a child, then scenes started flashing of him in a uniform, first at school then through training. She gasped at the sight of Eric in a clinch with a young woman. Her hand jerked back and the flood of sensual memories stopped. The sense of having invaded Eric's life didn't. She winced. She really hadn't planned for that to happen.

"Oh boy."

So, there *was* more to his girlfriend issue. Still, not her place to ask. Curiosity just might kill her though. At least she was on the right track. Now to fine-tune it. "Remove all references to Eric's love life."

There was a pause, then her hand dropped and started circling lightly on the same picture. She kept her eyes closed and could only hope that the stylus was doing as requested. A quick moment later, she opened her eyes to find the folder showing, but the label now held a series of weird marks on it. She didn't know what it had done.

She thought about Eric's life and was relieved to see him as a child and in several other stages of his life, even as an adult.

Using her sketchbook, she fanned herself to cool off, finding it hard to remove the images she'd seen so briefly. Her attraction for Eric stemmed from a lot of different things. He was unusual, which was part of it. He also felt comfortable, easy to talk to. He had a sense of confidence that was very attractive.

She'd never considered it before. She'd wondered about sex a lot, had experimented some with Jeff. Then he'd moved away. She was an idiot thinking about sex at a time like this. Eric might perish in the war going on his world, and if he survived, his own father might kill him. She sat up straight again. She'd returned to her world. That meant the death sentence on Eric's head was in effect.

A groan escaped her. That so wasn't good. Why hadn't she thought of it before leaving him alone? Why was it that for every step forward she made, she ended up further back? It's what she didn't know that got her. Like her parents and their religion. Not quite believing she was planning on changing something she'd wished for ages, she realized it had to be their choice, not hers. Closing her eyes, she asked the stylus to reverse the changes she'd made to her parents' belief system. She didn't know what to say about her father's presence. Could she reverse that, too? And what if she didn't want to reverse it. Was that cheating?

Quickly deciding this wasn't something to fool with, she asked the stylus to reverse the changes she'd made unknowingly since this mess started. Hit the reset button, so to speak. Was there an undo function on this thing?

The stylus went to work. Then it stopped. The work was over so quickly she could only assume it was a minor fix in the fabric of things.

Or something beyond the scope of its abilities.

Had anything been fixed? Now wasn't the time to check, her parents would be asleep and she wasn't going to wake them. She needed to spend her time now learning what she could. She needed more information on the history of Eric's people and the Louers.

She settled into what had become a routine and let the stylus do its thing. This time she concentrated on gaining information so she was at least on equal footing with the others. A tiny niggle of worry bugged her. What had Eric said? Something about potential damage from crossing the veil. His people limited their research trips and monitored them closely. Was it for that reason they didn't travel back and forth on a whim?

Could this system of learning cause her physical harm? Was brain damage a consideration? Deliberately, she shut those thoughts down and replaced them with happy, healthy thoughts about how much smarter these sessions were helping her to become. And how harmless they were to her. She didn't know if it would work, but her parents' conversion had happened as a result of a random thought. She didn't dare take a chance.

A shiver went through the house.

She opened her eyes in shock and gulped hard. She hadn't done that, had she? Her hand rested on the side of the sketchbook like normal. The picture appeared to be of more file drawers, the information archives. What about the Louers? Please don't let that be them. She closed her eyes, "Stylus, did Louers cause that odd vibration?"

She read out the answer. "No."

Her shoulders slumped in relief. "Well, thank God for that," she whispered under her breath. Then it hit her.

A realization that chased all other thoughts from her mind. This experience had been taken to a whole new level. She'd *asked* the question – instead of *writing* the question. She gulped, her mind racing forward. For all the weirdness, it would make communication so much easier.

Quickly, she asked if it had information on how to stop the Louers from entering her world and how to get them out of Eric's world.

Her hand never moved.

She turned to a clean page and concentrated hard on the same question. Once again, nothing. Panic set in. What if the stylus didn't have the answer?

Where were the answers coming from anyway? The archives of Eric's people. Maybe, their archives didn't have the solution to the problem. Several questions and much reading later, she finally understood. At the end of the war between the Toran and Louers a portal had opened, accidentally it seemed, and the scientists at the time had taken the opportunity to force the Louers through in an act of desperation. But her files contained more than just that general information. In truth, the Louers had been tricked into going through the portal. Eric's people hadn't even looked to see what was on the other side. They hadn't known if the Louers could even survive the crossing.

They hadn't cared. They were trying to get rid of a problem.

Therefore, the Louers had been exterminated.

She closed her eyes and shuddered. The Louers had suffered. She knew it. The archives hadn't been specific, but she'd seen those bony fingers coming through her living room. They were *not* normal looking. They'd been forced to adapt, evolve under extreme conditions. She read more. Originally a larger boned people, normal looking, they had been peaceful at first. Now they were a war mongering species.

Why though? Why had the Toran people had such a problem with the Louers? What could the Louers have done that was so bad? With her eyes closed, she searched further. A few minutes later, she opened them again, her gaze hardening in anger. The Louers had been slaves. They'd attempted a bid for their freedom and revolted. Banishment had been their punishment, at least for the few that survived. She hurt for them.

Were they only mindless animals intent on revenge? Could they even remember their origins? What were the chances of that?

She closed her eyes and asked her stylus if it had information on how to stop the current war going on in Eric's world. Still no response. Then she ran through a series of questions that touched on the same subject. Could the Louers be captured? Could they be sent back home again? Nothing she asked made the stylus move.

Finally, she picked it up and inspected the stylus, turning it over and over. Did it need batteries? Maybe it had quit working.

She pondered the tool again, and then asked it for information on how to save Eric. Her hand jumped back to the sketchbook to race across the page. Keeping her thoughts focused on Eric, she watched as a picture of her bedroom emerged. She understood. Eric wasn't safe over there. He'd be safe here. The good news was that her world appeared to be the safe zone. She asked the stylus if, with all the changes they'd made, the gates to Eric's world were still functional. Could the people leave?

Could she bring everyone over here?

The stylus glowed in her finger tips. The writing on the side shone in the darkness. Storey realized for all her new information floating around in her brain; she didn't know how to read this language. How could that be?

Hadn't Eric been taught to read this language? Wasn't it part of their history? Or was it another ancient element lost to the ages?

She closed her eyes and asked the stylus for the information to understand the written word and symbols of its world.

It struggled with its movements, as if reluctant, but forced to answer. Was it truth bound? Not that she understood what that might mean. "Is there a reason not to teach me your language?"

The answer blazed in her mind. However, her hand wrote out the word *Yes.*

Wow. Direct contact. Almost beside herself with joy of discovery, she asked, "Why?

It's dangerous.

"I'm making dangerous mistakes because I can't understand what I need to know. Isn't that more dangerous?"

So few of us know the language.

Us? She stared at it curiously before asking, "Are you a person?"

No.

"A consciousness?"

Yes.

Storey dropped the pencil and jumped to her feet. "I'm so stupid! Why didn't I try this earlier? Everything will be so different now." She paced the room in an attempt to calm down. It made so much more sense now. Finally, she stopped. There was so much more she needed to find out. She snatched up the stylus and her sketchbook. "Stylus – are you alive?"

No answer. She kept her hand on the sketchbook but there was no movement. Okay, so more questions.

"Can you think?"

Yes.

"See?"

No.

"Feel."

No.

She frowned. Had there been a bit of hesitation there? "Reason?"

Yes.

"Okay, that makes you a computer-like thingy. I can live with that."

It stayed quiet. Of course it did. But talking with it made it a lot easier to communicate on her end. It must have built in microphone equivalent. "Stylus, do you know how to preserve your world?"

Yes.

Relief swept over her. "That's great. How?"

Remove the threat.

"Yes. Exactly." She shifted to sitting cross legged again. "How do we do that?"

The stylus was quiet. She rephrased it. "Do you know how to do this?"

No.

"Does anyone?"

Yes.

"Who is that?"

Paxton.

"Paxton knows how to get rid of them?"

Yes.

"Where can I find him?"

In the lab.

Damn. How could they get in touch with him? "Can we communicate with him from here?"

Yes.

Storey's eyebrows shot up. "Really? How?"

I can communicate with his stylus.

"Of course. He'd have one too, wouldn't he? Okay,

let's see if Paxton's stylus is responding, please."

There was a weird humming in the room. Storey scrunched her shoulders against data streams flowing into the air. This must be the way the Internet worked. That's exactly what she had right now – an intranet, like big companies had for their different offices to connect. Could the other styluses be reached too?

"Stylus, do your people know that you can talk to each other?"

No.

"Is this something you've kept secret?"

No.

"Are we causing any harm doing this?"

No.

She slumped back on her bed at that answer. Thank heavens for that. Ever mindful now about the consequences of her actions, she waited for the two styluses to talk. "Can I communicate with Paxton now?"

Yes.

Exasperated at the short answers and lack of instructions, she said, "How?"

Write the message and I will have the other stylus write the message in front of Paxton.

Story wrote, speaking out loud as the stylus formed the words, "Paxton, this is Storey talking to you from my world. According to my stylus, you know the way to stop the Louers. Please advise if there is something I can do to help. By the way, Eric took me to your world and then sent me back when we found your world under attack. Have you seen him? Is he safe?"

She waited a moment thinking about it. "Okay Stylus, send that message."

It went as you wrote it.

"Great. Every word?"

Yes.

"How will I know if he sees the message?"

His stylus has shown him already.

"Can you tell me his reaction?"

No.

"Of course not. That would mean understanding feelings, like shock. Horror, even." She pondered the situation. "Send him another message. Tell him he can write using his stylus and his stylus will send his message to my stylus, so I can read it." She waited another breathless minute then leaned forward. "Done?"

Done.

She waited chewing on her fingernails. "Damn it. Why doesn't he answer?"

He's answering.

"He is? Where? Oh." She turned the page and put the pencil to paper. Her hand jerked as the message flowed. She read it aloud. "Stay out of our world."

"Wow. After all that he tells me to butt out." What an ass. Her hand started moving again. *Eric is lost to us. Your fault.*

She gasped. "What? Eric's dead? No, that can't be." Hesitantly, she asked, "Stylus, is Eric dead?"

Her hand never moved. "I'll take that as a good sign." Paxton said lost to them. What did that mean?

"Stylus send another message, please. What does he mean 'Eric is lost to them'? Eric should have gone straight to the basement to meet up with them, as per the instructions he received while in his room." She waited anxiously, her pencil in hand. "Isn't he going to answer?"

He is.

There seemed to be a time lag of some kind before her hand started to jerk out the message. *Basement under attack. All thought to be lost.*

"Not possible. That was supposed to be the safe zone." What was that other place the guy said, Manshire?

Mansfield? Mansfield, that was it. "Stylus send a message, please." She quickly wrote down her question about where this place was, who could have sent the message, and where was Paxton himself that he was safe?

It took a moment, and then her hand started writing. *Mansfield was the location of the portal used to banish the Louers. The global feed must have told Eric that and sent him to the basement. The basement was taken early this morning. There were so few people left. The others had been rounded up. Possibly being held in Mansfield. I'm in lab monitoring the situation.*

"Global feed? I don't think I want to know. And Paxton's in his lab? No, not possible. We were there this morning. How could we have missed him?"

She quickly answered him and asked why they hadn't seen him earlier.

His response was swift and sure. "None of my business," she read aloud. "Nice. Not."

He either didn't see us or didn't want us to see him. Either way, his behavior wasn't cool.

"According to the stylus," she wrote, "You know how to stop this war. I need to know how."

The response wasn't long in coming. *No, I don't.*

"Stylus, how is this possible?" Of course it didn't answer. "Okay, let me try that again. Stylus, is Paxton aware of his knowledge on how to stop the war?"

The stylus quickly etched out the word, *no.*

Okay, so he wasn't lying he just didn't know he knew. "Great. So Stylus, what does Paxton need to do to access this information?"

He needs to go into his memory banks and find the system used last time.

"But the system last time was an accident. He's not likely going to be able to recreate that accident."

No accident. Council project.

"So, like a secret government research project, huh? Figures, the archives say it was an accident. Well, we have a few of those going on here, too. Tell Paxton that, please."

Already done.

"Really? Wow, fast." She sighed and sat back to wait. Her hand started moving right away.

How do you know about that? I can't remember those details. Will have to access archive. No time.

Her hand continued to write, *The styluses are like old computers with long memory banks. Ask yours for the information. That's how I found out. My stylus answers questions. Yours will, too.*

She waited and waited. Nothing. She wanted to get up and storm around the room, but didn't dare do anything to stop the ongoing communications. "Why isn't he answering? Does he not know? Doesn't care? Or is he no longer there to care?"

After ten long minutes her hand started writing again. *Going to access archives. Eric had crossed into the basement. Triggered alarms with his signature. No idea what has happened.*

"Can I go get him out?" Not that she was going to listen for his answers.

"Yes!" she read aloud. "Wow, what a surprise he actually gave me permission." She pondered a return to the other side. "Stylus? Will you remember this message in case I run into trouble from being in your world?"

Yes. All data is stored and transmitted.

"Yep. So, you are just like our computers. Only you use a pencil and paper instead of a keyboard. Cool." She hopped up and grabbed a thicker sweater out of her closet. It was her one chance to pick up anything extra. She'd yet to use the supplies in her bag, as it was.

The stylus in her hand started to vibrate. She raced

over to the sketchbook.

*Not quite like your computers. We were people once.
We were Louers.*

CHAPTER 14

S HE CHOKED AND then choked again. "Did…did you say you used to be a Louer? As in you used to have a body and a mind?"

Yes.

"What happened?"

Slavery. Given to a research lab where I was bonded to the stylus to support the old man who'd been bonded to it for centuries before me. The risks were high. So, slaves were used to keep the soulbound objects functioning. The old man was failing and the bond had weakened. I don't know how, yet the next thing I knew, I was locked inside, joined as one with the previous souls. Soulbound.

Heat flushed upward then drained in hurry, leaving ice behind. Soulbound. Not bound to her soul, but a soul inside, bound to it. She shifted the stylus, to hold it almost reverently as she stretched out the fingers on her right hand. "Oh my God," she whispered. "I am so sorry. I had no idea."

Her left hand jerked under the impulses of the stylus. She quickly moved it to her right hand and let the words pour.

No. Most people don't. I haven't communicated with anyone in centuries. It feels odd. To feel anything is…unique.

She winced. "A good odd or not so good?"

A good odd. Rusty. Some of my capabilities are returning.

"Is that good?" She wondered what the hell she'd released.

Yes. There are many of us here. We have merged into one – the voice and mind of the same stylus. Each of us adds something, and the stylus grows in power. The older it is, the longer is has survived, the more of us are in here to keep it alive. The handler adds another element. In this case, you have increased our abilities tenfold. We thank you.

She gulped. "You're welcome. I think. I hope this is a good thing. Those people, Paxton, Eric and the others, aren't really open to progress. Not sure they'll appreciate this type of change."

No. Over time they will.

On that note, she turned around and finished packing her bags. "So, Stylus, how can we transport into the basement where Eric is? There are no gates there. I've never seen the inside, so drawing a door into it is going to be impossible and possibly not a good idea. Suggestions?"

The stylus was quiet. She laughed and picked it up off the bedding. Placing it on the sketchbook, she repeated, "I need a codex to travel around your world. Can we make one – is that possible?"

Possible – not practical. There exist many in Paxton's office.

"Paxton. Right. I can get to the lab." She pulled out the drawing she'd used with Eric the last time and ten minutes later she found herself back in the lab. And face to face with Paxton.

She grinned at him.

The color drained from his face. "What? How are you here?"

She wiggled the stylus in his direction. "It hasn't failed me yet. Are you aware that souls are bound to this stylus?" She watched him straighten. "Or should I say whose *souls?* These are Louers. They were normal people, whose only wrong was wanting a better life for themselves – not one of servitude. The Torans kept them as slaves, as prisoners." Outrage stiffening her spine, she stalked toward him.

"I know what we did," he snapped. "I read the archives. That is ancient history. That we're paying for it today is unacceptable. We didn't force any of them to become bound to the stylus, they were volunteers. It offered them a chance to live forever. They were also well compensated for their sacrifice. We aren't monsters, you know."

"Then why banishment to another dimension?" She couldn't help feeling that something else must have been going on.

"How would I know?" His voice rose. "I'm old, but not that old. It wasn't during my lifetime."

She shook her head. This wasn't getting them anywhere. "Where were you earlier, when Eric and I were looking for you?"

He reared back. "I've been here all along."

With a shake of her finger, she said, "Nope, you weren't, because we searched for you. Even at your apartment."

His eyes widened. A faint blush rose as he swallowed. "I was in my apartment until I heard intruders. I hid, then raced back to my lab."

Storey's gaze widened in understanding. He'd been the one that had knocked over something in the living room. They'd just missed each other. It would be laughable if it weren't so frustrating. She refocused. "I need a codex and training to use one."

He pulled himself up to his full height and raised his nose into the air. "Absolutely not. There is no way. It will kill you."

Storey pursed her lips. Instinct drove her to pull the

small blank notepad out of her pocket and slip the stylus into her fingers. "Stylus, will wearing a codex kill me?" The words formed on the page instantly. She lifted the book to show Paxton while reading it aloud. "No."

It would have taken a better person than she was to hide her triumphant look. Her grin widened. "Didn't know they could talk, did you?" She waggled the stylus in her fingers. "You don't know the first thing about them, do you?"

Paxton took a tentative step toward her, his eyes locked on the stylus. "How is it you have learned all of this in just a few days?"

She couldn't be sure, but he sounded slightly mollified instead of angry. She hadn't wanted to rub this in his face. "Because I didn't come at it with preconceived assumptions like you did." She thought that was a reasonable answer. From the glacial look fired in her direction he didn't agree. Adults and their egos. They made life so difficult.

"So yes or no on the codex? I am willing to go and get Eric; however, I can't get to him without a codex – unless you'd like to come to unlock the doors?"

He shook his head widely, white tufts of hair flying in all directions. "No, no. I can't leave. I'm needed here."

"Then you have no choice." She held out her arm.

"These aren't toys. Extensive training is required to use these. You can't just put one on and expect to be a pro."

"I don't expect to. Show me the basics so I can get to Eric. We can use *his* codex from there. Can't you sync one codex to find his codex?"

Paxton's brows drew together in surprise. "Yes. Yes, I can." He busied himself at a desk piled high with metal pieces while she waited. She glanced down at the stylus and paper. "Do you know how to work the codex,

Stylus?"

Her hand jerked immediately. *Much of it.*

"Good. Maybe, we'll do well after all."

Paxton raced toward her. "Here's a simpler version. We use these for visitors." He strapped the smaller unit on her wrist while firing instructions on its functionality.

She turned her arm slightly, admiring the look. "This is way cool." And it was. She could use something like this on her own world. Not that he'd appreciate hearing that. Still, when this was over…nope, not going to happen, the FBI would never let her keep it.

"Now pay attention. I'm punching in the identity code of Eric's codex right now. As soon as I press this last button, you're going to arrive at his side. That could put you into many horrible scenarios. This codex can't save you." As if the force of his stare could infuse common sense into her, he upped the wattage and directed it into her eyes.

She blinked and pulled back slightly. "No, but my brains and my stylus might."

He snorted. "And they might not. This is war. People are dying. You might, too."

That stopped her in her place. "I wanted to ask you about that. What is the population of your city here? Millions, thousands or only hundreds?"

"Thousands here and millions over the planet. We don't have your overpopulation problem."

"Thousands only? Are there children here?"

Paxton reared back. "Of course. We have a natural order of things. Children here do not run amuck, like in your world."

"What's the average life expectancy here?"

His lips thinned. "We live much longer than you do. I don't want your people coming over here and treating us as lab rats to find out our secrets."

Understandable. Yet it was okay for them to do that to her? Not that they'd said so to her. She shook her head. "That's not my intention. What I was thinking about was that your people are extremely long lived, so death is an even greater loss here. With your peaceful life, you're also not used to the trauma of war, of living in fear every day."

"And you are?"

"Not personally, but I've been raised with the possibility of a terrorist attack any day. We learn to live well in spite of it. That doesn't make us naive."

"My people are innocent."

"Good." She smiled and headed to the spot Paxton pointed out. She tucked her stylus into her jeans pocket, grimacing down at her clothing. At home she'd grabbed a sweater, but why hadn't she considered changing her jeans or socks and shoes? Too late now. She checked out her location and the circle she was standing in. "Here?"

"Yes. There. Return as soon as you can – with Eric."

She nodded and pushed the button. Having traveled by codex before gave her some warning as to what to expect. It happened so quickly though, she didn't have time to adjust. When the blackness cleared, she blinked and spun around.

The room was empty.

Surely not. Had the correct identity number been punched in? She had to believe in Paxton that much. Then where was Eric? She walked the small area, looking for some evidence that he'd been there.

A desk and several chairs sat in the center of the room, undisturbed. She bent to look underneath.

Something twinkled below. She pulled a chair back and reached for it.

Eric's codex.

Oh shit. She stood up and spun around, looking for where Eric could have gone. There was no sign of a fight.

No disruption to the room. Just plain…nothing.

Weird. Where were the doors in this place? Hidden? Why was nothing ever easy on this side of the veil? She walked the room, dragging her fingers along the wall, looking for breaks to denote a door. There weren't any. She stared up at the ceiling. Nothing visible. The floor? It was covered in a deep red flooring that sat like a cross between tile and carpet. Unique. She studied it, wondering if there was some kind of level below. Did basement mean the same thing here as it did back home? She wished she could ask Paxton. She brightened. She could. She pulled out her stylus and sketchbook, muttering to herself as she wrote the note, "Paxton, the room is empty. No doors or windows. Only a table and chairs in the center of the room. No sign of anyone. Eric has lost his codex. It was on the floor under the table."

She waited for the stylus to show signs of an answer from Paxton.

Impatience gnawed at her. Finally her hand started moving. *Move the table. Door is opened by knocking on it. Eric couldn't have 'lost' the codex. He's been taken and either had it cut off or removed it himself.*

Not good. She walked over to the table and turned it to the right. A smooth, sliding noise sounded behind her. She spun around to find a large door had shifted to the side. It hadn't been discernible before. Hard to believe.

Standing in the doorway, she realized there was only a dark black space beyond. Where were the damn light switches in this place? "Stylus, how do the lights turn on?" Even as she spoke the lights flashed on. Apparently they were voice controlled. She studied the long hallway now visible before her. A single closed door waited at the far end. She walked down and pushed it open. It led to another large room. This one was also empty. Not knowing what else to do, she returned to the room where she'd found his codex. "So, Stylus. Where is Eric?"

She expected a quick answer. Instead she got a weird humming sound. What was that? It almost seemed like her stylus was thinking things over.

I'm not registering him.

"Uh oh?" She stared at the pen. "What does that mean?"

It means I can't see his energy signature anywhere.

Her stomach knotted. "What? What does this mean?"

He is no longer in this dimension.

ERIC TRIED TO sit up. Bad idea. He gasped at the sledgehammer in his head. Bile from his stomach climbed up the back of his throat. Then he felt his bare arm. His codex was gone. He vaguely remembered being grabbed and putting up a crazy fight before taking a direct hit on the side of his head. He could have lost it then. Or they'd taken it. Whoever 'they' were. The loss of the codex could also contribute to the headache. He groaned softly. Brutal.

"Eric? Are you awake?" A familiar voice spoke through the pounding in his brain.

Eric tried to open his eyes. Pain forced them closed again. "I'm here," he whispered to his father. "Where are we?"

"I don't know. I was hoping you might know."

Peering through slit eyes, Eric saw his father squatting down in front of him. "What happened, sir?"

Shifting to sit on his ample butt, his father said, "We had just finished the emergency Council meeting when the alarm sounded. Louers. Everywhere. Seemed like hundreds of them. I don't know how or why. They overran us in minutes. At least I think they're Louers. They look different, though. Not like they used to look."

"Different how? What did they used to look like?"

His father peered around nervously, whispering, "Like us. Exactly like us."

What? Eric shot him a startled look. He didn't ask the burning question he wanted to ask. Instead, he went for the one next in line. "What are they like now?" Moving gently, he struggled into a sitting position, heaving a sigh of relief when the room stopped spinning. The fear in his father's voice made him look up.

"Mutants. Deformed, weird looking things. Nothing normal about them now."

"That makes sense in a way. They've had to evolve to survive. Did you know what the place was like when your people banished them?"

"No and I don't care." Sitting like a rotund Buddha, his father placed his hands on his knees and glared at Eric. "They're killing anyone who resists and rounding up the survivors. We've been taken somewhere. I'm afraid it's off planet."

That stopped Eric in the act of trying to stand up. "As in across the veil?" Just then the smell hit him. He bent over, plugging his nose. He groaned. "What's that smell?"

"Louers. We're prisoners in the Louers' dimension."

Nasty. Experimenting, Eric unplugged his nose and shuddered at the rank aroma. All the archives spoke about a horrible smell at the gate. Words hadn't done it justice.

He struggled past it to refocus on the mess they were in. From Storey's history, he'd learned that every war sported winners and losers and the losers, historically, became prisoners. When able to cross dimensions, it wasn't hard to imagine returning the prisoners to your home. Particularly if you needed slaves.

"Are we being guarded? Has someone come to speak with you?"

"No." His father shook his head. "There's been no

one."

"Does anyone have a codex?"

His father leaned closer to whisper, "I do. I don't know the coordinates to punch in."

Eric could take care of that. His father's unit wouldn't be strong enough to take everyone back at once. "Are they taking the codexes away?"

"Don't think so. We were herded forward as a group. Outside of giving us a quick check, they haven't done a massive search. There's one codex and even a couple of taprins,"

"Good." But not great. The simple taprins were basic codexes but wouldn't have the power and functionality to help out here. There wasn't a weapon amongst them. Why would there be? Until now, there'd been no need. "Slip me your codex. I can get out and back with reinforcements in no time."

His father glared. "Not without me. If you're going, then so am I."

Eric grimaced. "It's best if we all go at once. The guards could come any moment." He studied their surroundings and the ragged group surrounding them. "How many of us are here, about twenty?"

"Closer to thirty."

"Marshal the others into a group. I know where to go." Eric accepted his father's codex, clipped it on, then punched in the coordinates for Stanshor mine. That would get them clear of here, then they could jump to another point. The mine was better for a large group like this. Paxton's lab could be the second jump. Not that it would help much unless it was secure.

"We'll try for the mine," he whispered to the group gathered around him. "Everyone squeeze in as close together as possible and hang on. We're trying to move a lot of people at once. I don't know that I can take everyone in one jump."

"You're not leaving me here," blustered a big man in the back, shoving the others in closer.

"Nor me." That was a young woman holding a young child.

"I ain't staying. No way. Those things are going to come back and I want to be long gone." An older man spoke, Eric vaguely remembered seeing him in the Council chambers.

Eric understood their feelings. "Who else has a codex?"

Two people held up their arms. "Darn." They were both simple versions. "Okay. Let's try."

He hit the button on his codex and waited for the sequence to run on both, picking up the signals of each other, building power in their connectiveness. Who knew if the codex worked in the Louers dimension? They could very well end up someplace else entirely. He figured anywhere had to be better than here.

Reassuring blackness swirled around them. He closed his eyes and willed the portal to open. A wretched smell filled their nostrils and the air became fetid, hot. He coughed several times.

"Is it working?" whispered one of them.

The blackness deepened until Eric couldn't see his father's face in front of him. Isolation often accompanied a dimension journey, with the cold an ever-present symptom. He closed down inside and waited. Uneasiness knotted up his stomach. They had so few options. This had to work.

"Are we there yet?"

"No."

Another long minute of frightful silence. A child whimpered. Her mother hushed her. "Shhhh. We'll be there soon."

"Will we? I've never been in such a long transfer." The grumbler was in the back of the group. Probably the big man who'd spoken up earlier. Eric didn't have any guarantees to offer. "Some of the gates aren't working well. Not to mention with this many people the transfer will take twice as long."

Just when he thought they were trapped, the mist started to recede. Sighs of relief washed over him. The air lightened, the others grinned. He turned to look around. "We're here. Where ever here is?"

As the mists dissipated, Eric realized they weren't in Stanshor at all. He didn't know where they were.

"What is this place?" Everyone stepped back to look around. Curiosity and relief wreathed their faces. Trees, trees, and more trees surrounded them. Blue sky and sunshine looked down on them. Eric had to wonder if they'd crossed to Storey's world.

"I'm not sure yet. I don't recognize it."

"I don't care where it is. It's not with the Louers." A murmur of agreement wafted through the crowd.

"I want to go home." The little girl huddled against her mother's legs.

Eric's father walked over to him hooked his arm and led him a little ways away. "Have you heard about this place before?"

Eric circled the area. "I don't think so." He walked a few steps further as his father watched. "It's possible we're in another dimension."

"You mean we've crossed the veil? That we might be in the human's dimension?" he hissed, staring around as if something might jump out at him. "Do you know how dangerous it is over here?"

Eric looked at him oddly. "Yeah, I think I do. I've been back and forth several times with Storey. Still...I'm not sure that's where we are."

"So how do we find out?" The self-elected group leader, the large, burly man who'd complained before, stepped forward. "Don't get me wrong, I'm glad to have gotten out of that place…where's home though?"

"Please keep in mind that the Louers have taken over our home. We don't want to jump back into the same situation. I'll contact Central and let them know we need assistance."

He tapped his codes, watching the colors shift in the right order. Reassured, he contacted Central next. No one answered. Sending off a message, he hoped someone there would see the flashing signal and hit the receiver. He didn't want to consider the possibility of no one being there to receive it. Using other codex functions, he tried to get a location for this place. The wrist unit beeped and flashed and in the end, came up with an error message.

Even the codex didn't know where they were.

CHAPTER 15

S TOREY STARED AT her stylus. "Eric is in the Louer's dimension?" He'd better not be. She didn't relish trying to find her way over there.

Her pencil jerked out an answer. Or somewhat of an answer. *Yes. No.*

She sighed. "Which is it?"

He was. He is no longer.

"How do you know?"

His father's codex has recently been recalibrated for Eric's use.

"Then where are they now?"

In another dimension.

"What other dimension?" Exasperation at the short answers and having to pull teeth to get information was draining her. "My home?"

Close.

"Close." She stopped puzzled. "There are only three dimensions here." After a moment, she added, "Right?"

Her pencil answered quickly. *There were only three, but now there is a fourth.*

"Oh no." She groaned and closed her eyes briefly. The onion. "You mean the one I created to make a safety net for my world? Is Eric caught in there?"

Yes.

"Which means I can't wipe out that dimension without wiping out Eric and his group?"

If you destroy the dimension, you will also destroy everything in it.

"Such as?" The stylus remained quiet. "Could we wipe out the Louer's dimension?"

Yes.

"Yes?" she questioned. "So that's one way to stop them. Wipe them out and everyone in it will disappear, too. Drastic but as a last resort…possible." Except how could she know who else might be over there at the time? If the Louers were taking prisoners, then they'd be destroyed as well – including Eric, if he went back to rescue his people.

"Can you talk to Eric's codex?"

The codex is a machine. It does not talk.

"Right." She knew that. "Can you program the codes on Eric's wrist to give him the coordinates to get back home?"

Yes.

"Then do so." She wanted to jump up and down. This would all soon be over. Eric would be home safe and sound. Paxton should be sorting through the archives for a way to get rid of the Louers and she could go home. She frowned. She might need to fix a few things there yet.

I put in the coordinates for Paxton's lab.

"Good. Let's head back and we should arrive in time to meet them." She studied her codex. Paxton had programmed the original destination, not a return trip. The plan had been to use Eric's codex to get home. "Stylus, can you send the coordinates of Paxton's lab to my simple codex? Paxton didn't program a return trip for us."

Done.

Thank heavens for that. Now to get back and stop this solo act. She punched the button she'd used last time and the wrist unit went off in a series of flashes and beeps.

The black mist rolled around her, bundling her in a tight tornado of swirling black. She closed her eyes, hating the sense of isolation this type of travel created. One could get lost in the mists.

A shudder rippled down her spine. Lost in-between. Not a nice thought.

The mists started thinning. She relaxed, closed her eyes. It would be over soon. Several minutes later, she opened them and frowned. "Why isn't this over?" Frustration and the beginning tendrils of fear twisted in her stomach.

She waited. The mists still surrounded her, but seemed maybe less thick? Or maybe that was her imagination. The weird black gate they'd used when re-entering Eric's world popped into her mind. That had had a similar feel.

Her uneasiness grew. Following her instincts. "Stylus, have we arrived?"

She could barely see the writing on the page, even when held up to her nose.

No.

"Damn." Something had gone wrong. How to fix it? What would happen if she stepped out of the mist? She'd most likely be torn to bits. She shifted her weight from foot to foot. Another few minutes went by and she checked her wrist codex again. The lights continued to flash with bright colors. Who knew what that meant? "Stylus, can we contact Eric in any way?"

The stylus hummed. *Not at the moment.*

"Can we contact anyone? What about Paxton?"

More humming. *Yes.*

"Explain the situation to him, please." He should know what to do.

The humming intensified then shut off sharply. *Communication has been disrupted.*

"Damn it. I can't just stand here in the middle of a transition. What can I do?"

No answer. Her stylus never moved.

She groaned at the silence. "What's the use of being able to communicate if you can't help me problem-solve?" More silence. The stylus, like any computer, could only answer direct queries. "Okay. Stylus, can I get out of the middle of this gate?"

Yes.

She brightened. "How?"

Time.

She snorted. "That's something I don't have." Just then the mist started to darken again. She spun around, terrified. "What's happening?"

The blackness deepened into a morass of seething energy unlike anything she'd ever seen before. It had taken on a powerful, negative feel. She cried out. "Stop. Stop. What's happening?"

The energy spun faster and faster. She screamed as the pressure in her ears built. She crouched down, covering her head with her arms. Pain ripped through her mind.

She collapsed to the ground.

"PAXTON!" ERIC GRINNED at his aged mentor. His disreputable looking group gathered around him, relief and joy on everyone's faces.

"Eric, Councilman. You made it." Paxton raced toward him, joy beaming across his tired face. "I'm so glad to see you are well."

The strain of the last twenty-four hours had taken its toll on the older man. His hair stood out in all directions. For the first time in Eric's memory, Paxton's robes were dirty.

"What's the status at Central?" asked his father, his massive bulk collapsing onto one of the many chairs.

"We're not sure. So far, you're the only ones I've seen. Except for Storey, that is. Communication's down everywhere." Paxton lowered his face into his hands and rubbed his cheeks.

"Storey? Did you say Storey was here?" Eric couldn't believe it. Fear and joy warred in his heart. She was supposed to be home safe, not caught up in this mess. "Where is she?"

"I thought you would know. She went to the basement to help you…then I received a garbled transmission a few minutes ago saying she was having trouble with the codex and needed help." He shook his head. "The transmission cut off."

"Where was she last?"

"We calibrated her taprin to arrive at your side, based on your codex. Only we didn't know it was lost. I tracked her until communications went down," he pointed to one of his monitors. "My stylus received only part of it."

Eric looked at him quizzically. "Your stylus?"

Paxton glared at him. "That little girl is too smart. She not only figured out how to use her stylus, but she also found out that the styluses can communicate with each other."

Eric's jaw dropped.

The Councilman leaned forward in shock. "What? An otherworlder discovered things about our way of life — our tools — that we didn't even know? How is that possible?"

Paxton faced him. "I'm not sure. She seems to have a very inquisitive mind."

"That's not good. Not good at all."

Before the discussion got out of hand, Eric stepped in. "She had to figure out what the stylus could do on her own. When you have training, you're told what you can and can't do. We never questioned what we were told. She's had to constantly question and test the capabilities of the stylus in order to understand it."

His father's bulbous face darkened like a tomato. "You can't believe she is smarter than we are. That's not possible. We are far more brilliant than those…those animals," he blustered.

Excited murmurs wafted through the group.

One tall, spindly man half-stood. "Otherworlder?" He looked around at several of the others. "Are you saying there's a girl from the other side of the veil here? Here, in our dimension?"

Eric winced. He'd forgotten they had an audience.

"Not to worry. She'll be caught soon. And terminated. I have a standing kill order in effect for her actions."

Eric's hands fisted in sudden fury. "Right. Her actions. And what actions were those? To pick up what to her was nothing more than a pencil? To have it become soulbound to her without her knowledge or permission? For that you've put a death sentence on her head?"

Silence.

Everyone turned to look at the apoplectic councilman.

"Lies. All lies. The Louers attacked us because of her. She's behind everything ill that's befallen us." His father stood, his bulk so rounded and unsteady that Eric wondered if he'd topple over any moment.

"She is not. She didn't let them in. We snuck into her world and carelessly left the instrument over there. Do you realize we've put their entire world at risk with our actions? She picked the artifact up. That's it. She never did anything to us. She even offered to help solve *our* problem, and you ordered her to be put to death."

Eric couldn't stop the bottled bitterness that flowed

with the unfairness of it all. "She came back to help us —
even knowing there was a termination order on her head.
The Louers went to her house. Did you know that?"

"And you know what else? She *stopped* them. That
little schoolgirl from the other side of the veil stopped the
Louers from entering her home and her world. We should
be thanking her, giving her an honored place for her
bravery. But no, you set the guards after her. Ordered me
to retrieve her, so you could dispose of her here. You're
being blind and foolish in trying to wipe out the one
person that could actually save us." His voice roared
across the room, stunning everyone into silence.

Paxton moved first. Racing to Eric's side, he laid a
hand on his shoulder. "Easy, Eric. I don't think that the
Councilman understood the situation."

Eric shrugged off his hand. His bitterness came out in
full swing. "Oh he knew. In his all-knowing arrogance, he
even ordered my death — the death of his only son —
should I fail to return her to face her sentence."

The murmuring moved from person to person in a
growing wave of unrest. They faced the Councilman in
collective outrage. "We have a visitor from the other side
and you want to kill her? Are you trying to start a war
with those people, too?" The big burly spokesman settled
into a wide stance, his hands fisted. His face reddened in
anger. "Am I to understand, we sent a team over to this
little girl's world and left a soulbound item behind?"

Someone else called out, "How is that possible?
Where's the soul it was bound to?"

The Councilman's red face swelled with temper. Eric
watched him struggle for control. His father was a born
politician, meaning a born liar. His father's face smoothed
over and he beamed at them, then proceeded to answer
their questions. "The person who owned the stylus fell
seriously ill on his research trip to the other side. He was

rushed back here before the team knew that it had been lost. We believe that the veil, combined with the severity of the owner's illness, weakened the stylus's bond. Since then it's been trying to come back home, using this young person as its vehicle."

A woman who'd been quiet up until now stepped forward, her little daughter clinging tightly to her hand. "Has she done anything to hurt us?"

"No." Eric jumped in before his father could. He faced the group, looking each person in the eye, trying to explain. "She's an innocent in this. We don't know if she had anything to do with the timing of the Louer attack, that's possible, but she's not responsible for this war. Even more importantly, a Louer entered her dimension by ripping through a wall in her house and I watched her banish him to the far reaches." He turned to face his father. "She came to help us do the same thing."

His father, the esteemed Councilman, snickered. "She came to help *you*. What is she, another of your disreputable friends?"

Eric's blood pounded at the insult. His father had never approved of his friends. Any of them. He'd gone out of his way to separate Eric from everyone. Thankfully, his father had never learned of his one and only girlfriend…ex-girlfriend. His jaw clenched. It gratified him to see his father backing up a step. Fighting for control, Eric finally managed to speak a moment later. "Of course you would put her down like this. She's never treated you with anything but respect, so I think you could accord her the same. I would be honored to count her as a friend. She has many qualities that I admire. Not the least of which is stepping in to lend a hand, even when her own life is threatened."

"That sentence can't be still in place," protested the woman. "That's hardly fair."

"No, it's not fair. Except my father, the Councilman, never rescinds an order. Even if it's wrong." His bitterness resonated throughout the room. He winced. He hadn't meant to let everyone know how deep this went. But then he'd spent a lifetime trying to live up to his father's expectations, even though he knew there was no way he ever could succeed. The dam had to break sometime. "It doesn't matter. I'll go find her and send her home again."

"Now wait. That's not right either," blustered the burly man again. "We need her."

The mother shook her head. "Not if it's going to cost her life."

The burly man turned on her so fast, she stumbled while trying to back up. She snatched her daughter up into her arms. "Why not?" he said. "Our lives are at stake now, too. Or do you want to go back into that black hole again?"

"That's enough." Paxton entered the fray. "Eric, regardless of her future, she's in trouble if she hasn't made it back yet."

"Right. Then it's back to the basement for me."

"No. She's left there. She's caught somewhere in transit."

"How's that?" Eric's heart hitched. With all the chaos around them, anything could have happened to her. Damn he wished she was here, safe and sound.

"According to the monitors, she left the basement over half an hour ago. She should have been here within minutes. I can only think with all the disturbances that codex travel is messed up. I have no idea where she is."

The young women stepped up. "Can't you contact her? There must be some way to reach her."

Paxton stared down at his stylus frowning. "She got her stylus to communicate with mine somehow." He turned his over a couple of times. "I've been soulbound to mine for over a century and never knew. Then, maybe mine can't. Stylus, can you talk?"

Silence.

He shrugged. "I didn't think so."

"How did she communicate with you?" Eric stepped up and stared at Paxton's stylus. "Did they communicate to each other?"

"Yes, except her stylus contacted mine. I don't know how to get mine to initiate a conversation."

Eric ran over to the desk and pulled up a stylus tablet. Holding it out to Paxton, he said, "Write down the question."

"This is foolish," he protested, but did as asked. His stylus made an odd scratching sound as he wrote, requesting it to contact the other stylus. "There." He glared at Eric, holding up the tablet for everyone to see. "Now what?"

"If she can answer, your stylus will receive a message."

Paxton snorted. "I doubt it. This stylus has been used in the same way for a long time. It's not going to open up communication just because I request it."

"No, yet it did at the request of her stylus, correct?"

"Which isn't going to help right–" His hand jerked. He gasped. Eric grabbed Paxton's hand and placed it on the tablet. The stylus immediately started to write.

"Lost." Eric read it out loud.

Paxton read out the last half. "Need help."

A gasp rose through the crowd. "How do we help her?"

"Stylus, can you get the coordinates of the other stylus?"

The stylus wrote down the word *yes*. Paxton's eyes bugged out. He spluttered, "This is impossible. You can't just talk to it. It's not alive."

"Why? It's your belief system that needs to shift

here." Eric didn't care if Paxton was uncomfortable with this or not. "Stylus, please write down the coordinates so that I can key mine to match."

Instantly a series of numbers showed up on the tablet under Paxton's astonished gaze. "There, see? Now…" Eric ignored him and punched in the numbers. "Considering that the codexes are whacked right now, I can only try. Let's hope I can reach her."

He stared at Paxton. "Then again, if you come with me, I'll be able to communicate with her no matter where I end up."

Paxton shook his head vigorously. "No, I can't do any more codex travel. Go. If it doesn't work, we'll figure something else out."

The options weren't great.

"Back in five, I hope." He walked over to the port and hit the button.

CHAPTER 16

STOREY ROCKED BACK and forth, her stylus in hand, sketchpad resting on her crossed legs. A chill had set in, forcing her to drag her sweater out of her backpack to stay warm. She'd tried to exit this mist on foot, in her mind, and through her pictures. So far nothing had worked. She turned to yet another clean page. At this rate she would run out of paper. Just the thought of it sent her flipping the book and writing on the back of the previous page. "Now what? Stylus, do you have any idea of how to get us home again?"

No.

She retried the same question as she had for the last ten minutes. "Can we communicate with anyone?"

A humming again. Well that had to be progress. "Who?" she asked, the words bursting free before the stylus had a chance to answer.

Eric.

She brightened. Yay, something had shifted. And for the good. Straightening her back she asked, "What do I need to do?"

Nothing.

What? "Is he coming here?"

"Storey? Are you there?"

Eric. She jumped to her feet. "Eric! I'm over here. Follow the sound of my voice." She kept talking, loudly. Inside relief spilled over to fill her right down to her toes.

She was saved.

"I'm coming. Keep talking." His voice sounded like it was right next to her, that she could reach out and touch him. A hand reached through the mist and brushed her arm. She shrieked. Then a face. Eric.

She launched herself into his arms. "Oh, thank God. Am I glad to see you. I couldn't go anywhere. I don't know what happened." She was babbling and couldn't seem to stop herself.

"Shhh. It's okay. I'm here now. You're safe. The codexes are gimpy from the rips in the veil. Let's see if we can get you out of here." He tried to back out of the mist. He could move through, yet the minute she tried, it wouldn't let her pass.

"Weird. The mist thinks it's taking you somewhere. It won't release you."

"That doesn't make any sense."

"No it doesn't. Still, it goes along with everything being wonky right now."

"Can we cancel it?"

He reached for her armband and frowned. "You've just got a simple Codex. That's no good."

"Wait." She reached into her back pack and pulled out his codex. "I have yours, too."

His face lit up. "Great. Then I can take off my father's." He exchanged the codexes. "Mine is a controller. I should be able to clear the codes frozen on your unit." Drawing his brows together, he punched a series of buttons before tapping in a series of numbers.

Storey couldn't help but grin at the familiar musical notes. Such a teenager thing to do. Just hearing something normal again made her feel giddy with relief. "I like your ring tones."

"Ring tones?" He glanced up briefly, confusion clouding his eyes. "What do you mean?"

"Like the cell phones in my world. Yours plays music when you use it."

With a shake of his head he went back to studying the unit on her arm. "Sorta. Each is a code though."

"Whatever." She didn't care if it played movies, as long as it got her out of here.

"There. Now when I code into the coordinates for the lab, the mist should disappear."

A few tense minutes after the sounds stopped, the blackness lightened.

"It's working," she cried out.

She threw herself into his arms again. Reaching up, she planted an enthusiastic kiss on his lips. As she pulled back, she realized what she'd done. "Sorry."

"Sorry for what?" he said, his voice husky and soft, his arms wrapped tightly around her. "There's not a man alive that would object to being kissed by a beautiful woman."

A delicate shudder worked down her spine, pooling in her belly.

"Are you all right?" He pulled back slightly to peer deep into her eyes, forcing her to close hers or let him see how much he'd affected her.

She burrowed deeper, mumbling, "Yes. Yes, I'm fine. Just cold."

He tugged her back into his arms, letting the heat of his body warm her up. "This should help. The mist is always cold."

Snuggled in tight, Storey couldn't help wishing that they could stay like this a little longer. "Good. I'm so glad you found me. I was running out of options," she admitted against his chest.

He nudged her chin up so he could look her in the eyes. "It wouldn't have happened if you'd stayed home. What possessed you to come back? You knew it would be bad."

"Yes." Then she remembered. Explaining how she'd learned to communicate with the stylus and how it had given the knowledge necessary to protect her world from the Louers, she added, "I think it might be the answer here, too."

He gave her a quick squeeze. "Paxton doesn't like that you can do more with yours than he can with his."

She grinned. "They can talk to each other. They were Louers once."

"What?" He moved her back slightly and gave her a little shake. "What did you say?"

It took a moment to repeat what she'd learned from her stylus. "According to Paxton, they were volunteers, except I'm not sure how much was really voluntary when compared to the promise of a better life than slavery. There are several souls bonded to my stylus, so it's no longer one person but a compilation of many souls together. After so long they've fused together as one unit."

"But Louers? They're our hated enemies."

She took a few steps back and lifted her stylus and whipped out her pocket notebook. "Says who?" she scoffed. "Stylus, were you an enemy of Eric's people?"

Her hand jerked. She held it up to him to see.

"No?" He looked at her doubtfully, and she realized he thought she'd written that answer herself.

"Were you perceived as their enemy, Stylus?"

Yes.

"Were you enslaved to them?"

"Yes," she read to him, holding up the stylus triumphantly. "See. They were Louers."

He stared at her. "How did they get from being slaves to this nightmare they've become today?"

"Stylus can you answer that question?"

Her hand immediately went to work. *The Torans be-*

lieved Louers were trying to rise up against them. They banished us. In the process, we fought back and tried to take some of our old owners as slaves.

Figures. History repeated itself, regardless of which side of the veil humanity inhabited.

"That's regrettable if it's true, yet how does it help us now?"

"I don't know, except all information is power." She turned around. "The mist is gone. Can we leave now?"

"Yes." He focused on his codex and tapped in new codes. Once again musical notes accompanied the flash of numbers and colors.

Please let it take us where we want to go this time.

Black snaked up her legs.

She stepped closer. "I hate this part."

"It should work this time."

"Should?" Was that squeak her voice? She barely held back a shudder.

"Like I said, we've been having trouble with the codex travel."

"You said that?" She didn't remember that. Everything else had disappeared from her mind in the excitement of seeing him. Storey closed her eyes at the brief vertigo that always accompanied the transition. Within seconds, the mist thinned before pooling at the bottom of their feet.

Paxton's lab.

"Oh, thank heavens for that." Her breath rushed out in a whoosh, only to be sucked back in shock. The room was full of people.

Staring at her.

"Uh, hello."

Smiling tentatively, she studied them. Tired, dirty and very happy, they appeared relaxed. What a weird combination, especially given the war going on. They smiled back. At least they were friendly. Her gaze wandered around the familiar room and froze at the sight of Eric's rotund father glaring at her. No, that was too light a word. Animosity oozed from him.

Storey glowered back. *Asshole.*

As much as she hated it, she couldn't stop her back from stiffening or the sense of vulnerability creeping in.

Would he order her to be hauled off to the dungeons? Or had the kill order been rescinded? She'd forgotten to ask Eric.

"Easy," whispered Eric. "This isn't the time"

"As long as he wants me dead, it is."

"There is some doubt about the sentence, in light of your actions." Paxton rushed to assure her.

Storey studied his features, realizing how much the current situation had aged him. She grimaced. "Nice thought, but excuse me if I don't believe you."

"Don't blame you. Not sure I do either," Eric muttered beside her.

He placed a hand in the small of her back and nudged her forward. "Give me the codex. It's not going to do you any good." Taking it from her, he walked over to Paxton and handed it over. "This is the broken unit."

"The energy tears will be the root of the problem." Paxton examined it, turning it over several times. "But I might be able to fix the unit."

"It's not worth it." Eric pulled his father's codex out of the backpack. He handed it over to Paxton as well, then turned to address his father. "Not sure this unit is in working order, either. Might need to be overhauled as well."

Storey watched anger blitz across Eric's father's face. The Councilman was not happy. She couldn't help warning Eric. "Uh oh. He's not happy with you," she whispered.

Eric glanced down at her in surprise, then studied the anger and frustration on his father's face.

"Is this her?" a tiny voice piped up, interrupting the conversation.

Storey turned toward the sound to see a waif peering around a tall thin woman. Storey grinned. They did have children here. And females. She'd started to wonder where the hell they were or if this was a male only society. "Hi, who are you?"

"Sammy?" A smile peeked out, followed by a tinkle of a laugh.

"Well, hello, Sammy. My name is Storey."

"Hi." She ducked behind the woman's leg again.

Storey wanted to bend down and talk with her, but a robust male stepped in, blocking her view. With his arms akimbo and jaw squared, she realized that not all of these people were open to her presence. Storey smiled. "Beautiful child."

"Hmmm." His eyes narrowed, studying her.

She lifted an eyebrow in question, keeping a relaxed smile on her face. Eric put an arm around her shoulders. "Everyone, this is Storey. She is from the other side of the veil."

Storey shot him an amazed glance. "You told them?"

"Yeah, that whole secretive thing wasn't doing it for me. Besides, I figured honesty might be the better approach, considering we're trying to lift the death sentence on your head."

"Yeah. How's that working out?"

"Half and half."

She shook her head. "Nice. Now that Paxton knows how to stop the Louers, maybe I could go home."

"What?" Everyone turned to look at Paxton.

He shook his head. "No. No, I don't know how to stop them."

"According to the stylus, you do."

"Well, the stylus is wrong," he snapped. "How did you stop them in your world?"

"I erased them." She grinned at the dumbfounded looks staring at her. Eric smirked at her side. "And when I went back last time, I added another dimension between the Louers and my world. Don't know how well that's working out though. It's a touchy thing making changes on a large scale. Some unexpected things happen."

"Dare I ask?"

She shot Eric a look and shook her head "No, let's just say I might have to fix a few things when I go back." What were her parents thinking about now? Wiccan, Catholic or maybe by now, they've converted to some no-name cult. Or had everything reverted to normal and her father was gone from her life again? She groaned softly. Just because she'd instructed her stylus to reverse all unintentional changes didn't mean it had. Or that the attempt had worked. Only time would tell.

"Erased?" Paxton's voice squeaked between them. "How is that possible?"

"With the stylus." At the puzzled look, she added, "The Louers ripped through the veil and tried to enter through my living room wall while Eric and I were there."

Several of the women in the crowd gasped and held their children close. She couldn't blame them.

The big man's thick busy brows beetled together. "Is that the first time they've made it to your world?"

She nodded. "I think so, but I don't know. I imagine they came through in that spot because it's almost the same place as the portal I accidentally created in the beginning."

Understanding lit up Eric's face. "Right. You jumped through the floor. And they came in at nearly the same place where you'd have disappeared." He patted her on her shoulder. "That's the first time I got that. Wow. That makes so much sense. So, when you erased that Louer, did you also erase the crossing?"

"No, I don't think so." She thought about it again. "Or I recreated it when I crossed over again."

"Hmmm."

Paxton lifted his hands and shook them in her face. "That won't work here. It's not possible."

Storey studied his anxious features. "I don't know about that. To make it work, I'd have to either remove every tear except one and shepherd them back throughout that hole and erase it afterwards."

Eric shook his head. "Hang on here. Let's go back to that creating a new dimension. How did you do that? And what's to stop them from crossing from that dimension into yours?"

"As I don't know what they're capable of, I can't say that they can't. Keep in mind they haven't before. And consider that that they may not want to for a couple of reasons. To start with, this dimension is a copy of our world, the world they left behind. It's nice and they might be happy there. And second, they may think that this new world *is* my world. After all, who'd be there to tell them the difference? Third, they won't know there are other dimensions to go looking for. Why would they? Their current world isn't very pleasant, is it?"

"No." Paxton shook his head. "It's a dark, damp place with only a few hours of light each day."

"Nice." She grimaced. "No wonder they mutated into something so different from the slaves you once had. You could try to understand them before slaughtering them."

Eric's father stomped to his feet. "That's enough. What do you know of our world? You come here and cause trouble, yet still come out smelling like royalty. You're not. You don't belong here. You don't belong with my son."

Storey turned to face him. His beady eyes glowed with hate. She lifted her chin. "No, I don't. I have my own world to go back to." She refused to let this man intimidate her after all she'd been through already. They had no idea.

"Then go home and don't ever come back," the Councilman snapped.

She snorted. "Would love to. Not sure I can, considering that the tears in the veils are making travel very iffy right now." That didn't mean she couldn't travel by drawing though. Not that she was ready to tell him that. They still hadn't solved the Louer problem.

Paxton nodded his head. "That's quite right. Quite right, indeed." He wrung his hands and shuffled his feet. "She can't travel now."

"So fix it. That's your job. Take care of it. Then ship her home. Today." The Councilman settled back and crossed his arms over his ample stomach.

Storey's heart, always willing to forgive, hardened. He was an asshole. She opened her mouth to give him a piece of her mind when Eric's hand squeezed her shoulder. "Steady," he whispered before turning back to face his mentor. "Paxton, any idea of how long it could take?"

Paxton shook his head vigorously. "Oh dear. I don't know. I just don't know. I can't fix the tears with the Louers travelling back and forth."

"So we have to stop the Louers first?"

"Right." His head bobbed up and down. "I think so."

Storey glanced over at Eric to find him studying her, a questioning look in his eyes. "I can't deal with them all. Not this way."

"I know. The problem, as I see it, is the lack of information. There's no way to know how many have crossed into our world or how many more might come in a second wave."

"We don't want that to happen. This has to be sorted out and fast."

A weird sound ripped through the air. Storey backed up. Her stomach dropped. She knew that sound. It ripped through the room again. The crowd of people, sprawled across the floor, just starting to relax, jumped to their feet and cowered in a tight group.

"They're coming! Save us!" Hysteria erupted and the group scattered, with some people trying to hide under the tables and chairs. Eric's father jumped to his feet and raced to the door. "Save me."

Storey snorted. "Figures."

The Councilman glared at her. "It's their duty. My life supersedes theirs." He turned to glare at Eric, still standing at her side. "Eric, take me to a safe place."

The ripping sound sliced through the room. Storey jumped at the noise and spun around. She couldn't see the Louers, yet past experience told her it wouldn't take them long to break through the last barriers. She wondered how many there were in existence. Paxton wouldn't know and the Louer population could have changed drastically over the centuries, regardless of how many had been originally banished.

The others screamed and crouched lower. Mothers huddled protectively over their children. Storey took out her sketchbook and stylus. She couldn't afford to hide. Besides, there was no place left. She sat down in her favorite position on the floor and opened to a clean page. She'd need a new sketch book soon. Could she use the back side of her drawings or would that mix two together and create something she really didn't want to see? Best to not try for now.

Eric crouched at her side. "What are you doing?"

"I'm getting ready," she whispered nodding in the

direction of the ceiling over the monitors. "They're coming in over there."

She spoke softly. "Stylus. I need your help. The Louers will be here any moment. How can I stop them from entering this room?"

Seal it.

She grinned. "Perfect. Let's do it." She put the stylus to paper and studied the picture slashing down at double speed. Her stylus raced across the paper, stopped, scribbled in place before continuing at a pace so fast she couldn't discern the lines as they appeared as part of the picture.

She tried to watch, but the frenzy of movement was just too hard to follow. Just like that, her hand stopped. She shook out her arm as she studied the image in front of her.

Eric leaned over her shoulder. The picture showed Paxton's lab, the full essence of the space down in a few strokes. A plastic layer appeared to cover the entire space.

"Sealant?" She laughed. Looking up she caught the panicked look on everyone's face. She bent her head. "Hey, Stylus. How about sealing each Louer and sending them back to their own space."

Too many.

"Hmmm. This world is also too large to seal, correct?"

Correct.

She rambled ideas aloud. "So how can we seal the space or the Louers? If we could do that, could we send them home any easier?"

Eric shifted his position to sitting on the floor. "You do realize you're sitting here in a life and death situation and talking aloud to a pencil?"

Casting a quick glance around, she realized her actions weren't exactly confidence building. "Eric, I have to toss out questions and see what rises for answers. The stylus isn't good at offering information. It answers my questions, though. Think of this as a brainstorming session."

He nodded. "Go for it."

Shooting him a quick smile of thanks, she returned to talking to the stylus. "Is there a way to put a tracking number or something similar on each Louer so that we can move them home as if sent by computer or codex?" She wasn't making any sense. She knew that, yet somewhere in there had to be an idea, a starting point.

"What are you thinking?" Eric frowned.

"I'm trying to figure out a way to track them all and then send them home before sealing the door, somehow forever. Then open a door to their new world. That's presuming they don't have technology that allows them to return here. And presuming that they like their new world enough to not to want to try to return here. Can we put a codex on each one and send them back or something similar? Obviously not that, as it would give them our technology."

"We can't go and catch them all in order to do that."

"Maybe we don't have to." She asked the stylus, "Stylus, can we do something like that?"

No.

"Okay. I can't just erase them one by one. I can't seal every room one at a time. There has to be something more global."

"Like what?"

"The stylus can track each one," she stared at her pen. "Stylus, that's correct isn't it?"

Yes.

Storey nodded. "Eric, do you have a way to move supplies across dimensions? Or large items from one spot to another? Like supplies to another city?"

He pursed his lips. "Yes, we can. We place codes on the items and send them through the gates, using codexes to set the destination." He studied her face. "Where are you going with this?"

Excitement bubbled through her. "Now we're getting somewhere. Why can't we can track them, slap on codes and ship them home? The next issue is how to subdue them? And how do we stop more from coming over?"

Paxton interrupted their musing. "I can fix the field so they won't be able to come across without getting injured. They might try it once or twice, but by the time they figure it out I could have the tears fixed."

Eric stood up, stretched then squatted beside her. "That could take a long time."

"I know. I was hoping more people would have styluses and could help. Either that or have Paxton's stylus give us all locations and teams can go out at the same time. I doubt there are more than a dozen here at one time."

There were fifty in the first sweep. Her stylus moved freer on its own.

"How many are still here?"

One dead, seven wounded and taken home. Two escorted the injured home. Forty left on this side.

"Forty isn't so bad." She winced. Just forty opportunities to be captured or killed.

"I want to help." The burly man from the group stood up. "She's created a safe place for everyone, so they can stay here while we go hunting. I want to do my part."

"And me."

"I'm helping, too."

Before they realized what had happened, all the males in the group had stepped forward. Eric studied them. "Are any of you trained for codex use?"

"I'm in the reserves," said one of the younger men.

"I still think this is a bad idea," protested Paxton, facing the group. "You have no weapons, and they are bigger and stronger and meaner. None of you know what you're doing."

"Has anyone got a better idea? Do you have an army here? Security forces?" She asked the room in general. "We need to solve this ourselves before they return in greater numbers, now that they know how minimal your defenses are. Paxton, with the help of your stylus, can you organize teams to rescue your people from the Louer's dimension? If we can get them together in groups and send over teams with codexes, you could take them home very quickly. We need to make sure the Torans are here and the Louers are back on their side. Then we should be able to seal the tears while opening up the dimension in-between."

Frustrated, Eric ran his hand down over his face. "We're going to have to coordinate this very carefully. It could be dangerous. Storey, I don't want you in the middle of this."

Sadly she looked into his dear face. When and how had he become so important? So special to her? "I already am," she said simply. "Any of us could die on this mission, including you. There's no choice. The window of opportunity is now. Their numbers are down. Paxton might be able to reduce the numbers crossing over but if their numbers grow, there won't be any stopping them."

"She's right. If we're going, let's get a move on."

Eric looked around. "Two trained in codexes? No more?"

"Send one over to retrieve your people. Make sure more codexes are taken over there. Let the men who are prisoners use them. You'll move people much faster that way," Storey said.

Eric glanced over at his father, as if considering his

participation, then shook his head. Storey agreed. The man had to have some redeeming qualities. He was the leader of Eric's people after all. It seemed to be her that brought out the worst in him. And once he'd slid down into that level, well…he seemed to revel in it. Maybe they could make peace when this was over.

"Fine. Two codexes, then two teams. One to do retrievals and pull in more men and the other to start dealing with the Louers until more teams can come to help."

"Right. Can we find a way to speed up the process? I won't know how long things are going to take until we get started. Paxton is needed here, otherwise I'd say take his codex as well."

"What about his stylus?" The same burly man took several steps toward Paxton, who backed up ahead of him.

"That won't work, his is soulbound, too." She lifted her stylus. "Can you give us coordinates right now for several Louers, a small group? Preferably in close proximity to where we are now?"

A distinct, deep humming filled the air. Several women ducked even though Storey tried to reassure them all was well. "It's my stylus. He's locating the Louers."

Her hand jerked, and the message appeared as if by magic. *There are nine Louers approaching the Center.*

"Nine in one bunch. A bit many?" She bit her lip, then shook her head. "The location means we need to take them first before they take over the rest of the building." Storey stood up and walked over to Eric. "I think we should go as a group and see how we fare. Four of us against nine of them is completely doable, particularly if we have the element of surprise," she added with a grin.

Eric looked at the eager faces around them and gave in. "It's almost a quarter of them. Not exactly a small group. We'd be better off going for a couple at a time."

Paxton shook his head. "No time."

"Right." Eric shrugged. "We'll give this a try and evaluate after this test group."

"Stylus, do the Louers have guns?"

No.

"Where is the best place to capture them?"

In the basement.

"Except that's where they caught all of us." Eric stood with his hands fisted on his hips.

"True. Where and how, Stylus?" Humming picked up as the stylus computed information. In the meantime, Storey checked over her backpack, making sure she was as prepared as possible.

In the anteroom of the outside entrance to the basement. They will enter there.

"Eric, do you have weapons to use?"

"Some."

"Stun guns? Tranquilizers? Something along those lines? You keep saying how advanced you are, so what do you have?"

"We *are* more advanced," Paxton spluttered.

Exasperated, she said "Then you should be able to subdue these things before we even see them. Don't you have gas you can put into this small anteroom? For that matter, you should have the ability to pipe gas into the ante room without us ever venturing near." She turned to the Councilman. "You run this place. Do you have defensive measures in place?"

He stared at her, disdainful fury marring his pudgy face. "No. Why? We've never needed anything like that before. We don't live in your society where you make war on each other all the time. We've never worried about our safety until you came here."

Storey groaned. "Not that again. You know what the

problem is with your world? You're all talkers with no action. You'd talk yourselves to death if given a chance – at least that way you wouldn't have to worry about the Louers finishing you off."

She snatched up her bag off the floor. "I'm going down to the basement to do what I can to slap codes on these nine. Then we can ship them back where they came from. Either come with me and help or stay here on your fat butt and do nothing like you always do."

She strode to the door, pulling her small notepad from her pocket. "Stylus. Directions please."

Go through the door and turn left.

"Wait," cried out one of the women, "What about the sealant on this room? If you go out it'll break the seal and we'll be vulnerable again."

Hmmm. As much as she had no use for the Councilman, the women and children didn't deserve a life of servitude with the Louers. "Stylus, can it be resealed?"

No.

"Can we leave without disturbing the seal by using codexes?"

Yes.

She spun around searching for Eric. "Eric, are you ready?"

"Yes, just checking the status of the armory."

"How come you have an armory if you don't need such a thing," she asked mockingly of Eric's father. That pompous windbag really pissed her off. She wouldn't mind if he was captured again. It's not like he was doing anything to help save his people.

Eric shot her a sideways look. "Because at one point in time, we did need it. Therefore, for a long time we kept the training and weapons current. Then the threat died off and well…" He shrugged. "That could be a problem too. The weapons might be there, but I'm not sure what condition they are in." He motioned to the other men. "We'll go there first."

"Then let's move or we'll be too late."

He walked over, that wide cocky grin back on his face. Reaching out for her arm, he nodded to the others. "I'm dialing now. Step over."

The group rushed over in time for the black air to swirl around their feet and block out the rest of the room.

About damn time. This place would crumble with old age before anyone got down to business.

"Still as impatient as ever, I see," murmured Eric beside her.

She bent her head to hide her grin. If he only knew.

CHAPTER 17

A T THE BASEMENT, they split up. Eric took several men and headed to the armory. Storey and the remaining two men headed for the anteroom. She didn't know what they could do on their own, but hoped something would come to her on the way. The burly man strode at her side. The younger, pimple-faced, barely adult male loped along on the side. The teen smiled at her. She smiled back. "What's your name?"

"Horath."

She raised her eyebrow, "That's an interesting name."

He straightened, even his smile brightened.

"My name is Jendron." The burly man grinned knowingly at her. "Neither of us is mated."

What that had to do with anything, she didn't know. She knew enough to keep her mouth shut though.

She was grateful to see Eric ahead of them at the entrance to the anteroom. His nostrils flared. He lifted his head, almost sniffing the air. "They're here already."

"Good," she murmured. "Let's get in there and take them down."

He looked at her sideways. "How?"

"With the gun you're carrying."

His face broke into a half smile. "You've got that right. We have three stun guns. Old but still functional, I hope. Still, we'll be lucky if we shoot four or five. What about the others?"

Storey smiled and tapped her sketchbook. "I'm not without some resources."

"True. But it takes time to draw. You aren't going to have that time."

"No," she said. "I won't. Maybe you'll be able to handle them all and I won't need it." She didn't bother telling him she'd been working on an idea. She opened her sketchbook, stared at it and started drawing. She created the same door that started this whole mess from her bedroom. She fell into the project with the same intensity she put into all her drawings.

She barely noticed when Eric set up position and motioned to the others to be ready. One hand on the doorknob, he turned back to Storey. "Are you ready Storey? In three, two, one…"

Storey raised her head and watched. Her hand, stylus gripped tight in her fingers, sketched at a mad pace. The gate was almost done, the latch, the shading. Just another minute. She watched the men even as her hand, the stylus clenched tight, drew at a furious pace.

Eric reached for the knob. He kicked the door wide and jumped in low. Storey peered into the room. Darkness, complete and utterly blinding, greeted them. There should have been some light from the windows, at least. Nothing. All her instincts screamed at her.

"What's wrong?"

He cast Storey a frown and nudged her to silence. Pulling his weapon forward, he entered the darkness. One step. Two steps. All he could hear was heavy breathing from those trying to peer into the room from behind him. A bright light flashed. He blinked, then blinked again. Black smoke wafted at the floor level.

The smell hit him first. Sour and cloying, the fetid aroma filled his nostrils and threw him off stride. He bent slightly, gasping for air. The black smoke thickened. Then it hit him. He scrambled backwards. It was a portal.

"Watch out," he yelled in warning. "It's an active portal."

"I made it. Toss them through." Storey screamed back. "I didn't expect it to be that big."

There was a shocked silence. Several of the men turned to stare at her, disbelief twisting their features. Eric, his temper barely held in check, said, "Next time, how about a little warning first, please."

"Sorry." She hunkered down close to the floor. Not a good start.

Louers rushed through the charcoal fog. "Don't let them grab you. They'll be able to take you through to their world."

Storey scurried further back from the action, shaking so bad her legs couldn't hold her. Panic knotted her stomach down tight. She grabbed her stylus. She'd drawn the portal, but hadn't expected it to be so big or right in the front of the door. Making the best of the situation, sketching as fast as she could, she placed a stickman in the room, labeled it Louer, then tossed him into the portal. A rasping scream sounded from the room. She ignored it, desperate to send another Louer into the portal. The intensity of the fighting increased and screams echoed down the empty basement.

The smell seeped out to where she was. It caught her sideways, making her gag. She choked several times, her eyes watering.

The sounds of fighting went on around her. She coughed a couple more times.

"Storey, a little help please!"

Crap, that was Eric. Still coughing, and with tears running down her cheeks, she returned to her drawing, urging the stylus to increase the speed. Another male screamed. Sounded like Horath. She sank deeper into her focus and sketched faster. The hell going on in there was beyond her experience. That Eric may not survive hadn't been a serious consideration before.

This hadn't been real before.

Just then Jendron tumbled out of the room to roll to a stop at her feet. He groaned and lay there gasping in pain. Scratches raked from shoulder to elbow on both arms as if he'd been grabbed and had pulled free. She thought he might be seriously injured, when suddenly he let out a roar, bolted to his feet and blasted back into the center of the fight.

Gulping hard, Storey tore her gaze away from the fighting and tried to draw. Her nerves rattled making it hard to hold the stylus. Consumed with panic, she had to close her eyes to stay focused. Imagining Louers attacking Eric, she mentally picked them up and tossed them in, her hand mimicking her action on paper. It was as if she could see everyone clearly in the melee. Eric was there, so was Jendron at the back. Sketch, pick up, and toss. Repeat. Suddenly she realized that Eric was in the air and flying toward the portal.

"No," she screamed. She scribbled over the portal and Eric hit the closed wall – hard. She'd shut the portal. Shocked, everyone stilled and stared as they worked to catch their breath. Only two Loures remained. Eric bounced to his feet and shot them both. Stunned, they collapsed to the ground.

"Oh, thank God." Storey clambered to her feet and raced over to Eric, throwing herself into his arms. "You're safe."

He wrapped her up tight in his embrace, his chest heaving from exertion. "Thanks to you."

Rearing back slightly, she noted, "Yeah. Apparently as I become more bonded to the stylus, my abilities or the scope of my capabilities is improving."

"No, really." He grinned and leaned over to kiss her, hard. Just as she was enjoying the feel of his mouth on hers, he set her aside. Laughing at the look on her face, he grabbed her hand and walked a few steps to stare down at the unconscious enemies. "Now what do we do?"

The others shook their heads and walked around the two prisoners. Sweat now mingled with the noxious odor of the captives. Raw sewage couldn't have smelt worse. Storey looked from them to the attack party. At first glance, everyone appeared to be alive and accounted for, although Horath held his arm at a funny angle. The others appeared bloody, yet not seriously injured.

Storey stared down at the creatures she'd yet to see up close. Her throat seized. Lord, they were ugly. Nothing she'd care to see late at night, that's for sure. They had human features, but were disproportionate in size. And hairy. She could only see the face of one, but it resembled the pictures she'd seen in natural history class of early Neanderthals, with huge foreheads and thick jaws. Their palms were thick and ending in impossibly long skinny fingers. She took a step back. She couldn't stand to be so close, their very skin reeked.

"How do you attach codes to send your supplies where you need them?"

"We attach tags generated by the codexes."

"Will that work in this case?" She grabbed her sketchbook and asked the stylus to give her the sequence of numbers that the codex computer could pick up. Instantly, a series of numbers came up on the paper. "Okay, here they are."

"Do we just write this on their skin?" she asked.

Yes, but use me to write on them. Then the computer will have my signature.

Storey bent down to the thick arm in front of her. "Then we'll do that now. I'm at the first one. Let's repeat the first number." Once she touched the stylus to the Louer's skin, the stylus scratched out a complex series of numbers on his skin. No blood or obvious tissue damage. Weird. It was almost like a temporary tattoo when she was done.

She walked over to the other Louer and repeated the process. Then she stepped back and looked over at Eric. "This is your part now. Send them home."

Eric nodded and punched his codex several times bringing out the musical notes she'd come to understand. "Paxton gave me the destination code that he'd found in the archives used for Mansfield. Let's hope that's still effective." Mist started to swirl about. "Get out, everyone. The mist will take whoever is touching it."

The room filled with darkness. When Storey didn't move fast enough, she was grabbed and dragged out. The other men had filed out in front of them. They shut the door and waited.

Eric and Storey stared at each other. "Is this going to work?"

"It should. We send supplies to your world that way."

"Interesting." Something to keep in mind.

After a few minutes, Eric opened the door slightly, then threw it wide open. He grinned at her. "You did it. The room's empty."

She stepped in to look for herself. Turning back, she beamed a wide grin to the others. "I did it? This was a team effort." She kissed her stylus. "That leaves what, about thirty-one or so others? Let's go."

First though, they sent Horath and his broken arm back to Paxton for treatment. Now one man short, they needed smaller groups of Louers to keep the odds in their favor.

Using the stylus, they found a group of five Louers. This time they transported to within ten feet of their location, caught them by surprise and had them unconscious in minutes. The stun gun worked wonders now that the men were accustomed to using them.

Storey stared down at them in shock. "I haven't adjusted to arriving, and they're already out cold. This is great." With Eric's help they completed the code writing on all five. Standing back, Storey watched as Eric shipped them back to their old world.

"What's the chance of the other Louers being taken just as easily?"

Eric shook his head. "Not."

She grimaced. "Yeah, I didn't think so. Let's hope Paxton has closed those tears." She consulted with the stylus. "No more new crossings," she announced. "Still, we have another twenty-six to do."

The stylus came up with two in a group, and they were dispatched to follow their countrymen in a similar fashion.

"Two is about right, given how tired we are." Jendron said, adding, "Especially with there only being three of us now."

Eric nodded, fatigue pulling on his features. "Let's tell Paxton. He might have organized more teams by now. We're going to spend hours more doing this, otherwise. Not sure we'll be able to last."

Paxton reported everyone busy in rescue missions and fighting. It would be at least another hour before he'd have a second team for them, but he could send a couple of spare men for now. Eric's response was jubilant. "That's going to double our numbers. That's huge for us."

Coordinates were quickly sent and almost as quickly two more men, both big and broad, arrived. Storey grinned. Talk about a cool way to travel.

Feeling stronger with better odds, Storey's group repeated the process with another group of two and then one of three.

Jendron said, "This system works better with small groups." He wiped his brow, his voice deepening. "I don't know how many more we're going to be able to do. Now we need to find more this size."

"The stylus is looking." She glanced over at Eric. "How about an update from Paxton again. More teams would be wonderful."

He nodded.

"According to the stylus, the last of them are heading our way." She groaned. "Oh no, apparently three more have joined that group. There are now twelve Louers approaching. And no answer from Paxton."

Silence.

"Let's stay together and get the job done." Jendron had proven to be a great sergeant in this war. He took orders well and stepped up every time.

"Agreed," the group cried out, flushed with their success. Tired but willing. You had to respect the foot soldier.

Just then her stylus moved. Triumphantly, she read off, "Paxton is sending another team to meet us at the last location."

Watching the relief wash over the men, Storey could see how important it was for this last encounter to go fast and simple. She didn't want to consider failure and all that implied in this case. They'd been lucky so far. Horath's arm, a few scrapes and lots of bruises, but it could have been so much worse.

Just one more round.

The other team joined right in, catching on to the workable system. The battle was short and intense, passing in a blur of men, screams, and action. Storey, huddled out of the way, hadn't even needed her sketchbook. The men handled this one all on their own.

When the last one slammed to the ground unconscious, she jumped to her feet cheering. Eric threw his arms around her and swung her off her feet. They stayed like that for a long moment, both laughing in joy. It was done.

Well almost done. Using the same methodical system as before, they dispatched the last of them back to their homeland.

When it was done, she realized there couldn't have been a more anticlimactic ending. She smiled, a large, smug grin of triumph.

She didn't hear a thing before she was grabbed from behind.

"Eric!"

A vicious grip slammed her face against a hairy chest of an oversized Louer. The force of the blow knocked her breath out. She fought to fill her lungs with air, the arm around her ribs squeezing her tight. Christ he was big. She struggled futilely against the iron grip. Black spots crept through her vision. Just when she thought it was all over, the steel band loosened, her world flipped and she was thrown over his shoulder like a sack of dog food.

"Eric. Help!" Pushing against her abductor's back, she raised her head to see Eric racing behind them. The rest of the men were bringing up the rear.

Shit. She'd lost her sketchbook. She still had the stylus, stuffed uselessly in her pocket for safe-keeping. Now it was pinned between her and this massive shoulder. Using her fists, she punched the heavily muscled back and kicked out wildly. Her kidnapper grunted once, but never slowed.

Eric came fast. She could almost see his eyes. She couldn't miss the blast of the stun gun. It slammed into her attacker's ribs along his side, narrowly avoiding her. He stumbled. Storey bounced as the ground raced up to meet her. The Louer regained his balance, shifted her on his shoulder and struggled forward. She could respect his power and determination, but damn it, she was getting whiplash from all the bouncing.

Eric got off another shot.

The Louer slammed to a halt and swayed in place. Then he did a perfect face-plant on the ground. Storey was thrown on her back, her head slamming down hard and the heavy weight of the Louer crushing against her.

"Storey?" Eric raced to her side, his fingers gently stroking the line of her cheek and chin. "Are you hurt?"

She groaned. "I'm fine. Or I would be if you could get this asshole off of me, please." She coughed, struggling for air under the deadweight. The men hauled the attacker off, letting fresh air pour into her lungs. Lying still, Storey shuddered in relief. They'd talked about death and dying earlier. But it hadn't really sunk in that she might actually get hurt. She didn't have any problem imagining it now. Reality sucked.

While she recuperated, the men dispatched the last of the invaders home.

Reaching out a hand, Eric helped her to her feet. He handed her the missing sketchbook. Touched, she realized one of the men had retrieved it for her.

"Trust you to make things difficult, just when it's all over." He dropped a kiss on her temple. "I'm sorry he got the drop on us. We thought we had them all."

"So did I." Glancing around at the men gathered, she said, "We need to get back to the lab and make sure those tears are closed and fast." She sighed. "Then I need to open a portal from their world to the new copy I created somehow." She had no idea how, but knew she could do it with the stylus's help.

"Paxton's almost done with the tears. By the time we get there, he will be. Then you can do your stuff and it will all be over."

Over. What did that mean? Her heart hiccupped.

It meant the Louers were gone.

It meant Eric's world was safe.

It meant she wasn't needed any longer.

It meant – it was time to go home.

CHAPTER 18

ALL THE WAY back to Paxton's lab and the resounding victorious welcome waiting for them, Storey had trouble dealing with the fact that it was all over. That this nightmare she'd been living for days had finally finished. So much excitement. So much panic. So many emotions had rushed through her constantly. And then everything stopped. The chaos was over. Resolved. The change so sudden…she found it hard to believe.

It didn't feel right after days of living on a roller coaster. Days of fearing for her life and Eric's, the ranger from a different dimension. Now he was safe. She was safe. Everyone in his dimension was safe.

The stylus, the odd pencil-computer thingy with souls bound inside that she'd found, had opened a portal between the Louers' old and new worlds. Only time would tell if they'd make good use of it. Her stylus assured her the Louers were exploring their new world already.

Paxton, Eric's mentor and senior council member to the Torans, had monitors that tracked any activity through the areas where the dimensional tears had been repaired until they could all be reinforced. The process would take a bit longer, but like he'd said to her, they were on it.

They were on it.

As in she wasn't needed any longer.

They'd even managed a decent conversation over the future of her stylus. Now that she knew more, she understood his reluctance to let her keep it. Then he also understood her unwillingness to die in order to give it back. A truce had been made letting her keep it until they could figure out how to separate it from her safely. She kept the fake one tucked away. Just in case Paxton decided not to be as reasonable as he currently appeared.

Instead of feeling euphoric, she felt odd, uncertain. Almost as if she expected, no wanted, more chaos. And that couldn't be right. She wasn't a masochist. Why the hell would she want more war?

Because there'd been a certain attraction to being someone respected, looked up to. Someone who'd had answers. Someone who'd learned to do something others hadn't. Her pride and self-confidence had definitely had a good time here.

And it was coming to an end.

God, she was becoming downright depressed.

Off on one side, she watched the party going on around her. It was a standing-room-only crowd. Where had all the people come from? There were some seriously beautiful women here tonight which just added to her depression. She was still wearing her old jeans and sneakers.

Even the usually formal and uptight Paxton had let loose. He'd danced and hugged his way through the crowd. With so many well-wishers, she'd hardly had a moment to herself, hence her attempt at a time-out.

Eric found her a few minutes later. He slung an arm around her and held her close. "Hey, what's wrong?"

She relaxed against his shoulder, thankful he'd joined her. She needed this – him. "Nothing." With a light laugh, she added, "I was just ready for a couple of minutes of peace."

"That makes sense." He snagged a stool and sat on it without disturbing her position. "Are you ready to go home?"

"In a way. Then again, I finally feel connected to everyone here. We've been through so much, it's hard to leave."

"It's not forever. I'll be able to come over and visit, and you'll be able to come back."

"Will you though?" If she were honest, the fear of never seeing him again was behind the sense of letdown she'd been feeling all night. With his world safe again, it was over. There was no reason for Eric and her to meet anymore, except wanting to be together. They had a relationship – she just couldn't decide what it was. But she wanted to see where it could go. And how could she do that if they lived in opposite worlds?

If long distance relationships were hard to keep, then cross–dimensional relationships would have to be impossible.

And given his father's disposition, she didn't think she'd be welcome over here anytime soon. Everyone else had been friendly though. Several people had stopped to thank her. Some had stopped to ask her questions about her world and how long she was staying.

She needed to go home. Who knew what she still might have to fix back home yet? She'd left things in a bit of mess. And undone. Like the note on the inscription of the stylus she'd hidden on her computer. Not that it mattered any more as she could just ask the stylus about the lettering. Later, when she got home and had time to delve into all the unanswered questions.

"You look like you've lost your best friend." He bent closer to peer into her eyes. "Are you okay?"

"Yes." She gave him a reassuring smile, at least she thought it was. "I'm just sad."

"That's understandable. You've made some friends here. We appreciate all you've done. We might even be able to have you come over as a consultant on some projects."

"Really?" She brightened. "I figured I'd never be welcomed back – considering I had a death sentence on my head at one time."

"A fond memory of your visit." He snickered. "Even if they aren't interested in having you consult, I'll come visit you. I promise. There's no way I'm giving up our friendship."

She closed her eyes briefly. Then said with a lilt in her voice, "Boy, am I glad to hear that. I guess I was feeling a little blue, thinking I'd never see you again."

"Not going to happen." He stood up. "But I understand you need to go home. Did Paxton speak to you yet?"

"He apologized and thanked me." She smirked. "I think he's still a little miffed at me over the stylus stuff."

Eric laughed. "I wouldn't be surprised. He's been bonded with his for over a century. It can't be easy to be shown up by a young girl. Especially one not even from his world."

"I can understand that."

Eric pulled her upright and into his arms. He stared at her quietly for a long moment. His voice rumbled from his chest. "Thank you for coming back and helping us. I'm not sure we'd have survived without you."

"You would have, just in a different way." Storey nestled closer. "I couldn't see your world suffering when I'd figured out a way to help."

"And help you did. The Louers are gone forever and all because of you."

She lifted her head to caution him. "We don't know they're gone for good. It's too early to say. Paxton still has some work to do there. He has to make sure the portals are permanently sealed. We also don't know which dimension the Louers ended up in – for sure. We *think* we do, but…"

"Paxton will sort it out. He's nothing if not dedicated." As if to calm her worries, Eric bent and kissed her gently, then with growing enthusiasm.

"Arrumph."

They broke apart to find Paxton standing in the doorway. "I think it's time. Everyone wants to say goodbye to Storey and watch her leave."

"Oh." She brushed her shirt down and walked over to where her backpack sat on the floor waiting for her. "I hadn't realized."

They walked back into Paxton's lab to find a line had formed. Most of the Torans hugged her or shook her hand. By the time she'd reached the end of the line, she could barely hold back the tears.

Paxton gave her a codex. "So you don't have to travel by drawing portals everywhere. We all saw the result of that effort!" There was mixed laughter from the crowd, but it was the warm look on Paxton's face that made her respond with a big grin.

When the laughter died down, Paxton added, "This is a guest codex. It's pre-coded for your home, my dear. Thank you for all you've done."

Tears collected in the corner of her eyes. Storey smiled mistily. She really was going to miss him. "You're welcome." Impulsively, she gave him a quick hug.

Eric walked her over to the portal that his people used for travel and dropped a kiss on her cheek. "I'll pop over tomorrow to see how you're adjusting to being home again. Your mom has to be wondering where you've been all this time."

"True enough." Thinking about her mother brought her father to mind. Oh boy. What waited at home for her? Not daring to speak in case she broke into tears, she managed a brave smile. He reached over and hit the button on her wrist unit. The familiar musical notes sounded.

Storey straightened her back, determined to go out gracefully. Forced to sniffle back tears, she gave the crowd a quick wave good-bye. It had been a hell of a weekend. She'd miss these people. Definitely Eric and maybe even Paxton. With a final look around the room, she recognized Eric's father, the hated Councilman, standing in the far back corner, a malicious grin on his face. What was he up to? He looked way too happy for her comfort.

The black mist swirled up around her legs.

The Councilman gave her a wiggling fat sausage finger wave good-bye and opened his other hand so she could see what he held. Nestled deep in the rolls was a long thin object.

Her stylus.

The black swirling mist rose to her chest.

She gasped in shock.

It was too late to stop the portal.

His grin fattened.

The room disappeared into darkness. Panic threatened. Oh God. Was she going to die now? Could the esteemed Councilman have actually won? She closed her eyes, hating him and what he'd done. How could she contact Eric to let him know? Without her stylus she had no way to communicate with anyone here.

Just then the mists thinned and cleared.

She turned around. An oily darkness greeted her. The rank smell of death rose, overwhelming her senses. She wrinkled up her nose and coughed, then coughed again. "Oh God. I know that smell!"

Hearing something behind her, she spun around. A long meaty arm stretched through the darkness. White bony fingers reached for her.

DEADLY DESIGNS

(Book 2 of Design Series)

Dale Mayer

Dedication

This book is dedicated to my daughter Kara, who asked me to write books for her. The Design Series is the third young adult series I started for her.

Enjoy!

Acknowledgments

Deadly Designs wouldn't have been possible without the support of my friends and family. Many hands helped with proofreading, editing, and beta reading to make this book come together. Special thanks to my editor.

PROLOGUE

In Dangerous Designs we left off with this chapter...

ALL THE WAY back to Paxton's lab and the resounding victorious welcome waiting for them, Storey had trouble dealing with the fact that it was all over. That this nightmare she'd been living for days had finally finished. So much excitement. So much panic. So many emotions had rushed through her constantly. And then everything stopped. The chaos was over. Resolved. The change so sudden...she found it hard to believe.

It didn't feel right after days of living on a roller coaster. Days of fearing for her life and Eric's, the ranger from a different dimension. Now he was safe. She was safe. Everyone in his dimension was safe.

The stylus, the odd pencil-computer thingy with souls bound inside that she'd found, had opened a portal between the Louers' old and new worlds. Only time would tell if they'd make good use of it. Her stylus assured her the Louers were exploring their new world already.

Paxton, Eric's mentor and senior council member to the Torans, had monitors that tracked any activity through the areas where the dimensional tears had been repaired until they could all be reinforced. The process would take a bit longer, but like he'd said to her, they were on it.

They were on it.

As in she wasn't needed any longer.

They'd even managed a decent conversation over the future of her stylus. Now that she knew more, she understood his reluctance to let her keep it. Then he also understood her unwillingness to die in order to give it back. A truce had been made letting her keep it until they could figure out how to separate it from her safely. She kept the fake one tucked away. Just in case Paxton decided not to be as reasonable as he currently appeared.

Instead of feeling euphoric, she felt odd, uncertain. Almost as if she expected, no wanted, more chaos. And that couldn't be right. She wasn't a masochist. Why the hell would she want more war?

Because there'd been a certain attraction to being someone respected, looked up to. Someone who'd had answers. Someone who'd learned to do something others hadn't. Her pride and self-confidence had definitely had a good time here.

And it was coming to an end.

God, she was becoming downright depressed.

Off on one side, she watched the party going on around her. It was a standing-room-only crowd. Where had all the people come from? There were some seriously beautiful women here tonight which just added to her depression. She was still wearing her old jeans and sneakers.

Even the usually formal and uptight Paxton had let loose. He'd danced and hugged his way through the crowd. With so many well-wishers, she'd hardly had a moment to herself, hence her attempt at a time-out.

Eric found her a few minutes later. He slung an arm around her and held her close. "Hey, what's wrong?"

She relaxed against his shoulder, thankful he'd joined her. She needed this — him. "Nothing." With a light laugh, she added, "I was just ready for a couple of minutes of peace."

"That makes sense." He snagged a stool and sat on it without disturbing her position. "Are you ready to go home?"

"In a way. Then again, I finally feel connected to everyone here. We've been through so much, it's hard to leave."

"It's not forever. I'll be able to come over and visit, and you'll be able to come back."

"Will you though?" If she were honest, the fear of never seeing him again was behind the sense of letdown she'd been feeling all night. With his world safe again, it was over. There was no reason for Eric and her to meet anymore, except wanting to be together. They had a relationship – she just couldn't decide what it was. But she wanted to see where it could go. And how could she do that if they lived in opposite worlds?

If long distance relationships were hard to keep, then cross–dimensional relationships would have to be impossible.

And given his father's disposition, she didn't think she'd be welcome over here anytime soon. Everyone else had been friendly though. Several people had stopped to thank her. Some had stopped to ask her questions about her world and how long she was staying.

She needed to go home. Who knew what she still might have to fix back home yet? She'd left things in a bit of mess. And undone. Like the note on the inscription of the stylus she'd hidden on her computer. Not that it mattered any more as she could just ask the stylus about the lettering. Later, when she got home and had time to delve into all the unanswered questions.

"You look like you've lost your best friend." He bent closer to peer into her eyes. "Are you okay?"

"Yes." She gave him a reassuring smile, at least she thought it was. "I'm just sad."

"That's understandable. You've made some friends here. We appreciate all you've done. We might even be able to have you come over as a consultant on some projects."

"Really?" She brightened. "I figured I'd never be welcomed back – considering I had a death sentence on my head at one time."

"A fond memory of your visit." He snickered. "Even if they aren't interested in having you consult, I'll come visit you. I promise. There's no way I'm giving up our friendship."

She closed her eyes briefly. Then said with a lilt in her voice, "Boy, am I glad to hear that. I guess I was feeling a little blue, thinking I'd never see you again."

"Not going to happen." He stood up. "But I understand you need to go home. Did Paxton speak to you yet?"

"He apologized and thanked me." She smirked. "I think he's still a little miffed at me over the stylus stuff."

Eric laughed. "I wouldn't be surprised. He's been bonded with his for over a century. It can't be easy to be shown up by a young girl. Especially one not even from his world."

"I can understand that."

Eric pulled her upright and into his arms. He stared at her quietly for a long moment. His voice rumbled from his chest. "Thank you for coming back and helping us. I'm not sure we'd have survived without you."

"You would have, just in a different way." Storey nestled closer. "I couldn't see your world suffering when I'd figured out a way to help."

"And help you did. The Louers are gone forever and all because of you."

She lifted her head to caution him. "We don't know they're gone for good. It's too early to say. Paxton still has some work to do there. He has to make sure the portals are permanently sealed. We also don't know which dimension the Louers ended up in – for sure. We *think* we do, but…"

"Paxton will sort it out. He's nothing if not dedicated." As if to calm her worries, Eric bent and kissed her gently, then with growing enthusiasm.

"Arrumph."

They broke apart to find Paxton standing in the doorway. "I think it's time. Everyone wants to say good-bye to Storey and watch her leave."

"Oh." She brushed her shirt down and walked over to where her backpack sat on the floor waiting for her. "I hadn't realized."

They walked back into Paxton's lab to find a line had formed. Most of the Torans hugged her or shook her hand. By the time she'd reached the end of the line, she could barely hold back the tears.

Paxton gave her a codex. "So you don't have to travel by drawing portals everywhere. We all saw the result of that effort!" There was mixed laughter from the crowd, but it was the warm look on Paxton's face that made her respond with a big grin.

When the laughter died down, Paxton added, "This is a guest codex. It's pre-coded for your home, my dear. Thank you for all you've done."

Tears collected in the corner of her eyes. Storey smiled mistily. She really was going to miss him. "You're welcome." Impulsively, she gave him a quick hug.

Eric walked her over to the portal that his people used for travel and dropped a kiss on her cheek. "I'll pop over tomorrow to see how you're adjusting to being home again. Your mom has to be wondering where you've been all this time."

"True enough." Thinking about her mother brought her father to mind. Oh boy. What waited at home for her? Not daring to speak in case she broke into tears, she managed a brave smile. He reached over and hit the button on her wrist unit. The familiar musical notes sounded.

Storey straightened her back, determined to go out gracefully. Forced to sniffle back tears, she gave the crowd a quick wave good-bye. It had been a hell of a weekend. She'd miss these people. Definitely Eric and maybe even Paxton. With a final look around the room, she recognized Eric's father, the hated Councilman, standing in the far back corner, a malicious grin on his face. What was he up to? He looked way too happy for her comfort.

The black mist swirled up around her legs.

The Councilman gave her a wiggling fat sausage finger wave good-bye and opened his other hand so she could see what he held. Nestled deep in the rolls was a long thin object.

Her stylus.

The black swirling mist rose to her chest.

She gasped in shock.

It was too late to stop the portal.

His grin fattened.

The room disappeared into darkness. Panic threatened. Oh God. Was she going to die now? Could the esteemed Councilman have actually won? She closed her eyes, hating him and what he'd done. How could she contact Eric to let him know? Without her stylus she had no way to communicate with anyone here.

Just then the mists thinned and cleared.

She turned around. An oily darkness greeted her. The rank smell of death rose, overwhelming her senses. She wrinkled up her nose and coughed, then coughed again.

"Oh God. I know that smell!"

Hearing something behind her, she spun around. A long meaty arm stretched through the darkness. White bony fingers reached for her.

CHAPTER 1

T HE STENCH WOKE her. It spread deep into the recesses of her comatose brain like a shockwave. Storey Dalton slammed back to consciousness – and retched violently. Again and again. Finally, she groaned and collapsed to one side.

Coughing spasms came next. By the time that slowed, her thin frame stopped shaking and her stomach calmed down, Storey could lie in relative peace. Except for the smell. The sour reek of vomit now mixed with a horrible odor, almost like sulphur or rotten eggs. For a moment she just rested. Then her eyes shot open. She stared around in shock.

What the hell had just happened? Deep, depressing darkness surrounded her. She could see no lights, windows or moon around her, only complete, unforgiving blackness. She rolled to her right side and shifted to a sitting position. In a denseness where all other senses were deprived, the stench was almost enough to send her reeling to the ground again.

And ground it was. Dirt. Damp, black, hard dirt. If there were a hell, she imagined she'd found it.

Why?

How had she ended up in such a place? Events were as murky as the atmosphere around her. Eric. She'd been with Eric after helping to save his people, his entire dimension in fact, from the Louers. There'd been a party where everyone had joyously gathered around to thank her and send her off properly.

She'd been going home.

Storey struggled to her feet. Home. To her mother. And apparently after messing with the essential fabric of her own dimension, her father maybe as well. And that was so wrong. He'd been absent from her life for over a decade until she'd screwed with things. She'd tried to fix her mistakes, but hadn't had a chance to find out if her changes had been successful or not. Did her parents still believe that she attended a Roman Catholic school and did her homework on time? A snort escaped. As if. Given a chance, she'd spend all her time drawing.

She stilled. Drawing. The stylus. Eric's father, the Councilman, had stolen it. It had been in his fat hand as she'd disappeared in the portal. The mist had swirled up around her too quickly for her to yell for help. Could he have also changed her destination? Or was she being unfair? The unstable gates might have screwed up the destination. Paxton was making repairs but that didn't mean everything was working perfectly yet.

Then again, remembering the look on the Councilman's face she had to think he'd had something to do with her current disaster.

Shudders slipped down her back at the memory of long, bony hands reaching into the mist to pull her from the portal. Thank heavens she'd passed out. That's one memory she won't have to relive.

God only knew where the creatures were now.

And how was she going to get out of here without her stylus?

Hope surged inside as she remembered the fake stylus she'd created while still in her dimension. She'd made the decoy to fool those who might try to take the real stylus from her.

So had the nasty Councilman stolen *her* stylus – or the fake one?

For a furious minute she searched all her pockets. Empty. *Crap.* She whispered, "Are you here, Stylus?" She waited, hoping for that telltale tingling sensation. That sense of connectedness to the souls inside the stylus. Even though that connection hadn't been there that long, it had deepened, becoming a part of her.

According to Paxton, when a stylus became separated from its owner for a long time period, normally the owner died. Something to do with the soulbound relationship between the two.

Where was her backpack? It held her completed portals, jacket and sketchbook. Taking a few tentative steps, she tried to search around her. What's the chance her bag had been left with her?

Just then her foot banged into something hard, sending her downward where she cracked a knee against a rock. At least she assumed it was a rock. "Damn it." She jumped up and danced around in one place, afraid she'd hit something else.

"Would someone please turn on the damn lights in this Godforsaken place?"

Instantly lights blazed, blinding her. Instinctively she slammed her hands over her eyes as they burned with the severe change. "Shit," she whispered as she squinted between her fingers. The room glowed from a strange incredibly bright light source at the far side. Her eyes didn't know what to do with it. Keeping her eyes shaded, she turned slowly to look around. There was no sign of her backpack or her stylus.

The room appeared to be a huge underground bunker. Or a cave, maybe? Yet she couldn't see an entrance or an exit. And it was empty – except for her.

The reality of her situation set in.

She was a prisoner. But she had no idea where, or who held her here.

Or why.

ERIC WATCHED THE dark mist thicken, dread overtaking his senses. What could have caused that look of absolute horror on Storey's face? He stared hard at his father's rotund and positively gleeful face. Until he caught Eric staring at him. Then his fat grin slid off, his nose strutted up into the air and a look of superior disdain came over his cold features. Yeah, that's the normal expression Eric remembered.

The false face. It had taken Storey to show him the real man inside. It hadn't been easy to see. And even harder to accept. Now he just felt stupid. He'd spent his life respecting a man who deserved none of it. And adding to Eric's confusion was the realization he really didn't know this man.

His father was a stranger. Eric hadn't seen much parental love in his life. In reality, he'd had little contact with him. Since he learned to walk, he'd had respect and obedience drummed into him for a man he was only just realizing didn't deserve it.

How had the Council allowed this man to rule? What could his father have done to deserve their respect? And couldn't they see the man his father had become? Or had the changes happened so slowly that they hadn't been evident – until some major disaster when he'd shown his true self. Then again, he'd been the ruler for so long because there wasn't much to rule here. His decisions were mostly over little issues.

Still, Eric wondered about the man inside. Was he driven by power? Needing blind obedience from all like a dictator? Something Eric hadn't considered his society could have.

Storey's arrival had certainly thrown his father off balance. And had showed Eric a side of his father he'd never seen before.

Paxton on the other hand…. He glanced over at his mentor. Tufts of his white hair stood straight up, only this time from running his hands through it in excitement. Paxton was still on a high from the success of the day. His cheeks were flushed, and he appeared to be…dancing?

Eric continued to scan the partygoers. His people certainly were enjoying themselves. This mini war had restored pride they hadn't known was missing from their lives. They'd slipped into a passive type of existence. This had woken them up, stirred them to action. They wouldn't be quite so complacent about their lifestyle any longer. At least not for a while. And like them, Eric wanted to enjoy himself tonight. Celebrate today's success.

But…

Eric shook his head and spun around again to look at the spot where Storey had disappeared. He couldn't get the look on her face out of his mind. What could have caused it?

Paxton walked toward him, a lilt to his step, a bright look on his face. Eric had to grin. Paxton looked like he'd dropped twenty years off his shoulders.

"Eric! Still worrying about Storey? She'll be fine."

Eric shook his head. "It doesn't feel like she's fine."

Paxton narrowed his gaze. "Do you want to go after her? Make sure she arrived safely?"

Eric contemplated his sense of something being wrong. Did he want to go after her? Heck yes. "I wouldn't have to be gone long." He studied his feet. Was there really something wrong? Or was he just missing her?

Either way, he needed to know for sure. "I don't want to make a big thing out of this if everything is fine."

"We could just ask her if she's home safe and sound." Paxton held up his stylus, a wide smirk on his ancient face.

Perfect. Eric grinned widely, relief spreading throughout his body. "Perfect. Thanks."

Paxton grabbed up a nearby pad of paper, his movements easy and carefree, as if knowing this was for naught but happy to play along. He quickly wrote out a note to Storey. Eric read the simple message. "Hello Storey, please confirm that you made it home safely."

Lifting his head, Paxton beamed. "Amazing communication ability. I just love this. There's so much we can learn from these styluses."

He sounded positively chatty. Eric struggled to reconcile this Paxton with the grim, stern version from before the war. Talk about polar opposites.

"You know, my stylus knows all about the archives. Storey says they can access all the information from centuries ago. Do you understand how much we can learn from them?"

Eric raised an eyebrow as he finally noted the rosy cheeks and the overly bright shine to Paxton's eyes. Had his old mentor and friend indulged in a little too much to drink? Surely not? Eric couldn't remember seeing the man ever take a drink of wine.

But there was no doubt that he was under the influence of something. Maybe it was the power of success?

The stylus sat quietly as both men waited for an answer from Storey.

Eric's gaze narrowed as the moment stretched out longer and longer. "Could something be wrong?"

"Well, anything is possible, but it's unlikely. She's done this trip dozens of times."

"Ask your stylus if Storey's stylus is in her dimension."

"Why? We know it is." Some of the brightness dimmed in the older man's eyes. "You really think something is wrong?"

"If it isn't, then why hasn't she answered by now?"

"Maybe she's sleeping."

Eric blinked. Good answer. Why hadn't he thought of that? It was late. Storey had been on an incredible adrenaline rush, helping him and his men to save his world. Going home would have brought on a major crash and burn cycle. She might simply be asleep.

No! His mind screamed at him. Storey would have contacted him to let him know she'd arrived safely. She knew he'd be worried about her. There's no way she wouldn't do that.

"Please, just ask."

Shaking his head, tufts of white hair flipping out in all directions, Paxton picked up the stylus and wrote the question.

The answer was immediate. "No."

Both men shouted, "No?"

"Why not?" Paxton glared at the single word he'd written down. "She has to be."

Eric knew his father had been up to something. But what? "Where is her stylus? Maybe it's still here."

"Well, it shouldn't be. Not unless she's here, too." The answer came back immediately. Paxton read out the answer. "No. Storey and her stylus are not in this dimension."

The two men stared at each other in shock.

"We've been having problems with the gate so maybe something malfunctioned," Paxton mumbled.

"Ask where she is, please." Eric tried to contain his impatience. Though Storey had been willing and eager to find out information through her new pen as she thought of it, Paxton clung to the old ways and asking a simple instrument for help wasn't instinctive – or natural. The styluses could communicate with each other, but Eric thought Storey's was stronger and more capable. Or maybe Storey was stronger and more capable than Paxton.

He'd verbalized the questions before but now seemed to be only able to write down the questions. Either way, Paxton was working too slowly for Eric right now.

Paxton slowly wrote the question on the paper as if not wanting to hear the answer. The stylus never moved.

"See, there's no answer." Paxton sighed. "It must be a broken gate. Maybe it can't get a reading."

"What are you doing over there?"

Eric stiffened, a subconscious effect of his father's approach. He didn't dare look his sire in the eye, afraid that his suspicions would get the better of him. Surely his father wouldn't have willfully done anything to hurt Storey.

Yes, he would have.

This was the man who had once ordered her imprisonment and death. Eric's instincts screamed at him. Stay silent. Things were bad but they could get so much worse.

Paxton opened his mouth to answer and caught Eric's glare. Slowly, as if not understanding, Paxton dropped his gaze to study the paper in front of him.

"We were talking strategy," Eric answered calmly enough.

His father tilted his head upward. "Why bother? The problem's been solved. It's not going to happen again, so sure, hash over your success, then let it go. I won't have anyone wasting their time on such things now that the war is over."

"And if the war isn't over?"

"Don't say that," the Councilman snapped at his only

son. "It's over. That subject doesn't come up again, do you hear me?"

Eric struggled to keep back the words ready to blast out of his mouth. Setting his father off wouldn't do anyone any good at this point. With a clipped nod, and a last warning look at Paxton, he walked away from the men, determined to catch Paxton alone later. He needed to focus on Storey, now.

Keeping an eye on the happy partygoers still around, he checked his codex. How long had she been gone? One hour, not more. Too bad he didn't have a stylus of his own. It would be a great way to talk with her. How else were they going to communicate when they each lived in a different dimension? He had methods that worked in his dimension. Her cell phone worked in hers. But only the stylus was capable of crossing both dimensions. Checking behind him, he heard raised voices coming from his father and Paxton. *Uh oh, someone isn't happy.*

Well, neither was he. He strode back across the room to the two fighting men. His father saw him coming and rounded on him first. "I do not want to hear any more about that girl from you. She is gone and she is not allowed back in our world. Do you understand?"

Fury built inside Eric to the point that he could actually see black spots as he tried to find some measure of control. Releasing his rage at the Councilman, father or not, was liable to be a final step he wasn't sure he was prepared to take.

"No. That is not acceptable."

Eric blinked. What? Had Paxton really stood up for Storey? At one point, he'd been firm that she should return to her world and stay there. For good.

Paxton pulled up to his full height. In an authoritative voice, he stated, "Storey has been a valuable contributor to our world this past week. We have much we can learn from her."

"She caused the dratted problems in the first place. I do not want her back. Do you hear me?"

"I think everyone here heard you." Eric couldn't hold back his own anger, noting that half the partygoers were leaving and the other half were starting to collect around the arguing men.

The Councilman rounded on him, fire leaping from his eyes. "You. I've heard all I'm going to from you. I'm not sure why you think it's suddenly acceptable to argue with me, but there is no way I can consider your actions in any good light. That this young woman should have had such a disagreeable affect on you is unacceptable. You need to learn your place."

With narrowed eyes, he drew himself up to his full height. That it was many inches shorter than Eric's only made his action more laughable. No one within hearing distance could doubt that the Councilman was ready to hand out another final edict.

He opened his mouth.

"No." Paxton stood firm. "You will not punish him." Glaring at the rotund Councilman, Paxton shook his head. "You cannot. Eric is a hero to our people, as is Storey. They have become icons of hope, faith and courage. They deserve your recognition, your respect and even medals of valor for their actions."

As Paxton's words faded away, the gathering crowd picked up the energy and started to cheer, calling out Eric's name.

Eric. Eric. Eric.

Eric had to grin at the consternation on his father's face. The Councilman hadn't expected resistance. Especially from old Senator Paxton, a title the scientist never used, but still possessed; or from his own people. A red flush whispered across his father's face, his beady eyes going hard and bright with fury before sliding into cold determination. As Eric watched and waited, wondering what his father would do next, it was as if a switch had been thrown and his father settled back down.

Eric's suspicions rose again.

His father turned to face him, straightening to his full height. "So be it. We'll come up with some way to reward you for your actions, Eric."

Eric frowned. The words sounded right. The tone of voice definitely didn't. His father was up to something.

"And for Storey?" he asked, cautiously hoping his father would let something more slip.

"Oh, yes. Storey is getting everything that's coming to her."

Just then several things happened.

Paxton's stylus started moving in the air. Paxton raced to snatch up a useable piece of paper to write on.

His father grinned a sly, slow movement that sent shivers down Eric's spine. Then he turned and strode out of the room.

CHAPTER 2

STOREY SAT WITH her back against the dirt wall. Stumped. How could she get out of this mess? Her backpack was missing and her pockets were empty.

Panic sat on the edge of her consciousness, waiting to take over. She'd come to rely on the stylus and sketchbook so much that she found herself at a loss. Her simple codex, not like the high-tech one that Eric wore, didn't appear to be functioning either. That hadn't stopped her from pushing all the buttons several times, hoping to recreate the same musical combination Eric had used, but the instrument made no sound.

Had the Councilman switched hers for a broken codex? Or were the thick prison walls preventing the codex from functioning? It had been a hellish couple of days, leaving no time to study the wrist units. She'd figured Eric could give her some one-on-one training in a week or two. When things had calmed down.

Not great planning on her part.

And if she couldn't use her stylus to draw her way out of here, or portal her way back through the codex's abilities, she was literally stuck here with only old fashioned methods of escape. Now if only she knew what they were.

With no weapons or anything to make a weapon from, it's a good thing she had yet to see her captors. For all intents and purposes, she'd been dumped into a hole in the ground and forgotten.

A horrible thought and one she really didn't want to dwell on.

If only she had her stylus. She could only hope whoever had it was taking care of it. There were souls in there. Souls that needed care.

Wait.

She had been able to communicate verbally with her stylus, at least while she'd been holding it. She'd still had to write the answers down, but…maybe she could scratch a message in the dirt? Their bond was strong and they would eventually be able to communicate telepathically – when her skills developed further.

It was worth a try. But what did she have to scratch in the dirt with? The tab on her jacket zipper caught her eye. Made from hard metal, it had ripped half off already. With a hard tug, she pulled the tab off. Walking back to where she'd first regained consciousness, she squatted and scratched in the ground, *Stylus, can you hear me?*

Silence.

Pressing harder, she scratched again. *Stylus, I'm in trouble. Can you help?*

More silence.

Damn it. Fear started an insidious slide inside her mind. She tried again, harder, almost making her fingers bleed with the attempt. *Stylus. I need help. Contact Paxton. I need Eric's help to escape.*

Nothing.

What had she expected? She bowed her head.

Essentially, she'd been tossed into a hellhole and no one knew. Except…maybe the Councilman. The man was a power hungry toad. Remembering the look of satisfaction in his beady eyes as she disappeared to God knew where sent more shivers down her spine. It also had another effect.

Anger and pride rose to battle the loneliness and fear. She would not let him win.

She refused.

PAXTON LET HIS stylus move freely across the page. Eric crowded behind him, trying to read the message as it came through.

Storey is calling for help.

Both men gasped. Paxton quickly scratched out a question. "Where is she?"

Not here.

"We know that. Is she at her home?" Eric snapped, worry making his voice sharper than he intended.

No.

Paxton frowned. "Is she in her home dimension?"

No.

Horror rose in Eric's stomach and was matched by the horror in Paxton's eyes. "Do you know where she is?"

No.

"Then how did you know to contact us?"

Her stylus says she is trying to contact Eric.

Excitement whistled through Eric. He knew Storey would find a way to contact him. They'd rescue her yet. "Why can't her stylus bring her home?"

Silence.

With growing unease, Eric said to Paxton, "Ask if Storey has her stylus with her."

Eyes wide, Paxton did as requested. The answer wasn't long in coming.

No.

Both men shook their heads. Eric frowned, trying to figure out how this communication worked. "Then how did the stylus know that Storey is trying to contact us?"

Paxton's jumped in with another question first. "So Storey can communicate with her stylus, even though she's not touching it?"

With the souls in it.

Both men cried out in unison. "Soul bound."

Paxton then asked, "Then where is Storey's stylus?"

We don't know.

Eric pushed forward with the questions. "But you can communicate with it, correct?"

Yes.

"Then where is it?"

It doesn't know.

"Is it in this dimension?"

No.

"Is it in Storey's dimension?"

No.

The questioning continued until they determined that the stylus was in the same dimension as Storey, but not close to her. Close enough for her to communicate with it, but not close enough for her to see or touch it.

Eric ran his fingers through his hair. "Well, thank heavens for that. I was afraid she'd lost the stylus somehow. How long before their separation affects Storey's health?"

Paxton raised his gaze to Eric's. He frowned, intense worry developing in his eyes. "I don't know. That's why we didn't take it from her when she was first here, remember."

Eric straightened. "I thought I saw the Councilman with a stylus in his hand. I wondered at the time...but there's been so much going on, I didn't think about it any further."

"My stylus said it isn't here, remember." Paxton watched him. "But they are valuable. Priceless in fact." His voice lowered. "If he has one, I need to see it."

Eric's mind locked onto the memory of Storey creating a dummy stylus. *Could that possibly be the one his father had? Really?*

Storey might have let down her guard in the celebratory atmosphere after the battle, but she was pretty cagey. She'd have kept a firm grip on her real stylus.

He closed his eyes briefly, and bit back the curses that threatened to pour from his lips. Another side effect of having Storey in his life, no matter how briefly. People in his dimension didn't swear. It was considered a grave insult and showed a complete lack of respect to the person being spoken to. Unfortunately swearing appeared to be a natural part of her upbringing.

"Eric? What's the matter?"

Eric turned to look at his mentor. Paxton had been horrified by Storey initially, but had come to respect what she'd been capable of doing. After all, it was because of her they'd won the war. So fast and so efficiently, it had been a non-war, really.

"I'm remembering something Storey did when we were on her side of the veil. Using the stylus she created a copy of it, hoping the duplicate might fool the Torans who'd planned to separate it from her."

Paxton's mouth dropped then slowly closed as he processed the concept. "Did it work?"

Not knowing exactly what 'it' referred to here, Eric clarified. "The new stylus appeared to be identical but when she tested it, it didn't work. I'm not sure if we ever asked the stylus why, but we assumed at the time it was a dud. Although Storey wondered if it didn't work because it had no souls bound to it."

Paxton's face shifted and changed with understanding, finally coming to rest with a reflection of wonder. "How could she even think to try such a thing?"

Eric grinned. "That's the joy of Storey. The way she

thinks and processes problems and solutions is so different from us. It makes her ideas seem radical."

Paxton walked over to where the Councilman had been sitting. "He can't have a real one because your stylus said it wasn't here. Therefore he has to have the fake one, but *thinks* he has the real one."

The two stared at each other, letting the issues settle in.

Eric groaned. "Do we know if we can send messages back? We need to find her."

"I don't think so, because she hasn't got her stylus to receive the messages." Paxton pulled gently on his long white beard. "Although we can't underestimate her."

"Let's try to reach her anyway." Doing anything was better than doing nothing.

Paxton grabbed his writing tablet. "And let's see if we can find that empty stylus."

CHAPTER 3

S TOREY SAT BACK on the dirt and wondered what else she could do. She needed her stylus. Holding her zipper pull, she started scratching again. "Stylus, can you come to me?"

Her hand jerked.

No.

Storey gasped in joy. It was here! And responding to her. Excitedly she tried to marshal her thoughts and figure out her next questions in some kind of coherent manner. "Stylus, are you being held by another person?"

No.

"Stylus, are you close to me?"

Yes.

Yes. But not in this prison as far as she could tell. So the odds were good her captors, whoever they were, had her stylus and paper. "Stylus, has anyone attempted to use you yet?"

No.

"Do the people who separated you from me understand what you are?"

No answer.

Of course there was no answer. How would the stylus know what her captors understood and what they didn't? This wasn't getting her anywhere.

She also needed a washroom and couldn't see any such facility here. In fact, she couldn't see much at all.

The lighting was unique. Cool, but definitely weird. Still, it helped to keep back the chilling fear that the darkness let in so easily.

Now if only she could get the hell away from here before her captors returned. On the heels of that thought came the next pressing fear.

What if no one ever came?

WITH PAXTON CONTINUING to send messages to Storey's stylus, and hopefully to Storey herself, Eric decided to double check she hadn't made it home first, then gotten into trouble. Just to make sure. With Paxton guarding the lab, Eric crossed into Storey's dimension.

Opening his eyes on the other side, he realized the codex had sent him back to Bankhead mine where Storey had first crossed into his world. He retraced the well-traveled route back to Storey's two-story clapboard house. Approaching from behind, he checked out the back of her house. He couldn't see any sign that the Louers had ever been here. Had it only been days since they'd tried to tear through the dimensional fabric beside Storey's portal?

The lights were off in the house. Could he port into her bedroom? His codex had taken him there several times, so in theory, it should have the destination in its memory banks.

Punching the instructions into his wrist unit, he then waited for the black mist to wrap around his legs and transport him to her room. Thankfully, the darkness covered his actions in case any of the neighbors spotted him outside. The smoke dissipated quickly. Relieved, he noted the same childish posters on the walls and every-thing else that made a typical Storey looking bedroom. In fact, it didn't look any different than when he'd last seen it.

Not true. There was one big difference. Storey wasn't in it.

Hearing noises in the hallway, he quickly stuffed himself into her closet, overwhelmingly packed with years' worth of clothes and stuffed animals. And sketchbooks. Would any have her sketched portals? They'd come in handy to rescue her.

The sounds approached. Damn. He hoped it was Storey.

Just then the door pushed open and heavy footsteps sounded. A male voice muttered, "Damn lights. When are they going to come back on?"

"Storey? Are you in here?" The footsteps crossed the floor to Storey's bedside. "There's no sign of her."

"Are you sure? Oh dear." Storey's mother, at least he thought it was Storey's mother, stood just inside the room, enough that she could see the empty bed herself. "Where could she be?"

"Storey has never done anything rebellious up to now so maybe we're overreacting. What's the chance she's in the den like we found her last night?"

"Oh, I hope so. She's probably fallen asleep again with her drawings."

The lighter footsteps rapidly exited the room and headed down the hallway. The heavier footsteps followed.

Eric had his answer. Storey never made it home.

Damn. That meant she'd gone missing from his dimension.

STOREY'S NEED TO find a washroom had gone way beyond bad. When she had no other options, she had no qualms about going outdoors. But this prison was hardly outdoors. It also didn't offer toilet paper. She frowned and dug through her pockets. Tissues, three of them, lay crumpled at the bottom of her hoodie pocket. So that problem was solved, at least this time, but location wise, no. Nor did she have any idea if she was being watched. That possibility creeped her out.

She got up and wandered the large space for what had to be the umpteenth time. The light went on and off with her voice. She'd tried to order food and water the same way, with no luck. That there were no bodies gave her hope that she hadn't been dumped and left forever. Still, how long were they planning on leaving her here?

"Damn, why is there no door? There has to be a way in and out." The voice-activated lights meant someone had been here at one time. The concept of a door wasn't too outrageous.

"If there is a door, where the hell is it and why won't it open on command?" *Or had it?* Could it have opened silently? She might have missed it in the shadows. Anything was possible. With her hand in constant contact of the wall, Storey circled the room until she came to an open space. *A doorway.*

Was it a trap? It didn't really matter. She had to try to escape. With a deep breath, she snuck up to the doorway…then bolted through.

But to what?

More darkness. She couldn't see a thing. A round, metal, hand-sized button sat barely visible on the wall beside her. She slapped her hand on it. The door closed softly behind her.

Weird. Opened by voice and by hand. Double weird.

"Thank heavens for that," she muttered. "Now if only there were lights on."

Instantly the space lit up.

"Right. Voice controlled." Storey felt like an idiot.

But a quick scan showed this smaller anteroom was also empty. The only sign of another possible door was a second metal button on the far wall. Checking that there was nothing usable in the room she dashed to the button and slapped it. "Lights off," she added, not wanting anyone who might be on the other side to see her.

Although if they lived in this type of natural darkness, their vision had to be better than hers.

The door opened, smoother this time, and quieter. The doors were some sort of stone or compressed sand. Adobe maybe. She didn't know. It was definitely odd.

The next room had more lights, giving her a dim view of odd shapes.

Still, a pervading silence filled the air. Did no one speak? No music? Television? Thinking back, even the Louers she'd seen in the attack had been silent.

Yet the lights were voice, sound or movement activated.

Odd.

Taking a chance, she whispered, "Lights on half."

The lights pulsed on, dimmer this time, like fluorescent bulbs; chunks of luminosity lined the corner of the ceiling and shone on another large and empty room. So where the hell was everyone? Not that she wanted to see them, but she wanted to avoid a room full of them.

"Stylus, where are you?"

Not like it could answer her. Yet, she felt it. Sensed it trying to speak with her. A quick look around showed no stylus or paper. Everything appeared to have been formed from the same odd rock.

She could use her zipper pull again, if she had no other options. She fished it out of her pocket and held it tightly. As a weapon it wasn't much either.

Carefully, she slipped along the closest wall, willing it to lead her to safety…and to her stylus.

How was it she hadn't become sick without it? Or was it still close enough that she hadn't experienced any harm yet?

The wall went on forever. What an odd formation. Molded lumps rose from the middle of the floor as if they were furniture of some sort. Maybe this was a meeting area.

She tried to stay clear of the lumps. There's no way she wanted a repeat of her experience in Paxton's apartment where the furniture had shifted in its attempt to fit whatever sized person it needed to. Who knew what the furniture here could do? It might be made of natural materials, but that didn't stop things from doing weird stuff.

From the smell and the darkness, she'd assumed she was in the Louers' dimension. And if the Louers had already migrated to the new dimension, this one could theoretically, be empty. She brightened at that thought. Except they hadn't had time to migrate a whole species to the new dimension she'd created for them. Then again, there were only thousands of people here, not billions like in her dimension.

She couldn't imagine trying to move her people to another place. War would break out on a half dozen fronts. The first country across would probably claim the entire dimension as their own.

What a disaster that would be. How long had it been since she'd created that dimension? Hours or days. Had to be days. In the murky shadows, time had so little meaning. There were no sunrises or sunsets, no moon phases, nothing.

Storey closed her eyes and concentrated hard on connecting with the stylus. She could almost feel it. It was so vague, just a sensation really. She slid along the wall for another good fifty feet.

Where the hell was she?

ERIC CLOSED HIS eyes as the footsteps disappeared back downstairs. If those had been Storey's parents – a big maybe, because he remembered her saying she hadn't seen her father in over ten years – then something had gone majorly wrong in her dimension.

Vaguely he remembered her saying something about her family and how messed up things had become. If that man wasn't her father, then who was he and did it matter? Eric didn't want to deal with an angry male. Humans were more aggressive than his people. The Torans had evolved differently, choosing to use their psychic energy more, and had developed skills that were far superior to individuals in Storey's world. But his people weren't fighters.

Humans, on the other hand, had developed into warmongers. That's why the possibility of war on his side had stunned his people. They'd had no exposure to such violence. Only Storey hadn't been paralyzed. And she'd saved them all.

Now she was the one in need of saving.

CHAPTER 4

S TOREY CREPT AROUND another corner. Her mouth was so dry with fear she could barely swallow.

The silence unnerved her just as badly as if she heard the sound of footsteps.

Either this place was deserted or the Louers were professionals at staying quiet.

What about children? Did they have any here? Or were they in a different location? Not that she'd expect children close to a prison. Then again, she had so little information she couldn't afford to make any assumption. For all she knew, the Louers were herding her in a specific direction – like a trap.

Taking a deep breath, she rounded another corner, her back sliding along the wall. More blank walls faced her. She'd do a lot for a map of this place. Actually she'd do damn near anything to get her hands on her stylus.

A horrible sense of loss built deep inside her. The feeling so strong she had to consider that the stylus might be moving further away from her. It felt that bad. The nausea in her stomach made her want to heave. Yet, she didn't dare think that way. She had to find it. And fast.

Then the truth hit her, freezing her body in place. *Shit.*

The stylus hadn't moved – she had. In the wrong direction.

Crap. She really didn't want to go back, but the stylus

was her only hope of getting out of here. There was no choice. How could she pinpoint its location? Especially when the stylus couldn't tell her.

Either way the problem wasn't going to solve itself while she sat paralyzed with indecision.

Damn it.

She'd been communicating with the stylus somewhat. At least enough to kinda feel the answers to her questions. Could she do a hot and cold thing, like that children's game?

But she'd have to get a lot closer to test the idea out.

Groaning silently, she headed back to the entrance of the room she'd woken up in. The journey only took a few minutes. Her body didn't care; her heart had started pounding with the first step and her palms had to be leaving sweat marks. She could probably turn the lights on, but that didn't guarantee success at this point and would alert everyone as to where she was. Not that any Louers had come after her yet. And that didn't make sense either.

That just brought her back to the whole trap concept. Not her favorite one to dwell on.

The only sound was her heavy, rasping breaths. Damn. She'd never hear the stylus with that interfering. She took a deep breath and released it. Then did it again. That helped.

A bit.

At the entrance to the huge room, she peered around the doorway. Her eyes adjusted slowly to the deep darkness.

Still empty and open. That wouldn't be the most brilliant engineering she'd seen. Then again, just how far behind were these people? And yes, they were people, as much as it was hard to claim them as a relative of her own kind. The Torans, Eric's people, had developed more psychically than her own. Whatever that meant. It's not like she'd seen any examples of that.

Her people had developed differently as well. So in theory, the Louers could be more intelligent, more advanced than either humans or Torans. Or they could be the very opposite. Their living hadn't been the easiest but they had survived. Survival meant development of some kind.

She slipped past the door and headed the way she should have when she first escaped.

"Stylus, are you there?"

The faint sensation was a warm buzz in her head.

Thank God for that.

More confident now, she picked up the pace, trying to follow the warmth or coolness of the buzz as a directional signal. It grew stronger and stronger. A comforting sense of companionship. She wasn't alone. The stylus was here. Waiting for her.

Moving as fast as she could in the darkness, she passed a series of doors. Probably doors as each had a silver disc or button. She could only hope they didn't have any Torans or humans locked up in any of those rooms or she'd have to try and get them out, too. Damn, she needed her stylus.

Tuning into the buzzing noise in her head, she blocked everything else out and focused on following it.

Several long minutes later, she had no idea where she was; so focused on making the buzzing in her head grow, she'd followed the wall to what appeared to the be the end of the road. Another wall stood in front of her.

Mentally, she tapped into the stylus. *Can you feel me, Stylus?*

Nothing.

Damn. She snatched up the metal zipper pull and asked the question, this time she had her hand on the wall as it jerked with the answer. *Yes.*

Thank God for that. "Are you close to me?"

Yes.

And what did close mean? "Stylus, can you tell me the distance that's between us?"

Ten.

Ten what? Again, she had no idea of what measurements were used by Torans or Louers.

"Ten feet?" she asked cautiously.

Ten nacrons.

Shit.

"How long is a nacron?"

One nacron is ten sedents.

Double shit. Storey banged her forehead on the wall in front of her. Figures.

"Stylus, are there any Louers with you?"

No.

That was a relief.

"Are you contained in some way?"

Silence.

Stupid question, Storey. "Can you give me directions to find you?"

Follow the connection.

Connection? The buzz? Of course. That was how she'd made it this far, after all. She turned so her back pressed against the wall and closed her eyes. Where was the buzz coming from? The right. Great. That was the wall. No metal discs in sight.

"Stylus, I think you are behind the wall in front of me, but I can't see a way to get in."

Door.

"Yeah. That would be helpful." She thought hard. "Do they all have metal discs to show you how to open them?"

No.

Crap.

Backing up several steps, she took another look at the end wall. It made sense that there would be a way to open it, but how? The wall itself was about the length of her bedroom. And didn't that thought bring a pang to her heart? She missed her mom. That surprised her. But right now, a cup of tea with her mother sounded like the best gift ever.

Until she remembered that the last time she'd seen her mother, her father had been there, too. The same father she hadn't seen in a decade.

She shuddered. What a mess she had to clean up when she got home.

One mess at a time.

That meant getting out of here.

And that meant getting through the damn wall stand-ing between her and her stylus.

Shit.

Taking several steps back, she ran, shoulder down, straight at the wall.

ERIC SLIPPED OUT of the closet and studied Storey's bedroom. Surely if she'd been back there'd be a sign. Like her backpack, sketchbook or even her shoes could be here. Something would have been disturbed. The trouble was he couldn't tell.

From what he could see, she hadn't made it back to her home dimension. That matched the stylus's words and her parents' conversation. That left two more dimensions that he was aware of, both potentially full of the enemy.

Not good. He was very much afraid Storey was in the new dimension she'd created.

And if so, that could be a huge problem.

With a final look at her room, he set his codex for home and sent himself back to Paxton's lab.

Paxton waited for him as the mist dissipated. "Well," he asked impatiently, "Did she make it there?"

"No. I need to go to the new dimension. Make sure she hasn't somehow gotten into that one."

"Absolutely not. We can't have any energy moving between that dimension and ours. You know as well as I do that the more we travel the more the energy instinctively aligns into a pathway. If we go over there, the Louers could eventually find their way back here."

"If Storey is over there, we have to get her back."

"Go ask your father if he knows anything about her whereabouts."

Eric frowned at his mentor. "He's not likely to tell me, you know that." Paxton refused to meet his gaze. "You think she might be dead or at least dying, don't you?"

"It's a distinct possibility. Now hurry."

Eric strode down the long white hallway. It had taken Storey's comment about the white being everywhere to make him realize how odd his world must look to her. Her dimension swelled with color and chaos. Peace and quiet were hard to find, but the place buzzed with activity. At home, calm ruled and the most excitement on a normal day was watching the sun go down. Nothing ever happened – until Storey had popped in. She'd brought some of the same chaos and color to his world, too. He enjoyed the energy and he *really* missed the chaos.

Stupid.

He missed her even more.

His father's chambers lay at the end of the hall. As Councilman, his chambers were the largest and richest of any here. He was big on appearances. Not so big on sharing.

At a white door that looked the same as every other apartment on this floor, Eric took a deep breath, thought of Storey caught in a nightmare dimension, possibly dying, and knocked on his father's door. Hard.

The door opened under his hand. Eric entered expecting to see his father holding court with the other council members. The room was silent – and empty.

Eric frowned. "Father. Are you home?"

"Father?"

No answer.

He called out again, moving cautiously into the open space. The room appeared to be undisturbed. But if he wasn't here, then where was he? His father only frequented a few places. Council Chambers, his apartment and Paxton's lab. The only other place would be the private dining room. But at this hour of the morning? Not likely.

His father was a creature of habit.

So where was he?

STOREY HIT THE wall and bounced off. *Duh.* Rubbing her sore shoulder she glowered at the dirt wall. "This is ridiculous. Why doesn't anything work properly around here?"

She walked back and forth along the wall with her hand scraping the surface, looking for some kind of crack or door; any weakness would be a good start. There had to be some way to get past this barrier. And fast. *Shit.*

At the far end she turned to look back along the wall. Nothing had changed.

"Open sesame?" Stupid, she knew it was stupid, but she was willing to try anything. Nothing happened. Of course not. Still, she had to try. "Door open?"

"Please open the door?"

Nothing happened.

Like who said the Louers even spoke English. For all she knew they had a very different language. Not that having another dialect would make any sense, considering the Toran people spoke a basic form of English. They had some words she'd never heard of. Still, it was close enough to hers to be understandable. Unlike their portal technology. That's what she really wanted to take home. *Like that will ever happen.* Still, imagine being able to go to California for a swim and Hong Kong for a shopping trip and then ending up in Paris for dinner. Travel by codex was fast and simple. It was also green technology. At least she thought it was. It would eliminate the need for planes, trains, cars even. The air would be almost pollution free. So much nicer than walking along the street with all the car exhaust she had to breathe in now.

Well not right now. Right now she was in the Louers' dimension. At least she thought she was. Then she could possibly be underground in the new dimension, too.

Let's face it. I have no clue where I am.

"Enough, already. Door open."

A grinding sound filled the area. The wall in front of her slid to the side. She pivoted, crouching low only to see she was still alone. Then she slipped into the room and stopped just inside the doorway. Was it the tone of voice that mattered here? Odd, considering she'd heard no sounds here. In fact, the silence was starting to bug her.

"Lights on."

Instantly the same lighting system turned on, giving a low yellowish light over what appeared to be another empty room. "Crap. I like peace and quiet as much as the next person, but all the time? No. Are there any Torans here? Anything but Louers?" Silence was her only answer. Good thing, too, otherwise she'd have had a heart attack.

"Stylus, are you in here?"

She didn't have her zipper tab in her hand. Damn. Digging deep, she scrounged around in her pockets until she found it. From what she could see, there was nothing in this room. Turning to the closest wall, she repeated the question, her hand ready to write the answer.

Only there was no answer.

Shit.

"Stylus? Stylus, talk to me."

No answer.

Double shit. It had been here a minute ago. She knew that. Had felt that deep connection, so close, and now it was gone. Where and how?

Closing her eyes, she called out as strongly as she could on a mental level.

No response.

Somehow, within the last five minutes, she'd lost her connection to the stylus. Why? Her heart raced. She walked the perimeter of the room looking for anything that would show storage, another door, Louers…something to explain how her stylus could have gone missing.

And came up empty.

"Stylus, do you have a power source that has run out? Like a battery or something?"

No answer.

Fear crept down her spine. All alone was one thing, all alone without the stylus was a whole different problem. Up until the last couple of minutes, she'd thought she was close to holding it again in her grasp.

Now what?

ERIC STOOD IN the middle of his father's chambers.

Where was his father? Searching as he walked, Eric returned to Paxton. "My father isn't there. I can't find him anywhere."

Paxton lifted his head, concern clouding his eyes. "He can't be far. Everyone is still on alert. Just because the war is over doesn't mean the danger is."

Eric shrugged. "I couldn't find him. Ask your stylus."

Paxton frowned. "We can't be bothering it for every little thing. Walk the building and find him. He's probably in the dining room."

Studying his codex, Eric typed in a series of numbers to see if he could track his father. "I don't know. This doesn't feel right."

"Why?"

"The codex isn't picking up his wrist unit."

"I believe he has the broken one, remember? I tried to fix it, but he wanted it back before I completed the job." Paxton looked at the charts and papers covering his desk. Grabbing a blank page, he picked up his stylus. "Stylus, where is the Councilman?"

His hand jerked as the message came through. *Gone.*

"What does that mean?" Eric stared at the paper. "Gone where?"

"Stylus, has the Councilman left the building?"
Yes.

"There's no way. He almost never leaves. Ever." Eric glanced at Paxton, his uncertainty mirrored in his mentor's gaze.

Paxton shook his head. "That's not true. The Councilman prefers to stay inside, but he does leave when he has to."

"So where is he then?"

Turning back to the stylus, Paxton wrote, "Stylus, can you tell us where he has gone?"
No.

Paxton frowned. "No, you can't tell us or no, you can't tell us where he's gone?"

I don't know.

Both Paxton and Eric stared at each other in confusion. "I don't understand. Has something changed that you aren't getting the information you need?"

"Is it broken?" Eric figured to clear the air right away.

"No, at least I don't think so. Stylus, are you broken?"

No. Cloudy. Injured.

Paxton immediately laid it on top of the paper. "See, we probably overused it."

"No way. We have to figure out what's wrong. For all you know this is related to Storey's stylus. Maybe hers has been broken. They are all connected remember."

"I remember," he answered testily. "That's still a big assumption."

Eric tried to be patient. "I'm not assuming anything. I'm asking you to pick it up again and get more answers."

Paxton waffled then relented. He reached out for his stylus hesitantly. "I don't want to hurt it."

"Then ask it if you are doing anything to hurt it."

Paxton asked the question and his shoulders sagged with relief when the answer came back 'no.'

"Now find out who's been injured," Eric urged.

The ensuing conversation blew him away. He'd been right. Something had happened to Storey's stylus and it had gone into sleep mode. Leaving her alone and probably in the Louers' dimension.

"Sleep mode?"

We turn off and hibernate after a long period of inactivity...or if someone happens to pick us up that we feel we are better off to hibernate from.

Eric didn't like the sound of that. "Can it tell if something happened to Storey?"

The answer came back negative. But that could mean

it didn't know.

Shit. "I have to go find her. And her stylus apparently."

"I don't have a good feeling about this," Paxton said.

Eric's stomach twisted in agreement. "While I'm looking for Storey, maybe you can find my father."

Walking past Paxton's work desk, Eric snatched up a second codex for Storey, just in case. Last time he'd been in that horrible place, they hadn't had enough traveling power for everyone and that shortage had sent them into the newly created fourth dimension. Back then it had been empty. Now...it could be full of Louers. Securing the new codex to his right arm, he used the codes he'd thought to never repeat. The one difficult thing about codex travel, it needed coordinates. He'd only been in one place in that horrible land – a prison. Therefore, that's the only place he could return to.

As blackness swirled up around his body, he sent out a silent hope that he'd make it through this trip fine.

The last thing he wanted was to end up a prisoner – again.

CHAPTER 5

S TOREY PRIDED HERSELF on staying calm and rational in difficult circumstances. She'd learned a lot through the skirmishes in Eric's dimension and knew she needed to control the panic crouching on the edge of her mind. The bottom line to her situation is she *had* to find her stylus. It had been elemental to every successful thing she'd done so far.

Why had it stopped communicating? Did it have batteries to run dry? Or, as it was bound to her, maybe it needed to spend time with her to recharge. With a few short steps, she returned to the wall she'd tried to bust through. She'd been so sure the stylus had been on the other side, and that's the last sensation she'd had of it, then it had stopped.

Cracks went up and down. Cupboards?

Could it be?

Quickly she searched for some way to open them. "Cupboards open." Nothing. *Crap, this again.* "Storage open. Door open. Wall open?"

Nothing.

She pounded along the crack, hoping it might have a release lever. Again nothing. The longer she stared at the wall the more she could make out the vertical lines that had to be there for a reason.

It had to be a cupboard of some kind. Organized cracks filled the wall like the outline of a puzzle. It's like she looked at the backside of a storage unit.

That couldn't be right. On the other side she'd run her hand along the entire wall and there'd been no cracks or breaks at all. So between that wall and here, there had to be storage. And her stylus was in there. And if it was in there, someone had put it there. Now if only she knew who and how. Damn it.

With a heavy sigh, she reached up a hand and massaged her neck. Everything was starting to ache. And her stomach was growling from lack of food. Another growing problem. Food. And water. Damn, she shouldn't have thought of that, now her mouth was dry and all she could think of was cold, clear water. She closed her eyes and tried to focus. *Stylus? Please, are you there? I need to find you.*

Again, she heard nothing.

But...but what? A faint buzz, so faint she could almost persuade herself she'd imagined it. There it was again. With an ear cocked to one side, she walked toward the noise. It was coming from the corner of the wall. Reaching out, she touched the spot gently. Then harder. *Snick.* The cupboard in front of her opened up. She backed away. It didn't snap open or open by much, but it was as if some interior connection had released and there was now a big enough crack to pull the door toward her. She opened it, expecting to see shelves. Instead, a space, too big for the area she'd thought had been available for the cupboard stood in front of her. Big enough she could walk inside. And that thought made her stomach cringe. Because not only could she *not* find her stylus lying on the dirt floor of this cupboard, she also couldn't see a back to the cupboard. There wasn't one.

Because this wasn't a cupboard, but a doorway.

ERIC COUGHED, GASPED, then coughed again. The smell.

His eyes streamed and his chest burned. How could the Louers live with this stench? He coughed and coughed, almost retching as his system struggled to adapt. Bending over, he gave himself another long moment to adjust. The crossing had been easy enough, but the arrival had been tough.

Standing slowly, he searched the area around him. The darkness held a dense, cloying odor. He squinted. It appeared to be the same room he'd been in last time. It also appeared to be empty.

Relaxing slightly, he rolled his head and scrunched his shoulders slightly to ease up the tension in his back. He did a quick walk of the perimeter of the large room. No lights, no door, nothing. How did that work?

The Louers' technology had diversified from those of his own people centuries ago, so even though he might know some of their methods to make daily living work, chances are he wouldn't understand all of it. His father and Paxton assumed that the Louers had become even more primitive after they'd been banished to this hell, but he wasn't so sure. The two men held the same opinion of Storey and her people, and look at what she'd managed to do. If the Louers had developed half as well as the humans, they could have some pretty amazing technology.

The Louers he'd seen on his dimension had been brutish in looks, but they had been incredibly strong. They'd also crossed the veil and devised a strategy to try and take over his world. That they hadn't succeeded was due mostly to Storey and they couldn't have known to account for her in their plans. Who could have?

He grinned.

Good for Storey. Just being herself had been enough to make his people stand up and take notice. Teach them for acting superior and thinking all other people were inferior. He planned on not making the same mistake.

So…how to get out of here and find Storey?

With a hand held against the wall, he quickly searched for openings in the weird sandstone walls. Just because he couldn't see any light source didn't mean there wasn't one. Taking a chance on attracting attention, he called aloud for light. Instantly the room flooded with bright light. So they had that much. Great. Maybe this wouldn't be so hard after all.

"Door open."

Nothing.

Then again…

Using his best military sounding voice, Eric tried again. "Open prison door."

Nothing.

"Please open this door."

Nothing.

This was just going to make him mad. He'd assumed they had voice technology as his people did, so it made sense to have voice activated doors. However, if this was a prison then they wouldn't want the prisoners to get out, so chances were that the guards either had a voice print, word sequence or some other way of making sure only a select few people would be allowed to open the door. His people would do the same.

So back to Paxton's lab and see if his stylus would be able to get more information on the security here.

Frustrated, he tapped in the code to take him back to Paxton's lab, the musical notes filling the large space. The echo was surprising but with so little ambient noise it reverberated around the room. As he readied to enter the last digit of the sequence, he heard a grating sound. Whirling around, he crouched, ready for an attack…and saw no one.

A huge door had opened. But no one came in. Were they waiting on the other side? He crept up behind the door and waited. Nothing. Peering through the crack between the door and the wall didn't help, only blackness showed on the other side. Of course the light was on his side. Taking a deep breath, he slipped out of the room and melted into the shadows on the other side. It took way too long for his eyes to adjust to the darkness. When they finally did, he found he was alone in another large, empty room.

Could the notes of his codex…have opened the door? That would mean they had music here. Or the door mechanism had been triggered by his movements. That didn't make sense either. Prisoners walked around all the time. The only other explanation he could imagine was a failsafe mechanism that opened automatically after a certain length of time. So that no one was left in there forever. That concept was kind of reassuring. But not much.

Choosing to go left, he crept down the hallway.

Storey was here somewhere.

STOREY STUDIED THE cupboard passageway. Dare she enter? How could she not?

Closing her eyes she called to the stylus.

The faintest of buzzes answered her. Shit. It was down here. The many thick walls might explain the stylus's inability to communicate. Could it die? Maybe it went to sleep or something until a new soul could bond to it. Maybe that's why it had bonded to her so strongly when she'd initially found it. So it would survive. In which case, what if it bonded with the Louer who'd found it here?

That wouldn't be good.

Decision made.

Focusing on the buzz, she strode into the dark tunnel. "Stylus, hold on. I'm coming. Stay strong. Stay connected."

A hum sounded. Stronger than before, but still indistinct. Even though she couldn't see what she walked on or anything two feet in front of her, she knew as strongly as she'd ever understood anything in her life, she needed to travel this pathway to her stylus.

She could only hope she'd find it in time to save them both.

Picking up the pace, she trotted down the corridor.

The end of the road came up and smacked her in the face – hard. She tumbled backwards. "Damn." Sitting up she rubbed her head and right elbow, sore from cracking hard on the ground. Getting up slowly, she put out a hand to touch the wall or door in front of her. "Door open."

Silently, the door moved toward her, forcing her back. The stream of light widened. An odd shuffling sound came through, soft and gentle, but unidentifiable.

Was there someone in the next room?

She closed her eyes and tried to control her gasping breath. The last thing she needed was for them to hear her. On the other hand, if they had her stylus and thought they were going to keep it, they had better think again.

So not going to happen. Not here. Her mother would be devastated at never knowing what had happened. Chances were good that Storey would become just another runaway teenager that was never heard from again.

Peering around the corner of the doorway, she realized she'd reached a small anteroom. Maybe it would be a sitting room off a bedroom in her dimension. Another weird table sat off to one side covered in items she couldn't decipher. Almost everything had a neutral color to it. The sheer drabness of this world hurt her creative soul, her artist soul. Where were the reds, greens and blues?

Very odd. She quickly scanned the room. It was empty. But there was an open doorway ahead of her. Maybe the person had gone into there.

She crept over to the table, ducking out of sight at the slightest sound. Lifting her head slightly, she checked to see if she was still alone.

Yes. She reached up to the stack of items on the table and picked up one for a closer look. It seemed somewhat like a cup, except too big for her small fingers to hold comfortably. The next item appeared to be made of the same material, almost a thin sandstone slice. It resembled a tiny box of some kind. It was also empty.

Weird materials.

Weird items.

Weird place.

The items were odd sized, too. The table was higher than she was used to; not that she had to stand on tiptoes to look down on it but she'd have a hard time doing any work on it comfortably. What's the chance her stylus was in the jumble? She didn't recognize it. And she didn't want to move around too much and alert whoever was in the next room. Hunkering back down, she searched the area again, and spotted another wall of cupboards like the last one she'd entered. And this one was open showing shelves on the one side. Closing her eyes she called out to the stylus in a soft whisper, "Are you there?"

A buzz answered her. Stronger, clearer, but still indistinct because she had no way to write the answers. She grabbed her zipper pull and held it against what must be a seat butted up against the side of the table and asked again.

Slowly her hand moved. *Yes.*

Oh thank heavens for that.

"Where are you?"

Don't know.

Of course it didn't. Neither did she. But…it was a computer-like thingy so maybe it could send out a beacon. "Can you send out a signal, a noise to let me know where you are?"

Instantly, there was an odd ringtone going off in her head. Or in the air? No, surely not. She spun around looking for the source. There, in the cupboards. Within seconds, she'd raced toward the spot, scared to alert whoever was in the other room to her presence. There were deep shelves inside. She quickly searched them. The stylus just looked like an old carpenter's pencil. Dull and dark, it was hard to see in the dark.

The noise was definitely louder here. Excited, she dropped to her knees and checked the bottom spaces. The noise increased to almost deafening now. A good sign. The last few items were almost recognizable. A ball, maybe a bat? A bunch of toys like a ball on string or wire and a wooden post. Like a child's closet. Off to one side were tablets of some kind. Maybe for writing on, like miniature chalkboards. Even chalk would be a huge help. By the time she'd moved to the next cubby hole the music in her head changed from a weird ringtone to an almost soothing lullaby.

"Does that mean I'm almost there, Stylus?"

The lullaby increased in volume. It increased so much, she could hardly stand it. She shoved her hand into the jumbled mess and closed around a half dozen objects.

Something made her fingers tingle.

The lullaby came to a dead stop.

Warmth shot up her arm. She withdrew her handful

until she could see what she'd snagged clearly.

Her stylus!

Joy shot through her. *Yes!*

And then she took another look and stopped. How could this be possible?

There, clutched in her fingers, were three pencils that could have all been styluses. And maybe they were? Who would have stashed these in here, lost and forgotten? These gems could have saved the Louers so much hardship?

They might *not* be styluses, but as she studied each one, the magical lettering shone on the side of each one. Unbelievable. Did they have souls attached to them too?

And if there were three, what was the chance there were more?

It was important to find every one. How she knew that, she didn't know. But she did. Tucking those three securely into her pocket, she dove into the bottom of the cupboard and sorted through the mess. And found two more. Unbelievable. Now she didn't dare leave any behind. There were people in there, after all.

Knowing she didn't have the time to spare, but unable to help herself, she went back for a third and final search, and found one really old looking stylus jammed into the joinery at the very back. Six styluses. Pulling back slightly, a wary eye to the open door, she moved over and checked every cupboard, as fast and as systematically as she could in order to not miss one. Ten panicked minutes later, she held a broken one in her hand. No others though. Now to safety.

She ran across the room and back into the open doorway from where she'd entered.

Just as she hit the safety of the darkness, she heard a loud grunt behind her.

Shit.

ERIC'S EYES FINALLY adjusted to the dark as he paced forward, instinct keeping him moving in the same direction. He almost sensed Storey up ahead. Many of his people had strong psychic powers. His society used healers in their hospitals and people with an affinity for plants and growing in the gardens and greenhouses. Those that had a specialty were given the means to develop it as far as they could.

To the best of his knowledge, he possessed a weird navigational sense. It allowed him to find his way home from most places and could move toward something even if he had no idea where it was.

Unfortunately, he'd had little chance to develop that sense. And as it wasn't one of the known talents, his ability hadn't been given much training time. He'd yet to even mention it to Storey. She'd find it fascinating he was sure. And unlike his father, he doubted she'd laugh at it.

So he couldn't heal sick people or tell the future or lift items with his mind, like some of his people could, but surely being good at geography and navigation had to count for something. Of course, that's why he'd been put into Ranger training.

Eric's codex lit up like a Christmas tree. "What the…"

He kept running while trying to understand the odd number sequences and lights. Was someone trying to contact him? Or was someone trying to navigate toward his last known location? The codexes were capable of so much more than what they were commonly used for that he often forgot about their other capabilities. Still, not many people would know about those extras ei-ther…except Paxton.

Should he go back to the lab and check? Or could he

remember how to send a coded message? Something he hadn't done since his training days. Neither could he tap in Toranee code while running. Toranee was old in his world, and similar in some ways to the Morse code of Storey's dimension.

He wondered if one had spawned the other? Another piece of information his people had taken from her dimension?

That made it one of the more basic languages. And he couldn't remember much of it. Breathing hard, he came to a stop and crouched down out of sight. He lowered the volume on his unit and struggled to tap out a simple message to Paxton. It took several tries and head bangs, as Storey would say, to get out a quick note.

In Louers' world. On Storey's trail. Can't come back. Problems.

Eric sent it, hoping the last word would be understood. Then, hating the time he'd lost, he returned to trotting down the corridor. Storey was up ahead. Somewhere.

He had yet to see any Louers here, and that didn't feel right either. Surely they hadn't managed a complete migration already. They'd need time to move everyone and everything over.

Cold seeped into his arms and legs, even with the energy he was expending. The dark and the dirt, the smell and the cold, all combined to make this a very unwelcoming place.

Quite similar to Storey's first foray into his world actually. She'd landed in a big cave, a major crossing his people used regularly to move through dimensions and across his world. The crossing would have looked similar to what he'd seen here. Dirt walls, a room that went on seemingly forever – and all without seeing a soul.

Maybe this was a similar type of place in the Louer

world. It's not like he'd had a chance to explore to know for sure.

His respect for Storey zoomed up another notch.

Now if he could just find her.

CHAPTER 6

STOREY BOLTED THROUGH the dark tunnel, terrified she'd trip and drop the styluses. In her mind, she knew they could be just empty shells, but the personal connection to *her* stylus was real and precious. How could she desert the others – just in case?

She glanced behind her, scared she was being followed. Which didn't appear to be the case. Her footsteps slowed as she approached the next room. Why not?

Maybe they didn't mean her any harm.

Shit. She hated it when her softer side came out. For all she knew this was the last Louer here. Damn it. How bad could they be? They'd kept styluses and kids' toys. Kids' toys.

Her stomach twisted. What if that had been a child? A Louer child. Were there such things? Of course. They were people. Just a different kind.

If there was a child, was there an adult with it? Or had the child been left behind alone? By accident or on purpose?

With a heavy sigh, she realized she couldn't leave without knowing. Who knew if there was anyone left here to help them out?

Too bad all the styluses she'd picked up couldn't help. She held them gently in her hand. No heat emanated from them, like Eric experienced when he'd held her stylus. Would her stylus know if they were empty? Maybe.

Now if only she had paper. The wall might work again, but something softer would be easier. Like her missing sketchbook.

With her stylus in her hand, she delighted when the sense of loss, of being alone, shifted to a full sense of connectedness. That instant knowing that this stylus was hers. Although identical in appearance to the others there was no doubt in her mind that she held her stylus. There was a link between them – strong, clearer than before. She didn't understand why. And didn't care.

"Stylus? Are you okay?"

She placed her stylus against the wall and read the faint impression in the dirt.

Yes. Getting stronger.

"Do you need much longer before you are back to full strength?"

No. Not long.

Whatever that meant in terms of time for a stylus. Rather than wasting time trying to sort it out, she asked if it had been a Louer who'd put the stylus in the closet.

There was a humming silence. *Yes. Almost.*

Storey paused, her mouth open. "Almost?" she asked cautiously.

Child.

Oh shit. "Oh no. We can't leave a child alone, can we?"

Yes, we can.

Of course the stylus didn't know about balancing morals and right and wrong actions.

"Is the child alone?"

Yes.

"How many Louers are there in this complex?" That wasn't quite the right word to describe this place, but it was all she could think of.

One. The child.

That finished it. There was no way Storey could leave without making sure the child would be okay. Louer or not, the child was alone. "How old is the child?"

She's six.

She? It was a little girl. Storey definitely wouldn't leave her behind, lost and alone. But… "Is she a danger to me?"

A humming sound filled the air. *No. We don't believe so.*

Believe? Storey would rather have a more definite answer than that. "Will I be able to communicate with her?"

Somewhat.

Sigh. Why was nothing ever easy? "Where is the child's family?"

In the new dimension.

Well that's good. At least she had a family. "Can we return the child to her family?"

Yes.

Thinking of the less than ideal lifestyle some kids in her human world experienced, she had to know. "Is she a wanted child? Or did they leave her behind on purpose?

Accident. Her pet ran away. She ran after it.

"Pet? I've yet to see anything living here. What type of pet?"

A skorl.

Yeah, that was so not helpful. "Did she find it?"

Yes.

"Can she take the pet with her to the other dimension?"

Yes.

"And no one has come back for her?"

They can't reopen the portal to come back.

Storey straightened as understanding swept through her. How sad. At the same time, she felt much better about not having to worry that she'd be recaptured. "Was she the one I saw on arrival?" It was getting easier to understand the stylus. Some of the words seemed to form in her mind. As if she were only partly reading and anticipating what the stylus planned to say before it actually did. Weird. But a relief. She'd take any improvement to her situation at this point.

She saw you arrive, thought you were her people coming back for her.

"So she left me there and took my stuff?" Storey didn't like the sound of that. Typical.

She thought you were dead.

"And where is my sketchbook?"

With the child.

"Why did she take you?"

She'd seen others like me.

"Does she know what you are?"

No.

"I found six of you in that cupboard. Are there more?"

A heavy humming filled the air. Then it was joined by a humming of a different tenor, then another and another. Pretty soon the air buzzed as if a conversation raced around her. They were styluses then.

No. You have us all.

"Should I leave any of you behind?"

No. We are grateful to you.

"What about the broken one?"

We are grateful that you picked up the broken one. He is an important member of our group.

"Can he be fixed?"

Yes.

Good enough. She tucked them all safely away in her pockets then returned to the problem of the Louer child. "Stylus, can we write on her arm and send her to the new dimension like we did the prisoners from the war?

No.

She groaned. "Why not?"

I don't have the code for where her people are. If we sent her over she could end up anywhere.

Damn.

"So I'm all alone with a Louer child with no way to help either of us?"

Not quite.

Groaning a loud, she asked, "What's not quite right?"

You are not alone.

She spun around, searching for someone else to somehow, suddenly show up. "What do you mean? I thought you said the Louers were all gone except for the child?"

I did.

"So…"

A Toran is here now.

"Who?" But she knew. Only Eric would have come over and tried to help her.

Eric.

Yes! She turned around, listening for him. "Where is he?"

Not far.

"How far? Which way do I go to find him?"

You don't. He's following you.

"Perfect. So I can sit here and wait. Then he can help me deal with the issue of the child."

Yes.

A huge pressure valve inside eased. She wasn't alone. Thank God. "Stylus, are you okay now?"

Almost.

It had said that last time too. "What about the child, is she hurt?"

No. Hungry.

That figured. Weren't all kids? "Did the Louers get

settled into their new dimension?"

In progress. The Louers of this complex moved, but the others haven't been able to yet. The portal is damaged. Closed.

Uh oh. That couldn't be good. Did the Louers even know the child had been left behind? And speaking of children and parents…

"Are my parents okay? Still together." Her question slid out, surprising her.

Yes.

"That's not good."

Why?

"My father hasn't been in my life for a long time. When I created the new dimension I did something to *my* dimension. My parents are different. Their beliefs are different. I'm supposed to be different. I asked you to reverse what I did, but I don't think you changed everything back." She hesitated. "Did you?"

No. Your words and thoughts weren't as one. You twisted time.

"Yeah, that doesn't sound so good. Can I untwist it? Or twist it back again?

No.

She took a deep breath. "Why? I need to reverse what I did to my dimension without affecting the other good changes I made."

You can fix this.

She breathed a deep sigh of relief. Thank heavens for that. "Now if only Eric would show up, things would be great."

He's almost here.

Storey turned to face the door. Wouldn't he get a surprise when he saw what she'd found.

ERIC FOLLOWED THE wall deeper into the Louers' complex, wondering at the weird sounds coming from his codex. Was it broken? Maybe the Louers' dimension was the problem.

The light on his codex changed. And a series of symbols sat in the small display window. Mentally he converted it to something understandable. Storey. He came to a sliding stop.

Her presence was stronger than ever. And close.

Did he dare call for her?

If any Louers were here, he should have seen some sign or them by now. He'd almost have preferred it. This lonely darkness was unsettling. As was the constant looking over his shoulder only to find nothing, anywhere.

"Storey," he whispered, then shook his head. How stupid. It's not like Storey could've heard that. She'd have to be right in front of him to hear him.

"Yes?"

Storey's pale face flashed in front of him, a huge grin and sheer joy in her eyes. "Did you call?"

"Storey!" he shouted, and snatched her up into his arms. He twirled her around, holding her close. *Oh, thank you!*

"Finally! I've been so worried." With a big grin he put her down then pushed her hair back so she could look into her face. He stared deep into her eyes. "What the heck happened? How did you end up here? Why couldn't you leave?"

She laughed and jumped back into his arms. He held her tight, dropping his head to rest on hers. Joy rippled through him, so grateful to have her safe.

Finally she stepped back, her smile this time a little teary eyed. She sniffled and wiped her eyes. "Am I glad to see you." In a surprise move, she reached up and hit his shoulder. "That's for your lousy father." To be fair, as she had no proof, she added with a sigh, "At least I think this mess is his fault."

"I'm afraid it is too, but I don't have any proof yet." Eric bit back a sigh. He hoped his father was innocent. Except that concept was getting harder to believe. His father had to have been behind it. There'd been no one else with the motive, means and skill level to send Storey somewhere else. "You didn't even make it to your home, did you?"

"No. As I left the party, your father waved at me. In his hand he had my stylus. At least what he thought was my stylus. Oh, he gloated like he knew something bad was going to happen – something I was *not* going to like. And he was right." Storey shook her head at the memory. "When the mist dissipated, there were these horrible hands reaching for me. I don't know if it was crossing the dimension or what but I blacked out. When I came to, I was alone in a large cave-like room."

Eric closed his eyes. Damn. His father couldn't have known about her fake stylus. He'd intended to separate Storey from her stylus, thus bringing about her death. Could he have also changed the destination in her codex? Did he even know how to do that? The one was bad enough, but if he'd done them both...well, Eric didn't know what to think.

Could his father hate Storey that much? Or was this a desperate act of a desperate man? Could he have thought this was a way to regain his all powerful leadership status – using her as an example to others, perhaps? He'd never had to deal with outright defiance or a potential non-confidence vote before – until Storey. Could this be just about ego?

Or maybe fear was the basis of his father's actions. Fear of losing everything he had? Eric had heard mutterings from several displeased council members and presumed his father had as well. Would that have been enough to precipitate these actions?

Eric would have to let this mess roll around in his head for a bit.

Right now he had bigger priorities – like getting Storey home safely.

"It's going to be fine now. I have my codex and I brought another one for you." By the time he'd finished speaking, Eric had unclipped the spare on his left and snagged her arm to clip it onto hers.

He stopped. "What's this?"

"What's what?"

Eric tapped her arm.

"I can't see."

"Lights on full." Instantly the lights turned on, giving Storey her first real look at the large room. She couldn't believe the enormity of the space they were in. There had to have been many Louers living here to require a room of such size. It was bigger than the community center she'd gone to at home. "Wow. Look at this place."

"Wow," Eric said patiently, "Look at your arm." He grabbed her left arm and gave it a good shake.

Staring, Storey frowned at the intricate swirls decorating her arm. They traveled from the back of her wrist to her elbow and around the underside. She felt nothing as she ran her fingers over it. There was no burning, scarring or even loose ink to come off on her fingers.

"I have no idea. I don't know when or how I got these."

"It's also not *on* you; it's a part *of* you. Your people have tattoos inked into their skin. These are considered marks of honor in my home. I have no idea if the Louers have something similar in theirs."

"Marks of honor." She snorted. They were pretty cool looking. "That might have made sense if your people had given them to me on the night of the celebration. But not here and now. My arm was clean when I left your place."

"Somehow you've gained these marks in the time you've been here." He studied her face carefully, a hint of humor in his eyes. "You are the strangest girl."

"Oh," she gasped, "that is so unfair."

He grinned. "Only you could be banished to another dimension and come out with marks of honor without having any idea of how you got them."

She snickered. "I found a few other things here too." All humor fell away. Storey looked into his eyes, willing him to understand. "A lost Louer child for one. A little girl was accidentally left behind in the mass exodus of her people. According to my stylus there's something wrong with the portal and the Louers can't come back for her. She's all alone."

"What? A single juvenile? Oh, that's not good."

Storey nodded emphatically. "Exactly. I'm glad you understand. So, you'll help, right?"

Eric tried to figure out where Storey's lightning quick mind was going. A Louer child alone probably wouldn't survive and as much as he didn't like the idea, it might be a kindness to kill her now and prevent her suffering. But from the hope on Storey's face, he highly doubted he was going to like her solution.

"Help you do what?" he asked warily. Somehow he didn't think he was going to like her answer.

"Help me return her to her parents. In the new di-mension."

Oh shit.

STOREY COULDN'T BELIEVE Eric stood in front of her. Only now that she realized she'd been saved, did she admit to herself how worried she'd been. How alone —

how lost – she'd felt. Eric had become such a great friend with the potential to become so much more.

Unable to help herself, she reached out and hugged him again. As his arms closed around her, she finally realized he wasn't warming to her idea regarding the child. "Eric?"

"Hmmm." His husky voice against her ear melted her insides. Damn it was wonderful to have him here.

She pulled back slightly to see his expression clearer. "You don't think we should help her?"

"Have you seen her? Do you know how old she is? Can you talk to her?"

"According to the stylus, she's six." Storey frowned. Whatever that number meant to the Louers. "We can't just leave her. She'll die." She watched his conscience war with his upbringing. At least that's what she thought the fight going on behind his eyes was all about. The Louers were hated enemies of the Torans. It was natural for him to be concerned. But a child was a child regardless of her family. They had to help her. That was not negotiable.

What form that help took was up for discussion. "Can we pinpoint where the Louers are in the new dimension and send her to them?"

Eric frowned.

She grinned at his automatic reaction to something he wasn't sure about. But his morals were good and his common sense sound. He'd come around and probably with a better idea than she had.

"I don't know how to do that," he said. "Paxton or your stylus might though. The first thing we have to do is find a way to talk to the child. If she doesn't want to come willingly, it's not going to be fun for any of us."

He had a point. Storey turned back to the room with the cupboard-door-looking hallway.

"There's a weird hallway in this room. I think she's at

the far end."

"Show me."

Storey led the way back into the passageway. At the other end, it appeared as if the light was still on. There was no sign of the child in the first room. She motioned at the lit room ahead, then they walked quietly over to see if the child was in the second area.

The room appeared to be more of a bedroom than anything else Storey had seen in the place, but it didn't make much sense in layout. There were shapes similar to beds, but wider and shorter and they were stacked liked bunks. There was no bedding. Storey guessed everything necessary had been stripped. Since the Louers hadn't had much time for crossing over, it made sense that some belongings had been left behind for another trip. Although from what she could see, they'd done a decent job the first time around.

As she walked into the center of the room, she turned slowly, searching for the child. And found her backpack.

Yes. The bag sat on the floor, open and dumped. Even from where she stood, Storey could see the granola had been flattened. "I need to get my stuff," she whispered, nudging Eric's arm, she pointed to her bag. With a cautious look around, she raced forward and quickly grabbed up the remaining contents. Her sketchbook was missing. Figured.

Still no sign of the child. Or another door, either. Weird. Then again, what did she know about the doors here? They seemed to just appear. "Eric, I don't know where she is."

"Hiding most likely. It's what I'd do. Is everything here made of rock?" He walked over to the closest bed like structure and pushed down. "Looks like it."

"I wondered too. It looks like they've taken absolutely everything they could with them. Well, not quite. There are cupboards in the other room with some weird stuff left behind." Storey paused and spun around to face him, delight spreading across her face, as she remembered what else she'd found. "Guess what? I found more styluses. Six in all, including a broken one."

Eric spun so fast he almost knocked her over. "What? You found styluses? Like *our* styluses? Here? How?"

She pulled out two from her pocket. His look of astonishment grew. Flashing a big grin at him, she then tucked the items safely back away.

"Come. I'll show you." Storey led the way back through the tunnel. Inside the dark room again, she pointed to the shelves on the side. "They were tossed in there. I presume the child found mine in my backpack, recognized it and threw it in there with the others."

"Lights on." Instantly light filled the space.

Eric stared from her to the cupboard and back again. "Chances are that if they've been here all this time, they won't work now."

"Maybe." Storey bent to look, yet again, into the back of the cupboard. And found herself staring into a pair of eyes.

She screamed and jumped back, her hand to her throat. "Good God. What is that thing? A rat?"

Eric leaned over to take a look. And grinned. "I think it's a skorl. We have them at home, but they've almost become extinct."

Storey took another look. The animal's small, beady eyes were set wide apart with a small nose. The rest of the rodent-sized critter appeared to be covered in a large amount of dust covered fur. It held out a paw, the fur stopping before switching to brown skin covered digits.

"That's the girl's pet, then," Storey said. "According to my stylus, when everyone was moving to the new dimension, her pet was scared off and she ran after him and got left behind. Now with the portal the way it is…”

Eric looked from her to the animal. “Don’t tell me. We’re going to have to save the pet, too?”

She grinned. “I knew you’d understand.”

The small rodent with the big eyes sat on its haunches to stare at them curiously.

“I wonder if it bites?” he muttered.

“Probably,” she said cheerfully. “It doesn’t know you. If we could find the girl, she could retrieve it. Too bad they don’t have a cage to carry it. I’ve never seen such a pile of junk.” She pointed to the remaining contents of the cupboard.

Eric studied the almost empty shelves. “Think about it. They left behind…”

“…everything what wasn’t needed or useable.” Storey finished.

“Exactly. They might have more things stored in another location to collect later. If the portal is damaged, maybe they haven’t had a chance yet?” He cast another quick look around. “At least we know this group made it over to the new dimension.”

“How do we get the pet out safely?” She bent again to take a cautious glance at the animal still sitting at the back of the cupboard. “It’s liable to make a run for it if we try to capture it.”

Eric sighed. “I really don’t want to stick my hand in there and grab it. That thing is likely to take my fingers off.”

“True.” Storey grinned at the disgusted look on his face. “Do you think we should take the two of them back to your dimension first? Then figure out how to get her home to her family?”

He looked up at her from his squatting position. “Paxton would be horrified. Besides, you’re making a big assumption here. We might not be taking her anywhere.”

Storey refused to be put off. They'd faced much bigger obstacles and overcome them; this was no different. "Any better suggestions? We have to create a game plan. And to see if these styluses are okay. They're in hibernation, according to my stylus."

"You could contact Paxton and ask for advice. I'd hate to bring these two back unannounced."

"Except that I can't communicate very well with it." The backpack had been emptied. "No sketchbook, no paper. I can ask questions and he tries to answer, but sorting out what I'm writing on a wall in the dark isn't easy. And he's not back to full strength, although I'm not sure just what that means."

Eric stood up suddenly and reached into his back pocket. He pulled out two folded pieces of paper. "I found these in your bedroom. Use them."

She opened the paper up to find the several of the first portals she'd created. It seemed so long ago, but it had been...what...only a few weeks? Her fist pumped into the air. "Yes! We could be home in minutes." Homesickness hit, draining the excitement from her system. "You went to my place? To try and find me?"

"Yes."

"How..." Unexpected tears threatened to clog her vision. She cleared her throat. "How was my mother?"

"I am not exactly sure." He stared at her thoughtfully. "They know you're missing, because they came into your room while I hid in the closet."

"They," she said, her heart sinking. "My father was there?'

"Yes."

"So, the stylus was right again," she muttered, pulling the stylus out of her pocket. "Stylus, are you back to full working power yet?"

She didn't need paper to see her hand outline *No* in

the air. "Damn."

"What's that all about?"

"We were separated too long, so it went into sleep mode, power saver mode or something. Now that it's with me it's recharging – if that's the proper word for what it's doing – but it's not all there yet. I can ask questions, but I don't think he can reach Paxton yet. Every time I ask about how long, he just says soon."

Just then noises from inside the cupboard, followed by scurrying feet, had her jumping back and out of the way as the skorl raced out. Eric was faster. He scooped it up and tucked into the front of his coat.

The little creature struggled and squealed worse than a pig only in a much higher-pitched voice. The sound rose in volume like a damned siren. Storey clapped her hands over her ears. "Make it stop."

With a grimace, he said, "I don't know how." He looked around. "Find something to carry it in, will you?"

Storey raced to the cupboard. Surely there'd be a container of some kind.

The sound of running feet was her only warning, then Eric yelled, "Hey, stop that!"

Storey spun around to find the Louer child, at least she figured that's what it was, screaming at Eric and pounding on his chest.

And what a noise came out of her mouth. Storey had never heard anything like it. And didn't want to again. *Jesus.* The squealing skorl had nothing on her. "Eric. Give it to her. She thinks you're hurting it."

"What?"

Storey shook her head and raced over. Eric was getting pounded on from both sides. And getting madder by the minute. She couldn't blame him. Storey wrapped her arms securely around the child, who came up to her ribs, but was probably close to Storey in weight, and pulled her back off Eric. Then she clapped a hand over the child's mouth to try to stop the weird noise coming out of her mouth.

It helped, but only a little bit. "Eric, show her the pet. She needs to see that it is okay."

Eric rolled his eyes and reached inside his jacket for the squealing animal. As soon as the skorl saw the child and the child saw her pet, they both shut up. The child put out her arms and Eric placed the animal in them. The girl's arms squeezed the small animal tight.

Silence.

Except for a sniffling sound out of the little girl. Eric closed his eyes for a moment. "Blessed silence."

Storey couldn't agree more.

"Can you talk to her?"

He glared at her in horror. "I don't speak Louer. No one does."

"Wrong. My stylus does."

The child rained kisses on the matted varmint. And didn't the damn thing stay like it needed the affection as much as the child did? Storey shook her head and on a corner of the first of the two papers Eric had brought, she asked her stylus if he could write Louer.

"Yes."

"Can you write a note to this child that we mean her no harm and we'd like to help her, please?"

Her hand instantly started to move, writing out weird and wonderful characters in a close, tightly woven script similar to those on the side of the stylus itself. The writing had a delicate grace to the flowing characters. When she finally stopped writing, she'd filled the top quarter of the paper. And fast. The message was illegible. "Stylus, are you sure she can't read English?"

She's too young to read written English. Her native language speaks to her differently.

"Differently how?"

But she stood up to hold the paper in front of the child. Hoping she could understand it.

The child's eyes widened as she looked at the writing, some of the fear dropped off her face and relief filled her gaze. Her gaze went from Eric, to the paper and then Storey. Tears filled her eyes and she threw herself into Storey's arms, crumpling rodent and paper together.

Storey had to wrap her arms around her. But staring at Eric over top of the girl's head, she asked, "Do you have any idea what the stylus wrote?"

"Heck no."

Chapter 7

THEY'D AGREED TO bring the child to Eric's home. There they could enlist Paxton's help in finding the right way to return her to her family. At the moment, they hadn't been able to do even that.

Eric couldn't get his codexes to work.

The child – they so needed to find out what her name was – had curled up in a tight ball at Storey's feet. Sleeping as if she hadn't slept in months or at least since she'd been left alone. The skorl, although not asleep if the malevolent look in its beady eyes was anything to go by, had tucked itself into the curve of the girl's waist.

Storey studied the chunky looking girl. She could see the similarities to the Louers they'd banished earlier from the Toran dimension. They were a taller, stocky race, but she hadn't had an idea of what the females looked like. She still had the broad forehead, thick nose and flat high cheekbones. Yet there was a more delicate, feminine cast to her features.

Regardless of her misgivings, the child had to be returned to her parents. That's all there was to it.

And who knew better than Storey how that process would go? "Are the codexes really broken or are you looking for a way to avoid taking us back?" Not that she'd blame him if he was. She might pull that very trick if their positions were reversed.

He snapped, "The codex problem has nothing to do

with her. They worked originally, then there was a set of weird musical commands that I didn't, and still don't, understand. The last thing was a message in Toranee code that I finally understood to be your name. But before I could understand what or why, you were there, standing in front of me."

"The stylus. It probably contacted your codex to let you know my location."

Eric frowned. "Is that possible? Did he ever contact my codex before?"

It was Storey's turn to frown down at the codex. "I know it's tracked your codex, because that's how I found it when you lost it in the basement that time. But I don't know if the stylus ever tried to contact it directly. Then again, who knows."

Eric bent his head to the codex again. Once more he typed in Paxton's lab and once again, nothing happened.

"I wonder if the stylus did something so you couldn't go back without me. So I wouldn't be left here."

He glowered at her. "Then you'd better ask it."

With a soft groan, she pulled the stylus out of her pocket and grabbed the one piece of paper she had at her disposal. "Stylus, are you getting stronger?"

Yes.

She smiled triumphantly at Eric. "See. It even feels stronger in my hand."

"Yes, but is it ready to go? We need to get moving." He pointed out the sleeping pair at their feet. "We're going to have enough trouble when she wakes up. And communicating is going to be one of the biggest problems. Not to mention she'll expect us to help her and we don't even know what the stylus wrote in the message to her."

"Then let's start there with the questions." She twisteded the paper so that she had a clean corner to write on.

"Stylus, what did you tell the Louer girl?"

Her hand wrote quickly. *That she is safe now and that you were going to take her to her parents. And that she should trust you as you'd see her safely home.*

Eric groaned. "Why would it say that? We don't even know how to help ourselves at this point, let alone getting her home."

Storey stared at the words she'd written. "Maybe because that's how I felt." She gazed at Eric soberly. "The connection between us has deepened. It's almost as if I know what it's going to say. Maybe it has the same impression of my feelings?"

"That doesn't make sense. Why would it deepen when you'd been separated to the point where it almost went to sleep?"

"Maybe that's exactly why. To keep the connection there, to save the Louer souls inside from becoming a nothing shell like the other styluses that were outgrown, packed away and forgotten."

Storey studied the stylus in her hand. The connection did feel different. It was a little hard to explain but it felt deeper. Odd, but not unpleasant.

"Stylus, are the other styluses asleep like you were?"
Like I was in the process of becoming, yes.
"But there are souls in each one?"
Yes, especially the broken one.
She frowned. "What can we do for them?"
Nothing at the moment. Keep them safe.
"And later? Is there something we can do later?"
Yes.

Good. Glancing at Eric, she asked. "Stylus, did you do something to Eric's codex so that he couldn't leave without me?"

No. Had to change his codex to old programming to tell him you were here. His codex works but it needs to be programmed manually.

From the look of horror on Eric's face, she assumed the news wasn't to his liking.

"Stylus, can you revert the process on Eric's codex or reprogram it so we can return to Paxton's lab?"

Yes. But it takes time and energy.

Back to square one. The stylus wasn't fully up yet. Shit. The more she asked it to do, the more it wore down. And she was almost out of paper. Storey frowned. "Is there more paper here, Stylus?"

No.

"So, I have to go back to Paxton's lab to get something to write on?"

No. Go home. Paper there.

Ah. Storey sat back, an idea firing in the back of her mind.

"Why is it I don't think I'm going to like whatever you're thinking?" Eric's voice broke through her reverie.

"Let's go to my house. There's paper there, beds and food. I have no idea about my parents. We'll deal with that when we get there. Hopefully we can be there at least long enough for us to restock, reevaluate and figure out what to do. It's obvious we can't stay here. We have to go somewhere, and if you don't want to go to her new dimension, or take us to your dimension, then that only leaves my dimension." She thought she'd been the voice of reason, but from the frown on Eric's face, it didn't appear as if he agreed.

"And how are we going to get there? The codexes are on 'manual mode,' remember? Do you know how to program mine or your dimension on my codex so we can go anywhere?" he asked, the sarcasm thick on his voice.

She flipped the paper over and held up the portals. "We still have these." Although, she'd written on the portal to Bankhead mine, the other portal that she'd used to travel Paxton's lab from her bedroom, hadn't been touched. "I can change this so we can portal to my bedroom."

He closed his eyes and bowed his head. "It's not perfect, but it's better than staying in this hellhole. From there I can always go see Paxton and try to sort out the next step in this mess." With a nod toward the sleeping child, he said, "What about her?"

Storey was already working on adapting the one portal entrance. Thankfully it was almost perfect for here. She lifted her head from the sketch. "We take her with us. Believe me, I'd rather take her to her dimension right away, but not without a fully functioning stylus and lots of paper, thank you. Not to mention having your codexes working properly again." Storey shook her head. "No thank you."

"So, we hide away at your place until the stylus is stronger?" He cocked his head and waited.

"Unless you want to hide away in your dimension, instead."

"Paxton will see us. They've stepped up the monitoring of all crossings since the Louer invasion."

"Exactly."

"Fine. Let's go then. I don't know how we're going to keep her quiet though. That squeal of hers and her pet is going to cause a ruckus at your house."

"Another reason to have the stylus get back to full strength and to have more paper so he can write messages to her. If she understands we have to be quiet to get her home, then maybe – and I'm only saying maybe – she'll listen. I do know she's expecting us to solve her problems now and that includes me feeding her. Do you want to tell her there's no food when she wakes up?" She raised an eyebrow at him.

He stood. "Let's go now. I won't rest until we're out

of here."

ERIC GLARED AT the codexes. How was he going to fix them?

Storey nudged his arm and pointed at the child who was starting to stir.

With an eye roll, he said, "Let's go then."

Bending over, Storey laid the paper on the floor. "I think this should work."

"Think." He didn't like the sound of that. "What if it doesn't? Can't you draw a new one?"

"Not really." She studied his expression briefly. "The stylus is not up to full power, remember? We can't overdo it."

He couldn't believe how dependent they were on technology right now. He felt naked with his codex not working properly.

"Let's go." Once again, he studied the girl and her pet. "Do we pick her up and carry her?"

"It might be best. Except for her pet. It's liable to bite your hand off."

"Yet if we wake her…"

Storey grinned at him, that clear, honest, so open grin of hers. He couldn't help but smile back, his good humor rapidly returning. If nothing else, life with Storey was an adventure. "You're the ranger, remember. And you're the male here."

"She's no lightweight."

"So it's a good thing she isn't any older." Storey motioned toward the sleeping girl. "Now would be a good time."

Eric took a deep breath and caught up child and rodent in one scoop before either could wake. He took two

steps toward Storey and walked into the portal.

STOREY WATCHED THE three disappear into her portal and whispered a prayer that this path would lead them home. She grabbed a corner of the paper and hopped in herself. The last thing she saw was the dark, dank cold of the Louer world.

Good riddance.

She tumbled into sunshine. Sunshine and nothing else – no buildings and definitely no bedroom.

"Oh shit."

"Ya think?" Eric stood beside her, still holding the sleeping child. Her pet, now awake, glared at them. Maybe as long as it was being held tight in the child's arms he wouldn't take off. Storey would have much preferred to have had it in a cage.

First things first. "Any idea where we are?"

"No. You?"

"Not yet." She turned around, puzzled. "But I will. This can only be one of three dimensions."

"Great." Eric shifted the load in his arms. "If we get caught by Louers, this isn't going to look so good."

He was right.

Time to get serious, again. "Stylus, we need help and now. I don't know where we are. We're trying to get to my house. Help."

In a shaky script, the stylus wrote, *You're only halfway. Go through the portal again.*

Storey and Eric stared at each other in horror.

Eric spun around at her words. "What. We are? Here?" He shook his head. "As in the *new* Louer dimension?"

She put the sheet of paper with the portal back on the

ground. "Let's take another jump and see if it will take us to the right destination."

With a nervous glance around, Eric gave an abrupt nod and stepped in. Storey followed immediately.

And fell into her room.

"We're home," she crowed. She turned around a huge grin on her face. "Finally."

She couldn't believe how good it felt. Her bedroom. Different than she remembered, it looked like her mother had changed her bedding. Still, after all she'd been through, she was finally home. Clean clothes, a shower, food. Definitely food.

She motioned to the bed for Eric to lay the child down.

He did so carefully, asking, "What about your parents?"

Her smile fell away. "Right. That problem. Damn it." She studied Eric. How could she explain he was a ranger from another dimension and they'd brought a child of yet a third dimension and a weird pet home? What could she possibly say?

Shit. Instead of solving one problem, she had three more. Not that Eric was a problem. He was about the only good thing here.

Were her parents at home? How could she find out without drawing attention to herself and her entourage? She wanted a shower and a change of clothes so bad. The clothes she could grab. The shower – not if her parents were home. She looked out the window, realizing it was daytime. And likely early. She didn't know what day of the week or what day of the month it was, but at least the sun was shining. That meant there was a chance, a slim chance that her parents weren't home.

She opened her bedroom door and stuck her head around the corner. The house was silent. For the moment.

"Eric, I'm going to slip downstairs and see if we are alone. If we are, I'll search for food. Stay here with her."

Eric frowned.

"It's the only way. Don't wake her up."

Eric's gaze widened in horror, panic starting in his eyes. "You can't leave me with her."

"I'll be back soon." She closed the door softly and crept down the hallway to her mother's room. The door was ajar and it was dark inside. Empty. That was a good sign. At the top of the stairs, she cocked an ear and listened.

So far, so good. Skipping the second stair, which squeaked, she made her way to the first landing and poked her head around the corner. Nothing. And no one. Thank heavens for that. In the den, she stopped and frowned. Different furniture. Had they bought new furniture while she'd been gone? She crossed to the corner of the den where the Louers had tried to enter the house. A smirk broke free. Typical. Her mother had already repainted.

Just to be sure, she checked the garage and front driveway and breathed a sigh of relief. There were no vehicles in sight.

She headed to the kitchen. They might have lucked out this time, but her parents could return at any time. In the kitchen she tried to find food that she could grab easily and take to her hungry guests. She collected a box of granola bars, a pound of cheese and a loaf of bread. After further hunting, she found a package of ham, a bag of apples and a bag of mini carrots. There was also a full jug of orange juice. With her large haul, she raced back up to her bedroom.

Just in time.

A rising caterwaul shrieked through the bedroom door.

"Eric. Open the door." It opened immediately, making her suspicious he'd been at the point of coming after her.

His eyes lit up at the food. She came in and dumped the food on the bed. Immediately the rodent bounced to the middle of the pile sniffing the items.

Eric raced over. "Oh no you don't." He tried to brush the animal back. The little girl, whose eyes had grown huge at the sight of the food, opened her mouth, her bottom lip trembling. "Uh, Storey. Over here, uh, like now."

Storey walked over, smiled at the girl, and opened the loaf of bread, without any butter, she slapped some ham in between two slices of bread and handed it to the child. The girl took it, her eyes huge. She looked at the sandwich and then stared up at Storey.

"I don't think she recognizes it as food."

"I'm not sure I do either, but if you make one for me, I'll be happy to demonstrate."

Storey slid him a quick look. "You don't have ham and bread in your dimension?"

"Our bread isn't white. It's dark and full of seeds and grains. And ham, no, I don't know it." She made him one and handed it over. Eric held it up to catch the little girl's attention then took a big bite and chewed. Her face lit up and she tore into her sandwich.

Storey made herself one. Looking around her bedroom, her gaze lit on the glass of water she kept beside her bed. Getting up, she dumped the contents in the sad looking plant pot. She brought the glass over and filled it with orange juice and handed it to the girl.

"We need to find a name to call her," Storey mumbled around bites.

"Tammy."

Storey looked up at him in surprise. "Is that her

name?"

"Don't know. But she looks like a Tammy."

"That's fine with me, but that doesn't mean she'll answer to it."

"I think you need to show her what to do with that drink." Storey spun around to find Tammy had poked her finger into the juice.

"Oh crap." Storey lifted the glass to Tammy's mouth. Automatically, Tammy opened up and took a drink. And coughed several times. So much for being quiet.

Storey waited for a moment to make sure she was going to be fine, and held up the glass again. "Try it again."

This time Tammy drank eagerly, downing half the glass in one gulp.

"Any for me?"

She answered, "We can drink from the bottle."

Eric raised an eyebrow. He studied the bottle and lifted it to his own mouth. She watched the emotions play across his face as he tasted orange juice, and from the look on his face, maybe for the first time.

His face scrunched up, making her laugh. "It's orange juice," she said. "Made from oranges."

"Oranges?"

Oh boy. This was going to be fun. And she so didn't have time. In between bites of her sandwich, she explained. When done eating, she walked through her room and collected several changes of clothing, stuffing things into a much larger backpack she dragged out of her closet. Then she added several sketchbooks and a zip up jacket. Turning around, she perused her room taking in the familiar items of her childhood. Every time she left, she wondered if she'd ever come home again. "Is it safe to leave you three alone for a few minutes while I go wash up?"

Eric, in the middle of making a second sandwich, looked up guiltily. "Sure. We'll be fine." He slapped the second slice of bread onto the rest and Tammy snatched it out of his fingers. His look of astonishment had Storey laughing aloud.

"Good. Make yourself another one. Stay quiet, and I'll be back quick." She locked the door on her way out and headed to the bathroom. After one of the hottest, fastest, yet most satisfying showers Storey could ever remember having, she dressed in clean clothes, brushed her teeth and packed a travel bag. She didn't know when she'd be back again.

Once inside her bedroom, she paused. They were still eating. All of them.

The loaf of bread was almost gone. The meat was; the cheese almost was. Wow. She'd need to go raid the kitchen again. And soon. Yet, she couldn't help feeling that time was running out. They needed to go to Paxton's lab and get help.

She made a fast trip to the kitchen, constantly looking over her shoulder in case her parents came home. What could she take that they could eat while traveling? That she hadn't grabbed the first time, that is. The cupboard revealed grain crackers, flatbread and a package of tortillas. The second pass through the fridge harvested another package of cheese, leftover cooked chicken breasts, and more apples. Snatching up a shopping bag, she loaded it with everything. Then, going to the sideboard, she snatched up a bunch of perfectly ripe bananas. In one last pass, she collected as many of the packages of crackers as she could fit into the bag, a container of cheese spread, a spare jar of peanut butter, and a jar of jam. Snatching up several knives from the kitchen drawer, she hauled the groceries back upstairs and while the others all watched with great interest, she packed what she could in her backpack and then a second backpack for Eric to carry.

Heaving a sigh of relief she put on her sweater, and picked up another sketchbook before turning to Tammy. She realized that the little girl didn't have much to wear. Her face was badly in need of a washing and her shirt was grubby and torn. Would anything in Storey's closet fit her? Tammy was shorter but heavier, so…maybe. She rummaged in her bottom drawers for t-shirts and a pullover in case she got cold. Thank heavens it was still summer weather here.

"Eric, we need to get going. The bathroom is down the hall. I'm going to get her changed and pack a few spare items for her."

"Right. You do realize we're going to have trouble carrying all this."

Storey scanned the full bags. Was it enough? For how long? "I know. But did you see how much she ate? Do you want her running out of food and not be able to give her something? Not to mention her pet?"

He rolled his eyes. "Back in five."

Storey cleaned up the empty food packages, shaking her head at the sheer quantity of food they'd consumed. As she reached for the cheese, Tammy made a funny sound and held out her hand.

"More?" Tammy's voice thick and uncertain as the single word rolled out of her mouth. But it was understandable.

Storey grinned and broke off a decent sized piece for her. The rodent sat up on its back legs and looked at her expectantly. Storey sighed and broke off a smaller piece. She held it out and the rodent reached out to take it gently from her fingers. Maybe it was tame after all. They hadn't had a great first meeting and nothing since had endeared one to the other. But there was nothing like feeding an animal to make it a little friendlier. She wondered if Tammy had a name for it?

Standing up, she put the garbage in the can in her room, then packed the remaining food in the overstuffed bags. And went about trying to get Tammy into cleaner clothes.

Tammy didn't object, thankfully, but she made a weird mess of noises as she felt the different materials and colors. Her face lit up when Storey brought over the purple hoodie. Getting her into it and the zipper done up, was another issue altogether. Everything was so different to her; she kept playing with the zipper.

Leaving her to it, Storey spun around in her room, looking for something she'd had for her old guinea pig who'd died almost eight years ago. Stashed somewhere should be a small harness with bells and silver studs on it connected to a leash somewhere. Storey hadn't been able to get rid of it all these years. It really was time to clean up and clean out her childhood.

There. She grinned. The harness and leash hung on the back of the hanging clothes. Dragging it out, she eyed the rodent and the size of the leash when Eric walked in. His face lit up in understanding.

He grinned. "I'm so going to enjoy watching you put that on him."

"Him?"

"I don't know if it's a him or a her and I'm not checking, but you can do the honors."

Storey smirked, letting a little evil show through. "Except we really have to get going and Tammy needs to be taken to the bathroom and have her face washed. So which job do you want?"

His laugher fell away as he understood the choices. "That is so not fair." But he held out his hand in resignation.

Storey motioned for Tammy to come with her, and she led her out into the hallway, closing the door firmly behind them so Eric could do his job. In the bathroom, she spent more than a few minutes trying to show Tammy what she was supposed to do and how. Finally, giggling so hard she had tears in her eyes, Tammy got it. Storey grabbed a washcloth, warmed it up in hot water and set about scrubbing the little girl's face. By the time they were both done, the girls had laughed themselves silly. And the unmistakable odor surrounding the little girl was much improved.

Feeling better, Storey led Tammy back to the bedroom, ready to go to Paxton's place next. Opening the door to her bedroom, she found Eric sitting on the bed, the rodent happily playing with the leash, the harness buckled securely around his chest. Tammy grinned and ran over to look at the fancy chain and the colorful ribbons.

"If he's a boy, he might not appreciate the color," Storey said.

Eric looked at her, his head tilted to one side and said, "Huh?"

Storey rolled her eyes and said, "Forget it. A human joke. That's all."

He quirked one eyebrow at her. "So are we ready, or do you want to wait until your parents return?"

Even as the last of the words rolled out of his mouth, she heard the sound of a vehicle driving up the driveway. "Oh shit." Storey ran to the window to make sure, but there they were. She winced. Both of her parents were exiting the vehicle.

"Time to go. Eric, you first. And take Tammy and her pet with you."

"This is only going to take us to Stanshore Mine though, you know that. We might not be able to get out of there."

"Paxton will have the crossing monitored, and we'll be close enough to contact him." She gave him a little push, hearing her parents entering through the front door. "Go, go, go. I don't want them to find out. They'll never let me leave again."

"They won't be able to stop you as long as you have the stylus," he reminded her.

"Yeah, thanks for that." She was already scribbling a note on a piece of school paper. "What are you waiting for? Get moving," she whispered. Eric shouldered the largest backpack and held out his hand for Tammy. Storey picked up the rodent and as one they stepped into the portal.

In a flash they were gone. "Thank goodness for that." She took a quick look around. It was obvious someone had been in her room, there was no way to help that. Storey dropped the note on her bed. Hearing footsteps coming up the stairs, she grabbed the other backpack, and hanging onto a corner of her portal picture, she entered, dragging the paper through with her. She didn't dare leave it behind for her parents to accidentally fall through.

The last thing she heard, was her mother's hopeful voice calling her, "Storey, honey, is that you?"

And the sound of the door opening followed by her mother's gasp of surprise.

Then all Storey could see was blackness.

They'd gotten out just in time. As much as relief pulsed through her, so too did a pang of homesickness. Her mother didn't deserve this. Surely she could have stayed behind long enough to reassure her that everything was okay. But she wouldn't have understood and Storey couldn't explain, not now, and not in any way that would do any good.

Maybe that note would help ease her mother's pain.

Or maybe not.

Chapter 8

S TOREY LANDED OFF center and fell forward onto her knees. "Shit."

Eric stepped forward and grabbed her elbow. "Are you okay?"

It took her a moment, but then she stood up unsteadily, more from the panic of leaving and the remorse of hurting her family than her fall. "I'm fine. My mother walked in as I left."

"She didn't see you, did she?"

"No. I just heard her call and the door open as I went through." Storey sighed, already wishing she'd stayed and said something. "Maybe I should have stayed and explained things to her."

"Do you really think you could have?"

"No." And she didn't. Still, the warm concern in Eric's voice made her straighten and smile reassuringly at him. Fatigue lined his face. He hadn't had it easy either, this last week. Unlike her, he hadn't had a shower.

And somehow, Tammy had gone from standing beside him to riding piggyback. Eric didn't appear to mind, even when the rodent sat up on his shoulder to stare down at Storey.

She had to grin. Eric had gained two friends. Turning around, she scanned the familiar mine. "Any idea if your codex will work here?"

"It should. It's a number code only for there. If you're

ready, let's go before Paxton wonders what we're doing here." He started punching in numbers. The resulting musical ringtones made her chuckle. How many times had she heard those? They almost sounded like a home-coming party. Seeing the start of the black fog rising around their ankles, she stepped closer. "Hope this works."

Through the deafening stillness, he said, "Me too."

She shuddered at the thought of anything else going wrong. Honest to God, she needed something to go right for a change.

"We're here." Eric's warm, comforting voice had her opening her eyes to see his staring into hers, amusement lighting their dark depths. Her response was instant. A warm smile unfurled. "Sorry, I'm still not used to that." Tammy's huge saucer eyes staring at her, her arms wrapped in a vice grip around Eric's neck.

"Easy, Tammy. It's all right." Storey reached a sooth-ing hand to stroke Tammy's knee, feeling some of the rigidity leave her stocky frame.

He stretched his neck slightly, easing the tightness. "Is she okay? She's getting heavy."

"Harrumph."

Eric and Storey stilled and turned as one to stare at Paxton. Storey grinned and threw herself into his arms. "Paxton!"

He flushed multiple shades of white and pink, his arms closing awkwardly around her. "Storey, what happened to you?"

She pulled back, her smile flashing even brighter at his obvious embarrassment. She couldn't help looking around, delighted to see the familiar lab. Everything pristine white, all surfaces bare and clean, monster-sized monitors filling the room so he and his assistants could track all activity regarding dimension crossings.

"It's so great to be back here. I know I wasn't gone for long, but it seemed like forever."

"But where were you?"

"In the Louer dimension. Compliments of your leader, I believe," she added darkly.

His eyes widened in horror. "Oh dear. I'd so hoped he wasn't involved." Paxton lifted his head to look at Eric, his face pale, his eyes disturbed. "Eric?"

Storey was looking at Paxton when it happened. He bolted backwards, his eyes widening in horror. His jaw worked but no sound came out.

"Oh no. Here it comes." Eric tried to shift Tammy off his back so he could explain her presence to Paxton. Immediately the horrific wailing erupted from her mouth.

"Oh God, Eric, we have to make her stop." Storey raced over. "Tammy, stop. It's all right. Please stop."

Tammy buried her face against Eric's back and screamed at the top of her lungs. Storey reached into her backpack for the cheese she'd put in at the end. Ripping off a chunk, she held the piece out to Tammy. "Here, Tammy, cheese."

Tammy's head tilted her way, her nose wrinkled in spite of the piercing noise still coming out of her mouth. Her eyes opened and her gaze latched on to the cheese. Instantly the noise stopped as she started eating the treat with tiny bites.

Eric's shoulders slumped with relief. "I don't know what you gave her, but please tell me you have enough to keep her happy until she's returned to her parents."

Storey laughed. "Yeah, that I can't do. I'm hoping she'll take other food too, though." She held out her arms to Tammy and with a gamin grin, Tammy dropped like a stone from Eric's back and ran to Storey, wrapping her arms around her middle.

Groaning, Eric straightened. "She is not a lightweight."

"What…what is she?" Paxton cleared his throat several times, his gaze locked on Tammy's face. He shook his head. "No, she can't be."

Eric walked over to his old mentor. "Paxton, it's okay. She's only a child." He quickly explained, ending with, "She was the only Louer left in her complex. We couldn't leave her there."

Paxton's head had swiveled from Eric's face to Tammy's and back again several times. There was no softening in his features at the explanation, but Storey could see his mind spin with the options. "We couldn't leave her behind, Paxton. She had no food, no clothing, no one."

With another quick shift to look at Storey, Paxton asked, "Why didn't they go back and get her?"

Eric looked over at Storey. "According to Storey's stylus, there's something wrong with the portal. They can't return to their old world. Effectively cutting off both groups from each other. The complex where we found her is empty. I doubt she knows about any other complexes given her age. I'm sure she'd have died if we'd left her."

At Eric's last words, some of the rigidity in Paxton's spine and his shoulders relaxed slightly. Thank heavens for that. Paxton wasn't the boss here, but he held a lot of power.

"Thank you for understanding." Storey did appreciate it. As she'd already found out, having Paxton on her side was huge.

Paxton said, "You're going to take her home?" It wasn't a question as much as statement of fact.

"Well—"

But Storey cut Eric off in midsentence. "Yes. I'm going to take her back to her family."

Paxton nodded once as if he'd expected no less. "What do you need?"

Storey explained, "My stylus went into some kind of power saver mode while we were separated over in the Louer dimension, but it's taking a long time to recharge. I want to make sure it's fully functioning before traveling again. Also, because it was having trouble communicating, the stylus switched the codex to using Toranee code, or something." Storey turned to Eric. "Right?"

"The stylus can't reverse the change until it's back to full power."

"We'll need to reset the function panel." Paxton latched onto the one thing he could do something about. "Give it to me." Eric took off both machines and handed them over. Paxton bent his head, muttering to himself. "Yes. Interesting. Haven't seen this in decades. Hmmm." He walked over to one of the desks and pulled out a series of wires and odd black rubber attachments.

"Ah Eric, I think we need to tell Paxton about the rodent, too. Before he finds out the hard way."

Eric rolled his eyes. "Smart." He walked over to where Paxton worked. "Paxton, we forgot to mention that Tammy has her pet with her. That's the reason she missed the move to the other dimension, so we figured we'd better bring it too."

"Pet? What pet?" His gaze turned from Eric to Storey before latching onto Tammy's face. The rodent sat on Tammy's shoulder, his cheerful harness and leash looking bizarre against his dark fur. "Oh dear. Yes. Yes, please keep it on that leash at all times. Oh dear." He shook his head once and turned back to the table and the codexes in front of him.

Eric walked back to Storey. "See? Easy."

"We'll see about that. So far, nothing has been easy," he retorted, his wry grin belying the sharpness of his words. "How do we find out what the stylus needs to return to full health?"

Storey didn't need to think about that. "We ask it. But the more we ask of it right now, the less it can rejuvenate."

"What then?" Eric raised an eyebrow in question.

"Then we ask Paxton's stylus what it needs."

Eric sat back, a frown on his face. "Oh. That makes sense."

"Can we sit somewhere? I'd like to grab a sketchbook and see how the stylus is doing."

Eric pointed to the table where she'd sat toward the end of the celebration they'd had the night before. She stopped. Night before? Surely it had been longer. And it might have been. Time had become beyond screwy.

Leading Tammy over, she pulled out chairs for both of them and showed Tammy how to use one. Tammy grinned and bounced on the chair several times. Only stilling her antics long enough to watch curiously as Storey opened her bag to remove a sketchbook. Tammy grabbed it and tried to bite the end.

"No. This isn't food." Storey dove back into her bag and pulled out a red apple. She handed it to Tammy who looked at it and frowned. Storey took a bite, showed Tammy the inside. Tammy immediately bit into the apple. Her eyes grew rounder and she bounced several more times.

"I think she likes it," murmured Eric.

"Good thing. We know what happens when there's something she doesn't like." She hurriedly looked away as the skorl took a bite from the other side of Tammy's apple. Shudders rippled across her back. She so didn't want to share her meal with that thing.

Opening her sketchbook, she pulled out her stylus and studied the markings on the side. Now if only she knew what they meant. Something she'd have to ask her stylus about later.

"Stylus, we need information." She held her hand over the corner of a blank page of her sketchbook. "What do you need to get to full power?"

Time.

"Why is it taking so long?"

Damaged.

"Damaged?" Eric and Storey both bent to study the pencil. Twisting and turning it, neither could see any damage. "What kind of damage?"

Souls. We are getting older. Will need a new soul soon.

"Soon? As in how soon?" Storey frowned at Eric.

Within the next decade.

Storey and Eric both relaxed. "Good. That gives us a little time to figure that part out. Somehow. So it takes longer for you to recharge once we've been separated. Do the other styluses need new souls too?"

Yes.

"Are the ones in there still alive?" Storey couldn't imagine their existence.

We are always in stasis. New souls will blend and all will be well.

Eric looked at Storey and shook his head. "I don't think so."

Storey studied his features. "Don't think what?"

"It's not all going to be well. We don't know how to blend souls into the stylus anymore, and even if we did, it would be against our laws to force someone to do so."

"What about volunteers? Chances are someone would be interested in living forever."

He scrunched his face in disgust. "Not me."

Storey frowned. "If my life was almost over, it would be a heck of a way to extend it. To help out my people."

"Go for it. You're not locking me inside a pencil forever."

Storey had to laugh at the way he said it. It might not

be right for him, but if her people were involved she could see a long line forming almost instantly. Especially those with a terminal illness. To live forever was a much sought after goal with her people. The novelty alone would peak interest around the globe. She could see riots happening as people vied for the dozen odd positions.

Eric glanced over at Paxton working away on his codex. "It's not an issue right now, anyway. We need to find the correct codes to take Tammy home. Can the stylus help us do that?"

"Probably."

The longer Tammy was with her, the less she looked like a Louer and the more she resembled a normal child. Speaking of which…

"I haven't seen many children in your dimension?" Eric's face twisted curiously. "Don't you guys believe in families?" she said.

The faintest pink color washed over his face. "We do, but not large ones and many people are choosing to have no children."

She didn't know what more to say to that. Paxton worked at his desk on the codexes How much had he heard? He'd stayed out of it so far, but they knew so much more about her world and she knew so little about theirs. "Sounds like both of our systems need overhauling. Not that I know much about your world."

Paxton came over, the codexes in his hand. "And that might be for the best. If you are ever captured by your government and tortured for information, you won't have any to give them."

Stilling, Storey sucked her cheeks in. Was Paxton kidding? Not that she'd ever heard him do so before. Still the thought of her government trying to get information out of her made her skin crawl.

Her feelings must have shown on her face because

Eric reached out and placed a comforting hand on her shoulder. "That's not going to happen." He smiled reassuringly at her.

But what did he know?

A small hand crept under hers. Tammy. Storey put on a happy face for her. Keeping her voice light and soothing, she said, "It's okay. Everything will be fine."

"Hmpph. Says you," Paxton grumped, "You need to take her home before anyone else finds out she's here."

"I'd like to. The longer she's away, the harder it is on her, too." Storey pulled off her sweater and set it on the chair. She picked up the codexes. "So Eric will be able to use these now? Easily?"

Paxton went to speak then stopped. Storey stared at him but he silently pointed at the marks on her arm. She shrugged. "I don't know how, where, or when I got them."

Luckily Paxton stayed quiet, thinking heavily if his furrowed brow and distant gaze was anything to go by. Storey exchanged looks with Eric. He raised one brow but stayed quiet.

After a moment, Paxton continued as if the subject of her new honor marks had never been brought up. "Yes. I've recalibrated their functions. Everything is normal."

"Perfect." She watched as Eric picked up the closest codex, his fingers checking the systems until he was satisfied they were working properly. "Are you good now?"

"Yes." He clipped the first one on his wrist. Pushing the second one her way, he added, "Put that one on."

As instructed, she clipped hers on. Tammy made oo-ing sounds at the shiny look of it. Together the two girls admired the flashy armband. Tammy held out her arm. Paxton shook his head hard enough for his hair to fly off in all directions again.

Tammy's face puckered up.

Eric's voice cut through the room. "Storey, look out."

Just in time, Storey pulled a granola bar from her pocket. The shiny, brightly colored wrapper instantly caught Tammy's attention. Her eyes lit up and she grabbed it from Storey's hand. Turning it over and around, she admired all the colors.

"I don't think she knows she can eat it."

"You mean eat what's in it. We don't want her eating the wrap—"

Tammy shoved one end of the bar, wrapper and all in her mouth and bit down.

"Oh shit." Storey tried to take the bar away from her, but Tammy's eyes widened and her teeth clamped down even harder.

Storey dug into her bag and dragged out a second bar. Sitting back in front of Tammy again, she ripped open one end and took the flat bars out. Tammy blinked, watching Storey's every move. Then Storey took a bite of one of the two bars, and put the bright wrapper on the table.

In the sudden silence she realized several things. The first was that Tammy appeared to understand the concept of wrappers as she removed the packaged bar from her mouth and worked at ripping the end off like she'd seen Storey do; and two, the two men were staring at the spare half of the granola bar in her hand.

Her gaze widened as Eric swallowed. With a big sigh, and realizing that males appeared to be the same whether in her dimension or Eric's, she held out the unbitten piece to Paxton and the half with the bite taken out of it to Eric.

Both men accepted and bit into the treat; Eric, with obvious relish, and Paxton, with great interest but also trepidation. Eric had already eaten food at her house, whereas Paxton had very little experience with anything human – just her.

"It's okay Paxton. It might be different to you but it's perfectly edible."

He raised his gaze to her as he bit hard and the honey and almond flavor filled his mouth. He reared back slightly and blinked. "What is it?"

"We call it a granola bar. It's food that we use for traveling, snacks and even kids' lunches."

Eric hadn't wasted time on words, having finished his half in a few bites. "If you don't like it, that's fine. I'll eat it."

Paxton frowned at him. "It's good."

A small hand came to rest on Storey's shoulder. She turned to face Tammy to see her holding out the second half of her granola bar for Storey to share.

Storey's heart melted a little more. "Thank you, Tammy." As much as she didn't care to eat the granola bar, Tammy was clearly expecting her to have some. Deviating from that was likely to upset her. Storey reached out to accept it. She took a small bite then offered it back to her. Tammy's eyes lit up and her face beamed. She took the bar back and finished it in several bites.

"Whew. Good thing you packed a mess of food. That girl can eat." Eric's voice was an awed whisper that reminded Storey of the boys in her school back home. The more time she spent with Eric and Tammy, the more she realized that, regardless of their dimension, people were all essentially the same.

And saying that aloud wouldn't make her popular at all.

Storey considered just how much she'd changed over this last week. No longer was her mother an oddity, or her ex-boyfriend a devastating loss. High school was no longer something to get through, but an opportunity to learn.

She wondered if her school taught classes in outdoor living, astronomy, or navigation. All things she'd love to explore. Doubtful they'd have courses in alternative dimensions, travel by codex or Toran and Louer history.

She grinned at the thought. They'd be awesome classes though. Although the only human in a position to teach would be her – and her education in these areas was sadly lacking.

Maybe she could persuade Eric to come back and teach her people. *Not likely.*

"What are you snickering about?"

Storey dropped her smile. "Sorry. I was just thinking how hard it's going to be to go back to school. The courses I want to take won't be offered."

"It does make one consider how different reality can be." Eric nodded to Tammy.

Storey understood. "And like my stylus. That's so far beyond anything I'd have been able to imagine."

"Yet dimensions were totally believable."

Holding up the splayed fingers of her right hand, she counted off all the movies she'd seen with different realities and dimensions, "Star Trek, Inception, Harry Potter, Army of Darkness, Dinotopia." At the blank look on everyone's faces, she laughed. "They're all movies I've watched about different dimensions. We've been exploring the idea of you guys for decades. We have books and shows dedicated to such concepts."

"And how does reality match up?" Eric's eyes lit with humor.

Paxton stepped in. "I would like to know what shows and movies are?"

Storey opened her mouth to explain when the door opened to the lab and someone she'd met on her last trip raced inside. Memories flashed through Storey's mind of the cute young Toran fighting in the war against the

Louers. She stood and grinned at him. "Hi, Jendron."

He came to a complete stop and stared at her in surprise. His face lit up. "Hi. You're back already?"

"I didn't get a chance to go home yet."

Confusion clouded Jendron's face as he tried to work that out.

Paxton didn't give him a chance. "Jendron. Why have you come?"

His face cleared. "The Councilman hasn't shown up for the meeting. The other council members haven't been able to locate him. I've been sent to ask you for your help."

Eric stood up. "Paxton, is my father still missing?"

Paxton frowned, walking over to the control center. "Apparently."

Storey worked hard to keep her mouth shut. Inside she wanted to jump up and down for joy. Maybe the Councilman would stay missing. Lord knows, the Torans would be better off. Then she remembered that although nasty and mean, he was still Eric's father.

Paxton started working a series of keys. She wanted to go over and see what he was doing, but she suddenly became aware of Jendron's horrified stare.

"Eric."

Eric turned from Paxton's side to look at her, a question on his face. She nodded toward Jendron. Eric glanced over, then followed the direction of Jendron's gaze.

He sighed. "Jendron. Report to the Council that we are searching for the Councilman. As we are currently involved in a separate issue of the State, it is imperative that you speak of nothing you have seen here. That includes Storey's return at this time."

Jendron tore his gaze away from Tammy and her pet. His mouth opened as if to speak but Paxton glowered at him, effectively silencing any comments.

In a quiet voice, but one that brooked no arguments, Paxton said, "If you are unable to follow these orders, you will state so now, and work in another part of the government will be found for you. Do you understand?"

The huge Adams' apple in his long throat bobbed repeatedly. Finally, Jendron nodded. "Yes. I understand. My apologies."

He backed out of the room. As he went to close the door again, Storey called out, "Thanks, Jendron. It's good to see you again."

His grin flashed her way before the door shut.

ERIC WALKED OVER. "You shouldn't encourage him. He won't understand."

Storey looked at him in apparent surprise. "Is letting him know that I'm happy to see him encouraging him? I was just being friendly."

The clacking of keys came to a dead stop. Paxton turned in surprise. "What are you discussing?"

"Eric was just warning me not to be too friendly to Jendron." Her cheeky grin widened at Paxton's expression. "Guess you really wouldn't like that either, huh? No permanent residence here for me."

Weird noises came from Paxton as he continued to stare at her in dawning dismay.

Eric frowned. "Paxton are you all right?"

But Paxton's eyes were wide with shock. "It can never be. You know that, right?"

Walking closer, Eric reached out to his old friend. "It's okay, Paxton. Jendron knows the score. I just don't want anyone to get the wrong impression of Storey. She's unique. Brilliant actually. Of course the males are going to be interested."

He shot Storey a warning look as her snicker reached him. It was Paxton he was worried about. Obviously the fact that Storey was an attractive, dynamic female hadn't occurred to him or the potential problems that could arise. Eric didn't know what role he wanted her to play in his life; he just knew that he wanted her there. Only time would tell how strong the feelings were.

Life with Storey could never be boring. The relationships he'd seen between Toran mates were so peaceful and quiet that he didn't understand what kept them going. Did people talk together? Did they do anything outside of meal times? He didn't know. Paxton lived alone. His father lived alone. His peers were all like him. Young and single. The few married couples he'd met were on Council.

The decline in formal marriages might have had some effect on the declining population. He couldn't imagine being a father. Yet, he'd watched Storey with Tammy and she'd been a natural mother. He didn't think of any of the women he'd gone out with that could have handled the situation as easily.

Storey had definitely made him rethink what he wanted in a mate. And everyone looked drab and pale beside her color and energy.

"Eric?"

Shaking his head, Eric turned back to Paxton. "I'm here."

Paxton's gaze locked him in place. "Make sure you're here one hundred percent. Don't split your energies...or your loyalties."

Was that a warning? If so, of what? And why?

CHAPTER 9

"WE NEED TO get Tammy home," Storey said. "And soon."

"That's what I'm trying to make happen here." Paxton snapped. "We need to find the Councilman and you need to return that...that thing to her new home."

"That thing has a name – Tammy." Storey pointed out Tammy to the men. The little girl had curled up asleep on the floor. She never asked for anything and appeared to be comfortable without any creature comforts. Then, when she remembered the lack of luxuries in the Louer dimension, Tammy probably wasn't used to much more. "At least that's the name we've been calling her." And that was pretty arrogant of them. Pulling out her stylus, she asked, "Stylus, do you know the name of the Louer child we have with us?"

Louers' names are based on their parents' names.

She shrugged. "Does that mean you don't know then?"

I would need to know her parents' names.

"Are you feeling better, Stylus?" Storey got up to check the sleeping child for markings. Nothing visible. Walking back to the table and her paper, she said, "Tammy doesn't appear to have any marks on her."

Tammy? If you have her name why do you ask me for it? Yes, I am feeling better.

Storey chuckled. "Because it's not her real name, it's

just a name we made up." She turned toward Eric. "The stylus says he's feeling better."

"Good. Can we go then?"

"Stylus, are you now strong enough to locate this child's family so we can return her to them?"

Yes.

"Woot! Okay. How do we take her home?"

I can give you the location of where their portal landed.

"All of which is good news." Storey started to collect the few items she'd pulled from her bag in preparation for the upcoming journey.

"Can you give us the coordinates for Eric to program into the codexes?"

Yes. The stylus rattled off a series of numbers.

"Stylus, is there something I should know about trying to return Tammy to the Louers?"

A humming sound filled the air again. Just the sound perked her up. The stylus could make sounds but not speak. Knowing how and why would make her life easier. Then again, so would so many other things.

Her hand jerked so she put the stylus to paper and watched the words form. *They will not appreciate what you've done. Neither will they thank you.*

Great, so not fun. "Is there a way to deliver Tammy without upsetting them?"

No.

"Would they accept it easier if I went alone?

No. Once they understand that it was you and Eric who sent the other Louers back during the skirmish then they will capture you and keep you imprisoned.

"And their punishment would be what?" She didn't really want to hear this, but figured it was better to know what they were dealing with. Maybe it wasn't so bad.

Death.

She rolled her eyes. Of course. Eric placed a warm

hand on her shoulder. "Sounds almost familiar, doesn't it?"

"Sure does." For all the seriousness of the mission and potential outcome, she appreciated Eric's grounded humor. "I *can* go alone. There's no point in both of us getting caught."

"And that's enough of that. I should have taken you home last time. There's no way I'm letting you go blindly into something like this. We need to deliver her and get out. Fast."

"Sounds good to me." She stood and gazed into his eyes. "What's the chance of that happening?"

He frowned. "Not much, but we're not without resources. They won't understand what we're doing or that we're only trying to help, so there's no point in trying to make them."

Eric's words sounded good, but like her, he knew how much could go wrong. "Let's get started then."

FOR ALL THEIR good intentions, it wasn't a fast process. Eric needed to do a couple of trial runs with the codexes. Paxton couldn't find the coordinates given by the stylus and Storey needed to give Tammy more food. She'd tried to explain that they were taking her home to her family but Tammy just stared blankly.

Eric spoke up. "Why don't you get the stylus to write a note to her again?" He stood, hands on his hips watching as the stylus wrote a message in a language his own people didn't know. Paxton, once he understood what was happening, raced over to try and read the message himself.

He glanced at Eric, a question on his face.

"No, I don't understand it either." Eric explained,

"It's the same language that's written on the side of the styluses."

Paxton pulled his stylus out of his pocket to study the faded markings on his. "I'd never noticed."

"According to Storey, it has meaning as to the souls inside."

"Like the names of those soulbound?" He frowned and walked back to his desk. From the look on his face he was planning on researching any connection to his stylus he could find.

Eric finally turned back to Storey. Her bag was packed and Tammy bounced beside her, obviously happy with the message the stylus had given her.

"Is there any reason why the stylus can't write a message to the Louers and explain what we're doing and why?"

The look of surprise on her face irritated him. "I do get some good ideas, too, you know."

She flushed. "Sorry. It's a great idea." She dropped her backpack and pulled out her sketchbook. "Stylus, can you write a note for us to give to the Louers to explain why we have Tammy with us and that we are only trying to get her home. Would that work?"

It might.

"Good. We'd want her to have such a note anyway, as an explanation of how she'd arrived there."

The stylus scripted out a long message on the paper. After it was done, Storey carefully stored it in the outside pocket of her backpack for easy access.

"Okay, let's go." She picked up the bag and grabbed Tammy's hand. "We're ready."

Now if only Eric was. He couldn't help thinking this mission was a bad idea. Only there was no doubt that Tammy needed to go home. Damn. What happened to his old, boring life? Now look at him. Saving a child.

Helping a damsel to fulfill her quest. This was the stuff of heroes.

And he was going to be the hero.

"Eric? You can change your mind."

He grinned. "No way. I'm not going to miss out on any adventure available to me." *I don't want to go back to life like it used to be. It will happen soon enough. I'll take all the memories and store them away for the long future ahead of me.*

She looked up at him, admiration and pride washing over her pretty face.

Warmth spread through him. It felt right.

"Paxton, old friend, we're leaving. Please keep the lines open and your stylus on you at all times. This could be the worst mission ever."

Paxton's wrinkled face twisted with worry. "Are you sure you should be doing this?"

"No, but it's got to be done. Tammy needs her family and we need her away from here."

Eric held out a hand for Storey.

She placed hers in his. Trust. His back straightened. He grinned at her. "Ready?"

STOREY TOOK A deep breath as she waited for the black mist to rise up around her. Doing the right thing didn't always feel good. There was no doubt what they were doing was right for Tammy, but for herself and Eric, well…

A small hand crept into hers.

Another piece of Storey's heart melted. She looked at Tammy as she squeezed in between Eric and herself. Skorky, the name Storey had given the pet, sat comfortably on Tammy's shoulder. For all her inability to communicate, Tammy got her message across just fine. Outside of her couple attempts at speech, she'd stayed quiet – except for the horrific sounds that came out of her mouth when she was upset.

Squeezing the small hand, Storey found herself wishing she could hold Eric's hand. As soon as she'd dismissed the concept, Eric wrapped both arms around the girls. Tammy grinned and laid her head against Storey's chest. There was no sign of Skorky now. Oh there, it had slipped into Tammy's hood, its leash secure in Tammy's hand. Storey shuddered. She so didn't want that thing near her, but it would be worse if it escaped again. Paxton would have a fit.

Not to mention Tammy's reaction.

The blackness rose higher, making Storey's stomach heave. She'd been getting better at portal travel but this trip was unnerving to begin with. Still she'd made as many preparations as she could. Knowing they could end up in the middle of a group of angry Louers and have everything stolen again, she'd fashioned a chain with an odd piece of material that was similar to string, only more plasticized. With the stylus safely secured, she'd hung it around her neck to rest close to her heart. Just to be sure, she'd also folded several pieces of paper, stuffing them into her different pockets and hiding places.

The last thing she wanted was to lose her one advantage to getting home. The other styluses were safe with Paxton. He'd held them with such reverence; she knew they'd be safe with him.

The codexes had been preprogrammed to come to Paxton's lab. As long as she remembered to enter the numbers in the correct sequence. Eric had explained all that, but she'd only paid attention when he added it was a safety precaution in case they became separated.

Getting separated was *not* in her plans, but should

anything happen…

Eric's fingers squeezed her shoulder. Storey realized her eyes had closed and she'd tucked her head against his shoulder. She hated that nerves were eating her alive this time.

"It'll be okay, Storey. We can do this."

Her spirits lifted. When his gaze caught hers, she grinned. "You're right. We can. I just wish we already had."

The mist dropped away.

Her breath gushed out.

They were in a meadow. Brilliant clear skies shone above them. Warm fresh air filled her senses. Spectacular. No smog. No pollution. No Louers.

She turned in a circle as a thought hit her. "Do you build houses with your hands?"

Out of the blue and totally unrelated to anything – yeah, real smooth Storey. She sighed at the strange look on his face and explained, "I thought I'd created a copy of my world but maybe I created a copy of the original – without human interference. Although, given the vegetation, they must have an ecosystem of some kind. Hopefully that included wildlife."

"Really. We're here in the new Louer dimension, potentially facing grave danger and you want to know if I can build a house with my hands."

His astonishment had her laughing. She spread her arms wide. "Look around. There's no sign of civilization. For some reason I thought there'd be a city here but why would there be? They haven't had time to build anything. For all I know, these people are hiding in caves or tents."

His strange look got even stranger and then his shoulders started to shake. Finally loud guffaws erupted, his beautiful voice rolling over the hills. Not the smartest thing, considering the circumstances. Herding Tammy toward a large group of fir trees at the edge of the meadow, she demanded, "Just what is so funny? Geesh. You guys travel through dimensions like you're taking a Sunday stroll. Is it so strange to see that I might wonder if you can throw together cities in a day or two?"

He tried to answer, but his chuckles prevented it. He did, however, follow them to the relatively hidden position behind the trees.

Storey peered through the trees in all directions. Satisfied that no one waited to pounce on them, she turned back to Eric who still had a big grin on his face.

"So. How quickly would the Louers have created shelters for themselves?"

His laughter stopped to be replaced with surprise as if he finally understood the basis for her earlier query. "I don't know. But that's a good question."

She sighed. "Do you think they could have something pulled together by now? I'm just trying to get an understanding of what they might be doing at this point."

"I would suspect they've hidden away somewhere to assess their new location. The landscape is so different from their old home, they have to be concerned. Probably sent out a party to look around, and left the others behind. Alternatively, if they have some technology, they could have thrown up a temporary center already."

"Not helpful. Let's go." Storey lifted her backpack then held her hand to Tammy. The two started walking forward.

"Hey, where are you going?" Eric followed along. "Do you know where they are?"

"Nope. But I hear water. That's where I'd set up camp first."

"Oh." They walked in silence until the sound of rushing water was loud enough to really hear. Tammy tried to pull her hand free and run closer, but Storey wasn't sure she knew how to swim. There'd been no evidence of water in her dimension at all. Although there had to have been as Tammy would still need fluids.

"Hold on Tammy." But Tammy wasn't happy with that. She pulled and tugged harder. Rather than taking the chance of her starting to scream and bring a pack of angry Louers down on her, Storey increased the pace until she was almost running.

They crashed through small bushes to arrive at the edge of a small river. A small waterfall was the cause of the noise. Up above, where the water poured over the rocks, she could see the river widened into a wide, lazy stream. They could probably cross it on foot. Tammy was fascinated. She ran her fingers in the water and tried to splash around. Storey hung on to her with one hand and in the other hand she held the leash for the rodent. He'd survived the misty crossing and now wanted to explore. The two of them could do all the exploring they wanted – as soon as they were someone else's responsibility.

Handing the leash to Eric, Storey bent and scooped up water in her one hand and took a drink. Eric gave a shocked gasp. The second sip tasted even better. Raised in a small town like she had been, she'd often drunk from rivers and streams. Most city people wouldn't. That was their problem.

"What?"

"Is that safe to drink?" He almost shouted. "Just like that. You don't test it or anything?"

"Yes, just like that. I created this dimension to be a replica of my dimension. The water on my side is safe to drink, at least in many parts of the world, and without people to mess it up, it should be lovely and fresh. And it is." She lifted her hand toward him. "Try it."

He looked doubtful, but Tammy needed no urging, she went down on her hands and knees and put her face in the water like a dog and drank. Then she dunked her face all the way in and came up laughing. She shook her head, sending water droplets flying in all directions.

Storey and Eric laughed at her antics.

"There is so much I wish I could ask her. Like if she had water like this in her old home? Did they have trees and sky there? We saw so little and what we saw wasn't the most welcoming."

"I know. Do her people know what's edible over here? Do they know how to grow their food? Their population is so small, do they know how to survive here?"

"There is so much we don't know. They made a mass exodus from their dimension, but did they come with food, animals, tools, or hunting skills even, so can they survive here? Or have we just changed the type of prison they live in?"

"Stop feeling guilty. You've done a lot for them. They'll have to learn to help themselves, too."

"I know. I just can't help but wonder how they are doing. To have found Tammy as we did, well, I just can't imagine her being left there all alone like that."

"Well, she isn't any longer. We've brought her this far. We'll get her home."

He turned to look around.

"Uh, Storey."

"Hmmm." She was busy scooping handfuls of fresh water and drinking from her hand. Most of the water ran away before she could. But she didn't dare release Tammy's hand so she could scoop with two hands. Tammy was liable to walk out into the middle of the water. Tammy was well on her way to being soaked just from the shore.

"Storey?" Eric shook her shoulder. Gently at first. Then roughly. "Storey!"

"What?" she said in exasperation. Only his silence and odd stance caught her attention.

His tone of voice was hushed and wary. "Company."

Oh shit.

From her crouched position, Storey studied Tammy's face. Only the girl didn't appear to have noticed the new arrivals. What did that mean? She tugged on Tammy's hand, hoping to get her attention too. As Storey straightened, Tammy was automatically tugged upwards, too.

Tammy's face puckered. She turned to face Storey, a cry about to come forth when she froze.

"Oh shit."

"More like double shit."

CHAPTER 10

S TOREY TURNED EVER so slowly. She gasped. A quick scan of Tammy's face showed no joy either. Her bottom lip trembled. Not good. Her hand clenched Storey's and she snuggled tight against her side. Definitely not good. Were the strangers even Tammy's people?

The two people walking cautiously toward them were female and definitely made Tammy appear more childlike in comparison. Chunky, stocky, thick featured, they were similar to the males that Storey remembered shipping home to their dimension.

Did they know who Storey and Eric were?

They'd taken in Tammy's presence but their features in no way showed that they recognized her as one of their own people.

"Eric?" She kept her voice calm and quiet.

He answered in an equally low murmur, "Yeah. I'm here. Not sure what to do at this point."

Not liking the situation, she stepped closer to him. Tammy stayed glued to her side. "Tammy isn't liking this development."

"That's not good." He bent around her slightly to see for himself.

She waited, considering their options. The Louers were still a bit away. "Do we run?"

"Where?" he countered.

Damn. "Suggestions?"

"None."

"Aren't you the ranger here? Don't you speak multiple languages? Can't you communicate with them at least?" With a sharp motion, she tapped his codex. "Why are your codexes not translators, too?"

He lifted his arm. "That capability has never been needed before. I would have to ask Paxton about adding such a function."

"Right." The two were almost upon them. Storey stiffened at the stony looks on their faces. She tried smiling at them. No reaction. "Being friendly isn't helping."

"Pull out the message from your stylus."

"Oh right." Awkwardly, trying to keep an eye on the approaching women while working to open the pocket on her backpack, Storey finally managed to pull out the note. She straightened. Eric took it from her, unfolded it, then held it up in front of them.

The women stopped. Something flashed in their eyes. When they were still a good fifteen feet away, Storey called out, "Hello. It's nice to see you."

Both women had similar features, potentially making them siblings. Except one had short, dark hair and the hair on the other one was a lighter brown. The dark haired one glared at her.

"Great. Tammy doesn't speak verbally either. What's the chance they can communicate telepathically and sounds bother them?" she whispered.

"Noise didn't appear to bother Tammy. But telepathic communication might explain Tammy's lack of speech."

The women separated several feet as they approached. One came up on the outside of Eric and the other on the outside of Storey. Tammy freaked. Her mouth opened and the shrillest sound they'd heard yet came out of her mouth. Storey gasped and clapped her hands over her ears. From under her half closed lids, she could see the two women still strode forward. The noise didn't affect them.

"Maybe they're deaf."

"That would be wonderful right now."

Shuddering against the shrill tones, Storey bent to wrap her arms around Tammy. The shrieks reduced to whimpers. And Tammy locked her arms around Storey's neck – tight.

For a child, she was strong. Then she was going to grow into one of those Amazon women. Still, lifting her was out of the question. After a few moments, Tammy calmed enough to lift her face away from Storey's shirt.

Something poked her side. Storey turned to see one of the women had a long pole in her hand, and where that had come from she didn't know. Eric was receiving similar attention.

She frowned at the women and whispered, "What do they want?"

"To see how fat we are. To see if we're ready to eat."

Storey spun, horrified. "What?"

"Kidding," he muttered. "I think they want us to move."

He backed up closer to the water's edge, pulling Storey with him. Immediately the women poked them harder. Storey retreated more and the dark haired woman who'd been tormenting her, moved to the side and poked her more towards her back. "So do we go with them, or run across the water to the other side."

"I don't swim. Tammy probably doesn't swim. And we brought her here to find her people. How is running away going to help us?"

She hated when he was right. "Fine then."

Glaring at the woman poking her, Storey shifted her

bag on her shoulders and grabbing Tammy's hand again, she nudged her in front so they could walk forward. Tammy walked but she wasn't happy. She kept an eye on the women and the tears looked like they'd fall at any time.

"Tammy is so not happy."

"And what can we learn from that?"

"That's she not overjoyed to see some of her people?"

Eric whispered, "I got that. The question is why?"

With the two women now bringing up the rear of their little group, they walked for close to fifteen minutes. She was itching to drag out one of her portals and escape to Paxton's lab. Except, Eric was right. They'd come here to find Tammy's people. And they'd found them.

Only no one appeared to be happy about it.

Eric's words echoed her thoughts. "We don't know for sure that Tammy is wanted here."

She gulped. "Surely, anyone would be devastated to lose a child."

They kept walking forward. Storey's eyes searched from one side to the other. There was no sign of other Louers. No possessions. No buildings. No activity.

"Maybe, maybe not. They can't have it easy yet and Tammy is just another mouth to feed."

"So do we take her home again?"

"Your home or my home? You know how my people feel. We only have to consider Jendron's face when he saw her to understand that. Fear does that to a society."

"I don't know how my people would treat her. But it would be almost impossible to keep her secret. I'd have the government down on me in days. I'm sure her DNA would prove to be very different. That alone would make the scientists want to keep her under observation. What kind of life is that for her?"

"Not much of one. So forward we go then. For better

or worse."

ERIC DIDN'T LIKE any of their options. How many Louers were actually here? He had no way of knowing. What bothered him was Tammy's reaction. It's obvious the women frightened her, but why? Had she bonded too long and too hard with Storey that she didn't want to go back to her old life? Was she afraid of being punished for having run off and being left behind?

As with everything of late, there were more questions than answers. Why did parents play such a prominent role in their current difficulties? He had no idea where his own father had gone or what he could be up to. Then there was the problem of Storey's parents. Maybe they could find Tammy's parents and solve at least one problem.

Of course not.

Shepherded as they were, Storey didn't realize they'd arrived at their destination until they were suddenly surrounded by a large group of Louers. She stiffened as a large, angry looking male approached. *Oh shit.* "Eric, look at his arm."

Eric stiffened. The Louer wore a series of numbers on his arm. "Not good."

Surreptitiously, she grabbed one of the sheets of paper with a portal on it to take them back to Paxton's lab. "I don't know about you, but escape is starting to look like a good idea."

"You and me both."

Some of the younger members of the group reached out to touch Storey's long hair. Her bag was grabbed. She jerked it free, glaring at the offenders. "That's enough."

She nudged Tammy forward so everyone could see she had a Louer child with her.

Silence.

Tammy stared at them, her fingers clenching hard on Storey's hand. "Why does no one seem happy to see her?"

"I don't know." Eric held the note and slowly pivoted, showing it to everyone in the group.

"We didn't consider that there could be several different groups of Louers from the one complex. It's possible her family is in another totally different area."

"Then what do we do?" She despaired of finding an answer.

Just then a cry went up from the other side of the group. Tammy opened her mouth and an answering cry came from her.

Eric and Storey exchanged glances. "Now we're getting somewhere."

A smaller built Louer female squeezed in front of the crowd. She jumped up and down, her sturdy body vibrating in excitement. For the first time, Tammy dropped Storey's hand and ran over to the new arrival.

"Family or friend?" Storey asked in a low murmur.

"Don't know."

More Louers arrived from the same direction. What fascinated Storey was the sheer lack of expression on the faces of the others in the group. As if they were completely unaffected by the scene playing out in front of them. They continued to watch Storey and Eric. As if nothing else mattered. Storey also had the weird sensation of a low buzz going on in the ethers around them. Telepathic communication maybe?

Even the new arrivals failed to show any emotion. Storey hated it. Tammy had been through a lot and she'd done it with remarkable calm. Now she knew why. She'd learned from her elders.

Storey and Eric turned slowly as if to check out their surroundings, but were in fact wondering if they were knee deep in Louers on all sides. The answer was yes.

Storey sighed. "Suggestions?"

"We could run for it. Tammy has found someone to be with. Whether they are her parents isn't the issue. She's found someone who can help her more than we can at this point."

"So on the count of three, we run back toward the river and pop through a portal?"

Relief showed on his face. "Sounds good."

She grinned. "Can we find a way to get through this wall though? Or do we try to open a portal here and disappear without any of them jumping in too?"

Eric searched around. "We barely have room to open it. I say break through the line to the left."

Trying not to be too obvious, Storey checked out where Eric had mentioned. There were only a couple of Louers on that side with a space between them. She could go low and Eric could probably just bolt through.

"One, two and three…"

The blow came out of nowhere. Exploding on the side of her head like it did, she barely saw Eric crumpling to the ground as the ground rushed to meet her. A horrible cry erupted from Tammy.

Storey's cheek bounced twice on the ground then the world went black.

ERIC WOKE SLOWLY, his head pounding in agony. Bright sunlight beat down on his poor eyes, making it hard to open them. He gulped the fresh air, grateful it was not the stinky fumes of the Louers' old home.

After another moment, trying to remember where he was, he attempted to roll over. An explosion went off inside his head. He collapsed backwards. Getting his next breath became a challenge. Finally he succeeded, somewhere around the same time the pain became manageable.

He drew on his ranger training to try and assess the damage. Aching pain in the head, but…the rest of him appeared to be fine.

"Storey?"

No answer. With that the memories came rushing back.

Please let her be here. He did not want to have to chase around this dimension looking for her. And he wouldn't leave without her. With one, then a second deep breath, he rolled over slightly, this time managing the movement with minimal pain. With his eyes out of the direct sun, he tried opening them again. All he could see was bare ground. Casting his gaze while lying immobile he saw a line of trees further out. No guard within sight. Was he contained in any way? Or had he been left for dead? Any minute now, he'd grab his courage and try to stand up.

Now.

With uncoordinated movements, he made it onto his butt. Immediately he buried his head in his hands as the pounding took over. A head injury wouldn't do this, would it? Had they injected him with something? A drug of some kind? He had no idea what weapons the Louers had at their disposal, but whatever they'd used, it had brutal side effects.

Taking several shallow breaths, he finally lifted his head and looked around. He was alone. Left behind? Left for dead? Unwanted? Of no value? Relief mixed with worry and both were ringed with unaccountable anger. They'd taken Storey with them and had dumped him where he'd stood.

Unimportant, irrelevant, discarded.

Well, he'd see about that. First though, he had to check out what shape he was in. Giving his body a quick going over, he realized he was uninjured. That was the good news. The bad news was his codex was gone. As were the portals that Storey had insisted he stash in his pockets in case she lost hers or in case they were separated.

He had no way to communicate. No way to go home. And no way to escape.

Crap.

The loss of his codex bothered him. It was a part of him. A tool, but one that was also a lifeline to his home.

He felt naked without it. And lost.

STOREY CAME TO full wakefulness in a flash. She didn't move, instinct telling her she was in a new, unknown place. Her brain struggled to sort out what her eyes were seeing. She appeared to be in a small cave. *Again a cave.* The fresh smell reassured her she hadn't ended up back in the Louers' dimension. The top of the small space rose less than a dozen feet above her head. Light shone from the side, but in pale, weak rays.

There wasn't a sound. No Louers, no running water, no wind whispering through the trees. Silence filled the space, making it uncomfortable as anxiety filled the emptiness. And what about Eric? Was Tammy okay?

What about her stylus? Her hand slapped against her chest. Panic threatened to cut off her airways. Then she found it. The stylus was caught against the band of her bra. *Oh thank God.*

With the stylus, she had hope.

She rolled to the right and pushed onto her elbow to look around. Nothing and no one. The back of the cave stretched only a few feet behind her, offering nothing but more dirt and rock. Light shone in from the mouth of the cave.

With that, she did a personal assessment. She felt no physical pain and although stiff, she could move everything. Still, her codex was missing. Her backpack was missing. And her pockets appeared to have been emptied. Damn, she could use a granola bar right about now. And paper. Crap. All her paper was gone. Every pocket she'd manage to stuff a piece of paper in had been cleaned out. She groaned. Her stylus and no paper. Figured.

Well, she'd been there before.

Or…maybe not. She checked her bra. A silent woot went through her brain. She had one piece of paper still hidden.

Now where the hell had Eric gotten to?

Damn.

The entrance of the cave beckoned. Was she a prisoner? Was she even still in the same dimension? She peered around the edge of the rock face. Another big meadow. Trees. Blue sky and sunshine.

And no sign of Eric or the Louers.

Bouncing on her toes, her breath caught and held. Her blood pulsing with fear, she mentally counted down. Three, two, one… She bolted for the trees.

And made it to the cover of the first couple of evergreens. She hid behind the largest trunk and caught her breath. Still, no sign of anyone.

She studied the geographical area. The trees made it difficult to get a decent look. She needed to get higher. A large spruce tree with huge hanging boughs offered both protection and height. Seconds later, she'd slipped under the waist high branches and had a leg up on the next branch. Ignoring the stinging in her palms as the bark scraped her hands, she climbed from one branch to the next. Finally she made it close to the top, or at least high enough that she could look over the meadow and valley.

Cliffs dotted a large mountain off to the left. Hollows

on the side of the open faces reminded her of New Mexico and the cliff dwelling homes of the Anasazi people. She hadn't visited them herself but had studied it in school. A perfect spot for the Louers.

As she searched the area, she tried to find the river where they'd first met the female Louers. Maybe that was the shine off to the right. She was relatively safe up here and found herself relaxing to the point of taking her time and studying the area. It was almost familiar. Almost. Something about it though… Back home there'd been a place where she and her mom had often picnicked. She didn't have the same cliffs off to the side though so obviously it wasn't the exact location, yet it had the same effect of making her homesick.

Small towns like the one she'd grown up in, rivers, creeks and climbing trees were just a way of life. Being out here didn't make her nervous. It made her comfortable. Free in a way.

She hoped Eric felt the same way.

ERIC STUMBLED FORWARD, wishing his head would stop screaming at him. His stomach had already emptied once. His mouth would love a good rinse and his dry throat needed a drink.

He'd searched the area and there was no sign of anyone. The meadows and trees seemed to continue forever. Storey might struggle with all this openness being a small town girl. Unlike him. He was a ranger and was used to tough conditions. She was a schoolgirl without his training to fall back on. This couldn't be easy on her. On the other hand, she might be treated as a princess returning the lost daughter, enjoying a hot meal and a good rest.

Unlike him.

They'd emptied all his pockets. Too bad, he could use one of Storey's unending granola bars about now.

Why was there so much dratted country here? No buildings, no roads, no signs of civilization at all. How long would it take the Louers to build? Or would they live in caves? Make treehouses, or build structures of some kind? Was he to watch the ground for dugout type buildings, like into the side of a hill? Or could they throw up something instantly with a technology he had yet to hear about?

He had no idea. His people had technology that made building a relatively easy task. However, his people didn't do anything fast. They took, like Storey had once pointed out, a long time to make any decision. Therefore, although her people might need time to do the actual construction manually, they probably still completed their projects before his people, who could take years to determine and discuss the type, purpose, location, and size. It didn't take long once a decision was made, months maybe, but the decision making took years. Sad really.

And his people thought they were so advanced, so much better than the inhabitants of the other two dimensions. A thought that made him cringe as he remembered his dimensional lessons. Her world was always held up as an example of overpopulation, warmongering and power hungry politicians. Her world was theirs without controls, without regulations and with way too many people.

Everything was perspective.

CHAPTER 11

STOREY LEANED BACK against the trunk of the tree, grateful for the vantage point and somewhat safe position. Most people didn't think to look up when searching for something and she didn't think she could be seen from where she sat. All she needed now was Eric.

Settling back against the tree a little more securely, she pulled her stylus out from her shirt. Undoing the strap she'd used to tie it around her neck, she immediately felt the hum on her hand as the stylus woke.

"Hey, Stylus," she said, feeling a little odd without paper in her hand. "I have almost no paper to write your answers, so if there is another way to do this, now would be a good time to learn." Her hand slapped down on her jean leg. Immediately the words shone on her jean material.

Can write on anything.
"Good. That's excellent. Where is Eric?"
Walking.
"Alone?"
Yes.
"Close by?"
Yes.
"Where are the Louers?"
Hidden.
"Why?"
Scared.

"Is Tammy okay?"

Yes.

"Good. Then I can find Eric and go home. Right?"

Right.

Now she was feeling better. Except she didn't feel totally better. She stared down at her pant leg and realized she'd run out of space soon.

"Is Tammy with her family?"

No.

"No? Where is she then?"

With the Louers.

"Why not with her family?"

Her family isn't here.

Oh shit. That wasn't good. "They will they take her to her family, right?"

No.

She closed her eyes, her stomach churning with fear. "Why not?"

Tammy is the daughter of the leader of the Louers, but has been taken prisoner by this small offshoot group.

Oh shit. "Is she hurt?"

She's unharmed.

Right, to the stylus it was the same thing. Not to her though. "Is Tammy close by?"

Yes.

"Do we need to help her get to her family?" No answer.

What was she to do with that? Then again, the stylus couldn't make decisions for her… "I don't understand what these Louers want with Tammy?"

She's to be sacrificed if her father won't step down. Not all the Louers are happy about being in this dimension. With the portal damaged, they are cut off from the others and their means to survive. They can't go home. They are scared.

Home. Back to that dark, cold place. Yuck, but then

it's all they knew. "And Tammy's father? What does he want?"

He wants to stay and build here. Says it is a better place. The others want to force him to make a new portal so they can go back.

And this is where the problem lies. With a sinking heart, she said, "Only…he can't create a portal, can he?"

No.

So if he doesn't make one, they'd sacrifice Tammy. Not nice. "Why Tammy?"

Because they recognized her. As they hate him, they also hate her. So she's become a weapon to be used.

Double not nice. Who'd have thought the Louers would have dissident groups, too? "Why did the second group come over if they didn't like it?"

They thought it would be better, but to them it isn't.

"What do they want?"

Food, housing, the things they are used to.

That was understandable. Change was hard on everyone. Change without the means to adapt to their new place would be almost impossible. "So what can I do now?"

Find Eric, then find a way to go home and stay there, or help Tammy return to her people and find a way to make the Louers happy.

She groaned. "Make it easy, why don't you. How can I possibly make them happy? I already made this dimension for them, surely that's enough."

No. They need a portal so they can go back and forth and bring equipment over to help them grow food and build their buildings.

"So if I build them a portal, will that make them happy?"

The stylus hummed. *Maybe.*

Maybe? She groaned louder. "That's hardly good

enough. With a portal they can have some people living on both sides of the dimension. Then travel as they want to and have the best of both worlds."

But Storey knew the truth. People were people no matter the dimension. Never happy.

First thing first. Find Eric.

ERIC KEPT PUTTING one foot in front of the other. It's not like there were many options. He had to find Storey. With any luck she had the means to get them back home. It would be a long time before he'd be willing to come back to either of the Louer dimensions. He could only hope that Tammy and Skorky were with her parents.

Speaking of parents, and fathers in particular, where had his gone? His father might have gone into hiding. But where? And why? It's not as if he could hide out forever. At one point, he'd have to face the Council. Unless he hoped the issues would die down.

But they wouldn't. At least not while Eric was still fighting for Storey's side.

He studied the dry ground, green, tall grasses waving slowly in the breeze and the tree branches bouncing gently higher up. The tall treetops swayed gently. From the database on Storey's world, he'd read about people who built houses in trees. There'd even been movies of some of Storey's people playing in trees, kids climbing them, playing games in and around them. An odd, but fascinating concept. He'd never climbed a tree in his life.

His survival training had pointed out the advantages of getting to the top and having a better view of the area, but there were distinct disadvantages as well. Like being trapped and surrounded by the enemy.

Then there was the actual physical attempt to climb

one. He studied a large tree at his side. The first branches were above his jumping height. His training had included running, portal hopping, cliff jumping, rope work, communications, but as he looked around the woods, he understood there hadn't been enough wilderness training. He frowned, for the first time realizing how inadequate his training actually had been. In fact, when compared to some of what Storey's people went through, his had been a joke.

His people had never experienced war, never before been invaded and had never contemplated not being at the top of the food chain – a Storey phrase that seemed even more appropriate at this time.

His gaze went from treetop to treetop, shaking his head. There. His gaze caught on something as it went past. He returned to studying it, grateful his eyes were good enough to catch the slight movement.

Catch it but not understand it. He slipped around behind the trees and crept closer. That was another thing he had yet to see here, animals, wildlife of any kind. Storey felt she'd made a complete copy of her world, but had she included the animal world in that vision? An ecosystem of insects. Had she even thought to consider removing the human element here or was that another worry they needed to consider?

He crept a little closer.

And came to a dead stop.

It was Storey.

Sitting at the top of the tree, enjoying the sunshine – for all the world as if she had no worries. Relief and frustration whipped through him. Why did she always end up on top?

"Storey?"

She didn't notice. Dare he yell at her and alert anyone around to their presence? Well, he wasn't going to climb the tree after her. So…he opened his mouth and yelled, "Storey!"

Now he'd caught her attention. She waved madly at him. He laughed. Everything she did, she did with enthusiasm. He loved that about her. As he watched, she disappeared from view. The top of the tree swayed and wiggled under his fascinated gaze as she descended the tree like a pro.

Next thing he knew, she slipped out from under the lower boughs and was running toward him.

And straight into his arms.

STOREY LAUGHED AS Eric snatched her off the ground and swung her around. Finally, she pulled back enough to say, "It's so good to see you. You collapsed in front of me and then everything went dark. When I woke up, there was no sign of you."

"You saw me collapse? Did they hit me or something?" He reached up to rub his temple. "I've had this horrible headache since I woke up."

"I didn't see anything. Although I did hear Tammy scream. I've been worried. Have you seen her at all?"

"I haven't seen anyone." He wrapped her in a second tight hug before setting her away from him, his face grim. "While I was out, they took everything I had on me. Even my codex." He held out his bare arm for her to see.

"Me too." She showed him her am. "They also took all my paper, my backpack, all the food. But…" She shot him a huge beaming smile. "They didn't get my stylus or one sheet of paper"

He groaned with relief and raised his gaze skyward in relief. "Thank heavens for that."

"But," she cautioned him, "I don't know how to

make a portal. The paper is small. I'm not sure how to make it work."

He frowned. "So close but we're not quite there. That's okay, Tammy is back with her people, so mission accomplished there."

"Um, yeah that might be a problem." She stopped and shifted her feet restlessly, her gaze wandering the treed area. How did she tell him about Tammy? "You're right about a couple of things. The stylus does appear to be working well and with its help I'm sure we can figure out how to get home."

Relief washed over his face. "When you started to speak I was sure you were going to say something I wasn't going to like."

"I am." She winced, took a deep breath and explained what the stylus had said.

"What?" His outrage rippled through the trees. She just didn't know if it was outrage for poor Tammy or for her unspoken suggestion that they rescue her. "Also consider the codexes. Do you want to leave them here? Mine is supposed to allow me to get back to your dimension without much knowledge of how to use it…" she let her voice trail off as his eyes widened in horror.

"You don't think they would use it to go to my world?" The color drained from his face.

She didn't know how to answer. "Do you want to leave that as an option. I'm pretty sure no one in your dimension will be pleased if we return without them."

Eric stared at her, resignation and acceptance slowly making its way into his gaze. "I really didn't want to hear that. But there's no way I can leave my world vulnerable to another attack."

Soberly she answered. "And there's no way I can leave Tammy in danger either."

"OH NO."

"I'm sorry. But I can't. We brought her over here. For a chance at life. Not to ensure her death." Her pleading look was impossible to ignore. And he cared too much about her to ignore it. This mattered to her. And if he was honest, he'd have a hard time walking away and leaving Tammy to her fate. Now the rodent, yeah, that one he could leave behind. He'd never understood why anyone would have such a creature as a pet. That she had a pet at all showed a socializing structure he'd never have given the Louers credit for.

"No, we can't." Standing back, he considered the issue. The two of them obviously weren't considered a threat as they'd been left behind with no guard to keep an eye on them.

They would be able to find the Louers, most likely. However, locating Tammy, sneaking her away and finding her family was an entirely different matter. He reached up and rubbed the back of his neck.

"I saw caves in a hillside up ahead." Storey suggested helpfully. "Some of my ancient people lived in similar abodes. It's possible they've taken cover there." She pointed toward the north. "It's just a short walk."

Eric studied the area, nodded decisively then reached out and snagged her hand.

He smiled down at her. "I don't want to get separated again," he said. "So don't mind if I just hang on tight for awhile."

She squeezed his hand tight. "My sentiments exactly."

They walked in casual silence for several minutes.

"I wonder why I was left in a cave?" She looked at him. "Where were you?"

"I'm presuming I woke where I fell. It was a meadow

similar to where I remember being when we walked as a group.”

“Odd. They left you where you fell, and they carried me off and left me free to leave when I woke up.” She shrugged. “Why?”

“Maybe they thought you had value and then changed their minds. Or maybe they thought we died and should be left behind. Who knows?”

“I wonder how big this group of Louers is.” Storey had been trying to figure that out. “The stylus told me about the Louers plans for Tammy.”

“And how would it know?”

“He was a Louer, once. I presume he’s got a way to tap into what they are thinking. Although it would be best if we find out for sure.”

A few minutes later, hiding behind a tree and using her pant leg to write on, she asked the stylus how he’d known.

I heard them speak of it.

Storey sat back on her heels. “Of course. Just because I was unconscious doesn’t mean that the stylus was sleeping. It would have heard everything going on. And being Louer it understood the language clearly.”

She tucked the stylus back under her shirt. “Let’s go. We need to make sure they don’t have time to put their plan into action.”

The sun shone hot in the meadow, but the shade provided by the many trees along the edge of the field gave some relief. Eric didn’t recognize many of the tree species. The sheer variety of colors and types was fascinating. Brilliant. They came to the edge of the woods and stared.

Across from the meadow stood a high cliff dotted with black caves.

Eric pulled her back behind the trees.

“Look.”

STOREY PEERED AROUND the pine tree in the direction Eric had pointed out. She spotted movement by the caves. There seemed to be almost pathways between the caves. As she watched someone walked from one to the other. She hunkered down low. "Eric, are they Louers?"

"Who else would they be?"

"I don't know. I'd just like to make sure."

"No way to do that from here." He motioned to a large clump of trees that butted up against the base of the cliff edge closest to them. "Let's sneak over there."

Following his lead, they slipped from tree to tree, then raced as fast as they could through the open area to the relative safety of the shadows once again. Gasping for breath, Storey bent over trying to calm down. "That was fun. Not."

A strangled laugh escaped Eric as he watched her. He wasn't short of breath, she noted sourly. But he'd been cool and calm throughout this whole event. Unlike her, who'd gone from one extreme to the other.

Still, they were close now. She could see and feel it. Tammy would be hidden in one of those spots, maybe guarded and maybe not. The adult Louers wouldn't see her as a danger or in danger of running off. In fact, they'd probably have ignored her the whole time. They'd be more interested in the items they'd stolen from Eric and her. Especially if they understood what they'd found. Tammy would show them if given a chance.

If not, well, they might be able reclaim some of it.

"Do we have a plan of action?" she asked, hoping he'd figured out what to do from here. She didn't think the stylus would be much help. At this point, she couldn't see a way to use it effectively.

"I wish we knew where Tammy was stashed. That

info would help to find a way to sneak her out. As it is, they can see us as soon as we move. There's no cover. They've got a heck of a location here." His admiring tone made her turn to look at him.

"What? They do." He said defensively, "It's easy to defend and offers maximum protection."

She studied the layout. "It didn't help my people. They died out almost overnight."

"From what?"

"Who knows? They lived well for a long time, centuries I think, then they all disappeared. It's one of the great mysteries of my people." From the confusion on his face, she could see that didn't make any sense. This wasn't the time for a history lesson on the Anasazi people, especially since she had no answers. "Don't worry about it. I'll explain when we have more time."

He turned back to study the cave structure. "You know, if these caves go to the ground level, we might be able to gain access."

"I don't think they do. The whole point of living in caves like this is safety. To allow access from down here is to leave a door open for intruders."

"Were all your people about fighting and war? Surely it would make sense to have access for things like hunting and water."

"Yes," she said slowly, "but I wouldn't count on it."

He rolled his eyes and rubbed the bridge of his nose. "So...now what? We could go to the cliffs above them and try to climb down or we could climb up from here and hope we're not seen."

Storey studied the area more intently. "They had to have carried Tammy up there. I can't see her climbing that high on her own."

"That wouldn't have been hard. They're a large, strong people and she's a child to them. It would be natural for them to carry her."

"True." And that shot her idea down. Not that it had been much of an idea. There had to be a way to get to the first cave, which presumably was connected to the others inside the cliff.

She studied the cliff wall at her side. There were no cut-in steps on the face of the wall that she could see, but there must be some somewhere. They'd be hard to spot unless you knew of them. Hard to climb, unless you knew how. The best way to find them would probably be to walk along the ground, hands on the rock face, hoping to come across them by feel. She doubted they'd be easy to see otherwise.

It was afternoon, at least the sun was high and fairly warm. They couldn't wait that long for the sun to go down. Tammy was in trouble and...so were they.

Giving Eric a quick explanation, she slipped through the trees until she was as close as she could get to the cliff. She chose the first outcropping of rock, hoping it partially hid her from above. Checking the cliff wall carefully for Louers patrolling the top, she darted to the projection of rock and flattened against the cold stone. And froze. Did she hear something?

From the corner of her eye she could see Eric hiding in the trees. He gave her a smile. Okay. She'd made it. Relief rippled down her back.

The cliff appeared pockmarked like a lava rock but not as porous. Parts of the rock were smooth, others sharp. Varied in color and texture, the rock reminded her of the southwestern part of the States. Interesting.

She moved silently along the rock face, hugging the wall. In a moment, Eric joined her. Unless someone stood outside and stared straight down, they wouldn't be seen. They kept it up for another fifty odd feet when she stopped. Leaning her head close to the wall, she saw a pattern in the rock.

Could it be that easy? The pattern started at the rock ahead. Interesting. After giving her eyes a few moments to adjust to the multiple colors, she saw the beginning of the steps. With just a couple of steps, she'd climbed a good ten feet upwards. She heard Eric's gasp of surprise but kept going, knowing they were vulnerable on the open rock face. Besides he'd be following on her heels.

If anyone approached the caves from the woods or meadow as she and Eric had, they'd be spotted immediately. With that thought, she grabbed her courage and ran up the hidden staircase. Knowing Eric would be right behind her, she made it to the lowest plateau, where the first of the caves started. Ducking out of sight into the first cave, she gasped for air. Her heart slammed against her ribcage. She hated this. They could be found out any moment.

Eric joined her in seconds. The cave was huge. And empty.

They looked at each other. "I wonder if they're connected?" she whispered.

Knowing they could be found any time, they explored the caves with an eye to finding their way through the labyrinth of tunnels. The entire bottom row of caves appeared empty. There were connecting passages, and Storey couldn't believe how spacious the area appeared. If the weather stayed warm, the new inhabitants might actually have a cool place to live, temporarily or permanently. She thought it would be fun to spend a summer here.

But not with the Louers.

At the last cave on that level, noises finally penetrated the silence. Someone was close by. Working their way quietly through the tunnels, they tracked the noise deep within the cliff. Darkness shadowed the area. Maybe that worked in their favor too.

Walking slowly in the dark, the noise finally became recognizable. "That has to be Tammy."

"Or another child?"

"No." Storey knew that voice already like she knew her own voice. The noise was horrible. And Storey had nothing to give her to keep her quiet and happy. Damn. No one appeared to be rushing to keep her quiet either.

With the noise at an all-time high, Storey stuck her head around the corner of the last wall. Tammy, still wearing Storey's t-shirt, lay curled in the far corner. Alone.

Storey motioned at Eric to take a look. As she took a second look, Tammy's pet poked its head out from her arms and saw them. It raced toward Storey chattering in a loud voice. It still wore the harness and had a lead attached. Even as they watched, the rodent hit the end of the lead at full power and snapped back. It was enough to shake Tammy out of her crying jag. She sat up, and for the first time, Storey saw tear tracks on the little girl's cheeks. Tammy looked toward them, but Storey thought the girl probably couldn't see them in the dark cave. Storey took a step closer so her outline separated from the wall.

Tammy stared, her mouth dropped open as if to start screaming again. Storey slapped her hands over her ears in preparation. Instead Tammy scrambled to her feet and ran toward her. Eric stepped up beside Storey and grinned. Tammy opened her arms and launched herself at them both.

It almost took both of them to stop her assault. Still, for all her excitement and happiness at seeing them again, she was silent.

A wonderful blessing. Tammy squeezed hard, her arms wrapped around both of their necks in a group hug that Eric and Storey couldn't possibly escape. Eric spluttered several times. Storey looked over and started to laugh silently. She didn't dare make a sound, but it was hard to stay quiet. Skorky was jumping on Eric's head. Obviously he was happy to see them too.

Untangling herself from Tammy's arms, Storey walked over quickly to where Tammy had been lying on the ground, hoping some of her supplies might be there. There was nothing. *Damn.* Just one more break – that's all they needed – one lousy break and they'd be gone.

Back to Paxton. Back to her home. Anywhere was better than here.

"Storey." Eric's hoarse whisper had her walking quickly back to them.

"What?"

"Look." He held up a folded piece of paper. "This was in Tammy's pocket."

Excitement raced through her. Storey opened it up. "It's a portal to my house."

"Let's go." He almost jumped with impatience. "Just spread it out and I'll go through now. I think I hear someone coming. It's probably because she quit wailing."

Storey laid the portal on the cave floor. She didn't know if the dense rock would affect the portal's function or not. They didn't have much choice. They'd have to try it. As soon as she had the paper spread out properly, Eric, Tammy and the rodent still in his arms, stepped through and disappeared.

A loud shout sounded from the shadows. Shit. They were out of time. She snatched up the corner of the paper and jumped, making sure she took the drawing through with her. The last thing she saw were two of the big Louers coming out of the shadows.

CHAPTER 12

"**S**HIT."

Muffled groans and an odd shriek greeted her softer than expected landing. Tammy and Eric had cushioned her fall. She didn't even want to contemplate having squished the skorl. She scrambled to her feet and turned around, frowning. It looked like her dimension – sort of. If you expected to arrive in a storeroom of some kind.

At least they were alone.

"Where the hell are we?" Eric sat on the cement floor and stared.

Storey wished she had some idea. "It should have been my house, but..." she pivoted slowly, staring, "apparently not."

Eric hopped to his feet. "Oh great."

His voice sounded so disgusted and pissed; she fell immediately into apologizing. "Well, I'm sorry. I didn't exactly plan this. I don't know if something happened to the portal. Maybe they did something to it and gave it back to her, hoping we'd use it."

He spun around, astonishment on his face. "I'm not criticizing you. I'm simply wishing that for once things would go our way."

She waited a long moment for them both to calm down. "We could look on this turn of events as having gone very well." She let him consider that. "Just think, we snuck in, grabbed Tammy, and escaped – unscathed. Personally, I'd consider that things *are* going our way."

He shot her a frustrated look. "I know. It just seems like we go one step forward but then two steps backwards. Why? Why couldn't we have landed in your bedroom or Paxton's lab? Why here?" He gestured to the inside of a large empty room they were in.

"Why not here?" she laughed. "Okay, I know this isn't where we want to be, but it is much better than where we were."

Tammy made an odd sound, almost a prelude to her wailing. Both of them started. "Please not." Storey had nothing to appease her with if she started screaming. She walked over and hugged her. "It is okay, Tammy. We'll be fine."

"Will we?" murmured Eric. She shot him a warning look, nodding at Tammy.

He rolled his eyes at her. But restated in a perkier voice, "We will."

Tammy's lower lip trembled but the wailing appeared to have been averted for the moment, as if she understood what they were saying.

Keeping a hand on Tammy's shoulders, Storey stood up. "Good. Now, can we see about going home?"

Tammy looked up expectantly at both of them. Storey pointed at the door. "Let's see what's out there." Together the three of them trooped to the door. Eric pulled it open.

Outside, daylight shone bright and clear. Storey stepped out first. They appeared to be in a commercial storage unit where people could store their personal belongings. A couple of older trucks were parked outside the smaller sheds at the far end.

Storey searched the horizon for landmarks. Something to identify where they were. Casually, they walked through the front gates, not drawing any attention or curious glances. In fact, they were pretty much ignored. That worked for her.

Outside she found a sidewalk traveling in both directions on an average looking street. It could be any small town in North America. Or, it could be a street in Eric's dimension for all she knew — having never seen any.

A large blue pickup drove past, reaffirming her assumption that they were in her dimension. Tammy squealed at the noise, her arms wrapping tight about Storey. Right. This was probably the first time the child had seen anything even close to this. Storey hugged her tight for a long moment. Murmuring comforting words, she took a firm hold on Tammy's hand and led her forward.

Inside, her heart leapt with joy. This resembled home. Even that mountain in the distance looked familiar. A little different because of the angle but so close, she wanted to jump for joy. Ahead was a standard streetlight. She had to be home.

Maybe not home-home, but somewhere close. At least she hoped so. Even the street signs looked normal. They stopped at the corner of Main and Collingwood. That was an intersection in her town of Bankhead, but not an area she knew well.

"We'll go this way." She motioned toward Main Street.

"Do you know where we are?" Eric asked, staring at the lights and signs in confusion.

Glancing around again, she said, "I can't be sure yet, but I think we're in my home town."

Eric laughed. "This is nothing like your home."

She grinned at him. "You've only seen my house, the school, the mine and pathways in between. This could be the other side of town where the mill is. I don't spend a lot of time over here, so I'm not exactly sure yet. We need to keep walking so I can recognize more landmarks."

"Like those mountains?" He pointed to several snow capped peaks off the left.

"Yes, exactly like those." They walked in companionable silence for the rest of the block. Tammy never made a sound but her eyes were huge as she tried to take it all in. Her head swiveled from side to side. For her, this had to be a huge shock, but she was handling it well. Eric appeared to take it all in stride.

"Do you have towns like this, Eric?"

"Not like this." He grinned as an old van rattled by, large painted flowers in bright colors decorating its sides. "Definitely not like this."

She had to laugh. The next block was Cantor Street. Yes. Now that one she'd heard of for sure. She had to be several miles from home. She had to orient herself. The recreation center was over a couple of blocks and behind that was a trail to the high school. That would be the fastest way. With more energy in her step than she'd felt so far, she led them through the back way to her house.

Tammy stumbled. Eric reached out and helped her to regain her footing. Storey stopped to check her over. Tammy had to be getting tired. She'd been incredibly strong and valiant but at this point she needed food and rest. "We're almost home, Tammy. Just a little further. There should be food when we get there." Although what she had no idea; they'd wiped out so much food the last time. Had her mother had time to restock? Would she have gone out and replaced it? Or would she be waiting, pissed off, for Storey to come home?

Her house loomed ahead. Thank heaven for that. Luckily, she couldn't see the vehicle parked out front.

They walked to the back door of the kitchen. The door was locked.

Storey's switched her gaze from the closed door and back to him in amazement. "Really? We never lock our door."

"Yet, someone stole a whole pile of food while they were out one time, so I guess it makes sense that they'd lock it now?" Eric's sardonic humor had her grinning.

"Okay, fine. I'll run around and check the front door. Stay here."

Giving Tammy a quick reassuring grin, she ran around the house to the front door. It too was locked. Oh hell. She tried the garage. The inside looked different. Having a father around all the time could account for that. There were tools, shelves and cans of paint stacked in one corner. The inside door was unlocked.

Yes. She pushed it open and ran to the back door, opening it for Tammy and Eric. Ushering them inside, she said, "Take her to my room, quickly in case they come home. I'll look for something to eat."

Eric nodded, grabbed Tammy's hand and led her to the stairs. "Don't be long. She looks ready to pass out."

Storey cast a worried glance at Tammy. Her normal robust color was long gone and her shoulders sagged. Even her eyes drooped. Yet she'd been a trooper through-out all this.

"I'll be quick." Giving them an encouraging smile, she disappeared into the kitchen. The table was different. She hated the nervous energy bubbling in her stomach. She could only hope her mother was happier in this reality than she'd been in the other one. Personally, Storey wanted the old one back. There was nothing wrong with the other table, damn it. She'd liked it.

The fridge had been restocked. At least one problem was solved. Under the sink was a garbage bag. Storey hauled out cheese and apples again. There was a quart of milk, she grabbed that. Ten minutes later, her bag was full and she was hauling it upstairs. The colors of the hallway were totally different. Gone was the overly bright baroque look. Instead there was a neutral beige covering the walls. Boring.

She walked into her room, turning and locking the door behind her.

And stopped.

This was her room.

But this was not *her* room. She didn't recognize anything in the room. There were no personal items, no pictures on the walls, no clothes in the closet. If this was her bedroom, everything had been cleaned out and removed.

She didn't live here anymore.

ERIC STUDIED THE look on Storey's face, the emotions whistling across her features faster than a north wind coming through the mountains. The bedroom had been almost dehumanized. Was this normal behavior when a child didn't return home? He'd hate to see Storey tossed from her home because of this. From what he'd seen, she'd been close to her mother. A relationship she'd valued.

The room looked so much the same, yet different. His gaze fell on Tammy, curled into a small ball and fast asleep on the bed. The bed that had different sheets and blankets on it. A similar bed, just dressed differently.

Her art books were missing and that could be a huge problem. She needed her paper. *They* needed her paper.

The stricken look on her face was hard to gaze upon. He busied himself poking into the closet, the same closet he'd hidden in earlier. Finally he heard her speak.

"The house is empty."

Her voice, low and intense, showed such control and balance, he couldn't help but admire her. Again. He didn't know that he could do the same if the conditions were reversed.

"And I have food."

Food. Such a mundane necessity given everything else that had come to pass.

"Thank you. Do you think we should let Tammy sleep?"

Storey gazed at the child, her features softening. His heart warmed. If nothing else, having someone else to look after helped her forget her own troubles. Some matters had to take precedence.

"Yes, she's exhausted. I can't believe how good she's been throughout this." Storey walked over to sit on the bed beside her. Grabbing the folded blanket at the foot of her bed, she gently covered Tammy up. "She's not complained once."

"No. She's been surprisingly easy so far." Eric sat in the middle of the floor. "I, however, could use something to eat."

She opened the bag she'd brought upstairs. "I grabbed what I could. It's not the same as last time, but close."

"Good. Is there cheese?"

He grinned when she held out a large block of white cheese, then another loaf of bread. "Tammy will be happy."

"That's if we leave her any." Storey sorted through the food she'd brought. Eric made a simple sandwich and then watched her as he ate.

"Eric?"

He raised an eyebrow in question, his mouth full of food.

In a soft voice, Story asked. "What are we doing wrong? Everything seems to be getting worse."

STOREY COULDN'T HELP the wave of depression sweeping through her. Yes, they were warm and sheltered, with food at hand and they were safe from attacking Louers. But there were so many things wrong she couldn't begin to list them all.

Tammy's problem was the priority. How could she get Tammy home to her family? The stylus had at one time told her that she could delete the dimension she'd made but it would kill everyone in it. That meant all of Tammy's family and Tammy, if she were home at the time, would be wiped out. So not a good idea. She hadn't presented the idea to the Toran's because she'd figured they'd approve of the idea en masse. Getting rid of their enemy in one final drawing – yeah, they'd be all over that. Maybe not Eric, as he'd come to know Tammy.

They also had to go back and get the missing codexes. And her portals. She didn't like to think that one of them might jump into her bedroom. That made the hair on the back of her neck stand up straight.

"I'm thinking that maybe we should get Paxton's advice," Eric said.

She pondered that. "But we're no more welcome there than here."

"Did you ever consider that this…" he looked around, "might not be your room?"

The apple stalled midway to her mouth. "How do you mean?"

"What if we're in yet a different dimension? Or maybe a different time frame? Maybe your mother moved when you didn't return home."

Cold raced down her spine. She gasped in pain. "Oh, no way. I haven't been gone for that long."

"When you left the party, no. I don't know if time is

the same here as there. It should be but…we've twisted so many things we can't count on it."

She slumped back from her position on the floor to lean against the bed. Her gaze centered on the pile of food, not really seeing it. "Why is it that when I try to help someone, the situation gets worse?"

He winced. "It doesn't always. Look, we rescued Tammy."

Storey sniffled, hating the image of that whole female weakness thing, but she'd love to break down and bawl – just for a moment. Just long enough to release the pressure valve threatening to blow. She'd feel so much better. But not here and not now – and not with Eric watching.

The apple would have to do. She took another bite. She needed the food for energy. The thought of this not being her home, or worse not being her dimension, made her sick. She loved her mother. For all her mother's foibles, they'd had a good relationship. They still did, she corrected herself mentally. There's no way she'd accept that her life with her mother was over.

"Ask the stylus." Eric gazed at her, one eyebrow raised.

"Good idea. But I'll need some paper."

"Would they have paper downstairs?"

She shrugged and stood up. "I don't know. I'll have to go see." She didn't want to leave the relative safety and quiet of the room, but she needed answers.

The master bedroom was at the end of the hall, right at the top of the stairs. Even if her parents or whoever lived here came home, it's possible that by keeping the light off in her room, no one would know they were hiding there. She could create another portal but all these jumps were taking them somewhere…not quite right…and she needed to find out why.

At her mom's room, she was forced to turn on the light. And stopped, swallowed hard, and quickly moved forward. Maybe her parents didn't live here. The bedroom set was a heavy mahogany with dark drapes and dark carpet. Terrible.

She strode to the night table and checked the drawers, hoping for a pad of paper. Nothing in the first drawer and the second one only offered a small note pad. Better than nothing, but she needed sheets of paper if her big sketchbooks weren't available. At this rate, she'd be leaving them in all the dimensions. If there was an office downstairs, then a printer and printer paper would be possible. Slipping down the stairs, keeping the lights off, she walked through the rooms, coming to the den. Half the room had been established as an office. Again dark furniture, dark carpets and even darker caramel walls. She hated it.

Walking to the computer, she saw it was still on but asleep. The monitor looked different, too. A great, big, square unit. As long as it worked. She booted it back out of hibernation then searched for paper. At the printer, she found a pile of perforated accordion paper that had gone out of style years ago. The printer also looked old, huge and clunky. Weird. Still the reams of paper were perfect and because it was continuous she could draw as big a picture as she needed too. Several inches should do.

Back at the computer, she opened a browser, and tried to bring up a few of her favorite sites to see if there were any messages. And couldn't find any of the pages. Her throat started to close in on her. Surely what she was thinking wasn't possible, was it? Clicking on the calendar in the corner of the screen, the day was May 21st and that was certainly reasonable, but the year – she gasped.

Ten years ago. Ten. A whole decade earlier than she wanted it to be. This wasn't her house. It wouldn't be her house for another few months at least. That's why it all looked so different. She didn't remember if this is how the house had looked when she first moved in because, well, she'd been a kid. So much hadn't happened yet. She'd only be in first grade. Chances were good her parents were either newly divorced or in the process. A tough time back then for her family.

Unbelievable.

Once again, her arms full, she ran up the stairs. Eric looked up in surprise as she burst into the room.

Trying to keep her voice low so as to not disturb Tammy, she said, "Oh Eric, we've got a bigger problem than we thought."

He frowned, grabbed an apple and took a big bite. "What are you talking about?"

"We've gone back in time. Ten years backwards."

His brows furrowed and he stopped chewing in mid bite. He blinked several times as if trying to process the information. "What? How do you know that?"

"The computer downstairs."

"Could it be wrong?"

Could it? She twisted her lips and considered. "I don't know. Maybe? I never thought to double check. God, that was stupid."

"Is there any way here to check? Without having to go downstairs again?"

How could they check? A small radio sat on the desk. A clock radio. She walked closer. "This might tell us." After pushing the power button, she set the dial to radio. Soft music filled the room. "I don't know if they'll talk about the date, though."

Along the back of the dresser sat an old calendar. For the year 2002. She picked it up, turning to show it to Eric. He frowned.

She scavenged through the rest of the drawers, wishing there'd be a few articles of usable clothing. Nothing. The closet was just as empty. Crap. The master bedroom might have some, but she had no way of knowing what size the woman, if there was a woman living here, wore. There might be a front closet with sweaters or jackets, but she and Tammy could use a change of clothes.

Striding to the center of the room, she dropped to the floor and reached for the ream of paper. Pulling out her stylus, she started in on the questions.

"Is it possible that we've gone back in time?"

A hum filled the air. *Yes.*

"Can we get back to our normal time?"

The answer came faster. *Yes.*

Her breath gusted out and she couldn't resist looking at Eric. He grinned. "See. We can fix this."

She rolled her eyes at him and returned to getting answers.

"Stylus, how do we go back to our time?"

Go back through the same portal.

"The portal that took us here? I thought it was damaged so we shouldn't use it again." She picked up the paper she'd folded and tossed at the foot of the bed.

When damaged they still go to the same place, but might not hit the target right on. In this case the time line appears to be damaged.

"Actually we ended up not quite in the right spot either. We were close, but landed several miles away."

Exactly.

Storey snickered. "To you maybe. So if we go to the same portal, we'll arrive either back outside of the house or inside this room again. And it could take us closer in time, or might hit the right time?

Yes.

"Oh boy."

Eric stood and looked at Tammy. "I could carry her."

"We could we end up miles away again."

He grimaced.

Storey continued to talk. "Stylus, if we try to go back to Paxton's lab, will the time frame be wrong there?"

Yes. You would be moving through this time frame now.

"So we have to fix the time here first?" She rubbed her eyes. When would something be simple.

That is correct.

"So after we get back to the normal time, how do we find Tammy's parents so that we can portal to them and reunite them? We don't want to go back and risk meeting the wrong group of Louers again."

Eric stepped up behind her to read the stylus message this time for himself. He crouched down, his arm over her shoulder.

"Hey, are you reading this?"

Chapter 13

*O*NE THING AT *a time. Fix the time warp first.*

Eric rubbed the back of his neck, his other hand absentmindedly rubbing Storey's back as he thought about what the stylus had written. Like it made something so hard to even contemplate – easy.

"I'm so tired. Do we rest first?" She stared at his face, so close to hers, for answers.

"Or do we do this next jump so that you are at least back in the house that you actually live in – at the right time."

She rolled her eyes. *Oh right.* "Yes, that makes sense. It would be wonderful if walking through that portal takes us right back into this room. Then we could sleep for a few hours."

On cue, they both looked over at the sleeping Tammy.

Storey frowned. "I hate to disturb her."

"If we're just going to end up back in this room, then I can pick her up, walk through and lay her back down again.

"Why is it I don't think it's going to be that simple?"

He grinned. "Because it never has been?" he suggested, straightening. He glanced around the room at the food still lying out in disarray. "I guess we should tidy this mess first."

"Definitely. It would be better to not leave any sign

that we've been here."

"And I'm getting hungry again."

Storey groaned. "You're as bad as she is." She hopped to her feet and began cleaning up the food, absentmindedly making him another sandwich while she was at it. Bagging their food and garbage, she added the computer paper to their collection and put on her jacket. Finally, she laid the portal drawing on the floor. Glancing over at him, she watched as he carefully bent over Tammy and her pet, scooped them up like they hardly weighed anything. The skorl glared at him for disturbing his sleep but never cried out or tried to run off.

Straightening, Eric walked to where she stood. "Ready?"

Taking a deep breath, she said, "Yes." She stepped back as he hopped through, Tammy still asleep in his arms. He disappeared from sight.

"Please let this work."

She grabbed the corner and fell once more into the portal, taking the paper with her.

ERIC OPENED HIS eyes and studied his new location. It wasn't Storey's bedroom. Unfortunately. Tammy still slept in his arms and he'd have loved to have been able to lay her right back down. He waited for Storey to show up. And waited.

"Anytime Storey. I don't want to be lost in time without you and your portals, thank you very much."

The words had barely left his mouth when she arrived behind him.

She flopped back onto the pathway. In a hoarse whisper, she said, "I'd really like to be in bed right now."

"So would I." He waited a beat. "Any idea where we

are?"

She groaned but staggered to her feet. "Not a clue." She brushed her pants off and straightened to look around her. "In theory, we should be closer to the house than last time."

"And we need to be because I won't be able to carry Tammy very far."

He shifted the load in his arms impatiently.

Determinedly, she spun around as if trying to orient herself. "Right then."

Eric watched the emotions flash across her face. Her face showed everything. She was so honest in her expression. There was no deceit. No subterfuge. You saw exactly what she was thinking. It also meant she couldn't lie to him.

A refreshing change. He didn't know many eligible women in his world and as a ranger, and worse, as the Councilman's son, he wasn't treated the same as the other guys. The women were more formal with him; more on the lookout for a long-term relationship instead of just a fun evening. In his world, he was considered a catch. He suspected Storey would laugh at that.

"Well," he prompted, hating to show he was tiring, but Tammy was a heavyweight. "I need to put Tammy down soon."

Storey spun around, a huge smile on her face. "I think I have it. Let's go." She took off ahead of him. He followed at a much slower pace. So much for believing he could do anything. The longer he carried Tammy, the more he realized he was going to need to bulk up his muscles if trips like this were to continue. As much as he hated the thought of not being invincible…

Then he saw it.

"Is that your house?" He looked around. "We came in from the other side." He brightened. "That's the path to the school where we first met, isn't it?"

"Yes, it is." She almost raced to the house, a lively bounce to her step.

"Storey, wait." He hated to blow her joy but someone needed to be the voice of reason here.

She spun around. "I'm sorry, what? I'm just so hoping this is it. That I'm home."

"I know that. But did you ever wonder if there might be another Storey in this house? In this dimension or this time?"

The smile fell off her face. Horror filled her gaze. "There couldn't be, could there?"

"I have no idea. It's just we're back at the same house, your house, supposedly in the time frame that you were living here back then…so where are you?"

She tilted her head back to stare up at the sky. "I'm getting a headache."

"And what's the chance the house is empty? Do we even know what day it is anymore? Are you in school today? Does your mother work? Did you consider any of that?"

"Of course, I didn't," she snapped. "I can't think straight anymore. But inside is a bed, my bed, where you can lay her down."

He considered that – for a heartbeat. "Right. Lead the way."

Again, she walked to the back kitchen door. He wondered why she never used the front door.

At the back, she found the kitchen door unlocked. "That's more like it."

"You aren't worried about intruders here?"

"No. Small town and all that." She pushed it open wide enough for him and Tammy to enter.

"Small town, two women who live a distance away from any neighbors?"

"Let's just say that up to now, it hasn't been much of an issue."

He nodded, but doubted it would stay that way after life returned to normal. She'd changed. Become more self-confident. More secure. But with the confidence came more awareness of all the things that could go wrong. A loss of innocence, in a way.

It was both good and bad, and it was a sign of maturity.

Inside the kitchen, he stopped and watched her assess her surroundings. Her gaze narrowed on the calendar on the wall. It said May, a relief. From where he stood he couldn't see the year. He could only hope they'd arrived on time. "Storey."

When she didn't respond, he repeated it, "Storey."

"What?" She spun around when he didn't answer right away.

"I need to put her down."

Her gaze widened. "Oh geez. I'm so sorry. Come on, let's go up."

By now he knew the way, but suspected she wanted to see what her room looked like this time. He didn't care. His muscles were screaming and fatigue had taken over. He needed rest, too. At this rate, Tammy would wake and they wouldn't be able to sleep themselves because they'd need to look after her. His back was killing him, but there was no way he'd let Storey know. He was a ranger. They had an image to uphold. So how come there'd been no mention of rescuing damsels and children in distress anywhere in their manual?

Oh wait, what manual?

Storey opened the door and stepped inside. And stopped.

He groaned silently. Now what?

"SO?" ERIC'S STRESSED voice prodded her forward.

"It looks the same." *Thank God.* "I can't tell you how glad I am to see that."

"But?"

She turned back toward him, confused. "But what?"

"You haven't entered fully," he snapped. "If everything is all right, let me in."

Finally, the impatience, fatigue and frustration in his voice hit her. She stepped aside quickly. He had to be exhausted. "Sorry, I'm tired too."

"And that's going to have to be something we address immediately." At the bed he leaned over to lay Tammy down. Storey rushed over. "Hang on." She pulled the covers back. "Now, lay her down. Maybe we'll be lucky and she'll sleep long enough for us to rest as well."

"I doubt it, but I need to crash regardless. I think the time travel stuff finished my system." Straightening, his gaze fell to the open floor. "I'm going to lie on the floor with that blanket if you don't mind?" He pointed at the one half falling off the end of her bed. Storey snatched it up and held it out to him.

"I'm thinking to lie down beside Tammy, actually."

Eric didn't even look at where she pointed. He'd stretched out on the floor, pulling her blanket over him. "Go ahead. I won't sleep long. A couple of hours should recharge me."

"Good for you. I doubt that little bit will do me," she muttered. Storey locked her bedroom door, turned out the light and curled up behind Tammy. The rodent opened his eyes, glared at her, realized she wasn't moving and returned to his spot in the crook of Tammy's arms.

She was so tired. Yet the thought of another Storey walking in on them was enough to keep her mind buzzing. She needed rest. She needed solutions. She'd needed this to all go back to normal.

Somehow.

While her mind pondered and fussed, Eric slept deeply on the floor beside her. His snores wafted gently through the room, making her smile. Then she was jealous. He could rest so easily. As if there weren't a million problems pressing in on them. She desperately needed rest, too. And a shower and a change of clothes and…she fell asleep.

"STOREY." HER SHOULDER was jostled. She frowned and tried to burrow deeper into her pillow.

The insistent voice wouldn't let up. "Storey, wake up."

She grumbled, "Too tired."

"I know you're tired, but there's a problem."

Storey's eyes slowly opened as that information filtered in. They were safe. They were home. So what was the big deal? Her mind flooded with memories. She sat up slowly, hating the screaming going on in her head, and felt tempted to ignore everything and go back to sleep. Her brain screamed for more sleep. "Eric? How long did we sleep?"

"I don't know. A couple of hours, maybe."

A dull daylight shone through the window. She stared out the window. The sky had turned black and clouds had gathered. "I think time travel must be harder on us than normal portal travel. I still feel like I have lead inside my bones." She yawned. "I just hope we're in the right time frame."

"Yes." His voice was grim. "But we have a bigger problem."

"What's the matter?" She studied his face.

"Tammy's missing."

She blinked. Once. Twice. Then panic hit. "Oh my God. Are you serious? I locked the door. I know I did."

"And she unlocked it."

Storey made it to her feet, swaying only slightly. She looked around and pointed out signs of Tammy's activities. A block of cheese sat on the desk, a large chunk ripped off, and an open package of pepperoni was almost gone. "She's found food at least."

Eric stared hungrily at the items. Storey rolled her eyes. "Grab it then. I'm going to go outside and see if she's there."

She stood up, searching for Tammy. "How long has she been gone?"

"I only woke up a few minutes ago. So I can't say."

"We have to find her," she said urgently. She stumbled to the door.

"I know." He said, explaining patiently. "That's why I came and woke you."

She checked her mother's bedroom. Empty. Downstairs, she checked out the various rooms and couldn't see any sign of Tammy. Out on the front deck, she searched the front of the house. Thankfully it appeared her parents hadn't returned. At least there were no vehicles at home.

At the outside chairs she found a stub of pepperoni. "At least we know she came this way."

Eric walked up behind her. "Great. So where'd she go from here?"

"I wish I knew how long she'd been gone. That would give me an idea of how far she could have traveled." Storey glanced out into the dark cloudy skies and ran her fingers through her hair. "I feel like I haven't slept in days."

"We haven't really. Portal travel, stress and even panic

as we run for our lives, none of that is exactly easy on us, you know."

"I hear you." And she really didn't want to hear the details right now. Hadn't he mentioned brain damage in an earlier conversation? Nasty. She so didn't want to go there right now. She turned back to the real issue. "I really wish Tammy hadn't gone missing. I so don't need this."

"Actually...I'm not sure she has." He placed his hands on her shoulders and turned her gently. "Is that her? It looks almost like she's swinging on something like a suspended tire?"

Sure enough Tammy sat facing the other way on an old tire swing at the back of the neighbor's property. "Well thank heavens for that. One thing solved. Let's bring her back."

She started walking forward, Eric at her side, a chunk of cheese in one of his hands and a stick of pepperoni in the other. "You really love protein, don't you?"

"Protein?" He looked at the food in his hands.

"Meat. You could have grabbed an apple you know. Round out your food choices a little."

He grinned taking a big bite of cheese. "I'm good."

Males. She called out, "Tammy?"

Tammy spun around, saw them and a big grin lit her face. She opened her mouth and for the first time, a normal, or almost normal sounding voice came out. "Toey."

Storey grinned. "Almost. It's Storey with an Ssss sound."

Tammy tried again, her round face wrinkling with concentration. "Storrey."

"Close enough." Storey held out her hand. "Come on kiddo, back to the house."

Tammy hopped off, whistled sharply – at least her lips pursed the right motion, but it sounded more like air rushed out instead. But didn't the dratted rodent come running. He looked livelier too. He was dragging his leash behind. Tammy bent and grabbed the leash in one hand and her pet in the other.

The rest had done them all good. Storey had to admit she'd prefer to rest here for a day or two. Just sleep, shower, eat and repeat.

"I'm going to turn on the computer and check the dates."

"Will that tell you for sure?"

She frowned. "I can check the news and see what's happening. Computers are very exact nowadays."

"Hmmm."

"What are you thinking?" she asked curiously.

He glanced her and then away quickly. "I'm wondering about going back into time before the Louers crossed to their new dimension and make sure she's there for that crossing."

Storey's steps slowed as she considered the idea. "What would happen if we did something like that? Would we be messing with their future?"

"With Tammy's future maybe, in that she wouldn't remember any of this as it wouldn't have happened yet – in theory at least. If we returned in time to a point before Skorky ran away…and somehow stopped her from leaving the group…then she wouldn't have been there for you to find when you did."

"And I would have woken up still with my stylus and backpack and made a quick exit home. None of these last days would have happened." Her voice rose in excitement.

"In theory."

"And…would we remember it all? Or would we just not have those memories because we wouldn't have had these days?"

Eric shook his head. "I have no idea."

"It's a scary thought. It might be the best way to deal with Tammy's situation but is that the way to deal with anything else?"

"I don't think we can use it for much else though, at least not without messing with a lot of stuff."

It was her turn to say "Hmmm, I suppose." But her mind wouldn't let go of the concept. If it would return her world to normal that would be huge. But how could she do that without messing up the Louers' dimension?

Back at the house, Storey took everyone back to her room and turned on her laptop. It sat under a pile of clothes. She'd forgotten about it in their last few crazy trips. Once up, with Eric and Tammy crowding around, both of them eating apples this time, Storey checked the date. May 17th. Close enough. Checking out the news, as far as she could see, they were back where they belonged.

"Thank heavens for that," she murmured, relief slipping off her shoulders.

He wrapped one arm around her shoulder and squeezed. She smiled. Behind her, a telephone rang. She turned, a frown forming. Should she answer it or not?

"Aren't you going to answer it?" He dropped his arm and took a step back.

"It won't be for me. I have a cell phone."

But her feet walked in that direction. Slowly, she picked it up. "Hello."

"Storey? Where the hell have you been?"

Storey didn't recognize the irate voice. "Who is this?"

"Your father, of course. Who do you think?" Sarcasm dripped through the phone line. "Where have you been?"

"Um, doing homework?" she wrinkled her face at Eric, whispering the identity of the caller. He frowned at her.

She shrugged and spoke into the phone. "When are you coming home?"

"I'll be there in three hours, maybe four. I want you there when I get back, do you hear me? You mother and I have been worried sick. There's been a mess of weird storms going on, communications have been down all over the place. I know our phone hasn't been working but that's no reason for making us worry."

Storey didn't know what to say. Thankfully she didn't appear to need to say anything as his irate voice rolled right over her. "Stay home. We'll get there as soon as we're done working. I'm going to phone your mother right now and let her know you're okay."

Storey made what she thought might have been the appropriate response as he hung up a few seconds later. She shook her head. "What the heck. He said they've been having weird storms, communications down? That's not because of us, is it?"

Eric waved as if to brush off the idea, then paused, his hand in the air. His face twisted with concentration. "I'd have said no, until I remembered the time travel." He stood with his hands on his hips contemplating the flooring. "With that, it is very possible. Think about it. We can't just move through time-space without a reaction of some kind. Energy has to shift and change, atmospheres have to adapt, the time–space continuum has an order and we've disturbed it." He shrugged as if expecting her to understand all that he'd spouted off. "Weather anomalies could easily be experienced with those changes."

She winced. "Great. So we're screwing with the weather patterns, too. Is nothing going our way?" she muttered the last bit under her breath, but Eric still heard her.

"We're doing fine. We're back to the time period we belong in, now the stylus can help us to get Tammy home."

She brightened. "Let's ask. My parents are going to be home in three hours, four maximum. Possibly earlier. We need to be gone, and hopefully back again before they get home."

Eric motioned toward the bedroom where Tammy stood in the doorway a worried look on her face. Storey rushed forward, a reassuring smile on her face. "It's okay honey. Everything is fine." At least her tone of voice had to help even if Tammy didn't understand the words.

Coming up behind both of them, Eric ushered them into the bedroom, closing and locking the door behind them. "Let's get this done."

Storey pulled out her largest sketchbook from the closet. Seeing an older backpack stuffed in the back, she grabbed it too. Then she sat cross-legged with her stylus. "Stylus, we need to get Tammy back to her family. Not just any Louers but to her mother and father. How do we do that?"

The stylus jerked in her hand, Storey slapped the tip on the paper. She read the answer out to Eric. "Going back in time is dangerous. Going to her family in their new dimension right now is also dangerous."

Eric shook his head. "Staying here isn't an option. Tammy needs her family and because of you, she trusts us to take her home."

"Which option do you want to choose?" She studied Eric's face looking for an answer.

"Which is the least dangerous?" Eric countered.

Going to her family now. You won't have to factor in all the dimension shifts from a time change.

"Fine. Let's do that then. Give us the coordinates for her people, preferably her parents, so that we can land, give her to them, and get out again. This time in and out. No landing us in weird spots or other time frames. Clean and simple."

Storey took note of the determination in his jaw as he spoke. She wished it could be so easy.

The humming filled the air, this time louder, more intense as if the stylus was trying to actually transport them there himself. Storey looked over at Eric, one eyebrow raised. He shrugged. They both waited.

Tammy sidled closer, slipping her hand into Storey's hand. The two girls leaned against each other as they waited. She figured the stylus had to be communicating with the other styluses. Or it was recharging. Shrugging it off, she concentrated on the problems at hand. Time was running out.

"We'll need to change clothes," she said abruptly.

"Why? I haven't."

"You can't," she said wryly. "There aren't any other clothes here that will fit you."

An odd light flashed in his eyes and it matched the grin flashing across his face. Standing, he pulled a flat object out of a weird side pocket just below his knee of his ranger pants. "I forgot. They missed this when they emptied my pockets. Not that they'd have known its value anyway." At her frown, he laughed. "Exactly. You have no idea what this is, do you?"

She studied it for a moment. As it was too small to be anything but a plastic business card or credit card, she couldn't see any other purpose to it. Especially being as thin as it was. "Nope."

With a huge grin, he said, "Watch, you're gonna love this." He pulled a clip off the outside of his pants pocket. It was the size of a small cell phone. She'd thought it had been a decoration. Typical. He connected the clip to his small envelope looking thing, then tapped the small flat surface several times. Musical notes sounded, almost in a melody she recognized. Even Tammy came rushing over at the tune.

Then Eric held the small package slightly away from his body. The package, apparently unlocked by the music, swelled and reshaped into a large rectangle as if folded under pressure. By the time it stopped moving, the package was now several feet long and a good foot wide.

The process had taken less than a minute.

Her astonishment made him laugh. "If you tell me that there is a full change of clothes in there, I'm so going to get me one of those."

Eric laughed as he opened the package to pull out pants, a shirt and what looked like socks. "I've got several spares on me all the time."

She gasped. "And you didn't offer me the same thing?"

He said apologetically, "I never considered it. I wondered why you were putting all that stuff into your bag. But it's your dimension, your house, your system. I've been trying to learn how you do things here."

"I did that because I didn't have another choice," she snapped, exasperated. She stopped, a cool idea coming into her mind. "Does that only work with material?"

He frowned, not understanding.

"Could you do that to my sketchbooks, papers, food, anything?

"Everyone in my dimension carries things this way. And yes, we could carry blankets, clothing, sketchbooks. I don't know about food as I've never tried."

Storey bent and upended her bag of collected goodies. The mess rolled everywhere. "Go for it."

Eric gave her a shuttered look but bent obediently and separated the items into perishable and nonperishable. The nonperishable items he converted to a small bagful almost immediately. Once he had things sorted, he took the same cell phone thingy, clipped it to a corner of the bag, tapped several different spots, producing a different musical tune and the magic happened in reverse. While Storey watched in amazement, a long brown film stretched over the end of the stack and within seconds it had compressed and shrunken to a small envelope size.

Eric stood and held it out to her.

She studied it, turning it over and over, all the while shaking her head. "Wow. I don't know how much you can put into a package like this but my world needs this technology."

"It's tied to our codex technology. This way people can carry what they need to travel."

"Right." Her frown deepened. "So we can't have it. How can I open it without that little musical thingy? What's it called anyway?" She couldn't believe how fascinating and practical this system was. She so wanted one of those tools.

"It's a codin." He laughed lightly. "We all have them. Several in some cases."

"Is there a way to open it if we get separated?"

His grin flashed again. "I suspect the stylus would be able to open it for you if I'm not around."

"Except I need the sketchbook in here to communicate," she said in exasperation.

"Not quite. You seem to do fine even without paper. I wonder if there's a way for you to become telepathic with it?"

"Yes. I just don't know how yet." Unfortunately. "Can you do another of those little packages up? To hold spares of everything and another for food?"

Eric pulled another clip from his knee pocket and attached it to his codin.

Boy did she want to have that technology for herself. "Do you know how much easier it would be to travel if I could do that with all my stuff?"

"It has limits, but for the most part, it's a wonderful

convenience."

She snorted. "Ya think? What's the limit for this type of thing?"

Eric assessed the food stacked in front of him. "I've only used it for packing clothing and personal items." He grinned sheepishly. "That spare has been in these pants for awhile now. We could have done this so much earlier, but honestly, your system worked so well, I never considered looking for an alternative."

What could she say to that? Nothing. With time marching against them, she quickly drew a portal to Paxton's lab while Eric packed clothing and food in separate parcels in case they were separated or captured again. In the packets Storey included two portals that they could use. The one they'd use to bring them home and the one to Paxton's lab.

Now, prepared with these, Storey had to admit the concept of going back with Tammy wasn't so daunting.

The deck was stacked in her favor for once.

CHAPTER 14

"ARE YOU SURE you want to leave before your parents get home?" Eric waited for her answer patiently.

She'd been warring with herself for the last ten minutes over that same issue. "Yeah. I can't even begin to explain you three being here." As much as she'd like to smooth things over and leave on a good note, how could she without bringing up more problems? She didn't even know this man who called himself her father. He might use the same name…but that didn't make him the same man. Which he obviously wasn't as he'd stuck around in this reality.

Making a sudden decision, she walked over to her desk and wrote a note on the pad of paper sitting there, reading it out as she wrote. "Sorry. I have to leave. I'll be back in a couple of hours."

Staring at the message for a long moment, she decided it would have to do. Hopefully she'd be back in time to ditch the note before they ever saw it.

She marched back over to where Tammy, holding Skorky tucked firmly under her arm with her hand in Eric's, waited for her. At Eric's questioning look, she shrugged. "I don't know what else to do."

His lopsided grin flashed. "It's pretty messed up, isn't it?"

"Ya think," she sniffed. "Do we know what we're doing this time? Do we need to meet with Paxton? Get another codex?" Eric frowned, considering. "It would be a good idea. If nothing else we should report in."

Storey glanced at Tammy. Paxton wouldn't be happy if she returned with them. "Before or after?"

He grimaced as he understood her meaning. "Before would be better, but afterward would be easier on Paxton."

"We can't forget the missing portals and codexes. A second team to retrieve those would be easier on us."

This time excitement lit Eric's face. "Now that would be awesome."

"I know." Still she felt a cautionary note was needed. "Do you have any idea what happened to your father?" She frowned and walked over to the pad of paper on her desk. "Stylus, please send a message to Paxton letting him know where we are and the problem we had of the time dimensional issue."

"He knows," she read out loud. "I've kept him informed." She shook her head. "Oh. Good, I guess. So he knows we're at my house with Tammy still?"

No. Telling him now.

Storey waited. "Could you also ask if Eric's father has been located?"

No sign of him yet.

Storey and Eric exchanged worried looks. "I don't know if I should be worried for you or happy for me," she said in a wry voice. "I don't want anything bad to happen to him, I just want to have him be nice to me. Or better yet, have nothing to do with me."

Eric bent his head to the paper, as if waiting for another immediate communication. "I know. I don't like this though. It's been days. There's no place he could go."

"Could he go to another dimension?"

"He'd be scared to come here, and the Louers, well,

he was in a panic the one time I helped him and the others escape from there. I can't see him willingly going back."

"So where could he be?" Storey shook her head. "I'm an idiot. Stylus, where is the Councilman?"

She rolled her eyes at Eric. "How could we not have asked it?"

Humming filled the air. It fascinated her as the stylus had no source of power or speakers. "How can it make that noise?"

"Just another of the wonders of the stylus."

The humming stopped and Storey's hand jerked as it started writing. She closed her eyes, almost seeing the message in her mind. With a little practice she could probably get the message without needing paper. But to create portals she'd still need paper – at least she thought so. At the rate her skills and knowledge had developed, who knew?

The Councilman is not in Eric's dimension.

"Oh shit."

She stared at Eric in shock. "Stylus, which dimension is he in?"

The new Louer home.

Eric reached out a hand and gripped Storey's shoulder. "What? Is that really possible?"

"Stylus? How did the Councilman get over there?"

He was taken as a prisoner.

Storey closed her eyes. Her stomach sank. This conversation was not going to be good. "What? How?"

He contacted the Louers to have them take care of you. You escaped, so they snatched him instead.

Swallowing painfully at the hard truths, Storey asked, "Stylus, please relay this information to Paxton."

Eric stumbled back several feet to the window. Storey knew if the truth had hurt her, it had to have devastated him.

"Which group of Louers took him as prisoner? And how did he contact the Louers?"

The ones that grabbed Tammy. Paxton entered the new coordinates from Eric's codex into the database. The Councilman used those to program his codex.

Storey sighed and stared at Eric. So much for a quick in and out trip. "How could he possibly communicate with them?" Storey wondered aloud. "Then again, we didn't try to talk to them very much, did we? We judged their communication abilities based on Tammy."

Most Louers have baseline English. An older version than you would know, but still understandable. Between themselves they use telepathy.

The stylus started moving faster. *Storey, this is Paxton. It's imperative that you rescue the Councilman from those people.*

It was on the tip of Storey's tongue to ask why when the asshole had contacted the Louers to take her out. She couldn't come up with one good reason why she should. From the fury on Eric's face, neither could he. "Stylus, is the Councilman in the same caves where we found Tammy?"

Yes.

"Oh shit." Storey looked at Eric. "Tammy needs to go home. She can't get involved in this. You know the Louers would love to recapture her. We can't take that chance."

Paxton sent another message. *This is a crisis for our people. Eric must come and plan the Councilman's return.*

"Eric, what do you want to do?"

"Leave my father to the fate he created." Eric's glower had Tammy creeping behind Storey, her hand slipping into Storey's pocket.

Storey patted her on the shoulder.

"That's what I *want* to do, but I don't know what we *should* do." Eric stared off into the night, the anger fading slightly from his eyes as he considered the problem a little longer.

Storey couldn't see an immediate solution either. She really didn't want to rescue someone who had tried to get rid of her. She valued her life. Why would she save his so he could try and take hers – again?

Still this was Eric's call.

Eric nodded. "We should leave him there. It would serve him right."

"And would that serve your people's needs, as well?" she asked curiously. There was much she didn't understand about the way his world worked, his government processes or even the way someone came into power. "Was your father born into his leadership position?"

Eric spun around. From the look on his face, she'd take that as a no. "Of course not. He was elected to the Council and then voted to the head."

"So he can be voted off? Removed from his position because of bad behavior?" She watched the change of emotions ripple across his features.

Eric hitched his hands on his hips, his head cocked to one side. "It's possible, but I've yet to see it happen."

"No one has ever been voted out?" Her astonishment sharpened her voice. Were they nuts? "How long has he been in power?"

"He's been the Councilman all my life. I've never known a time when he wasn't."

Something was wrong with that system. The Councilman was an unbalanced individual who'd allowed his own feelings to direct his actions. Actions that didn't make him look good. Maybe he'd been a good man, a strong leader…before Storey had jumped into his life. She had to believe he'd served his people well at one time.

It's not as if her society didn't have prejudices them-selves. To Eric's father she was an offworlder. An alien, almost.

"I want to leave him where he is for a while," he snapped. "But I can't. And that makes me mad. He should stay there. After the despicable things he's done, he deserves to suffer."

She could so understand. But like him, she knew it wasn't the right thing to do. "What's the chance he's learned his lesson?"

"Not him." Eric shook his head violently. "He's very powerful here. Believes he can do anything."

"Because you've all allowed him to think that way. He's been like a king over you all."

Eric shot her a disgusted look. "I know. But it's not going to be that way anymore."

"Not if you leave him there." She grinned. "You could make it a condition of helping him return."

He studied her before grudgingly nodding. "Not bad. I could slip home and talk to them, maybe organize a back up team to help us, then come back here."

Storey hated to see him go. He might never come back. But a second team would be a wonderful idea. "Go. At least to meet with your Council and determine what's to be done. I don't want you to go at all." She gave him a lopsided grin. "But it's something that you need to do."

He tilted his head and narrowed his gaze. "Yes, I do, but I want you to come to me in an hour. That way I won't have to worry about missing my meeting with you or worry about you going over there without me. I'll tell Paxton you three are due to join us in one hour. Don't be late," he warned. "Your arrival will be the necessary impetus to get them to talk. To actually make a decision about what to do."

"I'll need a portal to Paxton's lab though, please."

Rolling her eyes, she quickly sketched out a new one, then dropped it on her floor. She took a step back.

"Remember, one hour."

Tammy clung to Storey's hand. Storey confirmed, "We'll be there."

He gave them a long look, then stepped through and disappeared.

Just like that, they were alone.

ERIC HATED LEAVING Storey. Pressure squeezed his chest tight. It wasn't so much the separation, although that was part of it, but more the fact that everything was screwing up – no matter what they did. He didn't know if it was the stylus, the damage to the dimensions, or something worse. With everything so unstable, he hated leaving her behind. And Tammy.

The black mist dissipated. Eric looked around, frowning. Paxton's lab was deserted. Not all that unusual, but given the unpredictable events that had recently occurred, it didn't make him feel any better. Striding to the conference room, he found Paxton and the Council members in session.

Paxton broke off speaking, relief washing over his face as he caught sight of Eric. Standing, he cried, "There you are." A worried look slipped onto his face as he peered around behind Eric, "Are you alone?"

Eric glanced over his shoulder, only realizing as he did so that Paxton was asking about Storey…and maybe about Tammy as well. "Yes," he said brusquely. As Paxton sat back again, relaxed and happy, he added, "but not for long. Both Storey and Tammy will be here in less than an hour."

He'd have laughed if he could have at the look of horror on his mentor's face. "You called me back here, remember. We were having some big issues over there."

Paxton's white wispy hair bobbed as he nodded. "I understand that. But they can't come here. You'll have to stop them."

"No. I'm not going to. I'm not sending Storey and Tammy back to the Louer world alone. That's just foolish. We tried once and that ended in disaster."

The Council had listened with rapt attention to this point but no more. First one then another piped up with questions.

"Who is Tammy?"

"What disaster?"

Paxton glared at him. Eric shrugged. "Maybe they should know. The girls will be here soon. Besides, you brought me home."

"Know what?" Council member Eragin spoke up. Middle-aged and portly he had a self-professed air of importance like the other Council members, but he'd always been straightforward in his dealings with Eric.

Eric raised a brow in question to Paxton. Paxton held a unique position here. He had more seniority than many of the members added together and he headed the science and technology institute, but essentially he lived in the lab. He'd also been Eric's mentor and dare he say – friend – for most of Eric's life. He was a much bigger influence in Eric's life than his own father. That had to be a good thing, considering the mess his father was current-ly stirring up.

Paxton sighed, ran his fingers through his hair, then nodded. "Let's have everything out in the open."

"Good." The telling took a bit, but Eric finally brought the members up to speed on where he and Storey had been and the problems they'd encountered in the process. With another look at Paxton, he asked, "How much do they know of my father's situation?"

He was almost sorry for asking. Paxton aged in front of him, his wrinkles deepened and the look in his eyes…well, for that alone, Eric was sorry he'd mentioned the subject. Paxton's eyes flattened to black and the sadness Eric saw there would have made him weep on any other day.

"I'm sorry," he said gently, hating that his father could do this to such a good man. "If we're going to stop this vicious cycle we have to get things out in the open and keep them there."

"I know." Paxton cleared his throat. "I'll explain this part."

That was good. It not only allowed Eric some assimilation time, it also allowed him a chance to observe the reactions of the six council members. Their expressions ranged from horror to fear and one older fellow, Marxel, just didn't get it. Even after several explanations he still didn't seem to understand what the Councilman had done.

By the time he did, they'd wasted precious minutes. Eric couldn't resist checking the time for the umpteenth time. Now Storey would be there in a half hour. "The meeting needs to get on track. The girls will be here very soon." He waited a moment and then said into the silence, "What do you want to do about my father?"

There. It was out in the open. His father had made some bad decisions and someone needed to make an official decision. This was personal for Eric. He didn't really want his father left over there, no matter how tempting an idea initially.

"I do however have several stipulations to put forth. If I go to rescue my father, I won't see him return to his position of power. He abused his station and he's tried to hurt someone who has only been a friend to us. Should your decision be that the Councilman will regain his title once he has been rescued, then—"

"No, the Councilman has lost his title. I confronted your father. He admitted to changing Storey's codex to send her to the Louers' dimension. Based on that the council held an emergency meeting and told him he was done. He disappeared shortly after that." Paxton ran a hand through his wispy hair. "I suspect he's done this to extract revenge on the person he blames for everything that has gone wrong in his life."

Eric settled back on his heels. That actually made sense.

"We need to vote on his replacement – something that hasn't had to be done in decades. So while he still holds the title, it and he are now powerless."

Eric gave a short nod. "Good. So plans?"

The discussion became hot and heavy as suggestions were offered and rejected as the top brains and strategists of Eric's city put their heads together. He listened carefully, happy when his lowly opinion was asked for and his suggestions listened to. During the meeting several of his supervisors came and went as potential actions were considered by everyone.

There was no consensus. The various suggestions were problematic. Eric knew that to cross over with large numbers as a show of force could cause problems with the dimensional energy again. It was also liable to destroy the Louers and only a small portion of those people were responsible for either of the kidnappings. As with every civilization, there were small renegade groups that gave the other people a bad name. His father had just become an example in his own society.

"Stealth is required," he said, his voice firm. "A small force. In and out. Using our codexes, we should be able to travel close to the group, rescue the Councilman and slip home before the Louers know what's happened. If we go in with a large force, we are asking for trouble and…" he paused, thinking about how he and Storey had woken up after somehow being knocked out, "they may have a weapon or skill we can't compete with."

At their outraged looks he filled them in on what had happened.

Paxton interrupted, "Are you sure they didn't knock you out?"

Of everyone, he seemed the most upset. Eric wasn't sure if it was because of the treatment he'd received or the fact that the Louers might have superior technology. True, his people had amazing technology, but they'd achieved it through industrial espionage. If Storey's people had the same technology he had no doubt they'd have developed it much further than his people.

"No, I was not knocked out physically. It might be a telepathic weapon, since they communicate this way most of the time."

That set them off again. Eric sat back and tried to let it wash over him, their voices like the cacophony of a rising hurricane.

As in the eye of the storm, silence descended.

Then horrified gasps sounded.

The eye lasted barely a few seconds, then the storm hit.

Eric opened his eyes to find the council standing and almost shouting as a group, their arms pointing at the doorway. Eric turned.

Storey. And Tammy. And Skorky.

CHAPTER 15

S TOREY LOOKED OVER at him and rolled her eyes. Eric gave a shout of laughter and went to stand behind them, an arm on the shoulders of each girl. He waited for the men to calm down. For Marxel, it seemed as if the shock was almost too much. He sat, a gray cast to his skin, and seemed barely able to open his mouth. Eric motioned at Paxton, who immediately rushed to his old friend.

"I'm fine. Or I will be when I get rid of this abomination."

Storey's back stiffened. How dare he? Tammy clung closer, almost crawling up Storey's legs. She frowned at the elder. "Would that be me, Tammy or Skorky that you are calling an abomination?"

Eric squeezed her shoulder. "Easy," he whispered.

The elder's mouth opened and closed several times but no words came out. Storey nodded once and released her gaze on the hapless man to stare at Paxton.

Paxton rushed to speak. "Now, Storey, remember to see a Louer here in the chambers, particularly after the recent problem, is going to cause some distress."

"Of course," she said coolly. "As long as everyone is aware she is a child and a victim here. Not an aggressive warrior. She deserves our help. Not our hate."

The rumble of dissent had her sticking her jaw out.

Speaking loudly to get over the din, she said, "You

called Eric home when we were going to make another attempt to return this child to her family. If we can rescue the Councilman, something I'm not terribly in favor of given his behavior toward me, then I'm game to lend a hand. Otherwise, my priority at the moment is getting Tammy home."

All eyes focused on Tammy.

"She's a juvenile Louer?" One of the men at the back of the room spoke up. With so many staring at her, Storey didn't know which one.

"Yes. The animal is her pet." Taking advantage of the calmer atmosphere, she quickly gave an explanation as to how she and Tammy had met.

Understanding lit some of their faces, others showed no softening.

"How can we use this?"

Again, Storey couldn't see the speaker. "The group that grabbed Tammy is the same group that is holding the Councilman. She can't be taken back there. Her life is in danger."

"We should trade her. We'd get rid of two problems at once."

Storey gasped, unwittingly squeezing Tammy's hand. Tammy opened her mouth and the noise that screamed out of her mouth had everyone in the room clapping their hands over their ears and crying out. Storey slipped off her backpack and with Eric's help dug in to find a granola bar. Pulling it out, Storey held it out for Tammy who snatched it up with teary eyes. The noise shut off immediately.

"Good God, what was that?"

"That was the scream of betrayal for an adult who'd trade a defenseless child for a lying, cheating, vindictive Councilman," she snapped, her fury so great she doubted she'd be able to control what came out of her mouth if anyone said anything else about throwing Tammy to her death.

The room full of men stilled.

Behind her, Eric whispered, "I think that's the first time they've ever been told off."

"It's too bad," she bit off, "that this attitude is allowed to permeate through your people. It doesn't show any of you in a good light."

Knowing the others heard her, she added, "Reminds me of the actions of the same person you're asking us to go save." Her smile, grim and ferocious, beamed as she added, "That was also a death sentence."

Silence. The elders looked at each other, then down at their various papers. Paxton didn't appear to know how to answer that.

Eric spoke up, his tone placating, as if hoping to soothe the storm. "Time is an issue here. They were prepared to sacrifice Tammy within days. My father could face the same fate."

Paxton bolted to his feet. "You must go. Return Tammy then travel to where the Councilman is being held. While you gain intelligence, we'll pull a party together to meet you there. Time it to the minute. The team will port in, rescue him and all can return home. With enough codexes, the trip will take only minutes."

The rest of the elders sighed happily. Obviously, with a proactive plan finally put forward, they were prepared to jump behind it.

"Good. You do that." Storey turned abruptly and tugged Tammy back into the other room. Tammy followed obediently, still munching on her treat. Skorky sat in her hood, delicately working on his piece of bar.

"Hey wait, what's the matter?" Eric called out behind her, racing to catch up.

"Nothing," she said. At least nothing more than all of

the things wrong in her world right now. "We're so far behind schedule. If we stay here and do nothing but let them rant, Tammy will be our age before they get the plan moving. This way, we can take care of one problem, while they work on another problem."

She spun around, wondering at his silence. "Right?"

"Right." He grinned. "I'm just thinking we should have you attend all the Council meetings to get things done."

She shot him a horrified look. "Do you hate me that much?"

His grin flashed wickedly. "No, I like you that much I'd like to find reasons to keep you closer."

"Oh," she brightened. "For that reason alone, I'd consider it, but I can tell you right now that those old farts in there wouldn't let it happen."

He wrapped an arm around her shoulders and chucked the ever silent Tammy under the chin making her laugh. "I'm up for anything that keeps you in my world."

"Are you talking to Tammy or me?" At his look, she snickered. "Come on, let's return Tammy to her family, although I'm going to miss her something awful. And to think we're going to rescue your father now."

"He might learn something from this adventure." He laughed and tugged her toward the corner of the lab where the portal was.

"Yeah," she said darkly, "he might be worse now!"

Before she knew it the black smoke had risen to her waist. Tammy snuggled in close.

"I wish she could talk."

In the back of her head, a small voice said, "I do talk. Why can't you hear me?"

Storey shot a startled look at Tammy. Then blackness took over and she couldn't see or hear anything.

ERIC JUST BARELY caught an odd look on Storey's face before everything went dark. He tightened his arm around her shoulder, reassured as she cuddled closer. Tammy's arms wrapped tight around both of them. He had to admit, it wasn't going to be easy to say good-bye to her. Not being able to speak had kept them from learning anything about her people or lifestyle, but had maybe made the visit a little easier on them if her speech and communication abilities were anything like her screaming.

That noise she made had to be a lethal weapon.

The black fog started to recede.

The trip seemed longer this time. They'd had so many problems traveling lately that he no longer had the same assurance that all would be well. Still, if one didn't understand all the things that could go wrong, then it was impossible to be prepared.

Maybe that was a good thing.

He studied the familiar looking trees. "Looks like we're here."

"Hmm. Wherever here is?" Storey stepped back and checked out the sky and the surrounding hilly terrain. "It looks different than the last location."

Eric checked out the trees that dotted the landscape. "It's similar – we could be close to the last spot – but I don't recognize the area."

"Let's head over there." Storey pointed to the grove of evergreen trees in the distance.

"Why trees again?"

"I don't know. I guess I'd feel better if we weren't out in the open like this..."

"Got it." He was good with that. "First things first. Give me your codex." He unclipped both of them, and a quick glance toward Tammy, he dropped them into a different pocket on his left leg. With Tammy busy looking around, she never even saw the movement. He gave a soft chuckle, then led the way, trying to keep an eye on the open fields around them.

The closer they got to the trees however, the more nervous Storey started to act. She turned to look behind them several times, even to the point of turning around and walking backwards to check out the area.

"What's the matter?"

"I don't know," she admitted. "It's like a weird buzzing in my head. Sometimes at my home, when I walk beside a large hydro station, I can hear a similar sound. I almost recognize it, but it shouldn't exist in this location."

"Hydro station?"

She shook her head. "Creates electricity for our cities."

"Electricity?"

"Yeah, you know lights to see by, stoves to cook with, monitors to keep an eye on crossings; they all plug into wall outlets that provide the necessary power to make them run." She walked a few moments in silence then sighed. "You don't have that kind of power, do you?"

He shook his head. "Not like that. We have fuel cells that keep things running. But I think our requirements are much less than yours."

They'd almost reached the grove of trees, when Tammy started. She tugged on Storey's arm until Storey looked at her. "What's the matter?"

Tammy pointed.

Storey spun around but Eric was way ahead of her. "Louers."

STOREY STIFFENED. MEETING the Louers was why they

were here, but after their last meeting, she didn't trust them. The buzz in the air deepened. She studied Tammy's face looking for some sign that she might recognize the approaching Louers. Her face appeared normal. Not fearful, not worried, and yet, not happy. Very frustrating.

Eric whispered, "Careful."

That's when Storey realized she'd been retreating steadily. "Sorry." She glanced at him. "What is that noise? It's getting worse."

He frowned. "I don't hear it.

"Tammy appears unaffected."

Eric bent around Storey to check out Tammy's face. "So does that mean she knows them or doesn't know them? It's so frustrating she can't speak. We know she has healthy vocal cords and lungs."

Storey studied the approaching group. None were familiar. The buzz in her head deepened. She had to consider the idea that had trickled into her consciousness earlier. "I think the buzz is her people using telepathic communication. I heard it last time too."

He gripped her shoulders then relaxed slightly. "I can barely hear it."

The newcomers kept walking toward them. "They probably used a form of the same ability to knock us unconscious, too."

Eric walked several steps to the side to study Tammy's face. "She's busy doing something. If it isn't communicating with the approaching group then I don't know what else it could be."

"When we were in the portal, I thought Tammy spoke to me in my head." Storey hoped it had been her. She'd love to be able to talk to her.

"If it was her," Eric suggested, "that could mean you are receptive to their method but need to have the distractions filtered out so you can hear her."

That made sense. Just the thought of being able to communicate with Tammy was exciting. "Is the energy thinner, different in the portal?"

He nodded. They'd come to a dead stop, waiting until the Louers walked closer. Keeping his voice low, he answered, "Yes. The portal blocks everything else out."

"If I could learn to communicate with her, then in theory, I could learn to communicate with my stylus. That would be perfect."

She kept her eye on the leader of the group, a large overbearing male who strode slightly ahead of another dozen in their group. At least he didn't have any numbers on his arms. "I'm not liking this."

"Who is?"

Storey alternated between studying the group and then Tammy's face. "I don't understand why they have no facial expressions. It's like they are emotionless."

"Until you look them in the eyes."

At his words, Storey shifted her gaze to study the leader's eyes. Huge, deep set and dark, so dark it was hard to see if he had the same eye biology she had. She hadn't noticed any difference in Tammy's eyes.

His eyes weren't cold though; dark, curious, wary, yes. Certainly not emotionless. Interesting. She kept her hand resting on Tammy's shoulder – nonthreatening but protective. She didn't know what was about to happen but if anyone made a crosswise move against her…Storey planned to bolt – with Tammy. If she couldn't be assured of Tammy's safety, she wasn't leaving her behind.

Not that she had any idea of where to take her. *So please let everything work out.*

As the group approached, she watched all eyes zero in on Tammy. The buzzing in the air pumped up. Tammy started bouncing, her fingers were clenching Storey's hand so tightly, Storey didn't realize she was squeezing back so hard, Tammy couldn't go to see the others even if she wanted to.

Finding it difficult to do, Storey forced herself to let go of the little girl's hand. As if freed by an elastic band, Tammy shot forward and launched herself into the lead male's arms.

Eric and Storey inched closer, watching as Tammy was caught and held in a tight grip.

"Well, that's good news."

"It looks that way. We don't know that this is Tammy's father, but I guess it's safe to say that she's happy to see him."

"And he her." The group continued to march toward them, only now Tammy was wrapped tight in the leader's arms.

Her back straightened as the group stopped several feet in front of Storey. Storey didn't want to break eye contact with the leader but at the same time, she wanted to make sure Tammy was happy. Giving the little girl a quick look, she found her staring back at Storey. Storey couldn't help but smile at her.

For the first time, Tammy's lips curved upward in response.

"Tammy, that's perfect. I'm happy to see you smiling."

Tammy wiggled and the man holding her let her go. Tammy came running over to Storey and threw her arms tight around her waist. Storey bent and hugged her back. Skorky ran around Tammy's shoulders as if too excited to sit still. The others watched.

Tammy released Storey then hugged Eric in turn. He grinned at her. "I'm going to miss you, Tammy."

She ran back to the big male and stood at his side.

Then she turned to face them, waved at them both.

The world dimmed.

Storey watched as Eric crumpled to the ground in front of her.

"No." She struggled to stay on her feet.

The ground rushed to meet her.

CHAPTER 16

ERIC WINCED AT the sound. Someone was groaning, retching in a rhythm he recognized but didn't want to. The fumes of heavy stomach acid hit his nose just then and it was all he could do to not vomit himself. He had no idea who was sick, but he was about to join them if they didn't stop soon.

Then he heard a sound, just a faint moan, but it was enough. "Storey."

"Oh God, I hope not. That would mean I was here, caught in this no man's land still. Why couldn't it be like my clone or something?"

Eric laughed. Even feeling like crap, with her voice so woozy, her spunky attitude made him laugh. She might be sick but she wasn't screaming in pain and if her sense of humor was still there, things couldn't be that bad.

He opened his eyes. Where were they?

"Storey, are we prisoners again?"

"I have no idea. I can hardly move for the pain in my head."

Eric tried to sit up, and a hammer-sized boom exploded inside his head. Groaning, he collapsed back down. "What did they do to us?" he whispered when he could.

"I have no idea. We're in some kind of cave again. At least that's all I can see. There's no opening and it kind of reminds me of the Louers' old dimension except for one huge thing missing – the smell."

Eric sniffed the air experimentally. The last place he wanted to find himself was back in that horrible dimension, but if the Louers could do things like they'd done to Storey and him without them even letting on how they'd been done, he'd be happy to leave and never come back.

And he still had to rescue his father.

Gritting his teeth, he sat up very slowly and looked around. The air was murky. He could make out Storey but not much else.

"Wise of you to take it slow. I made the mistake of jumping up." Storey tried to smile, but gave up the attempt. "After that the contents of my stomach came rushing up, too."

"At least we're together."

"True." she agreed. "If you're awake enough, and my stomach has settled enough, can we port away from here? It looks like we're still prisoners and I'm really not wanting to be around when they come back."

Eager relief swept through him at her words. "Did they leave us a portal?"

"If we still have the packets, then I think so. I hope so."

Eric checked his ranger pants. Good. He still had the same packet that they'd missed last time. It should have a portal.

Storey found hers, too. "Looks like we're good. I'm surprised considering Tammy saw us pack up these. I don't know how much she understood of codexes and portals. I'm really hoping she didn't comprehend much."

Eric winced, realizing just how much an older Louer would have understood if they'd seen what Tammy had seen. "Let's hope she's too young to give an accurate account."

"Yeah, you think?" Storey handed over her traveling

packet. "Codex or portal?"

Within seconds he had it open. She grabbed the spare shirt from the package.

"Codex." He pulled two spares out of the pockets and held them up with a big grin. "They didn't take these."

"Yay!" Storey turned her back to him, quickly changing her shirt.

"Why are you changing?"

She snorted. "My shirt took a hit when my stomach emptied. I don't really want to be wearing my lunch for the rest of the day, thank you."

Turning back, she asked, "Eric, can you repackage all this?"

Eric looked up from his codex, frowning. "Yes. Have you got everything you need? We should have thrown your backpack in there."

"Practice makes perfect," she muttered. He was right, but she didn't need to be reminded of it. Fascinated, she watched the clothing and other items, minus her sketchbook, shrink into a tiny packet. She so needed that technology. Every female did, no matter what dimension they occupied.

"Are you ready?"

Storey looked over at him. Her travel pouch was safely stored away. "Yes."

Even as she spoke, she heard the sounds he'd obviously already heard.

Footsteps.

"Shit." She raced over to his side. "Let's go."

As she finished speaking, the black mist wrapped around her feet. Eric's arms came around her shoulders, tugging her close. "Say good-bye to Tammy."

"Oh." Storey leaned back. "I hope she's going to be okay now."

"She should be fine."

That's not quite what she wanted to hear, but as the mist rose, the choice to change things disappeared. They still had to find a way to fix the portal between the old and new Louer world. If such a thing were possible. Should she leave a note for Tammy's father, explaining the portal's new functionality? Maybe she'd get the chance to say good-bye then.

"She'll be fine," Eric whispered against her hair. "Tammy is with people that know her and we're going to believe that she's loved."

Storey knew he was right, but...even though she'd seen Tammy held high and happy in the leader's arms, she felt like she'd deserted her. And Skorky.

"I'll miss her," she whispered.

"I know." His arms tightened around her. "So will I."

She squeezed him tight and waited for the trip to complete. Being snug tight against his chest made it easier. "Sure wish we were going home."

His arms tightened.

Storey rested her cheek against his chest. How nice to be held by him again. He smelled so masculine and seemed so strong. It had been a long time for her. She could hardly remember what it was like to be in a relationship. As for her old boyfriend, well, she could hardly remember what he looked like either. Eric had taken his spot in her life.

"Are you okay?"

With a warm sigh, she rubbed her cheek against his chest. His arms squeezed and released. She did it again. He gripped her tight. "Witch, that tickles."

She giggled. "Sorry. Shouldn't tease you."

"Teasing is fine, but I'd just as soon be back in one of our dimensions where we might be able to do a little more than tease," he responded gently.

Storey cuddled closer. She hadn't known Eric long

enough to be comfortable taking the next step in their relationship. But she wasn't far off. She'd almost made it there with her ex before he'd moved.

The black mist seemed to last forever. Considering this was a short hop distance-wise, not even leaving the dimension, she didn't understand why it hadn't been a short port. Sometimes though, it seemed like the Internet; the more users, the slower the speed.

Although there was only she and Eric traveling here at the moment, there could be any number of people traveling this way in Eric's dimension. And hadn't Paxton said something about still having trouble with tears and gates?

Finally the mist lowered. Storey found herself regretting it. The tiny space was peaceful, almost intimate in a way. As if there were no other beings, no other pressing issues to deal with – just the two of them.

"Looks like we're back to saving the world again." Storey did a slow turn to make sure they were alone. She kind of recognized the area, but couldn't be totally sure. A group of trees lined the left side of the meadow they now occupied, and she thought the creek would be down a ways but in the same direction. "Can we determine where your father is from here?"

"I think so. Being the Councilman he has a tracker chip embedded in his arm. It was done decades ago. With any luck, it's still active and the codex can read it. It's always an iffy thing in another dimension as you don't know what might have been screwed up with all the traveling. The energy is going to affect it somehow, at least over time. This is my father's first offworld travel though, so it should be okay."

"Let's check first." She kept an eye out as they walked toward the trees again. Seemed like that's always the first thing they did when they arrived at one of these dimensions. Still, shelter was shelter.

After what seemed like a long time, but was probably only minutes, he said, "Got it."

Storey tilted her head, hearing a steady beat coming from his arm. "Straight ahead."

At the trees, they stopped to check the beacon again. Following the same path, they came to the creek. Storey had a drink, but kept glancing around, ever mindful of the women who'd come upon them last time. Neither of them saw anyone walking around this time, and the tracking system was leading them back to the caves in the cliff.

"Well, at least we know we're in the right place." Storey ran a hand over her hair, wishing for a long hot soak and for this to all be over with. She was feeling melancholic over leaving Tammy behind.

As they approached the cliff's edge, they stopped at the same bunch of trees as last time. She surveyed the cliff dwellings, thankful the sun was behind clouds. "The place looks deserted."

"I wish, but so not likely," Eric snorted. "I sent a message to Paxton. Haven't heard back from him yet."

"We could use that backup team."

"I know. I asked. We need to have portals out at the ready this time, too."

Storey, winced, remembering how they'd had to jump, or in her case tumble, through the last portal as the Louers rushed them. "Yeah, I'd like to not have a repeat of last time, thank you."

"Me too. We'll wait here a bit longer until we hear from Paxton."

"In that case, there is something I need to ask the stylus. I should have asked him earlier." She plunked down on the ground, and removed the readymade portals she'd stashed in there and some blank paper. "Stylus, we need to fix the portal from this dimension to the Louers' old dimension. Then Tammy's father will remain the leader and these people can travel back and forth at will."

Yes.

Immediately Storey's hand flashed and danced on the paper. She watched, fascinated, as her stylus created something so advanced and difficult in mere seconds, that it was more like science fiction to her than reality. Moments later, her hand stilled.

"Is it done?"

Yes.

She gave Eric a wide smile. "We're good."

Eric crouched down to stare at the mess on her paper. "Does that mean anything to you?"

Giving the paper some serious study time, she finally shook her head. "Not at all." She turned the paper around slowly, looking for anything identifiable within the weird scribbles. Nothing. "Stylus, is the portal now functional?"

Yes.

"Can you tell Tammy's father that the portal works?"

A weird buzzing filled the air.

"It can't do that. Can it?" Eric's puzzled voice spoke right at her ear.

"I have no idea. I was going to ask it to write a letter and explain everything about Tammy and the portal, but…" the buzzing became louder and louder. Just as she was ready to clap her hands over her ears, the noise stopped.

She exchanged a surprised look with Eric. Cautiously, she asked, "Stylus, what was that all about?"

I spoke with the leader.

"Um, just like that? You can communicate with him? Why did you not say so earlier?" she asked in exasperation. "We could have told them about Tammy before. And set up a way to return her."

Yes. I, too, am a Louer.

She exchanged an irritated look with Eric. She'd have to think on the implications of this. Later. "So does he understand about Tammy and the fixed broken portal? About our visit and the new dimension?" It sounded too good to be true, but given all the other things the stylus had done, it seemed on par.

Yes.

"And he won't interfere with our mission to rescue my father?" Eric asked, doubt, turning to almost disbelief in his voice.

No. He will deal with the other group after we leave. Now that the portal works, he will be able to get their tools and the rest of their people over.

Eric pursed his lips. "Really. And they will leave my dimension alone?"

He says they want nothing to do with your people. They want to be left alone to build a new life here.

"I'd like that, too," Storey muttered. "Now we just have to muzzle your father so he stops interfering with the Louers!"

That was the leader's request. Take your father home and keep him there.

"And we'd be happy to. Just as soon as we can rescue the Councilman." She sighed. "Stylus, please make sure Tammy knows how much we miss her." Her stomach growled. Talk about a reminder of Tammy. Storey groaned silently. She'd love a home cooked meal right now. Her mom was a great cook; she just didn't have much time or inclination to do much these days. Come to think of it, her mom hadn't dated in years, either.

Storey had been grateful to not have to deal with a long line of "uncles" but still, she had to wonder if her mom was happy or if she'd abstained from the dating scene on purpose as Storey had gotten older. She'd never taken the time to ask her. *There's nothing like having your perception of reality blown apart by crossing dimensions to make you take a hard look at who you are.*

"Heavy thoughts?"

Storey glanced up. "Lots. Just looking back on my life."

He grimaced. "I've been doing a bit of that myself. Once you uncover one lie, like my perception of my father, it's almost impossible to not dissect the rest of your life looking for more."

"I think you should contact Paxton again."

Eric frowned. "I've been contacting him every ten minutes. There's no answer."

Storey frowned. Figures. "So are we going in without them? Waiting longer? What could be wrong?" She was pulling out her stylus as she spoke. Grabbing one of the small pieces of blank paper, she asked the stylus, "Contact Paxton and find out what the holdup is, please."

Her right hand jerked immediately. Even after all this time, she still watched in fascination as the stylus communicated through to Paxton in an alternate dimension.

He's under attack.

"What?" Eric stared at her before pulling the sketchbook away to read the message himself. "Surely not from the Louers again, right?"

At Eric's question, the stylus jumped to answer. *Yes, they attacked after you left. They are holding the Councilman hostage in the new dimension.*

"If we rescue the hostage, will that stop their attack on Eric's dimension?"

No. They are there now.

Eric, anger glinting deep in his eyes, added, "That also means that the force here is small. We will have an easier time rescuing him."

"Sure, but why would we?" she couldn't help but

mutter.

"I understand your feelings, but imagine what trouble he could stir up for us if left here for a week or two."

She'd give him that point. "So what do you want to do? Go home and help fight the Louers off, stay here and rescue your father?"

"Damn."

Storey's gaze widened. A hint of laugher sounded in her voice as she said, "Now I know you're upset. That's like the third time I've ever heard you swear."

He frowned at her. "Now is hardly the time."

Storey sat back down. "Stylus, how many Louers are left guarding the Councilman?"

There are twelve adults here.

Twelve. That wasn't so bad. "What about women and children?"

There are no children here and that count includes the females. They are guards in this group.

"The stylus has to be communicating telepathically with the Louers to know this stuff." Eric stared at Storey and her sheet of paper.

"That would mean he's still more person than computer – right?" The concept confused her. She'd assumed and was sure that she'd clarified the issue at one point. She'd believed the stylus was more computer thingy than alive. That assumption made it easier for her to deal with the concept of the prisoners held indefinitely inside the pencil.

An intense humming filled the air. This time there was an unpleasantness to it. Storey looked around uneasily. Up to this point, the humming had always had a benign feeling to it. "Eric, the buzzing is stronger."

"Yeah. I'm hearing it, myself." His voice was grim, his eyes never still, darting from place to place. "Are they coming toward us, then?"

"I'm wondering. At only twelve left behind, I doubt they are all approaching." Turning the stylus around in her fingers, she asked, "Stylus, are the Louers approaching us?"

Yes. A group of four is approaching from inside the cliff.

Storey's voice rose as she bolted to her feet. "How did they find out about us?"

The stylus's answer came quickly.

I told them.

Eric's jaw clenched. Storey felt betrayal sweep through her, although she fought it, didn't want to believe it would have done such a thing.

It's the fastest way to find your father and get you home to help the rest of your world.

Storey took a deep breath and let it out slowly. She gazed into Eric's furious eyes. "We might not like it, but he's right." A muscle twitched on the corner of Eric's jaw. "If we can rescue him, we can jump through a portal together."

"We *had* the element of surprise. Not now. We have portals but only for the moment. Remember last time?"

"Shit." She didn't know what to do. "Stylus, how can we get in and out without being caught?"

Port in.

"What?"

Port to where you found Tammy.

Her mouth dropped. She should have considered that. With Eric supporting the paper on his back, she quickly drew an image of the cave where they'd rescued Tammy from. "Almost done."

"Then draw faster and make sure you're drawing this location or something similar so we can get out cleaner."

"Except for the time travel issue."

"Right. So scrap the second portal then. We'll codex out."

Her hand flew as her pulse screamed at them to run.

Eric continued to talk while she worked. "We need to search for the stuff they stole from us last time. Though I've been thinking. Would they have gone through a portal or used a codex when they didn't know where they were going or how to get back?"

She frowned. There's no way she would.

Eric twisted slightly to see her. "We used the one portal to go to my world, remember. The others, although which ones I don't remember exactly, would have taken them to your world."

"And they would have had to deal with the time travel issue," Storey said, not raising her head. "Maybe they used your father's codex? With his help?"

Finally she finished. It felt like a half hour but she'd whipped the sketches together in minutes.

The buzzing in her ears was getting louder. Almost a bee sound. Incredibly hard to listen to. She smacked the side of her head. "They have to be close. Let's go."

As if the approaching Louers could sense what they were planning, the noise became deafening.

"Hurry, they're trying to knock us out before we can leave."

Storey dropped the portal on the ground, almost pushing Eric into it. He grabbed her hand. "I want you with me. Let's not get separated."

Warmth wrapped around her heart. "I'm here. I have to make sure we grab this portal as we go through. We can't take any more chances."

The pressure in her ears built up. She gasped at the pain, dropping to her knees at the edge of the paper. "Go, go. They're almost here."

Holding her left hand, the corner of the paper clenched in her right, Eric jumped in and pulled her with him.

Blackness surged through her consciousness as she fell into the hole.

CHAPTER 17

Someone moaned.

Storey wished they'd stop. Her headache boomed deep inside. "Easy, Storey." Eric's voice split right through her skull. She shuddered.

"It's over now, but we almost didn't make it. We're still feeling the effects of their telepathic weapon."

Storey sat up in a panic, grabbing her head as it threatened to explode. "Did the portal come with us?"

The large sheet of paper landed in the dirt in front of her. Groaning, she dropped back to the ground. "Thank heavens. I don't think I'd be able to run anywhere right now."

"Too bad," snapped an angry voice behind them. "You took so long to get here, we don't have a choice. We have to leave now."

Storey closed her eyes. Damn. The Councilman still lived.

"Hello, father." Eric struggled to his feet.

Storey didn't bother. Besides, she wasn't sure she could. The pounding inside her skull had eased slightly, but not enough to make movement a good idea yet.

"Storey? You can recuperate back home."

Home? Her eyelids popped open. "That much effort might be possible."

"Better yet," the Councilman snapped, "we leave you here. You're responsible for this mess. Let's go, Eric."

"No." Eric's harsh voice left no doubt about his seriousness. "She comes with us or I leave you here."

Storey's gaze landed on the Councilman's face long enough to see the hate glazing his eyes. He obviously hadn't come to terms with her presence in his world. At least back at Paxton's lab, she knew they'd take care of him. With false energy, she struggled to her feet, but was forced to stay bent over for a long moment to adjust to being vertical.

"Can you see any of the other codexes? Portals?" She studied around the dark space. It appeared empty. But in the darkness, who could tell for sure. And they didn't have time for a full search right now.

"Father, is there anything left here with you?"

"No, they didn't understand and ruined them with water and they are wearing the codexes. That's how they went home." He snorted as he scrambled to his feet. "They didn't need much guidance on their usage."

Storey exchanged an appalled look with Eric. How much did the Louers know of Toran technology after their session with Eric's father? "If Paxton can shut them down that might be the easiest way to deal with any that can't be retrieved."

"And if he can't?" Eric glared at his father. "Did you really help them use the codexes…against your own people?" His jaw worked furiously. "Have you so little regard for your home? That you would bring something like this on them?"

The Councilman turned his back on Storey to glower at Eric. He sniffed hard and lifted his nose into the air. "It was the only way to secure my safety."

"Jesus," Storey muttered under her breath. "Eric, are you prepared to trust his word about the portals and codexes?"

Running a hand through his short cropped hair, Eric

frowned. He walked the small space where his father had been held. There were small pieces of paper on the ground at the doorway to the next cavern, soaked and damaged beyond use. "He's correct about these." Eric pointed to the fragments. "Let's hope Paxton *can* disable the remaining codexes."

Storey walked over, the portal in her hand. "I'll ask the stylus to disable any still functioning portals as well. Soon as we get somewhere safe."

"That makes sense."

"Enough already," snapped the Councilman. "The guards will be here any minute. Let's go."

Even as the words left his mouth they heard heavy sounds of someone running. Then another set of running footsteps.

"Shit." Storey stepped back to give Eric room. "Hurry."

Eric bent over in agony, his hands clasped to his ears.

"My head. The pain. I can't think."

That same horrible noise built up inside Storey's head. Damn the Louers' and their secret weapon. "We have to go. Punch the codes." Storey gasped as the pain increased.

"Hurry up," snapped the Councilman. The noise twisted his features, but didn't seem to be crippling him the same as Eric and her. "Why can't we travel by codex? Or portals?"

Time. That's why they couldn't go by portal. "It has to be codex. Time is a problem with portals." Storey yelled to be heard over the pounding in her head.

Eric's gaze widened as he understood her. "Right. I forgot." He took a deep breath, pulled back his sleeve and tapped a sequence of numbers.

The Councilman stepped closer, his nervous gaze searching the darkness around them. Hissing, he said,

"Hurry."

"It takes a moment." Eric's face twisted against the unbearable noise. He bent over gasping for breath. Mist swirled up from the ground. Storey struggled to remain conscious as pain turned her world black. She didn't know how Eric was faring or why the Councilman seemed unaffected. Unless his sheer size had something to do with it.

Gratefully, she realized that the higher the black mist, the less the noise penetrated. It didn't take long before she could stand up straight. Over Eric's shoulder she watched several Louer guards race into the chamber. "Uh, Eric? How far does the mist have to climb before it's too late to reverse?"

She nodded behind him. He turned his head, his shoulders relaxed. "It's too late now."

The Councilman glared at her. "Don't be telling her any of our secrets."

"It's hardly a secret, Father. Besides, it's nothing to what you've told them."

Keeping a wary eye on the two Louers, Storey held her breath until the mist blocked her view. They were safe.

The black mist was damn freaky. She didn't under-stand how the system worked. If she was in the middle of the haze, would it only transport part of her? If the Louers had tried to jump in, would only part of them make it? That thought shook her.

Still, they'd gotten away clean. Eric was here with her, Tammy was home and they were even bringing the Councilman back. There might be some skirmishing going on in Eric's dimension, but his people were perfectly capable of taking care of that problem now. Maybe she could finally go home. In truth, she wanted a hug from her mother. She couldn't believe how much she'd missed her.

The mist closed over her head.

"Thank heavens for that," she whispered.

"We're fine. Almost home now."

She closed her eyes and waited for the endless darkness to lighten. And waited. "Eric?"

"Another moment. The codex has stopped signaling."

His comforting tone of voice reassured her almost as much as his words. She breathed a sigh of relief. "Good, I was afraid something else had gone wrong."

"No. Everything's fine. Almost there."

The stiffness eased from her shoulders and her insides relaxed.

Just then two hands reached out and gave her a shove – hard. She lost her balance.

A shocked shriek escaped her.

ERIC REACHED OUT to grab her and yelled, "Storey? What's the matter?"

There was only silence.

And empty space.

DARKEST DESIGNS

(Book 3 of Design Series)

Dale Mayer

Acknowledgments

Darkest Designs wouldn't have been possible without the support of my friends and family. Many hands helped with proofreading, editing, and beta reading to make this book come together. I had a vision, but it took many people to make that vision real. I thank you all.

PROLOGUE

In Deadly Designs we let off with this chapter…

S OMEONE MOANED.

Storey wished they'd stop. Her headache boomed deep inside. "Easy, Storey." Eric's voice split right through her skull. She shuddered.

"It's over now, but we almost didn't make it. We're still feeling the effects of their telepathic weapon."

Storey sat up in a panic, grabbing her head as it threatened to explode. "Did the portal come with us?"

The large sheet of paper landed in the dirt in front of her. Groaning, she dropped back to the ground and picked up the paper. "Thank heavens. I don't think I'd be able to run anywhere right now."

"Too bad," snapped an angry voice behind them. "You took so long to get here, we don't have a choice. We have to leave now."

Storey closed her eyes. Damn. The Councilman still lived.

"Hello, father." Eric struggled to his feet.

Storey didn't bother. Besides, she wasn't sure she could. The pounding inside her skull had eased slightly, but not enough to make movement a good idea yet.

"Storey? You can recuperate back home."

Home? Her eyelids popped open. "That much effort might be possible."

"Better yet," the Councilman snapped, "we leave you

here. You're responsible for this mess. Let's go, Eric."

"No." Eric's harsh voice left no doubt about his seriousness. "She comes with us or I leave you here."

Storey's gaze landed on the Councilman's face long enough to see the hate glazing his eyes. He obviously hadn't come to terms with her presence in his world. At least back at Paxton's lab, she knew they'd take care of him. With false energy, she struggled to her feet, but was forced to stay bent over for a long moment to adjust to being vertical.

"Can you see any of the other codexes? Portals?" She studied around the dark space. It appeared empty. But in the darkness, who could tell for sure? And they didn't have time for a full search right now.

"Father, did they leave anything here with you?"

"No, they didn't understand and ruined the portals with water. They are wearing the codexes. That's how they went home." He snorted as he scrambled to his feet. "They didn't need much guidance on their usage."

Storey exchanged an appalled look with Eric. How much did the Louers know of Toran technology after their session with Eric's father? "If Paxton can shut them down that might be the easiest way to deal with any that can't be retrieved."

"And if he can't?" Eric glared at his father. "Did you really help them use the codexes...against your own people?" His jaw worked furiously. "Have you so little regard for your home? That you would bring something like this on them?"

The Councilman turned his back on Storey to glower at Eric. He sniffed hard and lifted his nose into the air. "It was the only way to secure my safety."

"Jesus," Storey muttered under her breath. "Eric, are you prepared to trust his word about the portals and codexes?"

Running a hand through his short cropped hair, Eric frowned. He walked the small space where his father had been held. There were small pieces of paper on the ground at the doorway to the next cavern, soaked and damaged beyond use. "He's correct about these." Eric pointed to the fragments. "Let's hope Paxton *can* disable the remaining codexes."

Storey walked over, the portal in her hand. "I'll ask the stylus to disable any still functioning portals as well. Soon as we get somewhere safe."

"That makes sense."

"Enough already," snapped the Councilman. "The guards will be here any minute. Let's go."

Even as the words left his mouth they heard heavy sounds of someone running. Then another set of running footsteps.

"Shit." Storey stepped back to give Eric room. "Hurry."

Eric bent over in agony, his hands clasped to his ears.

"My head. The pain. I can't think."

That same horrible noise built up inside Storey's head. Damn the Louers' and their secret weapon. "We have to go. Punch the codes." Storey gasped as the pain increased.

"Hurry up," snapped the Councilman. The noise twisted his features, but didn't seem to be crippling him the same as Eric and her. "Why can't we travel by portal?"

Time. That's why they couldn't go by portal. "It has to be codex. Time is a problem with portals." Storey yelled to be heard over the pounding in her head.

Eric's gaze widened as he understood her. "Right. I forgot." He took a deep breath, pulled back his sleeve and tapped a sequence of numbers.

The Councilman stepped closer, his nervous gaze searching the darkness around them. Hissing, he said,

"Hurry."

"It takes a moment." Eric's face twisted against the unbearable noise. He bent over gasping for breath. Mist swirled up from the ground. Storey struggled to remain conscious as pain turned her world black. She didn't know how Eric was faring or why the Councilman seemed unaffected. Unless his sheer size had something to do with it.

Gratefully, she realized that the higher the black mist, the less the noise penetrated. It didn't take long before she could stand up straight. Over Eric's shoulder she watched several Louer guards race into the chamber. "Uh, Eric? How far does the mist have to climb before it's too late to reverse?"

She nodded behind him. He turned his head, his shoulders relaxed. "It's too late now."

The Councilman glared at her. "Don't be telling her any of our secrets."

"It's hardly a secret, Father. Besides, it's nothing to what you've told them."

Keeping a wary eye on the two Louers, Storey held her breath until the mist blocked her view. They were safe.

The black mist was damn freaky. She didn't understand how the system worked. If she was in the middle of the haze, would it only transport part of her? If the Louers had tried to jump in, would only part of them make it? That thought shook her.

Still, they'd gotten away clean. Eric was here with her, Tammy was home and they were even bringing the Councilman back. There might be some skirmishing going on in Eric's dimension, but his people were perfectly capable of taking care of that problem now. Maybe she could finally go home. In truth, she wanted a hug from her mother. She couldn't believe how much she'd missed her.

The mist closed over her head.

"Thank heavens for that," she whispered.

"We're almost home now."

She closed her eyes and waited for the endless darkness to lighten. And waited. "Eric?"

"Another moment. The codex has stopped signaling."

His comforting tone of voice reassured her almost as much as his words. She breathed a sigh of relief. "Good, I was afraid something else had gone wrong."

"No. Everything's fine. Almost there."

The stiffness eased from her shoulders and her insides relaxed.

Just then two hands reached out and gave her a shove – hard. She lost her balance.

A shocked shriek escaped her.

ERIC REACHED OUT to grab her and yelled, "Storey? What's the matter?"

There was only silence.

And empty space.

CHAPTER 1

STOREY COULDN'T BREATHE. She bent over and gasped, desperately trying to force her chest open to let air in. The pressure was killing her. She didn't dare pass out in case she didn't wake up. She gulped air like a grounded fish, trying to take in as much oxygen as she could. With each breath her lungs expanded easier, faster. Finally, some of the tension slipped off her shoulders and her muscles eased slightly. She stretched her neck and willed the rest of the strain away.

Wherever she was, she lay surrounded in a dense gray fog. Not shadowy, like the Louers' world, but a completely empty type of gloominess. In spite of her attempts to stop it, shudders slid down her spine in a continuous tremor. What had happened?

Then she remembered. Of course. They'd almost made it home – her, Eric and the Councilman. Then she'd been pushed out of the portal.

Damn.

"Eric?" She called out tentatively. No answer. She called out louder. "Eric." Still nothing. She yelled his name next, and when only a deafening silence answered, she screamed at the top of her lungs. "Eric! Are you there?"

Silence. And not a normal silence. A total absence of…anything. Beyond weird.

What had she expected? Why was it she hadn't seen

this coming? Not that she'd expected decent behavior from the man that had tried several times to have her killed, but to actually do the dirty work himself? That surprised her.

Stylus. She slapped her hands over the stylus, her pencil-like computer thingy. "Stylus, can you hear me?"

Yes.

"Oh thank you, God," she murmured. She closed her eyes. She wasn't alone. She could do this. With the stylus, she could do anything. Taking a deep breath, she let it go gustily, feeling her sense of optimism settle in. This was going to be okay. Feeling better, she asked, "Where are we?"

In-between.

Uh oh. Cautiously, she asked, "In-between what?"

Time and place.

She winced. That so didn't sound good. "What does that mean?"

It means we have no location.

No location? How could that be? She existed. Some-where. Therefore there was a place. It was here. "Sooo…" she pressed. "How do we get out of this?"

We don't have that information.

Okay, so maybe this wasn't going to be so easy. She shook her head, more to clear the negativity than in denial. Although denial of the circumstances was there – by the bucket loads. "So not a good answer. We'll have to find the information. The longer we stay stuck like this, the harder it's going to be to get home."

So saying she took a deep breath and stood up. Her surroundings looked the same. She placed a hand out into the dense space in front of her, but there was nothing there. And that freaked her out more than she cared to admit. She crouched down and studied her feet. Her shoes were muddy and showing signs of damage after the past week. She'd have to find new ones soon. She winced. She was focusing on her shoes to avoid thinking of the fogginess around them, in front of them…under them. Yet she could see her feet – barely. She straightened. In the Louers' mine she'd at least been able to tap the hard surface of the floor and recognize that she'd come to the end of whatever drop she'd taken.

Here…she stretched out the tip of her right shoe and tried to tap the space in front of her left shoe. Her shoe went below her left foot. She gasped and pulled her foot back. She tried to stand on her right foot like she had been a minute earlier, only now there was nothing solid beneath it. Her foot slipped down until she caught herself and leaned all her weight onto her left shoe. Slowly she moved her foot around and tested the ground behind and in front of her. Only there was nothing there. Oh God. Oh God. *Oh God!*

She straightened and rested her right foot on her left foot and closed her eyes, trying to concentrate on her balance. Why wasn't she one of those agile gymnast-cheerleader types who could stand on one leg for hours? She breathed in and out, in and out. Somewhat balanced, but knowing she couldn't keep this up, she called out, "Stylus…a little help here."

When there was no response, she snapped, panicked, "Like now!"

Researching our database. Our records show some people going In-between.

She brightened. "That's good right? So how did these people get out?"

They only traveled to In-between as part of the journey to their end destination.

"In other words they didn't stop in…In-between. Which really means it doesn't apply to us," she said in exasperation. "Has anyone gotten stuck In-between that you know of?"

Of course. You.

She groaned and leaned her head back. Her left leg was starting to ache. She wasn't going to be able to do this much longer. She spread her arms out to stabilize her footing. "Anyone else?"

We are continuing to search the archives for more cases.

Damn. "So best guess? Am I going to continue to fall if I put my weight on my right foot?"

It's possible.

"Possible? Yeah. I know it's possible. But is it likely?" She'd woken up here. Surely she hadn't been sleeping standing up? What if she tried to sit? Did she dare? Did she have any choice?

Her left leg trembled. Beads of sweat formed on her upper lip and the headache she'd had since she woke, minor pounding until now, started to kick her butt. She groaned with the effort to continue standing on one foot.

You could fall. See where you stop.

Well, it couldn't be worse than this. Could it? Oh boy. She so didn't want to try it out and see. The fall could knock her out again too.

But…maybe she could sit very close to her feet? There had to be something there for her foot to stand on. She ignored the fact that there had to have been something for her right foot initially too. She hadn't heard anything drop away either. In fact, she could barely hear anything.

She took a deep breath and crouched down slowly, swearing at her unsteady movement. With her bum down as far as it could go, her arms wrapped tightly around her legs, she dropped her weight onto her backside, as close to the heel of her left foot as possible.

And sat down.

And fell backwards.

"STOREY! WHERE ARE you?" Eric spun around inside the confines of the portal. Only his father stood at his side. "What happened to her?" he asked him, a hard knot of suspicion forming in his gut.

His father opened his eyes wide, and held his hands out in innocence. Eric's suspicions solidified. "She must have fallen," his father said, his voice holding just that perfect mix of concern and confusion that he'd used so many times before.

And Eric knew. "You pushed her, didn't you?" He watched as surprised anger lit the depths of his father's gaze.

"I did not."

"Did too." Eric didn't care if he sounded like a two year old arguing the point. In truth he wanted to break down and cry. Things couldn't get much worse. For the first time, he didn't know what to do. Somehow, this seemed too big to deal with. How could he possibly help Storey now? And all because of his father.

His father snorted. "So what if I did. Good riddance I say. Her influence on you was nothing less than a disaster. You'd never have spoken so disrespectfully to me before." He stabbed the air with his index finger. "I blame her for the mess my life is in."

Eric glared at him, emotions welling up. He wanted to punch that smug look off his father's face. He balled his fist and pulled back his arm. A red wave of anger and a need to hit out at something overwhelmed him.

"Eric. Don't." Paxton's sharp voice caught Eric just as the power built in his upper arm. Eric stopped, frozen, a fierce welling of denial inside. This wasn't fair. His father deserved to get his ass kicked and Eric was just the one to do it.

"No! Not you." Paxton seemed to read his thoughts. "He will be punished. I heard what he said. We all did."

Releasing his breath in a heavy gust, Eric let his arm drop and turned to face his mentor and friend and a dozen of the council. He tried to school his features back into the non-emotional, calm expression his people were used to. He knew he didn't make it when Paxton took a small step forward, his hand outstretched toward him.

"He pushed her out of the portal," he cried out, anguish cracking his voice. "He pushed Storey out into the In-between. After she went and risked her own life…again…to rescue him."

The look of horror on the collective group of faces made him realize he wasn't alone in his shock and dismay. These people knew how final such a move was. How absolutely wrong it was. His people were peaceful, serene. Acts of violence were few and always shocking when they happened. But this…that their leader, even one that had been recently deposed…had done something so horrific to the visitor who'd saved them all…

If nothing else, it was satisfying to see the repugnance in their faces as they stared at his father.

Paxton ordered the Councilman to be taken under guard. Eric almost snorted at that. They didn't have much in the way of guards. At the rarely used underground dungeons, there might be a few on retainer, but they were hardly in prime condition.

"Throw him in the dungeon. That way he can't bribe anyone to let him out." Eric caught the outrage in his father's face. He turned. "Did you really think such an act would go unpunished? That you could return home a hero? That all your problems would go away if you could just get rid of Storey? Because I have to tell you, your problems are just starting. I for one will be asking for the death penalty."

At the shocked outcries from the others in the room, Eric strode as far away from his father as he could get and headed to Paxton's workbench. He had to focus on Storey. There was little information in the archives about In-between, the layer of nothing that existed between dimensions. Growing up he'd been fascinated by the early trials of portal travel. There'd been a few people who'd lost their lives in the development process. But he needed to go back and see if they'd ever rescued anyone who'd gotten lost In-between. Maybe there was a way to retrieve Storey. Or to help her find her way home.

Of course there was. Her stylus. Eric spun around searching for Paxton in the growing crowd. Where had all these people come from? He watched as more people rushed in to confirm the news. Had Storey really disappeared In-between? They'd talk until they had no more words to say, but that wasn't going to help Storey come home. He caught Paxton's eye, motioning him to come to his workspace.

"Everyone, let's move this discussion into the conference room." Paxton opened the double doors and motioned the crowd out of his space and into the large common room. "I need to speak with Eric first, then I will give you all an update as I know more. Please go in and get comfortable. We'll find a way to handle this mess."

"You'd better," someone called from the crowd.

"Storey needs our help. She helped us…"

"And the Councilman must pay for what he's done." Shouts and raised voices followed the group as it made its way into the larger room. Finally Paxton closed the main doors to the lab, locking them, and walked over to the workbench. "Now maybe we can have a few moments."

Eric strode over to the adjoining conference room door and shut it behind the last person moving through the lab to join the group mingling and talking loudly. This and the recent battle with the Louers had given them something to talk about for decades to come. Too bad most of it was at Storey's expense.

Paxton hurried toward him. "Now Eric, are you sure she's lost In-between?"

Eric ran a hand through his hair as he thought on what had happened. "She was in the portal with us. I could see her, then there was a small rush of wind, she shrieked and was gone. I searched the blackness, but you know you can't see very much at all during a transfer." He stopped for breath, and closed his eyes briefly. Would the echo of Storey's scream ever fade? He almost hoped not. He needed to keep her alive…until he could find a way to bring her back.

"We'll find a way to help her."

"We need to contact her stylus," Eric said. "See if it can communicate from In-between. If it can, we might be lucky and get a way out of this fast."

Paxton was ahead of him. He already had his stylus in his hand and an electronic tablet on the desk. In seconds his hand flowed over the screen. "My stylus is already checking. Our connection is growing every day." Paxton shook his head. "It can hear and anticipate my needs now."

Eric snorted. "After all this time? Unbelievable."

"I wished I'd known about their abilities earlier," Paxton admitted. "If it hadn't been for Storey…"

"Exactly. She's done so much for us," Eric muttered, peering down at the tablet. He couldn't read what Paxton's stylus was writing.

"Eric, back up. I can't see what I'm doing." The exasperation in Paxton's voice made Eric smile. He stepped back to give his friend room to work.

"It says it can hear the stylus, but there is great distance between them. Communication is splotchy."

Eric laughed with relief. Splotchy meant there was still some communication. "That sounds like Storey's vocabulary."

Paxton snorted. "Another of her influences."

There was no arguing with that comment. Storey had dropped into their world – literally – and they were forever changed. They needed to get her back safely to where she belonged. "But we can communicate. First off, let's make sure she's okay. I'd hate to think of her lying somewhere with a broken leg."

When there was no answer, Eric glanced at his mentor. The confusion on Paxton's face had him asking, "What's wrong?"

Paxton held out his hands, palms upwards. "There is *nothing* In-between. It's empty space. In theory she couldn't be hurt. There's nothing for her to have hit in the fall – unless she was carrying something. By that same logic, she should be unconscious from the pressure. The absence of atmosphere...I'd think." But he looked doubtful. He turned back to his stylus. "Let's find out what the stylus knows."

Not much was the answer that trickled in a few minutes later. The stylus said it was caught In-between, and had no information as to how to get home. It did confirm that Storey had been pushed from the portal just before the arrival at Paxton's lab and that she hadn't been physically hurt in the process. Just as Paxton started to ask another question, the communication was cut off.

Instead of feeling better, Eric paced, his mind full of more questions. Unfortunately, uninjured from the fall didn't mean she was *still* unhurt or if she'd suffered emotional or mental trauma.

Paxton seemed to think both were inevitable under the circumstances. But to Eric, Paxton was once again underestimating Storey. She was tough mentally. Stronger and more adept than any other female in Eric's acquaintance. But not even she could withstand atmospheric pressure issues like Paxton had described. If there was no atmosphere, she wouldn't be able to breathe either. And that meant it was all over. The stylus might not even know that yet. Eric shook his head at the puzzle. Did the stylus know when its owner was unconscious? Dead? It must, because the bond between stylus and owner would break. That was how the stylus had come to be Storey's in the first place – the bond between it and its previous owner had broken when the owner became ill. But if it was no longer bonded, could it still communicate with other styluses?

He shuddered. So many questions and no answers.

"Oh dear." Paxton murmured. "We need to be able to talk to her stylus."

That definitely understated the problem. Eric glanced at the monitor in front of him. "Why can't we access our archives here and see if there is anything helpful?"

"My stylus is looking for answers." Paxton rubbed his face. "We just have to be patient."

"Patient? Storey could be dying right now."

"Actually," Paxton took a deep breath, looked up at Eric, and in a low voice said, "It's more likely that she's already dead."

CHAPTER 2

S TOREY FELL INTO nothingness. Again. She twisted in panic as her body went into freefall.

The thing was…she wasn't falling fast like a six story drop. More like she was on a slow descent – almost as if there was little to no gravity. And it appeared endless. What the hell? No wind whistled past her ears, but her hair floated gently upward from the force of changing altitude, not streaming her like she'd expect.

And she should have stopped by now.

Suddenly she did.

"Ohhmph." She groaned at the shock as much as the pain. Her face had smashed flat against a hard surface. An invisible surface.

"Stylus what is going on?"

The humming in her head reassured her. That at least was normal. She paused, her thoughts hiccupping on the idea that speaking to a pencil was *normal* and having it answer back was *normal* too. 'Cause neither would have been something she'd have considered 'normal' any other time except this last week. Lord her life had changed!

"Stylus, what am I lying on?"

Nothing.

"I can see that. How is this happening? It's like the rules of normal reality don't exist here."

They don't. You aren't in the Louers', Torans' or your home world. In theory there might be no rules here. Or you might be able to create the rules you want.

That made her stop and think. The suggestion didn't feel wrong. As she considered the strangeness of what had happened to her since she'd arrived, it started to make even more sense. "Like stopping?" she questioned. "I was wondering about why I hadn't stopped falling, when all of a sudden, I stopped."

Maybe.

She closed her eyes, took a breath and said, "I'm falling."

Instantly her body dropped, leaving her stomach back where she'd been resting. *Shit.*

"Stop!"

She stopped, coming to another jarring slam against nothing. She laughed. How freaky cool was that? She rolled over and sat up. On nothing. "Now that's weird."

It would seem this reality answers to your thoughts, even instructions.

"And how cool is that?" Still, playing here for an hour or two was not the same thing as being stuck. But was she stuck? Could she get out the same way she'd stopped falling? She wouldn't know until she'd tried.

"I want to go home." Nothing. Then, getting all the way back to her reality might be a bit of a stretch. How about the one she'd left to arrive here? "I want to go back to Eric's dimension."

Try instructions not requests.

"Take me back to the Torans' dimension." Old habits rose to the surface and she added, "Please."

Nothing changed. "Okay, maybe there's a time delay?"

I don't think so. Everything is instant here.

She frowned. "Then what am I doing wrong?" She stood up and turned around. "Is anyone here? Can anyone hear me? Hello."

A faint echo sounded.

Hello.

She frowned. "An echo means something has to be here. Sound bounces off objects in order to create an echo. Right?" She couldn't remember much about the science behind the repeating sounds, but she was pretty sure they couldn't exist if they didn't have something to hit and rebound off. She vaguely remembered hearing an echo when she'd been screaming for Eric.

"Hello!" she shouted.

Hello.

There it was again, faint, but definitely an echo. Excited, she strode off in the direction of the sound. She kept her gaze in front of her so as to not look down at the endless nothingness beneath her feet. New reality or not, some fears needed to be kept submerged before she created them accidentally. "Stylus, is it possible that there could be people here? Like yet another reality? Maybe there's a whole new species of people who live in this In-between dimension. I mean, why not? I'm breathing and speaking. Thankfully I don't have to go to the bathroom or have an appetite right now, cause that's just not going to work out too well…but maybe there are others like me here." The concept brought a smile to her face and a lightness to her footsteps.

We don't believe so.

"But you don't know – do you? And if you don't know, you can only guess." She laughed. "This is new for both of us. Not just me."

Since meeting you, there has been much new for both of us.

She stopped, considered the stylus's words and nodded. "True enough. Well, together we can find whatever the sounds are bouncing off of. Maybe that will lead us to a way out."

Or lead you further from your point of entry.

Ah shit. She hadn't thought of that. She spun around and looked back the way she'd come. Of course, she could see exactly…nothing.

And she'd lost track of how long she'd been travelling. "Do you think I need to keep track of where I landed?" She chewed on her bottom lip, worrying away on that new concern and wishing she'd thought of it earlier. "Did you keep track of it?"

We have noted the coordinates of your entrance point to this dimension and your exit point from the Toran dimension.

She brightened. "So we can go back there at any time, right?"

In theory, yes. However as our knowledge doesn't cover this instance, we can't confirm that.

She pondered that. "I think you should keep track of every step I take here. On all levels. Because we fell a long way in that first drop. Add the other couple of smaller falls and the vertical distance could be huge. It might be hard to get back up there."

You should be able to think yourself back there.

She nodded. Theoretically that might be possible, in reality, well, that remained to be seen. Should they try to regain their same starting position? But she'd tried that back when she'd first entered the Louers' dimension. She'd ended up in a whole different location.

And if that happened here, she'd lose track of where the echo had come from. She spun around only to realize she wasn't at all sure she was facing the right direction anymore. Damn it.

She stood for a moment, hands on her hips and studied the thick endless fog around her. "Hello?"

No echo. Although there appeared to be something. She turned slightly and called out louder, "Hello."

No echo. Maybe it wasn't an echo? She turned to the other side and yelled, "Hello."

Hello.

And damn it. That didn't sound the same at all.

Still, she didn't have much choice but to go forward and find out.

"HOW IS IT that we have no idea how to help Storey?" Eric refused to contemplate that she was dead. She'd find a way to survive. She was unlike anyone else he'd ever known. And she'd get out of this mess just like she'd gotten out of any number of her other chaotic disasters.

She had to. Anything less was unthinkable.

Paxton opened his mouth…hesitated and closed it again. Then he took a deep breath and said, "I don't think she's alive."

"I do." Eric was stalwart in his stance. "There's no way she's not." He glared down at the stylus in Paxton's hand. "Ask it more questions. There has to be a way to track her."

"And what good will that do?" Paxton stared at him, concern growing in his gaze. "You can't go in after her. That's not possible."

Eric studied him. "It is you know. If we can track her on this side, I can set the coordinates, port to where she is, then port home again."

But Paxton was shaking his head. Tufts of hair flying in all directions. "No. No. That's not possible. You could be lost in there with her."

"And I could get her back again. We owe it to her. I owe it to her. It's my father who sent her there."

"We can't lose you, too. No." Paxton lifted both hands to his head and tugged on the ends of his hair. "No.

You can't go after her."

"Then find a way to leave breadcrumbs for her to follow so she can get out on her own."

Paxton brightened. Eric could only imagine at what he was thinking. His mentor had been impressed with Storey, but he'd sacrifice her in a heartbeat if it meant keeping Eric safe. Unlike his own father, Paxton cared.

But now Eric had to get Paxton to care about Storey. Enough to help her to get out. And this could be the way. Have him help Storey in order to keep Eric safe. "Let's ask the stylus to track her?"

Paxton sniffed. "I already have."

Eric rolled his eyes. But not so the older man could see. "And?"

"It's trying to contact Storey's stylus. The communication is getting worse."

"Could she be moving further away?"

"Or she's…fading." Paxton shot him a quick look. Eric glared back at him. "But we won't go there yet."

Paxton refocused on his paper and the stylus in his hand, busy writing down a message. "The stylus has a location for Storey."

Eric grinned. "Good. I knew this could work."

"But…" Paxton held up a cautioning hand. "The location is changing."

"Of course it is." She wasn't dead. Relief washed over him. He'd been right. "She's going to be moving around. Trying to come back."

"Maybe, but she needs to be back at the same point she arrived at in order to leave. Otherwise time will have changed."

"Oh, shit." Not that whole time thing again. Last time they'd messed with time, things had gone from bad to worse before they could get back where they belonged.

Paxton spun around and stared at him in shock.

Eric shook his head. "Sorry. I don't mean to swear.

It's Storey's influence, I know. I'll stop."

Paxton thrust his nose up at an amazing altitude even for him. Then his hand jerked on the paper as the stylus started to move.

"Her stylus has the coordinates of where they landed. It says Storey can see nothing. It's like being in thick fog. The place is empty. She heard an echo so is looking to locate the reason. The stylus is tracking her movements."

Eric laughed. "That's Storey. She's off exploring."

"It's dangerous." Paxton glared. "She should have stayed put."

Paxton didn't understand. Eric did. He admired Storey's courage. Her sense of making life happen instead of standing by and watching it happen. He needed to do more of the same. He should go over and help her. He frowned, remembering something else Paxton had said. "There were other men lost In-between, you said. Is there any chance they could still be alive?"

The speed with which Paxton spun around stunned Eric. He backed up a step. "Whoa. I was just asking."

Paxton stared, his thoughts obviously engaged elsewhere.

"Paxton? Is that possible?"

He pursed his lips, then shook his head regretfully. "No. It's been much too long."

"What's been too long?" Eric studied the emotions rippling across his friend's face. "Did you know someone who was lost?"

"There have been very few people lost there. Mostly in the beginning when portal travelling was being worked out. Most died from being half in and half out when the transfer completed. Since then, only one, no two, have been lost completely In-between. One because he had a heart attack while travelling and fell out of the portal. We're pretty sure he was dead first though. And then there was a young man whose foolish behavior sent him through the portal into the In-between during travel."

Eric winced. Not a great way to die. Paxton looked as if he wanted to say more, but he closed his mouth, his lips pressed firmly together.

"What aren't you telling me?"

Paxton sighed, then broke down. "That young man has been In-between for over a century and a half." He paused, swallowed loudly and added, "He was my younger brother."

"Your brother?" Eric stared at him. "I didn't know you had one. That must have been terrible." He shook his head. Unbelievable. "Have you tried to get him back?"

"He was a young man at the time, but always acting the fool. We were a group of six, and he was trying to impress the ladies and tripped and fell In-between." Paxton frowned, his eyes losing focus as if gazing back into the years past. "We've never had a way to go in and find him. Or find what was left of him."

He picked up the stylus that he'd laid down on the tablet. "If only I'd known about this back then. But I'd just bonded with it. We were still getting to know each other. It was all so new. And I was so full of myself and my new status." He shook his head. "And our knowledge was so limited."

"Maybe we can track your brother down. At least find his remains and bring him home."

Paxton looked hopeful for a short moment, then shook his head. "No. There's no way to know where he went over. He could be anywhere and after so long, he must be dead. I can't imagine there is food or water there." He sighed heavily, as if he was letting go of a long held wish. "No, death should have come immediately and if not, then within days to a week at the most."

Eric wasn't so sure of that. If there was anything over there to find, Storey would be the one to find it.

CHAPTER 3

"HELLO?" STOREY CALLED out, her head cocked to hear the echo. There it was, faint, but solid. She walked quickly toward it. As quickly as she dared. In the dense nothingness, she didn't dare look up or down. She focused on the sound, her hands out in front, and tried to keep a steady course forward. In her mind, she held to the thought of finding whatever created the echo.

She didn't understand how this place worked and with the stylus still not up to full strength... Were her messages to Paxton and Eric even getting through? She hadn't heard anything in response. And that wasn't good. She was running out of options. She had to find a way to boost the Stylus's power. Fast.

And she had to figure out if there was anything useful in this In-between dimension to make that happen. She called out again, and again, each time getting closer to the source of the echo. She felt like a fool, but there was nothing new in that. She'd never have tried to go through the portal in her bedroom floor if she'd been worried about what other people thought of her. She knew she was 'different.' Tough. Who said different was bad?

She dropped her arms and picked up the pace to sprint forward and smacked into...something...hard.

"Oomph." Storey groaned as she stumbled backwards, tried to regain her balance and fell on her butt. She shook her head and looked up.

And looked again.

"Hello," she said cautiously. There appeared to be a person in front of her. A man. But he was tilting forward several feet in front of her. In fact he was leaning so far forward she didn't understand what kept him upright. Then remembered where she was.

The fog was so dense, she could barely see his features. She edged forward and studied him closely, noting his Toran style pants and shirt, his brown hair and oddly preserved-looking features. He couldn't be more than mid-twenties, but there was something off to his face, as if it were weathered, like an antique. He slowly shook his head, as if waking from a deep sleep.

Yet he didn't straighten. He opened his eyes, blinked several times, then closed them as if to snooze off again.

She was both relieved to see someone here and yet at the same time…discomfited at his oddness. Even after all she'd seen. Still, having another person to talk to, to bounce ideas off of, to show her how to manage this new dimension was huge. Her breath gusted out and her shoulders relaxed. She was not alone.

"Hello," she repeated quietly, not sure what else to do, but not wanting to freak him out.

His eyes flew open and he twisted his head enough to see her. Now he looked really odd because he still leaned so far forward.

Storey walked in front of him, hoping he'd straighten. And he did, slightly.

"W…who…are you?" he asked, his voice a whisper of sound in the air.

"I'm Storey Dalton. I just arrived here." She grimaced. She sounded like a damn tourist. She took a deep breath. "Who are you, and how long have you been here?"

He blinked, yet the rest of him remained eerily still.

Now this was going to get irritating. Storey hadn't

realized how much of a get up and go person she really was until she'd started crossing dimensions. And how different she was from others. And not only her own people. The Torans with their endless discussions, the Louers with their communication system that didn't include her and now this brain fogged sleeper. Nothing moved as quickly as she'd like.

"Hello? Are you in there?" She leaned closer, gazing into his eyes. She was hoping to see some kind of light come on. A sign of comprehension – of knowledge that he needed to wake up – and proof that was going to happen.

She got another blink.

So not helpful. She reached out a tentative hand and watched as his eyes tracked her movement. Talk about creepy. She gently squeezed his shoulder, a little surprised to find him solid. She'd begun to wonder if he was real or as insubstantial as the rest of this world.

"Stylus, who is this person. And what's wrong with him. He appears to be barely conscious."

He should be unconscious.

"Why? I'm not?"

He's been here much too long to remain conscious.

"Well he might have been unconscious before, but I did run into him. Hard. Could that have woken him up?" She bent to look into the man's face again. "Sorry about that by the way." He blinked. She grimaced. "Stylus, I think he hears me and sees me, but I'm not sure he's doing much comprehending."

It may take him time to come around. He could have been here for centuries. We have found only two men recorded to having fallen In-between in the last quarter millennia.

She straightened. "Centuries," she repeated, hating the tremor that wavered through her voice. Hell, her whole body was starting to quake. "Surely that's not possible. How could he survive here all that time? His body needs food and water…doesn't it?"

This is not a physical reality. Time does not exist here.

Time. She was really starting to hate that element. It kept screwing up her world.

But in fact, you are the one that keeps…screwing…with time.

She grinned. "Hey stylus, you're really loosening up. Good on you."

You have introduced new words and language patterns. We are attempting to integrate these into our knowledge base.

She had to laugh. "Not sure that's a good idea, but hey, you will always remember my influence on your world this way. Nice to know I'll be remembered."

You will always be remembered.

Her thoughts turned melancholy. Would she? If she stayed in here? Eric would mourn her, Paxton would put her into the archives and the Councilman would cheer. Her mother could already be past the worst stage of grief. For all she knew, her old life was gone – maybe had never even existed in the first place if she'd truly twisted up time like it appeared she had. In which case, she most likely would never have been born. And if that wasn't a mind-bender to consider.

She so had to go back and fix that.

But first she had to fix this mess. She couldn't help but feel like it was all getting to be too much. She really wanted to just go home. Something she'd been trying to do since…well, forever.

This man had to know something. Therefore he was just going to have to wake up enough to share it. To that end, she reached over and gave him a hard slap on the shoulder. "Wake up. I need to know how to get out of here."

He blinked.

Was he in there? Conscious? Normal? She peered at him, wondering. Maybe he had brain damage. That fear jumped inside and wouldn't let go. She closed her eyes and prayed for patience. She opened them and tried again. "Please, tell me how to escape from here."

His mouth opened and his voice, rusty from disuse, whispered, "There is no escape."

ERIC RETURNED TO his home and packed. He didn't know what exactly he might need, but was determined to make sure he had as much in the way of supplies as possible. Storey could get into trouble like no one he'd ever known. But she always got out of it. It's just sometimes she needed a little help. He loaded a pack with emergency food rations, water, clothes and first aid supplies.

This was one of those times. He pulled the codin clip from his belt and connected it to his pack, then sucked the pack into its envelope form. Storey loved this technology. It let him shrink wrap almost any household item down to a packet the size of a small envelope without damaging the contents. Just thinking about Storey made him remember something else. He tucked the pack away in his back pocket, then pulled out an empty one. Storey might need extra paper. Not something he had here. He returned to Paxton's lab to find his mentor at the workbench. "Any news before I leave?"

Paxton's back stiffened. "Leave?"

"Paxton, I have to try and rescue her. She would do the same for me. She *has done* just that. I can't sit by now when she's trapped In-between."

The older man's face grayed and although already sitting, he seemed to shrink into himself. "I know," he whispered. "I'd hoped I could make you see reason but…"

"I may not need to if we can help her rescue herself." Eric motioned to his table full of stuff. "But I'm preparing to go just in case."

He eyed the stack of codexes. Navigation was an inherent skill for him. Except in the In-between nothing might work – tools or instinct. The last thing he wanted was to get over there and wish he had brought more equipment. He added several to his pocket. He precoded them to save time.

"Eric, look here…" Paxton stood up and pointed to the big monitor in front. He had some kind of blank screen set up with only lights flashing to show anything existed on it. "The top marker is the location Storey entered In-between, according to the coordinates given by her stylus. It has kept a running guide of her travels. As you can see, she's all over the place." The screen rotated to show Storey's progress from various points of view, eventually morphing into a three dimensional picture.

Eric walked closer. "I don't understand. Why are some of these higher? Is this a map?

Paxton's head bobbed. "That's the issue. She's not moving north or south *only*, she's also moving up and down. The system is tracking the changes in her altitude."

"Are there mountains there?" Eric didn't understand. Yet even as he watched, the signal moved again. This time slightly higher. He tapped the screen. "So you are saying that this little jag up in her pathway is actually an altitude change and not a few steps to the north?"

"Exactly. On the whole she is moving toward the north. But you could walk for hours following her tracks and never see her because she could be above you or below, out of your line of sight. And the fog is likely all encompassing. You wouldn't see her until you hit her."

That just reminded Eric of finding Storey in the Louers' dimension. His codex had locked onto hers and he'd tracked her all the way through the Louers' housing. In fact, she'd jumped him out of the darkness as her stylus had told her he was there already. He pointed that out to Paxton.

"Yes, but there's no guarantee that the codex will function there." Paxton replied. "If north isn't north and gravity is nonexistent, all the machinery will be off too."

Yeah, he got that. He stared down at his codex. The arm band covered the bulk of his forearm. An essential tool of his work and lifestyle. And he'd been forced to use the codex in so many ways lately. For travelling, communication, even tracking. He hated knowing that it might not be there for him In-between. "Can we do anything to make my codex more adaptable? Boost it in some way. Give it an alternative navigational system? Alternate power? Something else?"

Paxton stared at him, his brows narrowed in concentration. He stood suddenly and walked to his workbench on the side. "We can boost the tracking system. That will help us to know where you are at all times."

Eric wasn't sure that would help. It would drive Paxton nuts to be able to track Eric, but not know how to bring him home. "What about the stylus? Does it have any suggestions on how to adapt or strengthen the codex?"

Paxton shrugged, but picked up the stylus and his tablet. The stylus immediately started to write. Paxton read the message out loud. "We didn't always have portal travel. In the beginning, to establish the pathways, we had to learn how to go In-between."

In-between? Paxton and Eric stared at each other. "I'm sorry. Did you say you had to go In-between to make the portal travel system work?"

The stylus started writing. *That's how it works. You go between time-space reality to land in a new place. We made many mistakes early on. But it was one of us who created this process.*

"One of you?" Eric stared at the stylus. He still couldn't get over the fact that there were souls inside the tool.

One of us not in here.

And wished, not for the first time, that they'd speak clearer and with less riddles. "If not one of you in there, then who?"

He who exists in the broken one. He is much revered by us all. He had been lost to us until Storey saved him.

Storey again. She just kept gaining admirers. Eric turned to Paxton. "Where are they? The styluses that Storey rescued," he explained at Paxton's blank look. "She gave them to you for safe keeping."

Paxton was already up off his chair and racing to the far side of the room. He unlocked a cupboard and removed a large box. Carefully he placed it down on his desk and opened it. There inside, on a purple cushion, rested the styluses Storey had brought back from the Louers' dimension.

Paxton grabbed up his tablet and stylus, quickly asking which of the styluses could help.

Before the stylus could give instructions, Eric had rummaged through and found the thick broken one. It looked similar to the others, but older, more crude in design. Like an early prototype. "Got it."

Yes that one.

Eric looked down at the stylus in Paxton's hand. "How did it know which one I was holding?"

Paxton's hand jerked. *We can see. And feel. As you touched the others, we registered the change in temperature. You hold the correct one.*

See? The stylus could see. See what? Everything? The more he learned, the more bizarre these tools became. Seeing, however, could be very helpful in finding Storey.

"How can we wake this broken stylus up?"

It is damaged. He is too weak.

"No. See, I'm not going to accept that. He has information that Storey needs to escape her prison. As she saved him, he needs to save her."

The air filled with a high level buzz that had Eric spinning around in panic. It was too reminiscent of the Louers' attack on Eric's world, before Storey created a whole new world for the Louers.

Even Paxton seemed to shake nervously. "It's the stylus," he exclaimed. He dropped the tool on the tablet and backed away. "Maybe it's going to blow up. Maybe we did something to it. Broke it somehow?"

Eric took a step closer and the buzz intensified. He held out the broken stylus and again the sound intensified. "I think…they are talking to each other."

Paxton rushed forward. "Why so loud? They've never done that before."

"Because this one is broken and…old." At least that was the best answer Eric could come up with. He looked at Paxton and shrugged. "This one might be damaged, but that doesn't mean his information isn't good."

"Then it should be in the database and archived with the rest of the information. It's unacceptable that one stylus should still contain sole ownership of any information." Paxton looked so affronted at the breach in protocol that Eric had to laugh.

"You might want to consider that it might be so old that it was created *before* the rules became protocol. They might have been just guidelines back then. Also consider that it might have been broken before the information could be sent to the archives."

"Harrumph," Paxton said. He glared at the two styluses. "How long is this noise going to keep up?"

Even as he finished speaking the buzz in the air eased down several decibels. "Makes you wonder if they heard your complaint and decided to tone it down a bit."

"They are instruments. Not reasoning beings," Paxton said testily.

Eric slid a sideways glance over at his mentor. Even with all he'd learned about his stylus, Paxton still didn't get it. There were people inside. Real souls. Not living breathing souls as in walking, talking Torans, but real, functioning, thinking souls without a body. But Eric himself might not have understood if it hadn't been for Storey and the way she'd communicated with her stylus. The damn thing *could* read her mind at this point. And apparently, she'd be able to read its thoughts soon, too. And if that didn't blow away all their beliefs about a stylus being only an instrument, what would?

"Could Storey communicate with the broken one?"

"How could she? She's not bonded to it."

Eric wondered about that. Storey, he knew, would have something to say about that kind of narrow thinking. Paxton just didn't know what few limitations she'd found with her own stylus. If this stylus had information they needed…

Taking a chance, he slipped the broken stylus into his pocket.

CHAPTER 4

"THERE HAS TO be something here." Even the sound of Storey's own voice failed to reassure her. She was in deep shit. In the grim fog surrounding her, everything was amplified. Including her fear. Damn. She stopped, closed her eyes and took a deep, calming breath. She had to stay in control. She had to stay composed. She didn't dare let fear take over. She'd end up as mindless jelly.

This could be the end of everything, but she didn't dare focus on that. Especially here. She might create that end before she understood what she'd done. Then she'd never get back to Eric's world. She'd never make it home. She'd never see her mother again. Or fix the mess she'd left behind. That so couldn't happen. How could her life be cut short before she'd done what she needed to do? She had yet to live. Had yet to love. Had yet to be loved.

There's no way she could die.

She refused.

And laughed. If insisting something could make it so, then she had this place beat. She wasn't going to knock the value of positive thinking. She'd had too much of it drilled into her from her mom, who believed anything could happen if a person wanted it badly enough. Right now, Storey desperately wanted her mother to be right.

'Cause positive thinking was all that she appeared to have available to her.

Damn.

"Stylus, is there any way to draw in the air – versus on paper like I normally do – and have you take us out of here?"

No.

"Well then, let's draw on my jeans again. Although I don't think I can port through those – or could I?" She looked down at her already doodle-covered jeans, then pulled her shirt up. She didn't remember writing on her skin last time, but this time she'd do it in a heartbeat if it meant getting the hell out of here. She stared at the glowing gold pattern on her skin. Honor marks, Paxton had called them.

In the darkness, they were a bright beacon. If anyone were looking for her.

It's not the surface. It's the medium, the atmosphere, that is the problem. I can't move us through this to another dimension.

Storey shook her head. At least she could just talk to her stylus. Saved on writing surfaces. "See that doesn't make sense. We drew portals from the Louers' dimension to my dimension. Sure, we ended up back in time then, but we still managed to travel."

I don't have the coordinates.

Storey stopped. "Yes you do. You have the coordinates for Eric's place, my homeland and even the Louers' world. Take us to anyone of those."

I can't. I don't have the coordinates of where we are here.

"But you said that you were going to keep track of the coordinates of where we landed before I started to move to where I thought I heard the echo."

Yes, I have the location of where we landed, but we don't have anything to measure those against in this dimension. I have to have a map of this dimension in order to calculate a way out of it. A point of origin. To move anywhere, I need to know the point we are starting from.

"Then get it from Paxton!" She was beside herself with excitement. They could do this. They would do this.

Communication is faulty. And there is no guarantee that they will have this location. No one has been here before.

She sighed and rubbed her eyebrows. "You mean no one has returned from here. So what do we need to do to improve the communication?"

An odd hum filled the air. She grinned. A welcome sound. It meant the stylus was thinking about a solution.

The sound cut off.

We need more power. This place is difficult, more complicated.

"Fine. How do we get more power?"

More of us. We are damaged.

She rolled her eyes. She'd heard that a lot lately. "And how do you expect us to do that?"

"We don't."

"Can Paxton help?"

No. Communication is faulty.

She sighed and pinched the bridge of her nose. Okay. Back to the same problem.

The faint cough at her side made her look up. Right – the odd guy she'd found. "Hey, you don't have any idea how to increase our power here, do you?"

He stared at her, a blank look in his eyes. As if finally understanding she was serious, he shook his head. Even that motion appeared to pain him. It was like his body hadn't moved in many years. And she didn't know how that could be.

"Stylus, can we do anything to help ourselves from this side?" The stylus was quiet. Damn it. Storey wanted to pound something but in this foggy land of nothing, there was nothing to pound.

She turned to the almost asleep-on-his-feet man. "Are there others here?"

She had to nudge him and repeat the questions. He shook his head and in a voice barely above a whispers, said, "No. Not since a long time."

She jumped on that. "Since a long time? What does that mean? Are there other people lost here?"

He gave a slight shake of his head. "I don't know. I never saw anyone."

"Let's find out. If there is someone here, maybe they can help."

If they had a way out, they would have left.

Storey wasn't sure when the stylus had started to get a personality, but this dimension appeared to bring it to the surface. "But they didn't have you."

The hum started again. Storey glanced over at the man. He appeared to be asleep again. It was odd. Had he slept through the last century? Did he have food or water? And if he did, that meant body functions. Still, there appeared to have been little to no aging in all the decades or centuries that he'd been stuck here. Had time stopped for him? And if so, what would happen to him when it started again?

Stylus, she asked mentally. *Is he okay? If he's been here all these years, can he survive in the Torans' world now?*

He's been comatose for all this time.

Right. Was that good or bad?

Does that mean we can take him back or we can't? I don't want him to die when we get home, but... She chewed on her bottom lip. This was a new concern. Originally, all she'd wanted was to get home. Now she wanted take this poor man with her and...she was very much afraid he couldn't go back. That was a horrible concept...and one she had to question in her own case.

We believe he will die.

Will he? She glanced over at the sleeping man. *Are you sure?*

Yes. And if you stay here, it will be your fate too.

ERIC FINISHED PACKING, doubled checked that the broken stylus was safe, then tucked it away in his inside jacket pocket. He didn't mention it to Paxton. The scientist was protective of all the styluses, and Eric didn't want him to refuse to let it go.

Still, if there was any chance this one had information for Storey, then all the more reason to bring it to her. Just because Paxton said she couldn't access the information, didn't mean that was fact. As he was quickly learning, Storey knew a lot more about some stuff than most Torans.

A fact that would irritate them all. Especially his father.

"While I'm gone, you'll make sure to keep my father locked up, right?" When an answer wasn't immediately forthcoming, Eric spun around, "Right?"

Paxton nodded. "Yes. Still, I wish you wouldn't go."

"I know." But that wouldn't stop Eric. "So help me minimize the danger."

Paxton held out a weird instrument. "Just in case there are no landmarks or sky to work with, I'm going to give you a different type of tracker." He stood up and walked over to his workbench. He opened a drawer on the left side. Inside the drawer was another locked box. Eric leaned over. He'd never seen this box.

Paxton opened the box and pulled out a small, pill-like object. "Here. Swallow this."

Eric stared down at the thing. His stomach heaved. He didn't like the sound of this at all. "Do I have to? I can't imagine what it could do in there."

"This tracker will flush out of your system in a few

days. In the meantime it will track your body heat in case we lose communications."

"But you already can track me. Look…" He pointed at Storey's moving pathway. "Track me like her."

"I'm tracking her stylus, not her." Paxton waited patiently.

Eric looked from the pill to his mentor and back again. "Fine. But I don't like it."

"You never did like to take your medicine, did you?"

Eric rolled his eyes at the mention of his childhood behavior and tossed the pill into his mouth. With difficulty he swallowed it dry.

"Good. Now we'll set it up and it should go live in a few minutes." He turned back to his monitors, his fingers busy on the keyboard. "Do you have everything you might need?"

"Paper? Something for Storey to write on if need be?"

Paxton found a spare tablet in a different drawer by his knees. He held it out.

"The only thing is these are small. She has these huge paper sheets that work well. And being electronic – will it even work over there?" Eric stared down at the tablet. He didn't think it would work to jump through the same way as the many paper portals Storey had drawn.

"We gave up paper decades ago," Paxton said testily.

"And that's why I was wondering if I should port to Storey's bedroom and grab more of her sketchbooks. Her closet has several of them." Storey'd had everything she needed for the last trip to the Louers' dimension, and as far as he remembered, she'd still had her travelling pouch during that last jump with his father. But…that didn't mean she still had it. What if she'd lost her pouch in her fall? According to what he'd learned so far, that could mean the pack was there, but just out of sight.

Besides, the more supplies the better.

The more he considered it, the better he like the idea. He might be able to scoop up some of her never ending stash of granola bars, too.

"I don't like all this traffic. You know it creates tunnels between dimensions when we do too much of it. That's why visits to her dimension are so carefully regulated."

"I understand that. But we have to do what we can to make sure that we have all options covered. If her paper can create a portal to get us out – like she created to allow us to rescue my father – then we should have more in *this* situation." Maybe the gentle reminder of how many times Storey had used paper to save their lives would help nudge Paxton. Eric didn't know if cross-dimension travel was an issue based in reality or just another of Paxton's unfounded worries.

How could anyone know?

"Then make it quick. In and out. Let no one see you and get back here immediately. Time is running out. If you're going to try and find Storey, I think you need to go there as soon as possible. The damage to her system, providing she's even alive, will increase by the hour."

Crap. "I didn't need to hear that," Eric muttered. "I'm going to run. Back within the hour."

CHAPTER 5

STOREY TOOK ANOTHER look at the man leaning at the impossible angle. If she'd found one person, would she find more if she stayed here longer? And how? She couldn't help but think it was only dumb luck that had brought her to this man in the first place. He still hadn't given her his name. She'd feel better talking to him if she knew what to call him.

She leaned across and nudged his shoulder. Then nudged it again – harder.

He blinked at her. Damn that was irritating. "Hey, remember me? What is your name?" She spoke clearly and slowly. Maybe it would help him understand.

"Dillon." He frowned as if surprised by his answer. "I think."

"Dillon. Good. That's a good start. How long have you been here, Dillon?"

His frown deepened. "I...don't know."

"Right. That probably wasn't the best question to ask you as time doesn't seem to matter here. Okay, Dillon, do you have any family back home that might be missing you?"

She winced. Probably not a good question either. But she needed to find out something about him. Just in case they could find a way to keep him alive. She refused to entertain the concept of failure in this case. Any information she could find would help Paxton sort this out.

And let Dillon's family know what had happened to him.

"Brother," he said faintly, closing his eyes and swaying as if the effort had taxed him.

Excellent. His brain was functioning. "Good. You have a brother. He might be still alive too. What's his name?"

Dillon looked at her in confusion. Not that she'd seen many other expressions from him yet. She did get the impression she was disturbing his sleep. Something he was falling back into every time she stopped talking to him. So she kept talking. "Dillon?" she sharpened her voice this time.

He straightened ever so slightly. But it helped. His face had a familiar look to it. But, then, the Torans looked like humans.

"Yes?"

"You have a brother," she prompted, trying to hold in her exasperation. "What is his name?"

"Paxton."

"Paxton! Your brother is Paxton?" What were the odds? She shook her head. "Wait there must be more than one man with that name in your world. Hell, we have thousands of guys named Eric in mine. It must be a different man." But wouldn't it be cool if it was the Paxton she knew? She'd love to reunite the brothers.

If this one survived the trip. She wasn't even sure he could walk. What would happen to his body in a normal dimension? Whatever 'normal' meant. Space travel in her world apparently did horrible things to the human body. Something to do with radiation and no gravity. She couldn't imagine the gravity issue being any better on the body here.

"Stylus, we can't leave him behind. That's so not going to happen."

Dillon raised his head slightly. "Leave? There is no

way to leave." His face crumpled. "I've been here for so long."

"What about water and food? Have you eaten anything in all these years?"

Dillon's eyes widened. "No. Sleep. I've been asleep. Until you came." He straightened a little more and looked around. "I remember hoping, waiting for rescue. When it didn't come, I slept. Until now."

"Until now? Really?" So not good. "Stylus, is that possible?"

In a comatose state similar to an animal in hibernation, yes, I believe so.

"Yes, but even a bear wakes up and comes out of his home when he's hungry. Dillon's system shut down. Completely."

Not completely. He is waking up. Slowly. If his body had shut down, he'd be dead. But there will be more problems as his body comes back to a more normal state.

"And is that going to mean his bodily needs are going to wake up too? I doubt I have enough food and water for a century long appetite." She'd reverted to speaking to the stylus out loud instead of in her mind. The sound of her voice was more appealing than the smothering silence. The normalcy of hearing her own voice somehow added balance to yet another bizarre situation.

"Stylus...I was thinking. Can't we just go back in time to before I was pushed out of the portal?"

They'd gone back in time accidentally before, but they'd survived that trip and she had no doubt that she'd survive it again. Staying here didn't look very survivable – not if Dillon was anything to go by.

No. I don't believe so.

"But that's not the same thing as no. Is it?" she prodded.

No. As the air here is different, I can't say that anything will work. We have no archival information of this.

"You guys did time travel before, right? Because you helped us last time."

But you didn't use my help to go back in time. I helped you find a way forward.

Splitting hairs as far as she was concerned. Time travel was time travel. Although technically the stylus was correct – again. That didn't mean it was *always* correct.

She sat down in front of Dillon. "I should have some paper and rations. I think." She pulled out the shrunken pack Eric had made for her in triumph. "And I have this." She waved it around. Eric should have the other pack – maybe. "Stylus can you open this?"

Yes.

"Good. Um…how? What do I need to do?"

Even as the last words tripped off her lips, a weird set of musical notes that sounded familiar rang out. And how the stylus could do that without speakers she didn't know. She laughed. "That's perfect. How come you don't play music to lighten the air?"

How can music lighten the air?

Storey shook her head. "It's a figure of speech. Music makes people feel good. It lightens their moods, their souls. Makes people happy."

Interesting.

She stared at it. "That's all you have to say? It seems much of your education is missing."

Education? We have had no education. We are Louers. Slaves. We received no education.

That whole ugly history thing again. She sympathized, but this was so not the time. "Back to the problem then. I have a piece of paper. Why not just draw a portal back to Paxton's lab?"

We don't have a location for where we are at.

She pursed her lips, finally starting to understand

there were limitations to the stylus. She hadn't come up against them before, because she hadn't really understood how the stylus had done what it did. Now she realized it had need of certain information to follow through on some of her requirements and for the first time they were both in new territory and neither knew what to do.

"What if we try it anyway?"

She pulled out an old portal she'd stashed in the pack a long time ago. Unfolding it, she found it led to Paxton's lab. She grinned and stood up. She placed the portal on the ground and reached out a hand to Dillon. "Dillon, step on this paper, please."

He blinked. He reached out a hand. Grabbed hers and stepped on the paper.

ERIC STUDIED THE trees and bushes of Storey's world as the black mist of the portal dissipated. It looked the same as the first time he'd ventured here. The size of the trees and the season all appeared to fit. But with the time shifts and new dimensions being created – he no longer trusted what stood before his own eyes. And how sad was that.

Before meeting Storey, life had been simple and complete…and boring. Now he felt so energized and alive. In ways he'd never experienced before and could hardly explain. But life thrummed through his veins now. Sure, so did worry and fear, but that was better than ennui.

And the weird thing was, he hadn't realized how lacking his previous life really had been. Ignorance really was bliss. He'd read that saying in the archives and had to admit there was some truth to it.

He walked the path to Storey's house, keeping a wary eye out. He should be in the right dimension and the right time frame, but as Storey had messed with things here, twisted time as the stylus had put it, he didn't know what to expect each time he came.

That brought back memories of Tammy, the little Louer child they'd rescued from her old home dimension. He grinned at the memory of her insatiable appetite. And her scream. He shuddered. That was very forgettable. At least he wished it were.

The house loomed ahead of him. He walked cautiously around to the front to see if any of the metal boxes Storey called cars were there. None. His breath gusted out in relief. That didn't mean no one was home, just meant there were likely less people at home. He stepped back into the trees and punched the coordinates for Storey's bedroom into his codex. He could have done it this way from the beginning, but the thought of porting into a stranger's bedroom while they were there made him cringe. With Storey having shifted time, there was no guarantee that he was in the same time as when Storey had lived here. The less he had to explain the better. And according to Storey, he should avoid capture at all costs. Something about not having the right identification or history. He shrugged. The black mist rose up around his shoulders, quickly blocking out the world around him. When it cleared he smiled. This was still Storey's bedroom.

The same bed, pictures on the wall, sketchbooks and paper tossed haphazardly around the room. So much of her personality permeated the room it made him smile. And then he froze. This was exactly like the first time he'd seen Storey's room. When only her mother lived with her here.

What had happened to the time twist where Storey's life had shifted, creating an alternate form of the reality she had lived? In the new reality, her father, whom she hadn't seen in a decade, now lived as if he'd never separated from her mother. And the family's religious beliefs and lifestyles were all different. For Storey, it had been incredibly unnerving. For Eric, it was just plain fascinating. Who knew how many realities co-existed out there.

But time was wasting. He stepped through and grabbed up anything he thought Storey might need. Some larger sheets of paper folded within a smaller sketch book and a sweater. She'd had everything she needed for the last trip to the Louers' dimension, and as far as he remembered, she'd still had her travelling pouch during that last jump with his father. But…that didn't mean she still had it. He still had his packets. He checked to make sure, but they were both there. Good. Now what else could they need?

As he rummaged through her desk he found several of her granola bars. Perfect! He snatched them up and wondered at the sensibility of going downstairs for more food. She had to be hungry and not knowing how long they'd be before getting out, he crept down the stairs and into the kitchen. The room was empty. He pulled cupboards open and studied their contents. Nothing looked familiar. He shrugged, and started filling his package with anything that looked edible. Then he opened the fridge and grinned when he saw a block of cheese. Tammy would be in heaven. As would her pet, Skorky. Those two had eaten anything and everything, but especially cheese.

He snagged the block and several apples and decided he'd taken enough time. He slipped out the kitchen door and ran to the treed area. Once under cover, he coded in Paxton's lab. Within minutes he stood inside the normalcy of his world, his mentor still huddled over his key board.

"Any news?" He asked striding forward.

Paxton swiveled, his features brightening as he saw Eric. "No. Nothing."

Damn. Even as he registered the swear word, he realized using it no longer mattered. The simple rules he'd lived by all his life were overshadowed by the urgency of Storey's situation. "Then we have no option." He walked over to the monitor, noted the coordinates where Storey currently stood and punched them into his codex. "I'll send you a message as soon as I land."

Not giving Paxton a chance to argue, Eric walked to the portal station and hit the button on his codex to take him to Storey. The last thing he saw as the smoke rose quickly to take him away, was the stricken look on Paxton's face.

CHAPTER 6

STOREY STARED AS Dillon stood on the paper. On, not *in*. She groaned. She *needed* the portals to work. "Stylus, it didn't work."

No. It can't.

"But I need it to work. This one was going to Paxton's lab. Would it be better to try for my dimension?" She searched through her packet for a portal to her bedroom.

No.

She sighed, trying hard to hold back the frustration and fear from overwhelming her. This couldn't be. "Okay," she said slowly thinking, "We came from the Louers' new dimension. Then it makes sense to return that way. That pathway has to be relatively fresh – as compared to one which Dillon traveled so long ago. So in theory, we should have an easier time going back there."

And she'd take that place over this one any day.

Silence.

"Correct?" She snapped, her voice sharper than she'd intended. Shit. Fear ate away at her nerves. She ran her fingers through her hair.

Possibly. We have no data to confirm that. Based on dimensional travel history, we do know it is easier to move through a pathway already forged.

Storey brightened. "Of course it is. Same as any path. The person who walks in the lead breaks the path and the person who comes behind will be able to walk easier. So therefore, we should take the same way back to where I was. In the portal between the Louers' caves and Paxton's lab."

Excitement surged between her. She knew there'd be a way out of this. She just had to get her mind wrapped around the concept.

In theory.

She laughed. "Stylus, you are getting downright maudlin."

We do not like the lack of data. Decisions should be made on facts.

"Sure, but like you said," she added cheerfully, "We don't have any to go on. We will be the first. Therefore we are creating the data for you to store for others."

She couldn't be sure, but it was almost as if the air lightened. She grinned. There was more personality from the stylus every day. There *were* souls in there. Such a fascinating concept.

"Now to test that theory, we have to try from the point where we arrived in this dimension." She hesitated, then asked, "Do you agree with that logic?"

Yes.

She smiled, feeling much better. It always felt better to have others agree – even if they were both wrong. "Okay. So…we need to return to the physical location where we arrived. You have those coordinates."

Yes.

Storey turned to look at Dillon. He had fallen asleep again. On the damn paper. She sighed and nudged his shoulder. He slept on. She nudged him harder. "Dillon? Wake up."

He snuffled.

At least that's the way it sounded. Bizarre. "Dillon. It's time to go. Wake up please. I need to pick up that piece of paper."

Dillon opened his eyes. Looked down, and stepped back. "Sorry," he whispered. "So tired."

Returning wasn't looking so easy. Storey started to realize just how much of a problem she had on her hand. She didn't know if Dillon would survive the trip. The biggest concern was that his physical body couldn't handle the travel or even worse, couldn't handle another reality. Gravity, atmosphere, and whatever else was different here would suddenly impact a body held in stasis for over a century. His muscles – would they even hold him upright after all this time? If she managed to get him out of here would he collapse and die in her arms?

Was he better off here? He was alive this way. If his existence here was life. Maybe down the road, Paxton's people could create the technology to come back here and find Dillon.

No. He's almost gone.

Shit.

"I'm his only hope, aren't I?"

We believe so.

Believe? Such an odd word for the stylus. Everything the stylus had spoken of before had been definite, based on facts. It had been sure, almost computerized in its analysis of problems and optimal solutions. Until this mess. This was a new scenario for the stylus. And it had no answers. Only suggestions.

She shrugged. "First, we have to return to where we arrived in the In-between." And maybe in the meantime she'd come up with an answer. She spun around to reorient herself and grimaced. "Going back to where we arrived isn't going to be easy, is it?"

Consider this reality and your thoughts.

She paused and considered the stylus's words. And grinned. She scooped up the paper that Dillon had been standing on, grabbed Dillon's hand and closed her eyes. She took a deep breath and let it out slowly. Calmly. She thought herself back to the point where she'd arrived in the In-between. She let the knowledge that she could create her reality through her thoughts settle deeper into her psyche. Letting the memory resurface of having fallen because she'd imagined herself to be falling, and having stopped her fall because she'd told herself she'd stopped. Therefore she was back where she'd first arrived because she imagined herself to be.

With her eyes still closed, she asked, "Stylus, where are we?"

The stylus made a series of clicking noises then a long hum sounded. She didn't know if that was good or bad, but it felt…good.

We are back where we began.

She took several little steps for joy. "Perfect."

She glanced at the almost comatose Dillon at her side. "Are there others here in this dimension that I should be trying to save?"

We don't believe so.

"Can you run a scan and see? Maybe look for heat signatures. Something?"

We will do so. We can do more than search for heat signatures. And have been since we first landed.

"Good."

You are not alone.

She froze. "I have Dillon here, so I am not alone. Do you mean there is someone else here?"

A Toran.

She grinned. Then her grin fell off. "Of course there is a Toran. Dillon is here."

Dillon is a Louer.

"He's what?" she exclaimed. "He doesn't look anything like a Louer."

He is as they were originally.

Oh God. She stared in shock at Dillon. "But," she whispered, "He looks like Eric."

Eric is a Toran.

"So what's the difference?" She threw up her hands in frustration.

The faction they originated from.

Faction? Didn't that mean something political or religious in her world?

On Toran a faction is a Clan, a group formed of both family and political ties.

"So there were two groups of the same people. Half called themselves Torans and the other half called themselves Louers? The two fought, the Torans won and enslaved the Louers. The Louers fought back and were banished."

Yes.

Simple and sad. As she stared at Dillon, she realized he had to have been born after the war that enslaved the Louers. How had he been spared? "Stylus, how is it that Dillon is a Louer and free? Or was he a slave?"

He was free. No one knew he was a Louer. Dillon's name is in the database as having gone lost.

And his ancestors?

Again, a secret. Their ancestors were Louers that makes them Louers. Ancestral law states that you are of the same clan as your parentage. No one was allowed to change allegiance.

"But that's not fair," she cried. "Children have a right to choose what they believe. They shouldn't be punished by who their parents are."

Even as she said that, she could think of many instances in her own world where just that had happened and continued to happen. Those born into slavery, born in jail, born to different races. Each of those offspring had an uphill climb to get free of their heritage. It appeared to be no different here.

Unfortunately.

Shaking her mind free of those depressing thoughts and tucking the knowledge that Dillon was a Louer back into the corner of her mind, she turned to the more immediate issue.

"You said there is a Toran here. Who and where?"

Eric.

"Really?" she shouted. This time she danced around Dillon, joy rippling through every part of her. "We're saved!"

Dillon stared at her and blinked.

She groaned in disgust. "Dillon, it means someone is here to help us." She continued to skip in small circles. "I presume he's on his way to us? And we should stay until he finds us?"

He landed at our old coordinates, where you found Dillon.

She laughed. "I knew he'd find us. Does he have the new coordinates?"

Paxton has just given them to him.

"Good." She said with satisfaction. "Then he should be here any moment." Then she frowned. And tugged Dillon several steps over. "Just so he doesn't land on top of us."

She stared and stared at the spot. Nothing happened. She glanced around in case he'd adjusted the coordinates slightly and still nothing. She turned back to look at the original spot.

And there was Eric.

His grin flashed, huge and full of relief.

"Woot!" She launched herself into his arms. "I knew you'd come!"

He picked her up and swung her around and around. "Oh, I'm so glad to see you."

He put her back down and gave her a blistering kiss.

She pulled back slightly and beamed up at him. "Maybe I'll have to disappear again, if you're going to welcome me like that!"

"Trust you." He glanced around. "Man is this is a weird place."

She snorted. "Tell me about it!"

He smiled down at her, then froze and spun around. "What the…"

"Yeah, what a surprise, huh?" Storey glanced at the sleeping Dillon. "I still don't understand that whole 45 degree angle sleeping thing."

"He's asleep?" Eric dropped his to a faint whisper. He bent over slightly to look closer.

"Yes. I think he's been asleep since he arrived. According to the stylus that was a long time ago." She shrugged. "He's spoken to me a couple of times, but then always nods off again."

"Unbelievable." Eric shook his head. "How did he survive here?"

Storey wished she knew. "I have no idea. I think he went into a sort of hibernation. The stylus doesn't think he'll survive if we try to take him home though. That his muscles, after not experiencing gravity in so long, won't support him. And that's just the beginning of the problems. The thing is, I can't leave him."

Eric stared down at her. "This isn't a Louer child to return to her parents. This is an adult male Toran. If he dies while going home, surely that's better than this quasi-dead existence."

That whole death with dignity thing. She sighed. "I hate to kill the poor man. And speaking of family," Storey winced, not sure how Eric would react. "He says he has a brother, named Paxton."

Eric's head swiveled to stare down at her in shock.

Then back at Dillon. "It couldn't be."

"What?" When he didn't answer right away, Storey poked him in the chest. "What couldn't be?"

"Paxton did lose a brother when they were young men. He was playing up to the ladies while porting and fell In-between."

She gasped and turned to stare at Dillon. "Oh no. Then we definitely can't leave him."

"Neither do I want to take him home to his brother to die."

She didn't know what to say. "Stylus. Is there anything we can do for Dillon?"

His body won't be able to handle living in the other dimensions.

"But he's not alive here either," she said in frustration. Then caught Eric's look. Right. He couldn't hear the stylus.

Quickly she explained what she she'd heard. "According to the stylus, Dillon can't live in other dimensions, but it told me earlier he won't be able to survive much longer here, either. I don't want to believe that."

"But there is no other way." Eric wafted his arm in the thick soup. "Either desert him to this endless darkness or take him home and he will either live or die, but at least he'll be home again. Think of his family. This would mean tremendous closure for them."

Storey opened her mouth to speak, but a weird noise sounded.

What the hell was that?

A HEAVY DRONING noise, one Eric had initially taken to be a part of this strange space, increased like an amplifier steadily turning higher and higher.

"Storey, what is that?" He had to yell over the noise.

Then the noise cut off.

The look on Storey's face was…stunned. Yet…preoccupied?

"Storey? What's wrong?" No answer. Eric leaned in. Her gaze was intent, but focused inward. She had to be talking to the stylus. He'd seen that same look before. A part of him was jealous. To have that kind of connection – special.

Although, from looking at the contortions in Storey's face right now, he wasn't sure the process was particularly comfortable. He reached out and stroked her shoulder and upper arms. "Storey, are you okay?" He didn't expect an answer. In fact the air was so thick and dense, he had to wonder if there wasn't something else going on. He kept glancing at Dillon to see if he'd been affected by either the noise or the weird atmosphere, but Dillon just swayed in place.

Paxton's brother. After all this time. How could they help him? It would mean so much to Paxton.

With another helpless glance at Storey, Eric lifted his arm and sent a message to Paxton, letting him know what he'd found. The old tech communication system was one of the boosts Paxton had added to his codex – Toranese code. Awkward, but functional.

The answer was immediate.

Eric gave a short laugh as he read it off. *"Not possible."* He stared at Dillon for a long moment, realizing what a miracle it was that he should even be alive after all this time. It was as if time had stopped. So not possible. Yet the proof stood before him.

He painstakingly sent another message explaining that Dillon hadn't aged much in appearance, but appeared to exist in a semi-asleep state. Although capable of talking, he was confused. Writing on the codex was a slow and tedious process, but Eric did his best.

He added at the end that he didn't think Dillon could survive a return to any normal dimension.

Paxton replied, saying he'd confer with his stylus. Maybe they could come up with answers.

And that's when Eric remembered the big broken stylus he'd brought with him. He reached for it. As his fingers touched it, he realized the stylus was vibrating. He pulled it out to rest on his hand. The vibration pulsed so strongly the stylus physically rocked.

Damaged maybe. Dead…nope. It was foreign in a way. He hadn't had much to do with the styluses and this was the only one he'd touched that didn't burn him. Although there was a warning heat, it wasn't enough to force him to put it away. "Still trying to send out a warning aren't you? But you're not strong enough. What was I thinking in bringing you? How much help can you be in this state?"

"B…igg…er, tha…n you—"

Eric stared as Storey tried to speak again, but the words wouldn't come. "Storey?"

But she'd gone quiet again.

Too quiet. He stared into her eyes. All he saw was a reflection of the same look…from Dillon's eyes.

CHAPTER 7

S TOREY REELED UNDER an onslaught of emotion and
sound. It pounded at her from all sides. At first she'd
been too slammed to understand. Then a pattern had
formed in her mind. It wasn't just one external voice, it
was two, with several conversations going on at once.
She'd heard her stylus before. Many times. Its communication had an essence to it, a flavor that was her stylus.
And that made it very distinctive from the other thoughts
floating in her head. Plus it spoke with a certain rhythm.
A different structure to the sounds. But now there was a
new voice.

Speaking to the stylus and sometimes…maybe to her.

It wasn't Eric, though wouldn't it be cool if they
could speak like that. She shuddered as another wave
washed through her mind. She caught bits and pieces.
Not that she understood them, but there was something
recognizable and yet foreign at the same time in the
interaction between the voices in her mind. She didn't
dare get hung up on the concept of voices in her head. In
her dimension she'd be seeing a shrink for that. In Eric's
dimension…she had no idea. Most people couldn't get
their mind wrapped around such things.

For herself, well…apparently she was different. And
the longer she stayed out of her normal life, the more odd
she became. Or at least the more aware she was of her
differences.

A particularly sharp tone in her mind made her close her eyes. She knew Eric was trying to talk to her. But about what defeated her.

He pulled something out of his pocket. She wanted to laugh hysterically when the object registered in her sore brain. A broken stylus. *The* broken stylus.

Yes. Me.

Whoa. What was that…who was that?

"Are you speaking to me?" she asked out loud. She managed to shake her head slightly at Eric, hoping he'd understand that she wasn't talking to him. Carrying on internal and external conversations at the same time was impossible at the best of times; right now, though…

Yes.

"Are you my stylus?" Even though she knew it couldn't be, she had to ask.

No.

Then her stylus spoke. *He is our leader. You rescued him. We are grateful.*

Oh my God. She was speaking to the broken stylus.

That is correct.

Now she didn't know who had said that.

We did.

She'd have laughed if she could have. At the moment, she couldn't tell the two styluses apart. And that wasn't right. She had a connection to her stylus. This broken stylus defied the Torans' belief about bonding and communication. Or had it?

No.

She sighed. *So how then?*

The bonding increases the abilities between the holder and the soul bound stylus. Our broken leader is the best of us. He can speak slightly without being bonded.

Storey had to think about that. *What about the Louers? They have telecommunication. Why couldn't they speak to you? The Broken One was there.*

To communicate both parties must be open. The Louers lost many in the early years after they were banished. Much knowledge has been lost. The survivors over time discarded the styluses as childhood toys, broken and forgotten. Not as instruments of value. They would not see a stylus as something desirable. Or the souls within as valuable. If they even knew that we were within.

She shared the information with Eric.

"How sad." Eric frowned at her.

She nodded. This communication system was cumbersome. "Stylus, can you speak with Eric?"

Eric shook his head.

No. He is not open to such a form of communication.

Right. She asked, "Can't you two speak out loud so he can hear?"

No. We are not allowed to speak in such ways.

"Not allowed?" She pounced on that term. "But it is possible?"

A buzz hummed through her ear. And she realized they were speaking together, but not with her. So although she understood they were talking, she couldn't hear the conversation.

"Broken one, what do I call you?"

Broken one.

She winced. *Have you no name?*

I was once called Barrat. Many years ago.

A slow smile spread across her face. "Barrat. Lovely name. Are there more of you in there?"

No.

"That is unusual, is it not?"

Yes.

"And lonely," she suggested, sad for him.

Yes.

"Do you know how to help us leave In-between?" she

asked.

That buzz filled the air as the two stylus started again. While they were at it, she caught Eric up on what she'd learned.

"If they figure out something – good. Otherwise, since the longer we stay here the harder it may be to get out, I suggest we try leaving now." Eric pulled a second codex out from his pack and clicked it on Storey's wrist. Then digging into his pants pocket he pulled out a third. "I thought I was over doing it bringing more than two units, but now…" He stepped up to Dillon, snapped the instrument around Dillon's wrist in one smooth move. He needn't have worried. Dillon continued to sleep, swaying gently on his feet.

"How bizarre," he said, unconsciously mimicking her earlier words.

"I know." But to business. "Where are we travelling to?"

"Paxton's lab?" He cocked his head at her. "I know my father did this to you, but I hope you won't hold all of us to blame."

She just gave him a long look. "Never. And as long as I don't have to see your father again…all is good." Glancing around she shivered and added, "Besides, any place is better than here." Then she remembered something else. "The stylus said it would be easier for me to leave by heading back the way I'd arrived. I planned on drawing a portal back to the Louers' new dimension. Although we were closer to arriving at Paxton's lab when I was pushed out than the Louers' dimension."

He blinked.

She glared. "Don't do that. That's what Dillon always does."

"Sorry. I'm just trying to figure out what you're talking about."

"Oh, never mind." She threw up her hands. "Let's

just get on with it. But first, Stylus, did you two figure out how to get us out?"

The Broken One says he knows, but is trying to access his archives. He is damaged.

That again. "Okay Eric, let's try your way."

He shrugged. "Good. The sooner the better. This place is…weird." He tugged her closer to Dillon and made sure they were all crowded up tight together, then at his timing, they hit the buttons on the multiple codexes. Dillon just swayed in place, seemingly unaware of what was going on around him.

To Storey's relief, the black smoke swelled up around them. "Yeah, we're going home!"

"And how many times have we thought that in the past," Eric said with a grin, his head so close she could feel his breath against her hair.

"I know. I just want to go home and stay there."

"Speaking of which, I went to your house and grabbed more sketchbooks before coming to get you."

"Oh," she gasped. "How was it? Did you see my parents?"

"No. And, I think it was normal. Your room looked like it did in the beginning. There were no vehicles there and I didn't see anyone in the house."

"But my room looked the same?" How odd. She wanted things back to the way they were supposed to be, but she hadn't been that lucky yet. "Stylus, you did say fixing my home dimension was an easy job, right?"

Not easy, but possible. And the dimension will need to be realigned.

"Uh Oh. What does that mean?"

You will have to port out while the changes happen and port back in afterwards.

"How do I do that?"

Go to the closest dimension and then come back in.

Her stomach sank. "The Louers' dimension?" She felt

Eric stiffen beside her. Neither of them wanted to go back there again. Quickly she related the conversation so far.

Yes.

"Can we port to Eric's dimension instead?"

No. Not without more of us. We are damaged.

"Damn. I'm getting really sick of hearing that."

She'd been using the conversation to distract her from the portal travel and the fact that the mist hadn't dissipated. "Eric?"

"It's fine. Don't forget there are three of us here."

"And three codexes," she reminded him. "So lots of power."

"But not for this pea soup stuff. I expected it to take longer as the air is so different."

She was prepared to be patient. She was just so happy to have him with her. She'd been afraid she'd be lost alone forever. And that reminded her of someone else that had become very dear to her. "I wonder how Tammy is doing?"

"I'm sure she's fine."

She tilted her head back. "Do you really think so?"

He smiled down, the curve of his lips barely visible. "Knowing Tammy, she's having lots of fun."

Storey wanted to believe it. The last thing she'd seen in Tammy's face had been happiness with the man who held her in his arms and sadness at saying good bye to Storey. Or Torrey as she'd called her. "I'm sure Tammy was trying to talk to us telepathically in the portal that last time."

"She probably was. We know they have a higher developed internal communication system than we do."

On a whim, Storey closed her eyes sent out a loud greeting, "Hi Tammy."

Nothing. Then she hadn't expected there to be a response. They were somewhere In-between. Eric thought he knew what he was doing, but she was afraid this whole return to Paxton's lab wasn't happening. She opened her eyes. Black mist continued to surround them. She sighed. "Eric, I don't think we're going anywhere."

He lifted his arm to look at his brightly lit codex. "We're not at the same place we were however."

She brightened. "Oh good. As long as we're going somewhere. So do we just wait?"

"For a bit longer." He slung an arm through Dillon's. "I don't want to lose him again."

"Again?"

"Let me rephrase that. I want to make sure we get him home to Paxton safe and sound. For however long he's got."

"Right. Stylus, where are we?"

In-between.

"Still?"

Yes.

Damn. "But we are at a different point in In-between than we were before – correct?"

Correct.

Good. She smiled happily.

Ten minutes later she wasn't so happy. Nothing had changed. "Why do I get the feeling that we are caught in this portal now?"

"I'm thinking you might be right." Eric tapped his codex several times.

Storey watched him. "Can you change our destination while we're in here?"

"No."

She didn't want to bug, but this was getting them nowhere. Literally. "Isn't there a reset button or something?"

"I reset it a few moments ago," he admitted. "I don't think it changed anything."

"Great." So not. "Okay Stylus, are we still traveling?"

Yes.

Good. She lifted a hand to massage her temple. So much to consider. "Which is the closest dimension for us to land first?"

Louers' dimension.

"Fine. I'm happy to land in the Louers' dimension if it gets us out of the pea soup." She cocked her head in question up at Eric. He shrugged. Right. It's not like they had much in the way of choice.

"Stylus, can you help us land there then?"

Yes.

She grinned. "Good. Do I need to do anythi—"

Musical sounds filled the air. Eric lifted his arm as the codex flashed and sounded off in a weird sequence. "I've never seen anything like this before."

"Hope I never do again." But if it improved their situation, she was good. "Stylus? What are you doing?"

The Broken One is doing this.

She gulped. "Broken one? What are you doing?"

Changing the communication system to accept new coordinates. I have no other souls to help. I can only use what I have.

"Okay," she said slowly, "And that means what?"

There is a destination point In-between that we used to establish portal travel in the beginning. But my archives have only some of it listed. We need it all to be able to chart our way out.

"Oh, that's the whole point of origin thing," she said in excitement. "What do you need to heal yourself?"

Eric rolled his eyes at her. It had to be hard with the half conversation stuff.

"More souls."

She groaned. "And how do I help you get those?

Silence.

"And even if I had another soul for you, how would

they go into the stylus? Your stylus form is broken."

I would need to transfer to a new stylus.

Talk about mind boggling.

To transfer from one stylus to the next, we must have a third that is open to both sets of souls inside. A middleman. Both stylus souls join in the consciousness of the middleman. Then the old soul joins with the soul of the new stylus and transfers with it back to the stylus.

The Broken One's voice sounded thin and reedy as she listened. But his explanation sounded reasonable. And weird. But doable in a freaky way. "But how did the first soul get into each stylus originally?

We were sent In-between.

In-between? She shouted. "What? You sent souls to In-between then brought them back inside the new stylus?"

"Yes."

ERIC STARED IN shock at Storey's excited telling of what she'd just learned. That it was not reasonable nor feasible didn't seem to deter her.

"That's why all this technology has been lost. The Broken One was broken before his information could be downloaded to the archives. That's why you have so few styluses and no new ones. No one knew how to make new ones nor how to add new souls to old styluses." She danced in place, her hair bobbed with each hop she was so excited.

Could it be? Surely not. Eric looked around the fog that still surrounded them and had to wonder. They'd had little information on the styluses until Storey had dropped into their lives. Literally. And if she was right, what did it mean about them and their situation? Had people come and returned from In-between as people, or only as styluses? 'Cause he really didn't want to spend eternity inside a pencil.

At least not until he'd thoroughly enjoyed his current life. Dare he ask? He almost didn't want to know the answer, but given the situation… "Storey, can the Broken One tell you if anyone has successfully left In-between…not in a stylus?"

The smile fell from her lips as she understood what he was saying. An instant shadow of horror whispered across her expressive face.

"Don't assume we can't get out any other way." He rushed to say. "Let's find out for sure first."

She nodded slowly. Her gaze landed on Dillon as her mind, the fastest he'd ever seen, seem to flit from one answer to another. "It could be the saving grace for Dillon."

He turned to look at the sleeping man beside them. If that was possible, it would be one answer. He didn't know that Paxton would consider it a good one though.

Still, they didn't have much choice.

"Ask them. Ask them if Dillon could be moved to a stylus and if we can escape – with our bodies."

CHAPTER 8

STOREY'S INITIAL EXCITEMENT drained as if a switch had been flicked. Her emotions were all over the board. Living in a stylus might be an option for Dillon. But she didn't know how much of a good idea that was, transferring his soul to an inanimate object, given he was a young man who'd not had a chance to live yet.

But if death was the only other option… She quickly called out to both styluses mentally. *Can Dillon join a stylus? He's been here a long time, but according to my stylus he can no longer live in any of the other three dimensions.*

It's possible, said the Broken One. *Once safe, his soul will recuperate. Be as he was.*

In theory that was good news. But… *Are you both happy with your decision to be in a stylus? Is this something to be enjoyed or feared? I guess I'm asking if we would be doing him a favor or punishing him?*

It is an honor among us to assist in the continuation of our species.

And that's where she had trouble. They'd actually been continuing the existence of their enemies. Weren't they? Or did it not matter as they were in essence one species? Then she'd have to include the people from her own dimension as well. They were all essentially the same. She didn't doubt there were some differences, maybe even at the DNA level, but as far as she could see, Dillon, Eric and herself were all the same people.

Exactly.

She nodded thoughtfully. "And yet only Louers are soul bound to the styluses?"

Yes.

Interesting. She wondered on the perspective of each soul going into this arrangement. Still, for Dillon it might be the best answer. If not the only one.

"What do we need to do for Dillon to join a stylus? Can he join one of yours or do we need a completely different one? He is a new soul and you both need those, right?"

Yes.

From the look of understanding on Eric's face he was following the one sided conversation. "Eric, did you bring more styluses?"

He shook his head.

He need not have one with him. The process is in the porting home. He would be outfitted with a destination that is inside the target stylus.

"Cool." She laughed at Eric's frown and explained. The look of astonishment that followed made her grin. "Yeah, simple, isn't it.

Eric gave a half snort, half laugh. "The concept is simple. But we're missing just a little bit of information. Like how do we get the coordinates of the destination stylus? If we give the coordinates for where a stylus is at any given point, the person will land beside not inside it."

"They appear to want a coordinate from the inside of the stylus. With that information, would it work?"

He stared at her. "I have no idea. I have never heard sending people inside of something."

"Of course, you haven't," Storey said gently. "You didn't even know there were souls inside these instruments. This information has been lost to your people for a long time. Even Paxton isn't likely to know."

The Broken One said, *He does now. I spoke to his stylus.*

She titled her head. "Broken One, if you can speak to Paxton's stylus, why is it you couldn't speak to them from the Louers' dimension? And don't tell me you are damaged."

I was in hibernation. When you rescued me, your Stylus, as you call him, contacted me to see if I was safe. That started the waking process.

"And now you are functioning, but damaged. Right?"

Silence.

Then a hesitant voice that she had yet to hear from her stylus said, *We said you would help him.*

"Help him?" Storey frowned. What could she possibly do?

You can speak with us. Directly. With me, the Broken One said.

"I'm not sure how, but yes, that is apparently what we are doing."

I am using the connection between your stylus and myself, and by extension your stylus and you, to communicate with you.

"You can do that? Wow."

It is you who has made this possible. I thank you.

There was a lot of thanking going on and somehow Storey suspected there was something they wanted from her.

You are correct.

Storey...the Broken One needs to be saved. He is important to us.

"So you've said." A niggling suspicion had her stomach twisting tighter and tighter. Somehow she didn't think she was going to like what was coming. She held her breath.

We need you to save him.

She almost laughed. She'd saved him once already. What more could she do?

"Storey? What's going on? You look…ill." Eric's voice intruded into her confusion.

She took a deep breath and tried to reassure him. "Not really. My stylus wants me to save the Broken One."

In sync the two stared down at the stylus in Eric's hand. "How? It's damaged."

There was that word again. She wanted to hit him. She groaned instead. "Don't you use that word, too. I know it's broken. Damaged. In need of souls or whatever. But in this case, they want something specific. I just not sure what. Or how."

"Can't we just send a soul to this stylus?" He looked thunderstruck as he realized what he'd just said. "I didn't just say that, did I?"

"Absolutely, you did." She laughed. "See, it's almost normal to think this way."

"We don't have souls to give the Broken One, do we?" He winced. "I can't imagine forcing someone to this life. It would be essentially murder."

She shook her head. "That's why they used slaves. And some were happy to do this. I imagine others…not so much. And no, we don't have any other souls. Just Dillon. But I don't think that's the answer. From what I'm understanding the stylus itself is damaged. And not only can we not add a new soul, the Broken One needs to be moved to a different stylus or be lost altogether."

Eric reared back. "Is that even possible?"

As she thought back on the muddled conversations, she thought she just might understand. "I think…they want me to allow the Broken One to join with me, then through the bond I already have with my stylus, travel to my stylus. Using me as a middleman of some kind. A conduit, maybe."

"What? No way."

"It might be possible." She shrugged. "I'm just not sure what's involved and how dangerous it might be."

"Dangerous? That's it. You're not doing it." He shook his head violently, his hair flying out every which way. She loved the way he hooked his hands on his hips and widened his stance. So manly. And so not going to stop her.

"I don't know that it is or isn't yet. I'm only guessing here."

It is. That was her stylus speaking. *And you are correct. That is what we ask of you.*

She winced inside, careful to keep her reaction hidden from Eric. What he didn't know and all that. *How dangerous?* She kept the communication internal this time.

Silence.

Of course they didn't know. *How long will it take?*

Minutes, said her stylus.

That is for the first part of the process, added the Broken One. *The second stage will take slightly longer. This is new. We have information that it is possible. But I haven't done this process. I must learn too.*

Oh boy. *Does that mean you will be inside me? Cause that's very freaky.*

Yes. That is the only way.

She barely held back a shudder. She didn't know why it bothered her. Normally, she'd bend over to help someone in need, but this seemed more…private…more personal Almost invasive, and yet she was speaking to them mentally anyway. How much different would it be?

Not much different. Your discomfort would be small… The Broken One hesitated, before admitting softly, *And my need is great.*

We would honor your sacrifice.

That word gave her the willies. Made her afraid there

was more to this process that she wasn't seeing.

Eric interrupted her private concerns. "Paxton is worried about losing his brother again."

"Which way? In a stylus or by him returning to the dimension?"

"Both. Dillon will die if we take him home. But as the concept of souls bound inside a stylus is foreign to him, he's afraid his brother would be upset at waking up inside a stylus."

"Why don't we ask him?" She shrugged, "What can it hurt?"

She turned to Dillon and shook his shoulder. Dillon swayed in place, his hands hanging slightly forward. "Dillon, we need to talk."

Dillon looked at her, that same blank stillness on his features. Then his gaze cleared suddenly. "What?"

"We spoke with your brother, Paxton," she tried not to let her impatience show, but she really wanted to leave this place. And in order to do that they needed some answers. "We would like to take you back to him, but there is a problem." She tried to peer into his eyes. Make sure he was understanding, following her words so far. His big doe eyes gave her no clue, but there was something going on in there.

"I can't go back," he whispered. "It's been too long."

She winced. "I'm afraid that might be true. We can't know for sure."

"I thought it many times." His big eyes pleaded with her. "For so long. I don't want to be held a prisoner here…lost forever."

Oh boy. "That's why I wondered about another solution. You can't go back and you don't want to stay here, do you remember styluses from when you lived with Paxton? These instruments." She pulled hers loose from her shirt so he could see it.

His gaze locked on it, brightened. A look of recognition came over him. "You are one of the blessed. My brother too, the head of his field, was gifted with one such as this."

"Yes, I am blessed because of my stylus. But that's not what I meant. Inside these styluses are souls. Like you and me." At Eric's stifled snort, she shot him dark look. "They were willing to spend eternity alive, inside such an instrument to help their people, your people, develop into the future. Whatever that may be."

Dillon shook his head, she could almost hear the bones protesting the movement. "No. Not possible. It is an instrument. Only."

"Yes it is, but it is made powerful by the souls inside.

"Uh, Storey?" Eric called, "I don't think this is working."

She frowned. "Damn it. I just thought that maybe he would like to make a choice here. Death, stay here for the rest of eternity, or bond to a stylus and spend eternity being of use. He lost his entire life here. Wouldn't he prefer to salvage something from this?"

"But if he doesn't understand, he can't make that decision. And I'm afraid that understanding is beyond him at this point."

"For so long, I was angry, then sad that I should be forgotten and lost." Dillon said, his voice faltering and thin, but the adamant thread was clear. "I would like to have my life back."

"And that we can't give you." Storey said earnestly, "but we can give you a meaningful existence. Just not one you might expect."

Dillon blinked, his gaze slowly going from her to Eric to the stylus and back to her again. "You are serious."

"She is very serious." Eric stepped forward. "You would find a life of value, of contribution and bonding with other people and souls. Except you would only exist in soul form and be contained in a stylus."

"In other words you would physically be dead. Your soul would live on and interact on a daily basis with the people around you and technically, with your brother."

Dillon straightened. "Paxton. I could communicate with him?"

Storey looked at Eric. "There's no reason why he couldn't, is there? Paxton speaks with his stylus now on a regular basis and his stylus communicates with other styluses?"

Eric nodded. "True, but maybe confirm that with your stylus."

Right. "Am I right, stylus? Can Dillon speak with his brother once in the stylus?"

Yes. It will take a little time for him to adapt. But he will be able to communicate with us all.

"Dillon the stylus says you will be able to communicate with the whole community of them. You will be one of them."

Dillon smiled, a slow birthing of hope, and said. "I would like that."

ERIC'S HEAD SPUN as communication surged around him and over him. Stuck In-between, so thick in fog, he dared not step back. But he wanted to. To take a moment and regroup. But Storey was speaking with both styluses and they were speaking with Paxton's stylus who was in turn keeping Paxton and then Eric on top of what was happening.

Paxton had the suggested recipient stylus in his hands. He had coded in the destination coordinates to the database, given by the Broken One and with the Broken

One's help had downloaded the coordinates of the other styluses to the archives. Now the transfer was ready from Paxton's end.

Eric wasn't sure where his end was at. He'd tried to watch Storey, but the multiple facial reactions as she alternately understood or didn't understand what was being said telepathically fascinated him. He wanted to ask questions, but knew he'd slow the process down. It was better to wait it out.

He was happy that something was happening at last. They'd been standing here long enough. He wanted to leave this foggy half world and never come back. But he also wanted to make sure he got everyone home safe. He just didn't know if that was possible yet.

Paxton, once he'd heard Dillon's comment, had been all for the transfer. The Broken One had chosen the stylus most in need, but had emphasized that all needed new souls sooner rather than later.

He snorted at that.

"What Eric?" Storey asked, fatigue showing on her face. "Is something wrong?"

He smiled down at her. She looked so valiant right now, tired and wanting to be anywhere else but here, yet still game to do what she could to help others out. Even if it was dangerous. And he had no doubt it was. He also knew he wouldn't be able to talk her out of it.

She had this belief that she could do anything. So far she had, but life tended to deliver a major reality crash at some point. Not a reality check, but a complete flat out brick-to-the-face realization that you couldn't save everyone or everything.

"Are you sure you want to do this?" He tried to keep the worry out of his voice, but her reassuring smile said he hadn't been as successful as he'd hoped.

"I feel like I need to."

"You don't," he exploded. "Let someone else do this."

"Who?" she reached out a palm and cupped his cheek. He leaned into her soft touch. She was the most compassionate, caring female he'd ever known. So giving. And so resourceful. He both admired and cared about her. Too much to let her get hurt.

He'd come here to make sure she got out safe. But what did getting out safe mean if she walked right into another dangerous situation?

"Don't be so worried." Storey gave his cheek a pat before withdrawing her hand. "I'll be fine."

He frowned at her. She reached up and kissed his cheek.

"Will you?" he asked, his voice deepening with his heightened emotions, "Because I'm not sure I can take it if you aren't."

Her beautiful eyes darkened. She stepped back and said, "I will, but I think we need to help Dillon now."

Eric nodded, his stomach sinking with dread. "Yes, it's time." He lifted his right arm. "I have the coordinates here on my spare." He stepped around Storey and unhooked the codex on Dillon's arm and attached the properly coded one. There was a soft snick and it locked in place.

He stepped back, looking for any awareness from Paxton's brother of what was happening. Dillon's eyes were closed and once again he appeared to be sleeping. "Dillon, I've just put a codex on your arm. We're going to send you to the interior of the stylus now."

Dillon's lids fluttered. He nodded. His mouth opened, the words so faint Eric had to bend closer to hear. The words trickled out. "Not feeling too good."

Eric could just imagine. This needed to happen fast. Dillon was fading quickly. He shot a warning glance at Storey. He nodded in Dillon's direction. "The codex is set. He's running out of time."

A frown mingled with the worry twisting Storey's features. "I hope he lasts long enough to make the transition."

"Yeah, tell me again – how does he leave his body and go into the stylus? I'm just a little confused on that point."

She grimaced. "Actually so am I. Honestly I'm not sure I want to know, either. If this works then we've saved a life and reunited Paxton with his long lost brother."

She stepped slightly backwards. "I think we probably need to give him some room."

Eric lifted a brow, but retreated several steps, staying close to Storey. It was too easy to get lost in the fog. So thick he couldn't see more than a half dozen feet in front of him.

"Okay, now what?"

She looked over at him. And shrugged. "I don't know."

CHAPTER 9

S TOREY, AFTER MAKING sure Eric was what she hoped was a safe distance away, closed her eyes and asked, "What's next?"

Now we need to have Paxton run the program that will separate Dillon from his physical body and send him to the inside of his new stylus.

"I don't understand how this is possible. But if it's the only option…"

It became possible centuries ago, when some of the Toran and Louers developed psychic abilities involving astral travel. Much research and many experiments later, this was a process that could be followed by others.

Her insides locked down at the visual presented in her mind. Storey didn't know what to believe and her experience with styluses had her pondering life…and death. If death was only the end of the physical body in Eric's dimension, as proven by the people soul bound to the stylus, was that the same in her world? Was there something after death?

She didn't have time to work the angles in her mind, but realized at some point she'd have to sit down and clarify what this meant to her. And to her mother. It also showed her how lacking in beliefs she was. Without a strong religious background giving her defining guidelines one way or the other, she hadn't formulated any theories about death and afterlife herself. And now she'd experienced something so foreign to her world, that she knew she'd have no one else to discuss this with down the road. And that was sad.

"Storey?"

She took a deep breath. This so wasn't the time. With an attempt at a reassuring smile, she nodded. "Yes, let's do this."

The codex on Dillon's wrist started a series of notes that she'd never heard before. The sound achingly sad and heartbreakingly beautiful. Almost funeral. She spun a look at Eric and realized he was just as surprised as she was.

She watched as Dillon slowly appeared to sink in on himself. Fascinating. His features dimmed, his body slowly becoming fuzzy around the edges.

She'd expected the black mist to circle him and it did, but it seemed softer, more cloud like than she'd seen before. Instead of a hard port, dragging the body away to a new dimension, it was baby's breath gentle.

Tears welled up inside as she realized this was the end of Dillon as she'd known him. She could only hope he was traveling to somewhere so much better.

The music slowly faded as if moving a long way away. And it probably was. The fuzzy mist darkened to the point she could barely see anything within its depths.

Eventually the music died altogether. She waited. Would the mist disappear too?

It did, slowly. Dillon appeared to sway in place, then almost in slow motion his body disintegrated with the mist. Leaving nothing behind. Unfreakin' believable. And unfreakin' beautiful.

She was moved beyond tears. A warm hand wrapped around her shoulders.

"Are you okay?"

She smiled tremulously. "Yes. Or at least I will be soon."

"How long do you think before we know if it was successful?"

She'd like to know that herself.

"Stylus? Do you know if Dillon has arrived?"

He has.

A smile broke free, and Storey released the breath she'd held unconsciously. "Dillon is there."

"Really?" Eric's happy gasp made her laugh.

"Yes." Even she could hear the relief wreathing her voice as she asked, "Stylus, is he all right? Is he awake? Talking?"

Not yet. He will need time to acclimatize.

That wiped the smile off. "Any idea how long?" She reached up and squeezed Eric's hand at the worry etched on his features. Again, he couldn't hear all of the conversation. She gave him a thumbs up gesture.

He settled back slightly and waited.

This is an unknown. Depends on how long he needs to recuperate.

"Okay. Let me know, please, when anything changes."

She turned to Eric and relayed the information.

He shrugged. "We've done what we could for him. Now it's out of our hands. Do you think we can leave?" He looked around and shuddered. "I'd like to get out of here."

"Me too." She took a deep breath. "Stylus, what about us? Can we leave now?"

A heavy buzz filled the air.

A quick glance confirmed Eric heard it to. "I presume that's the styluses talking again. Not sure why that hum is so loud."

"If it helps us escape, I don't mind."

We don't know if the transfer for the Broken One will work in the physical dimensions.

Uh oh. Her next problem had appeared. "Eric, the styluses are not sure that the Broken One will be able to transfer in the regular dimensions. I believe they think the process might be easier if we do it here. They've always done the stylus transfers from In-between."

Not easier. But possible.

"Actually, they don't think the transfer can happen at all unless we do it here."

"So that's next?" His arm fell away, and he took several steps back. "Are you sure?"

"Yes."

She took a deep breath. "Okay, Stylus. What do we need to do?"

You don't need to do anything. Except remain calm.

Calm. That so wasn't easy. "Okay. I'm calm. Go ahead."

We need you to empty your mind. Just relax.

Empty my mind? How is that possible? she replied mentally, not wanting to worry Eric.

It will be easier for you if you are not trying to follow the process consciously.

Easier how?

There won't be a headache.

As soon as he mentioned the word, pain struck her on the back of the neck. She collapsed to her knees and held her head in her hands. "Ohhh," she moaned. "My head. It feels like it's going to explode."

Eric dropped beside her. He held her close. "Is this from the transfer?"

She writhed in place as the headache built higher, pounded louder, heavier.

She buried her face against Eric's shoulder shuddering in pain. "I don't know," she whispered. "I think so."

"Jesus." He leaned his cheek on the top of her head. "How long will this take?"

"No idea." Then she couldn't speak at all. A small cry escaped her lips. The pressure built and built until she couldn't stand to be touched. She fell back, away from Eric. "Don't..."

"Storey," he came closer, his hands out in front of him. "Please, tell me. What can I do to help?"

"Don't touch. My nerves. Sensitized." She gasped loudly. "So much pain."

"How long? Stylus? How much longer?" Eric shouted. "It's too much. She can't take this."

She groaned and swayed back and forth still on her knees. "Oh my God. It's getting worse."

She collapsed to the ground and curled into a tight fetal position.

ERIC HAD NEVER felt so helpless. He reached out to touch Storey, then let his hands drop away. If he couldn't help her and couldn't talk to the stylus through her, he still had Paxton. He lifted his codex and sent a message to Paxton, first checking to see about Dillon, then checking to see if he could get answers on Storey.

The wait for a response seemed interminable. When it came, he jumped to read the message. *No idea on Dillon. According to the coordinates, he has arrived. There is mass there. I can see it on the monitor.*

"Well, thank heavens for something."

His codex flashed again. *The transfer is in progress.*

"It's killing Storey," he responded to the empty air. "She's in terrible pain." There was no point in telling Paxton that. Neither of them could do anything to help. But he might know how long this was going to take. At least it was worth asking. But Paxton's response was no help. He had no idea.

"Damn."

Right about now, it would help to communicate with a stylus himself. He asked Paxton to check with his stylus.

Paxton wrote back: *I can't communicate with my stylus at this moment. They need everyone right now for this transfer. I don't understand it, but there is a horrific hum to the air.*

So it was a group effort.

According to Storey's stylus, they were trying to save a revered leader. Eric had no idea how they could have a leader amongst them. The thought that they could gather together, have a hierarchy, a society of styluses, really blew his mind.

He knew Storey would tell him off for denying them a community. And there was no doubt that's what they'd built.

Who'd have thought?

Just then Storey gave a high pitched squeal. Her head was thrown back on her neck into a rigid, backward arch. Her mouth opened and she screamed again. A long, painful wailing.

And then she fell silent. And still.

CHAPTER 10

S TOREY SLOWLY CAME awake. She lifted her lids ever so slightly and realized that much hadn't changed. She was still in In-between, caught in the never ending mist. She slammed her eyes shut again. So what was different? She considered it slowly. Inside was different. Her breath still went in and out in a relaxed rhythm. Her temperature appeared normal. She couldn't feel pain anymore, so that was good. Whatever had been tearing her skull in two was gone. She rolled her head to one side experimentally. That worked well. Hesitantly, she lifted her head to look around.

Eric was crouched in front of her, worry lines marring his face.

"How do you feel now?"

She opened her mouth. No words came out. She tried again. Nothing. She frowned. Why did she have no voice? She coughed and heard the hoarse sounds coming from a long ways off. So her vocal cords worked. She tried again. "Aggh." She waggled her tongue inside her mouth. It felt larger, thicker than normal. Filling her mouth unnaturally full. Odd.

"Storey? You're scaring me." Such concern, caring, poured from his gaze. As if by his emotion alone he could fix whatever was wrong.

She managed a weak smile. "I'm…here." That sound-ed better. Maybe she just needed a little more recovery time. She tried to sit up, managing to get her arm under her to prop herself up. Her arm gave way and she collapsed.

"Here, let me help." Eric grasped her under the arms and helped her to a sitting position. "Is that better?"

She nodded.

"You're having trouble talking?" Eric stared down into her eyes. She brightened and nodded.

A brush of relief whispered across his face. "Okay. What about the rest? Can you take a moment and check out the rest of you? Can you move? Think on your own? Is the Broken One in there with you?"

"Yes."

Storey's eyes opened so wide they hurt. She stared at Eric.

That hadn't been her voice.

That had been a man's voice.

Oh no.

She swallowed heavily.

"Storey? Was that you?" Eric leaned back and stared. "Or was that the Broken One speaking?"

"Yes."

Eric lifted a brow. "Yes, what?"

"The Broken One speaks."

Storey shuddered. God what a feeling. Her vocal cords rippled, her mouth moved, only she wasn't the one moving them. She wasn't the one in control. The Broken One had control.

Stylus!

Yes.

What is going on? she asked. *The Broken One is speaking using my body. You didn't say he would be able to control my body while he was in me.*

I did not know it would happen.

Well it did, she snapped. *Now I need to move him from*

me to you. I can't function like this.

There is some rest time required. This first move took much energy.

Then recharge. Fast.

It takes time. We are damaged.

She wanted to scream at that last phrase. *I know you are damaged. That's why we are doing this. But I am struggling here. How do I regain control?*

You never lost it. He is a visitor only.

And she, like a good host, had stepped aside. So he hadn't taken control – she'd handed it over. She closed her eyes and took a deep breath, letting it out slowly, softly in a long, meditative, drawn out sigh, releasing the old, dead air from her lungs.

As the last of the air exhaled, she smiled, feeling tension she hadn't been aware of drifting from her body. She felt…wonderful.

And peaceful.

Complete.

And that last thought scared the crap out of her.

Stylus…what is happening? I'm getting a little nervous here.

You have joined…us. Bonded to us all. Your soul knows it. Craves it, and now has that sense of belonging. You are one of us.

As the wonder and the shock of this revelation penetrated her confusion, she became aware of yet something else strange. A pain, running down the side of her neck and across her collarbone and back down her shoulder blade. She wanted to rub it, but at the same time it had a heat to it that made her pause. Even as her attention centered on the pain, it drifted away. As if her awareness of its existence was enough to remove it.

So not possible, but she wished it were.

It is.

She froze. That was the Broken One speaking — she thought. Hard to tell, as his mental voice was different than when he'd spoken from his previous location from inside the stylus.

It is I.

She nodded her head slowly, gaining confidence that the pain really was gone. *Are you saying I will be able to heal myself now? That's not possible — is it?*

None of this should be possible, but apparently she'd been wrong about that, too. She had the Broken One inside her physical body and if that didn't top the weirdness factor then she didn't want to know what did.

It is possible. To a point.

That's good to know, she said. *At least I'm going to have some benefits while you are visiting.*

There are many.

That peaked her curiosity. *Like what?*

You have access to my knowledge. As I have access to yours.

Her eyebrows shot up at that. *Really?* She couldn't resist peeking. She found his memories, like a vast room behind a door in her mind, and cast her thoughts back to the Broken One's earliest memories as a young boy. She'd thought he was male, but hadn't known for sure. She wondered if any female souls had been bonded to styluses.

The answer came immediately to her from…somewhere inside. No. Only males were allowed to bond.

That was hardly fair.

The Broken One said, *It has been that way, always. The Torans don't have females in power positions. They wouldn't allow Louers to have them either.*

Right. That made sense. She didn't like it, but it was logical. Women had some power in her world, but—

Not in all areas. I see much of your dimension is split on that issue.

She sighed. *Yes that is true. In many parts of the world, women are considered property and nothing more.*

There are many problems in your dimension.

She knew it couldn't be physical, but she felt a spidery, crawling sensation as the Broken One accessed her memories. She couldn't blame him. He was big on knowledge and she'd opened that door herself. There was such a duality to the moment. She had access to great knowledge, but there was also a hesitation to share her own. It was…private.

She almost laughed. Nothing would be private any more. The Broken One could see and experience everything in her life. As she could his. It wasn't intrusive, or jarring, just…odd? Maybe. She didn't know how to express it.

While she floundered to name her cascading feelings, a familiar face loomed close to her. Eric. She smiled. "Hey. I'm okay."

"You don't look it."

If his expression was anything to go by, she must look awful. His brows had pulled together into a dark vee and the angles of his face had hardened with worry. Even his lips were pressed firmly together. And the color, she didn't know if it was the foggy atmosphere, but his skin had taken on a gray pallor. Had she scared him that badly?

He snatched her up and hugged her tight.

She burrowed deeper into his arms. "Sorry," she murmured. "This is all so strange."

"Is that what you call it?" His attempt at humor fell flat. "Honestly, this is painful for me. I can't do anything, but watch." He squeezed her, then settled back a bit and stroked her back. He sighed, a deep welling release that she felt in her own body.

"I'm so sorry. This isn't how I'd planned to escape In-between."

He gave a gurgling laugh. She reared back to look at him. Was he crying? No. More of a choking laugh.

"I'm glad you had a plan. It would have helped to be filled in on it." He smiled. "Only you could call this mess a plan."

She moaned. "I know. I so have to work on that."

He smiled down at her. "You are one crazy girl. Now…do you have any idea what's next? I know I keep pushing the idea of leaving here, but I really want to go home."

"The styluses said that they need to recuperate from transferring the Broken One to me."

He peered down at her. "How long?"

She frowned. "I have no idea."

He closed his eyes and dropped his head. "Right. More waiting. And in this case, it could be a long time."

The Broken One spoke through Storey. "We can move now. The bond between you and your stylus is strong. We still need to wait for our power to regenerate for the next step, but we can do that in another dimension."

Storey brightened. *Really?*

"Yes."

Eric hopped to his feet, and carefully tugged Storey upwards. "Good. Let's go. I vote to go back to my dimension."

The Broken One spoke again, "That is not possible."

Eric froze. "And why is that?"

"In order to leave this dimension, Storey has to feel a strong bond to somewhere. Her bond to your dimension is tainted by your father. It would be hard to use that energy to successfully port home. However, she has a strong bond to her dimension that we could, possibly, build on."

That made sense and for all that she was sorry, the Broken One's assessment of Eric's dimension was true. She did have a negative feeling about that place and all because of the Councilman. Not a fair attitude and one she'd get over, but since her current predicament was because of him…

"Why can't we just port out?" Eric asked. "Now that you are here and functioning, and we have the coordinates of this place – point of origin – so to speak, why can't we just leave? Dillon did."

Storey wanted to hear that answer herself.

"Dillon didn't port out. Dillon's soul ported out."

Oh shit.

ERIC'S STOMACH HEAVED. Would this never be over? Whatever happened to an honest battle? He could handle that. Death, under those circumstances, was also understandable. He'd always known that every time he left his dimension in his capacity as a Ranger, he might never return.

This half world where neither life nor death existed was painful. He wanted to hit out at something and he couldn't even get into a decent argument with the stylus as it was ultimately Storey he'd be arguing with and that wouldn't work. He wanted to protect her – not hurt her.

And what he really wanted was to get them both out of this hell hole. This stylus deal had become so much bigger. What they'd just done with the Broken One…well, he couldn't begin to explain. But he'd kept the broken stylus just in case they'd need it down the road. As he'd come to realize, nothing was ever finished.

"What do we need to get out of here once and for all?

Intact. As in our bodies leaving with us."

Storey rolled her eyes at him. A quirky grin spread across her face. A lightness that only happened when she was around swelled inside. She could do that to him. Only her. Make a dark day lighter, sweeter. Just by being there. There was a special connection he always felt around her. A sense that it was just the two of them. That they were aligned against the rest of the world.

He relaxed. "I'm not trying to be pushy here. But I want a solution that keeps us alive and well, thank you."

At that Storey laughed. "Me too."

"Broken One?" he asked. "Have you a way out of this dimension?"

"We think so."

Storey lifted a brow as her mouth moved, but a different voice spoke.

Eric shook his head. It was so weird for him to see her, but hear the Broken One. That the stylus's voice was rougher, raspier, helped him to identify the speaker, but he couldn't imagine how Storey felt to have another soul inside using her vocal cords, her body.

"And what is that?"

Eric waited, hoping that the answer would be easy. He'd had enough of these puzzles that only seemed to embroil them all further.

"We need to have a strong energy connection that would allow us to build a portal to the other side. Storey's ability to draw would be instrumental in this. But she needs to feel very strongly about something in order for that energy, that caring, to be powerful enough for us to utilize the energy to power the process."

"Like my mother!" Storey laughed. "I so want to see her again. To be home again."

"Yes, that was our impression."

Eric waited, there was a 'but'…in there somewhere.

An uncomfortable silence filled the fog.

CHAPTER 11

"BROKEN ONE? IS there a problem?" Storey frowned. Her voice changed, deepened, as he said, "Your mother. There are some issues there. A time element that makes it difficult."

She groaned. Now that home had been mentioned as the ideal option, she couldn't stop the yearning inside to return to her own dimension. "Do what we have to do to get out of here."

"That might not be an ideal location with our limited power. Even with your strong feelings."

She closed her eyes and worked on bolstering her diminishing patience. "Then what is?"

"Someone else you care for, enough for us to build on the energy."

Her gaze flew to Eric. "Someone else is Eric. But he's here with us."

"Building a portal to him means a portal to here," said the Broken One. "Of no value."

She rolled her eyes. "Was that an attempt at humor?"

"We are learning. You have much laughter in your memories. Much joy. We would like to experience that."

"Don't you remember laughing?" As the question left her lips, she was bombarded with memories of his childhood. Sober, sad, alone with other slaves and working as he was given work to do. The life of a child slave hadn't been much fun. Although there were some times that were more lighthearted, she couldn't see any instances of real joy. There were no rocks being kicked around in a game, or running in sunlight just for fun. There were only solemn instances of work, discussion, aloneness and…not a hug in there.

"Were you abused?" She didn't think so, but…

"Not by your definition."

"Loved?"

"Not by your definition."

"Loving relationships? What about your mother? Father? Siblings? Friends? Lovers?"

"No."

His thoughts were clear, curious, detached. He had no experience with relationships. At all.

"Not true."

Right – he could read her mind. How weird was it that they were reading each other's minds, but were both speaking aloud using her vocal cords so as to include Eric in the discussion.

"I have a strong relationship with my community."

She smiled slowly, and inside her that sense of connectedness brightened. It was a strong, caring bond and she was glad he'd had that much. In fact, it was more than many people experienced in her own dimension.

"That is possible. I am not unhappy with my existence." He made an odd sound. "Especially now that you have saved it."

"And you are very welcome for that," she said sincerely. "Now I hope you can help me regain my life."

"We do too." He was silent for a long moment. "You need someone else you are connected to. Preferably someone where your feelings are still strong today. Not a relationship from a long time ago."

No one came to mind. She didn't know what to say. Who did she care about? Her mother, Eric, a few school friends. She had no siblings or nieces and nephews…she gasped. "Tammy!"

Eric looked at her in surprise. "You do really miss her, don't you?"

"I do and…" she emphasized, her voice rising. "Remember, I said she was trying to communicate telepathically with me? There is that bond as well."

"Will that be enough?"

The Broken One stepped in and said, "There is much affection for her. That is good."

"Is it?" Storey asked. "We can't see each other. I can't communicate with her and even though she's back home again where she belongs, I miss her."

"It's dangerous for us to go there." Eric groaned. "But it's still better than being here."

"And that is the emotional energy we can use to leave this place."

Storey paced a small circle. "What can I do to help?"

"And me?" Eric said. "There has to be some way we can both help."

Storey heard the answer like a faint echo in her mind. The two styluses were talking, but so low she couldn't understand the conversation. "They're busy doing something. I can barely hear them."

Eric squatted down slightly and pulled out one of his packs, expanding it. "I have your sketchbooks here. Maybe you can do something with them."

Storey squatted beside him. "I don't suppose you have anything to eat in there, do you?"

Eric laughed as his hand found the block of cheese he'd pulled from her house. He lifted it free and waved it around in front of her. She gasped in delight, but instead of going after the cheese, she dove into his pack. "What else have you got hidden in here?"

She found the granola bar within minutes. "Yes!" She

unwrapped and bit into it immediately.

The look in his eyes made her stop. She held it out to him. "Sorry, do you want a bite?"

"Go ahead." He shook his head and chuckled. "You need it more than I do."

Storey broke the bar in half and handed over the second piece. "Here. We both need our strength." He took it with a smile and popped the whole thing in his mouth.

She shook her head. She'd seen her male school friends eat like that. It always amazed her. How could so much fit in one mouth? But he wasn't worried about choking. He'd already pulled out his knife and was slicing chunks of cheese into her hand. Greedily she popped the largest one into her mouth. "Any chance there's an apple in there?"

Eric nodded. "Maybe the Broken One should use your love of food to mine the emotional energy they need. They could create a portal to your mother's kitchen."

She grinned. "I love it. It should be a cakewalk to mine a path to Tammy. Hell, if she knew I had this food, she'd be coming here to find us!" The smile fell away and she chewed very slowly. Both on the cheese and the worrisome thought in her mind.

"What?" Eric raised a brow at her as he popped more cheese into his mouth.

She swallowed the last of her mouthful, then stared at the slices in her hand. "Does this mean we're going to Tammy? And the rest of the Louers? The ones that held us prisoner last time?" She looked at him, knowing her fatigue and fear had to be showing. "They hate us. I'm not sure I can deal with all that again."

He reached out and grabbed her shoulder. "You can do it. At least there, we know what the problem is. What the solution is."

She nodded. "I'm just tired. I can draw a portal and

use it to escape as soon as we arrive."

"Why not do that now? We may not have much prep time before the Broken One has things ready." He pulled the sketchbook forward and handed it over.

Reinvigorated, she shoved the last of her piece of cheese into her mouth, wiped her hands on her jeans and reached for the book. She frowned at it. "Where did you get this?"

"From your room."

"I don't have any like this in my room. This is smooth paper. Silky. I prefer a rougher texture." She shrugged, not wanting to delve too deeply into why this book would be in her room. "Whatever."

She pulled her stylus free from around her neck. Opening to a blank page, she closed her eyes and asked her stylus, *What do I need to draw? Portals? Or Tammy's face?*

Her head started to vibrate inside. She squeezed her eyes shut, afraid her brain was going to bounce off the inside of her skull. A shudder drummed its way down her spine.

Stop it. That hurts.

The pounding in her head ceased. She took a shaky breath. *Thank you.*

We must work. It would be better if you slept.

I can't just sleep. I'm not tired. Well I am, but I can't just go to sleep when I want.

Yes you can.

Storey smiled. *It's not that ea—*

She fell to the floor. Asleep.

"STOREY? STOREY, WHAT'S wrong?" Eric knelt beside Storey. She breathed easily, her color remained normal.

He reached a hand to her forehead. Reassured that she was in fact still alive, he settled back on his heels to wait.

"Damn it, Storey. What the hell do I do now?"

Of course no one answered. Typical. But he could talk to Paxton. He quickly sent a message, bringing Paxton up to date. And asked about the status of Dillon.

He read the response out loud. "No information on Dillon. Why is she sleeping?" He snorted. "As if I know. And I'd like to."

He reached over again and stroked her hair back off her forehead. Surely this wasn't a normal sleep. She lay as if dead, not even shuffling or rolling over. She slept as if she hadn't seen sleep in days. Sure, she was exhausted, but this…it wasn't normal. He could only hope this place wasn't affecting her like it had Dillon.

All he could do was stand guard over her.

But for how long?

He waited and waited. And waited.

CHAPTER 12

S TOREY CAME AWAKE slowly. She opened her eyes and saw Eric sitting at her side. She had no recollection of falling asleep, yet she felt…rested. And depressed. She was still in In-between. Grey fog totally encompassed the two of them. Damn.

Her head was full. Her thoughts had some clarity though, as if the rest had been what she'd needed. She sat up slowly, happy to see there was no residual headache. That pain had been crippling. "Eric?"

He leaned toward her, his smile a bright light in the gloomy atmosphere. "Hi. Enjoy your nap?"

She winced. "I'd have enjoyed it more if I'd woken up in one of the other dimensions."

"You and me both," Eric said with a groan.

Feeling good, she could sympathize. "And that wasn't sleep as much as enforced rest." She explained what the Broken One had done.

His mouth formed a big O. "What? He knocked you out without your permission?"

She winced. "Permission is a difficult thing when you're sharing a body."

"You're not sharing. He's a guest. Remember that."

She struggled to her feet. "I'm trying to. And if I'm awake, I'm going to assume that he's done whatever they needed to do. Maybe," she glanced around, "we can leave now."

Eric stayed sitting. "I hope so. But I doubt it. Nothing is going as planned this trip," he said gloomily.

She laughed, reached a hand down, waiting until he grasped hers, and helped him stand up. "Are you trying to tell me that you actually *had* a plan this time?"

He grinned modestly. "Hey, I thought we could wing it. We've done that a time or two before."

She went to say something when a shutter blanked the words from her mind and the Broken One spoke using her vocal cords, his gravelly voice surprisingly deep. "It is time."

Eric shouted, "Yes!"

Storey was a little less enthused. She wanted to hear the details first. She asked, her voice surprisingly normal, "Broken One. Where are we going? And how are we travelling?"

"To Tammy's home. By your portal drawings."

Eric's brows shot up in surprise. "Tammy's dimension? Is that safe?"

"It doesn't matter. It is the only option."

Storey spluttered. It didn't matter? Is so mattered. His next word stopped her in her tracks.

"Tammy is waiting for you," the Broken One said.

She gasped in joy. She'd forgotten that the styluses could communicate telepathically with the Louers. Something about their combined abilities, adaptability and technological advancement. "You spoke with her? How is she?"

"She is well."

Eric said, "I still don't get this telepathic stuff."

"It is only language. And using energy as the translator."

With a shake of his head, Eric said, "I wanted to ask — is Dillon the first Toran to be soul bound to a stylus?"

"No."

Storey remembered Eric hadn't been in on the earlier conversation. He didn't know what Dillon was.

The Broken One added, "Dillon is not a Toran. He is a Louer."

She gasped, finally realizing what she'd missed earlier. She stared up at Eric.

Eric frowned down at her, obviously not understanding.

She didn't know if he hadn't put the dots together or if the connected dots really didn't matter. Cautiously, she said, "I didn't realize you have Torans and Louers intermingled in your Toran dimension. I'd assumed all the Louers had been banished."

He shrugged. "They were."

Storey sucked in her breath. And waited.

Eric shook his head. "I'm not dense, but the way you're looking at me, as if I'm missing something important, is making me feel that way."

She took a deep breath and hoped she didn't have to explain.

"Oh, hell." Eric shared at her stunned.

Yeah, he got it. Finally. He narrowed his gaze. "You're saying Dillon is a Louer. And he was in the Toran dimension. So therefore at one time, they were mingling."

"Dillon wasn't a slave."

"I remember that, too."

"And," she prompted.

He frowned. "And what?" His expression cleared as he finally understood what she'd been getting at. Then a thundercloud swept across his face. "It can't be. There has to be some mistake."

"I don't think there is."

"It's not possible. Paxton is Dillon's brother. If Dillon is a Louer, that means our top philosopher, our greatest scientific leader, the confidant of our Council and the eldest of all the council members – is a Louer."

Now he got it.

ERIC COULDN'T THINK. The facts, as he understood them, swirled into a dark, chaotic form that made no sense to his brain. Was it possible that Paxton was a Louer? Dillon looked like the same race as Eric or Storey, but then from what Eric had learned from her and the styluses about his people's history, Dillon would. The Louers' appearance had changed over time due to hardship – a hardship that Dillon…and Paxton…had missed. It boggled the mind.

How could it have happened?

"In all societies that employ slavery, some slaves hold higher positions than others. It's quite possible that Paxton's parents or grandparents were free people." Storey suggested, her tone quiet. "Maybe they had migrated from Louers to Torans and no one knew."

"It could change everything at home."

"If anyone finds out." She shrugged her shoulders. "I won't tell."

It wasn't that easy. Eric had no idea how he should feel. His mentor, the man he preferred to think of as his best friend, perhaps even as a father, was the enemy.

As if reading his thoughts, Storey said, "Just don't make the mistake of thinking that Paxton and Dillon are the enemy. Paxton has shown by his every action that he is as much a Toran as you."

Eric nodded. "I understand that."

"But?" Storey narrowed her eyes at him. "It makes no difference. You might want to also consider that given how long ago this could have happened, that Paxton might not even know."

Shocked, Eric studied her features. "How could that be? Of course he'd know."

"First off, his own parents might not have known. If they didn't, then he wouldn't have. It's not something you'd speak about normally. And even if he did know, Paxton has devoted his very long life to serving the Torans. He's kept you safe and helped in every way he could. You can't blame him for this."

"I'm not blaming him," Eric said slowly, "But there is a sense of betrayal."

That garnered him a dismissive look. "For not having told you? How could he? Especially once all the problems started. If he knows, he'd have to wait for the right time to tell you. And understand – there is no good time for bad news."

Eric didn't want to discuss it anymore. He couldn't. He had no idea of how to feel and certainly wasn't going to hash out the issue right now. He shoved it all away and tried to refocus. "The Broken One says it's time to go. Let's deal with that first. There will be plenty of time later to talk to Paxton."

Storey gave him a slow nod. "True. You and Paxton need some time alone to discuss this. Your father is already a big issue in your life. You don't want to do anything that would put a rift in your relationship with Paxton, too."

She was right. He knew that. Even the thought of losing Paxton brought a pang to his heart. But later. He'd deal with that later. Firmly, he said, "Let's get out of *this* mess first."

CHAPTER 13

WATCHING THE CONFUSION and turmoil on Eric's face, Storey realized how much she'd come to care for many of the Torans – especially Eric. He was special. And she'd even developed a kinship to Paxton. He was the only other person who'd bonded to a stylus that she knew of, after all.

Broken One, can we proceed?

Yes. Draw Tammy in her home. Make her happy and glad to see you. Connect emotionally.

That wouldn't be hard. Tammy had always been happy to see Storey. She'd been taken captive by a party of her own people hoping to force her father to take them home. Storey had saved her.

She picked up her stylus, and sank into the memory. There'd been such a glow in the girl's eyes when she'd realized she hadn't been deserted. That someone cared enough to help her. She's been so despondent before that, the contrast on her face had been emblazoned on Storey's memory. With that picture of hope, of joy, she overlaid the last glimpse she'd had of Tammy as her father walked away with her in his arms.

Her hand moved, slowly at first, carefully laying the picture down as she had it in her mind. Then she picked up speed. The stylus moved with such finesse and such accuracy, she knew she couldn't be doing it on her own. In fact, she'd have to admit this drawing was stronger, and more powerful than anything she'd done before.

Was that the addition of the Broken One?

Yes. We are one.

Stylus, this is only a picture of Tammy, don't I need to draw a portal as well?

We are doing that at the same time, her stylus said. The comforting sound of her own stylus made her sigh happily. Their connection was more than just instrument and operator. She'd like the think the sense of familiarity she had with her stylus was the beginning of friendship. She'd fought to keep her stylus. And even now couldn't begin to imagine life without it. Him. Them. She shrugged. She understood they were a collective of souls, but since she heard them as one voice, she thought of it as him. Right or wrong.

Of course being soul bound, if they were separated, she'd die.

Thank you.

She stilled. *For what?*

For feeling the sense of connection that has been missing in our world. As we have bonded to the stylus, we have also bonded to you. And you to us. That makes our relationship more than it has been before. It makes us whole.

But you were bonded to a scientist before, correct?

Correct. We bonded to him for our existence, but he did not bond to us.

Ah, she said. *So no mental, or emotional connection.*

Or respect.

She pursed her lips at that.

"Storey? Are you even watching what you are doing?"

She glanced over at Eric to see him staring at her in confusion. She blinked and looked down at her picture. She'd drawn a photographic image of Tammy in a dwelling of some kind. Her arms were open as if waiting for a hug and the smile on her face tugged at Storey's heart. She barely heard her own happy gasp at the look of joy in Tammy's eyes. The picture was stunning in its detail. And still her hand flashed and darted, adding a line here, a shadow there.

"I so want to keep this after we are done." She said. She stared at the warmth in Tammy's eyes. And saw, tucked into Tammy's hair, was her pet, Skorky. Storey chuckled. She'd even be happy to see the rat-like critter again.

"It's stunning, but look, you've got a door in front of her, one we can walk through. Except it's so small and the paper itself is small…how is this going to work?" Eric's tone was exasperated. Doubt twisted his lips as he shook his head. "This can't work. We've always had a piece of paper large enough to step into. Drawn the way you have it, it's a door like you did in Paxton's lab that first time, only you did it so it appeared at the end of a hallway. Like a perspective drawing."

"We can always use more paper," she suggested.

Not necessary. This is functional.

Storey lifted her eyebrow and repeated the stylus's words to Eric.

He turned to study the drawing in progress. Then got up, walked behind her and stared down over her shoulder. "Really?" he muttered. "If you say so. Then can we go? This damn place is starting to give me the creeps."

Storey almost laughed at hearing her thoughts coming out of his mouth. But he wouldn't appreciate it at this time. Or any time.

Then her hand stopped moving. Such an abrupt halt it startled her. She wondered if she could ever do art on her own ever again. With the stylus having become such a creative force behind her drawings, she'd never know what was her art and what was *their* art.

You will know.

Maybe. It wasn't the issue right now. She turned her attention to the sketchpad. She understood what Eric was saying. It didn't look big enough to be of use. Then this wasn't exactly a normal dimension.

Exactly.

"So how do we make this work?" She stood up. She held the picture out in front so both she and Eric could study it.

"Tammy looks so happy to see us, doesn't she?" And that made Storey anxious to see her. That little girl was special.

"Keep in mind – this is a drawing. The stylus can make her look as it wants her to look. That doesn't make it real. Or correct."

Ah, Eric's pragmatic approach to life. "Then let's find out."

"How?"

The stylus was silent.

Hmmm. Storey studied the picture. She looked up at Eric. "I think they're expecting us to know what to do with this."

He snorted. "Like that's going to happen." He waved an arm around. "We can't do anything here."

That wasn't quite true. They could do a lot. They just had to think differently. She created the rules here…somewhat. She wondered…could it be that easy? She remembered back to when she'd first arrived, and finding how falling and stopping worked, that so much of it was done by mental control. So if the perspective was the issue, then could she pin this paper to…the fog…and have it hang there?

Holding the paper gently, she detached it from the book and giving Eric a reassuring smile, she mentally, and physically, pinned the picture to the wall of fog.

It stayed there.

She grinned and stepped back. "There."

"Well it's hanging, but so what?"

As she studied the painting, she had to laugh. Unbelievable. Being a couple of feet in front of her, the fog had moved in, sliding a slight veil around the picture.

Giving it a distance. A perspective.

"Take another look at it."

Eric planted his hands on his hips and stared at the picture. She stared at him. And watched as he saw it. "The atmosphere here is making the perspective happen as if the picture is real and the fog is real."

"Right, we're approaching Tammy's home in deep fog conditions and look, there's a light in the picture."

He gave a short bark of a laugh. "So we just walk forward?"

"I'm guessing so."

She reached out for his hand. He clasped hers in his much larger one. Together they walked the short distance to the door. As they arrived, the door in the picture opened.

And they walked through.

ERIC COULDN'T HELP holding his breath as they entered the drawing. But just as with all the other strange portals Storey and her stylus had created, he stepped into a whole new world.

And a familiar sound had him dropping Storey's hand to clap both palms over his ears. He groaned, barely hearing Storey call out, "Tammy, hush. It's me, Storey."

The sound cut off instantly. Tammy's eyes widened. Then she launched herself from where she'd been sitting at Eric and Storey.

Eric, knowing the size of the bomb about to blast

them, tried to brace himself, but she knocked him back several steps, while they both knocked Storey over.

Storey cried out, then all Eric heard was her laughter. He disentangled himself from Tammy's legs and turned. He grinned. Storey was lying down and Tammy almost eclipsed her as she lay on top. Skorky raced over and around both of them, getting in the way as they laughed. Storey was tickling the chubby little Louer who wiggled frantically to get away, but at the same time, obviously didn't want to go anywhere.

"Torrey."

Storey, her grin splitting her face almost in two, hugged her close. Skorky dashed over Storey's head to take up residence on Tammy's shoulder, his beady eyes bright and curious. Tammy's over-bright eyes looked up at Eric. She sniffled happily. Something warm and fuzzy bloomed in Eric's heart. He'd never felt anything like it. At this moment, he couldn't be happier. They were in danger, had just survived what could have been an endless hell, yet seeing Storey and Tammy together made up for all of it.

He'd never thought to see Tammy again. Hadn't given any energy to wishing that any different. Now that he saw her, and her connection to Storey, he realized how much he'd missed the little girl himself. He'd just shut those emotions down, believing that a relationship wasn't possible.

Then Tammy scrambled to her feet and wrapped her arms around him. He hugged her tight.

Once again his world had shifted. Thanks to Storey.

CHAPTER 14

S TOREY FINALLY MANAGED to clamber to her feet. She took several deep breaths and rejoiced. They were free from In-between and they'd successfully reached Tammy. As Tammy and Eric enjoyed their reunion, she glanced around at Tammy's small room. Dirt walls again. Maybe that's all her people knew.

Or maybe that's all they'd been able to achieve so far. But Tammy appeared to have a bed, something like a small table and there'd been an attempt made to carve shelves into one wall. With Tammy's few things, like Storey's bag, she'd made the little room look like home.

On one wall were scratch drawings. Tammy's artwork, she presumed, studying the stick men in the picture. She walked closer. A small hand snuck into hers. Tammy reached out with her other hand and tapped the wall with the artwork.

Skorky ran across Tammy's arm to jump on a ledge and stare at them.

"Torrey." She tapped the wall and one skinny stick figure. Tammy grinned up at her. Storey was entranced. For the whole time she'd looked after Tammy, the child had shown little to no facial expressions. As if their race didn't use them. Over time, Tammy had learned to mimic more of the expressions she'd seen on Eric and Storey.

But this appeared to be her first spontaneous grin.

And it was beautiful. Storey bent, hugged the little girl, and said, "Thank you Tammy."

"Storey, do you think you can communicate with her again? Now that the styluses apparently contacted her?"

"I don't know." She straightened. "Tammy, do you know how to communicate with me, now?"

No response. She closed her eyes. *Stylus. Can you help me to communicate with Tammy?*

Don't need help. Tammy here.

Storey gasped and opened her eyes. She shared a special smile with Tammy, then turned to face Eric, excitement and that wonderful sense of connection flowing through her. "Tammy is here and we can communicate!"

"Telepathically, of course. Which means I'm only going to be able to get half the conversation again." He rolled his eyes in exaggeration, but his smile eased any sting.

She smiled back at him. "I'm sorry for that. Maybe you can learn to communicate telepathically as well."

Torrey?

Storey turned back to Tammy. *Yes?*

Are you in trouble?

Storey groaned loudly, but kept a smile on her face. *We are. This time you helped save us!*

Tammy danced several steps. Then her steps slowed as if understanding what would come next. *Are you leaving again?*

Soon. I need to return to my home first. Then come back here for another quick visit. Maybe if we can talk this way now, we can talk once I return home, too.

Tammy's face lit up.

"What brought that on?" Eric asked.

Storey laughed, holding out her hand to Tammy. "I was telling her that now we might be able to keep in touch."

"Do you think that would work across dimensions?" Eric frowned. "If that's the case, I might have to try to learn. Then we could stay in touch all the time."

"And if that doesn't work, you could get me a codex that allows me to write messages like you've been doing with Paxton. It wouldn't be as good as telepathy, but we would be in constant contact. Instead of planning visits." She chuckled. "Or better yet – you should get a stylus of your own."

"That's not likely to happen." He pulled up his codex and considered it. "I think both of these have that ability." He lifted her wrist, reminding her that she wore one already. "We'll test it later. First, are we going back to Paxton's lab or to your home world? As much as Tammy is happy to see us, I'm not so sure about her father."

Right. The leader of the Louers, Tammy's father, had knocked them out with their nasty telepathic weapon the last time they'd seen him. The horrible noise that made an unconscious state actually preferable.

She glanced down at Tammy. *Tammy does your father know we are here?*

She nodded. Storey gasped. *Did he know ahead of time?*

No.

So how does he know now?

Tammy cocked her head and frowned up at Storey in confusion. *He can hear us, of course.*

"Oh shit." Storey turned to Eric. "Her father apparently can hear this telepathic conversation so he knows we're here."

Eric immediately started punching coordinates that he'd used not too long ago to take him to Storey's dimension. "Tell her we have to go. We can't get into trouble with her father again."

As Storey relayed the message, Tammy's face crumpled.

"Ah Eric, we need to leave now. She looks like she's going to start crying."

"Hold her off," he said, urgently desperate to stop that horrible shrill sound of hell that would soon be coming out of Tammy's mouth. Then his codex started its musical notes, instantly distracting Tammy. The little girl reached out to touch the flashing lights.

"Whoa." Eric backed up. "Storey, get over here."

She quickly stepped right beside him as the black smoke rose up around his legs. She waved goodbye to Tammy, saying. *We'll be back soon, honey.*

Tammy's eyes filled with tears. She launched herself at Storey.

And the black mist closed around them all.

"STOREY, PLEASE TELL me that didn't just happen?"

Silence.

"Storey," he snapped. "Talk to me."

"I'm here. But so is Tammy." She added humorously, "I guess our visit wasn't long enough."

"Damn it." He couldn't believe it. Why did everything go wrong? This should have been so simple – get in and get out. No one should have even noticed.

A choked giggle slipped from Storey.

Short arms reached around his waist and Tammy snuggled close.

He glared into the mist, then sighed and wrapped an arm around Tammy's back. He reached out and tugged Storey in closer where he could see her face. "What are you laughing at?"

"You." She added, "You swore."

"Did not." But he had. And she knew it. Drat. She just smiled up at him. He'd always liked that about her. She never judged him. No matter what.

"What do we do now?" she asked.

"If her father finds out she came with us, there goes any chance of a peaceful relationship."

"Speaking of which, I'm thinking the stylus needs to contact Tammy's father and explain what happened."

He stared at. "If it can do that, why didn't it do it before?"

She shrugged. "Maybe it did."

We did not. We can.

Then please do so. It's our intention to return Tammy immediately.

A buzz filled the air.

"Uh, Storey?"

She wrapped her arm around him. "It's okay. It's the stylus doing something."

"That's what worries me!" Tammy's round face peered up at him through the gloom. She smiled, her empty hand reaching up to pat his cheek. "Ris."

"Eric." Eric covered her hand with his. "Eric. Try it again."

"Riss."

"I'm going to presume hard sounds like Ks aren't easy for her."

Storey giggled. "And what's her problem with E?"

The mist started to dissipate. A wave of relief washed through him. Maybe something would go right for a change.

The sun twinkled brightly overhead and green trees surrounded them.

Tammy's eye shone as she looked around with the mist almost gone.

Eric said, "Looks like she recognizes the area. You can

almost see the look in her eyes, saying food is around the corner."

At that Storey laughed again. "And she's welcome to it. I have never met anyone with an appetite like hers."

"Good thing she doesn't know about the rest of the cheese in my bag," he said smugly.

"Let's hang on to it. We might need your supplies for later." Storey headed off in the direction of her home.

Tammy followed, her hand securely held in Eric's.

Eric gave a last glance into the bushes around them and followed.

What would they find this time?

CHAPTER 15

S TOREY TILTED HER face to the sun. What day was it? The sun appeared to be high in the sky. If it was a weekday, then she might be lucky enough to find the house empty. If it was a weekend, then one…or both…of her parents could be there. And she so didn't want to meet them. Not in this time. Her mother, if things were back to normal…yes. She wanted to hug her tight and tell her how much she loved her.

But if it was the crazy life where she went to a private religious school and her father, who she hadn't seen in a decade, was home and still married to her mother, no way. Like how weird…and wrong…was that?

She admitted to being ambivalent on many of the issues, but she really didn't want to live the other Storey's life. That one did her schoolwork and never picked up an art pencil. This Storey would die under those conditions. Her art was her outlet. Her path to freedom from the world around her. She *had* to be able to draw.

And she would, no matter what. If what Eric had said was true about her room being full of art books she didn't recognize, then maybe the other Storey had already learned she needed to draw.

Maybe there was crossover, or bleeding from one Storey to the other. Time had twisted, but what else had twisted with it?

She reached the end of the trees and stopped. Her

home stood in front of her. Its familiar clapboard siding stirred pangs of homesickness inside. She desperately wanted to see her mother. The real one. Not the other one. Storey sighed. How did life get so confused?

Tammy tugged on her hand. Storey looked down at her trusting face, wondering at the child's sympathetic look. There was no way Tammy could really understand what bothered Storey at this time. But Tammy was offering what comfort she could.

And Storey was happy to accept it.

She smiled down at Tammy. "Let's go."

Tammy's smile kicked up a notch. They approached from the side. Storey led the way to the back kitchen door. She cautiously walked up the few stairs to the porch and tried the door. Locked. Damn. She left Tammy in Eric's care then slipped around the side of the house to the garage. There she crept into inside, relieved to find it empty. She crossed over to the inside door and found it locked too.

Rolling her eyes at fate, she whispered out loud, "You'd think there had been a series of break-ins where people raided the refrigerator or something."

Her mother had always kept a spare key under the freezer. She walked over to find the old chest freezer locked. But the spare key was still in the same old place. Gleefully, she picked up the key and unlocked the house door. She walked in cautiously. She couldn't be sure no one was home. At first glance the place seemed empty and that made her relax – slightly. Walking through the kitchen she unlocked the back door and let Eric and Tammy in. "Go on upstairs."

"What are you going to do?" Eric asked, already ushering Tammy ahead of him toward the stairs.

She rolled her eyes at him. "Look for food of course. What else?" She turned to the fridge. After all the times they'd raided this thing she wouldn't be surprised to find a lock on it. Not this time though. She studied the contents and realized there wasn't much that was grab and go. The kind of food she could offer without cooking it first. She did find a couple of oranges. In the pantry was a box of cookies and a box of snack crackers. She took both of those.

The problem was, Tammy could be expecting a mess of other food. She searched back in the fridge, but there was no meat that she could take up. She rummaged through the other cupboards and found an unopened package of beef jerky. Then she hit the motherload – a large box of Halloween mini-sized chocolate bars.

Perfect. Tammy wasn't going to argue with those. Not once she tried them.

She made a swift circle through the downstairs, rec-ognizing the furniture as being the same from her last visit. On the mantle, a family photo. With all three of them together. That meant her father was still in this life. With that confirmation, she ran up the stairs to her room. At the door, she stopped. Took a deep breath and kicked it lightly. Eric opened it immediately. His eyes lit up at her armload.

"Here let me help."

"No, it's okay. I'll just dump it all on the bed." She did just that. Tammy came running and jumped up beside the pile. Her chunky fingers immediately reached for the closest item. Storey snatched the orange back just before she bit into the rind. She tossed it to Eric. "This has to be peeled or cut into quarters."

She kept a wary eye on Tammy's face. Her mouth in a shocked O, then it crumpled. "Oh shit." Storey opened the box of snack crackers and pulled out several for her. She took the first one and popped it into her mouth. Tammy took several and shoved them into hers.

"Well, that much hasn't changed at least." Storey backed up several steps and turned to Eric. He was turning the orange over and over in his hands. She sighed. "Here give me that. I'll peel it." And she did, quickly and efficiently. Within minutes she split it into two halves and handed over both to the two people staring at her like she was going to be their next meal.

Eric bit into his half and his eyes grew rounder. He chewed, then bit again. "It's good!"

Tammy, after seeing Eric, shoved as much of the orange into her mouth as she could. Storey peeled the second orange. Then showing the two of them, broke it into sections and popped one section into her mouth and chewed it. Then popped a second one in. She split the rest into pieces for both the others. They followed her example and ate it slowly.

Storey left the two working their way through the food and went to the bathroom. She groaned at the picture in the mirror. Instead of things getting better, she was starting to look haggard. In-between obviously hadn't done anything good for her. She knew that when she closed her eyes to sleep, she was more than likely to have horrible nightmares of being caught In-between. Forever.

That type of fear would stay with her for a long time.

As would the 'what ifs' that kept going through her mind. What if Eric hadn't come for her? What if she hadn't found the Broken One in the Louers' dimension? What if she couldn't fix her own dimension…and things never went back the way they were supposed to be?

We can fix it. But we need time…and trust.

Thank you. Hot tears filled her eyes. She closed them, willing them not to fall. She needed to stay strong. Her stylus was right. They could fix this. She'd fixed so much that surely this was the last big one to handle.

She just needed to get it right. She was no longer

alone with this burden. Surely it would be easier with the Broken One to help. She smiled. Grabbing a washcloth, she scrubbed her hands and face.

And noticed the honor marks. Intricate golden scrolls across her collarbone and down her arm. Surely there were more now than before. So faint as to not be noticed on first glance, but now that she could see them… She rinsed her washcloth and stroked warm water over them. They warmed to the touch. She smiled.

They looked good. Great in fact. Mysterious and yet subtle.

She liked them.

Good. We are glad.

She took an extra few minutes, grabbed a brush and tugged the knots out of her hair. Refreshed, she headed back to the others.

She *was* hungry. A bite first, then she needed to get to work.

She wanted her life back.

"UM, STOREY, I appreciate the food. Honest. But I thought the plan was to turn around and send Tammy back. Immediately." He studied the strip of dark brown hard stuff. Odd. But he was game. He hadn't had anything from her yet that wasn't good. He really hoped to keep the cheese to take back to his dimension. That stuff was addictive.

She looked at him in surprise. Then grabbed a few crackers and stuffed them her mouth. He studied her for a long moment. "You don't want to send her back right away, do you?" A wave of bright pink washed up her face. He settled back. He understood, but they couldn't allow her affection for Tammy get in the way of what they needed to do.

With a telltale sigh, Storey dropped her gaze to Tammy's face and sighed. "She's special."

"Yes, she is." He waited.

Storey glanced over at him sheepishly. "It's just for a little while. How long are we here for? A half hour? An hour maybe. Then we have to go back anyway. I really want to fix my home before anything else goes wrong. And remember what the styluses, or was it Paxton, said? I can't remember who. Anyway, they said increased traffic between dimensions wasn't good because it creates a tunnel of energy that makes it easier for us to cross – but also for those that we don't want to cross."

He remembered that conversation and what she said was true, but she'd just pulled that out of her head as an excuse. In a gentle, but firm tone, he said. "Maybe figure out how to communicate with her using the stylus or telepathy and leave it at that. The visits can't continue. We don't want them coming to our dimensions and you really don't want them over here. That was the whole point of creating their new home. Remember?"

She nodded. "I know. It would be great to stay in touch with her, though."

"Yes. It would." He waited a moment. "But let's not forget her father, the group that kidnapped her or the lessons of my people. The Louers are a warring group. I'm not going to make a blanket statement and say they can't be trusted…but…"

Her knowing smile set him back. "You can't even begin to say anything like that. Paxton is a mainstay in your world. He's a pillar of the community. And he's a Louer."

"He might not know it either," Eric quickly defended his mentor. He wanted to ask him about that little bit of hidden history, but didn't want to do it at a distance. In person Eric would have a better chance of seeing the truth on his mentor's face.

He brooded on the consequences of the council finding out. Would it matter after all this time? Or could the reaction be even worse with the recent battle between the Torans and the Louers?

Was there any way to make peace with them all?

Having been raised with the shadowy specter of the Louers all his life, he hadn't noticed that threat on a conscious level, but on a subconscious level he had. His people were a simple folk. His gaze landed on Tammy. Like she was. She didn't deserve to be part of an ongoing war. Her people needed help to re-establish a new, better life in their new dimension. What was the chance he could help them do that?

Except Tammy's people were perceived as the enemy. Eric *might* want to see things workable between them. But he was pretty sure that other than Tammy, every other Louer would want to see him…dead.

CHAPTER 16

STOREY WATCH THE emotions flit across Eric's face. Normally it was hard to read what was going on inside in his head. But all this talk of Louers gave her a good inkling. Finding out about Paxton's history had to be a shock.

They needed to get moving on fixing her world. His world had been fixed – mostly. The Louers had a new world; they might need help to settle it, but they might also refuse to have anything to do with them. Then there was *her* mess of a world.

She opened her closet door and stared. There had to be dozens of sketchbooks on the shelves inside. She'd never had this many in her life. Not only that, she didn't think that this Storey drew.

"Stylus, why?"

The world is trying to reassert itself – to heal from the time twist. In your case, the Storey who lives here is feeling repressed. And having found a whole new hobby, she's driven to reassert that part of her personality. Your mother and father are also having some personal issues in this world as their personalities try to reassert themselves as well. In real time, they were divorced, so being together now is not easy. They are struggling with their relationship.

Storey took a shaky breath. "I really messed up, didn't I?"

Yes. That is one outlook.

She winced. "Thanks," she murmured. She reached into the closet and pulled out the largest of the sketchbooks. She sat on the floor beside Eric and leaned back against the bed. She flipped to through the pages. "The book is brand new."

"Does that surprise you?" Eric asked around a mouthful of food.

Storey shrugged. "I guess. I never had money for lots of sketchbooks. I'd have one, use it, then buy another one when I needed to."

"You never mention your currency or trade system here." He looked down at the beef jerky in his hand then back at her. "In fact, I know you call it money, but did you buy this food? All the times we've stocked up, did you need to leave some of this money behind?"

She stared at him in disbelief. Then laughed. And laughed. She twisted to see him better. "Now is a hell of a time to ask that question."

He flushed. He mumbled, "Yeah, I know. In my defense, we've been a little busy." Then he took another bite.

She grinned. "As it's my house, my mother's food, then no, I don't feel that we need to leave money to pay for what we've taken. The times where it wasn't my house, it would have been nice to have left money for them. But," she cocked a brow at him. "I didn't and don't have any."

His gaze widened. "Really? Why not?"

How to explain work and money. She had to think about it. She hadn't exactly seen any type of currency in his world either. Or a barter system for that matter. Maybe they didn't have the same system. "Well, I have a little, but not much." Her mother had given her money to go to the mall before this mess all started. And boy, did that seem like months ago. Then there was her almost empty bank account. "Do you have money?"

"Sure. We all do." He nodded. "We each get the same amount every month."

That stopped her. Wasn't that what the communist countries did here? Or some of them. Doctors and waitresses received the same or close to the same amount of money. Odd. And hardly fair. Then she wondered. "So you received the same amount of money as Paxton?

He nodded.

Weird. "And what about your father?"

He frowned. "I assume so."

She wouldn't. "I think you should look into that."

"Why would he have more than any of us?"

"What does the amount do for you?" She asked curiously. "Can you buy special things? Do extra things?"

He shrugged. "Somewhat. But we all have what we need. He does get different food and drink. His clothes cost more. So he probably needs more."

She had to bite her tongue. From her world she knew the extent people would go to for more of what they wanted. Greed was a powerful motivator. Maybe it was different in Eric's world, but she doubted it. Considering what his father already felt fully justified in doing to her, well, giving himself a larger portion of the pie would be nothing.

And then there was his size. He was way fatter than the others of the council that she'd seen. Maybe he had a thyroid problem or other health issue, but those hardly explained the triple chins. He ate more than he needed to and she suspected a richer quality food than the others too.

"You don't have much crime in your world, do you?" They must have some, because they had dungeons, but she'd not been aware of any kind of personal danger from the others there. Funny, she hadn't considered it. The only Toran she'd feared at all was Eric's father.

"No. There have been a few criminals over the years, but not many."

She nodded. Maybe their monetary system worked then. She refocused on the problem at hand. She'd have time to study up on the Torans' way of life later. When her mother was back to normal.

"Stylus, what do I need to do?"

We need you to think about the last time you saw your mother. The way your world was then. It will take some time to bend time back properly and allow that dimension to return to the way it was. You need to make sure you don't stop the process once it starts. This will be our only chance to fix this. Once we start, we must finish.

She looked down at her sketchbook and realized she'd written the message. This time, Eric leaned over and read it himself. "Scary."

"Yeah. So when I start, you have to make sure that nothing interrupts me. Got it?"

"Got it." He took in a deep breath. "Maybe we should take Tammy home first then."

Storey looked outside and realized how late the day was getting to be. "I don't think we have time. My parents could be home soon."

"That isn't good." He hopped off the bed and crouched in front of her. "I'm not going to be able to keep them out of the room if they hear us."

She nodded. "I know." With a deep breath, she added, "But I'm starting to feel a sense of urgency about this." She glanced at Tammy. "I don't want to put her in danger. If you have to, leave me and take her back alone. You can hop back here and get me out."

He shook his head. "Oh no. If it's going to be that bad, then we don't do this right now."

"We have to," she said earnestly. "Look at how

screwed up things are. Your world is almost normal. Tammy's is even better, although they might not think so yet, but my world is a mess. We're here and I can't help but feel the longer it stays like this, the harder it will be to change."

The Broken One spoke, shocking Storey as he once again took over her mouth, "She is correct. This must be fixed before it is too late."

"Damn." Eric glared at her, but she knew it was more at the Broken One than herself. "Fine. I don't like this, but the sooner we get it done the sooner it's over with." He looked around the room. "Maybe you should sit in the closet or something in case someone does come."

She looked at him in shock. "Why not just lock the door. I don't really want to sit in there."

"Because I presume your family could get in if they needed to. In the close—"

"They'd still find me. It's not like the closet opens to your world or anything." She thought about that. "Now that would be an interesting way to have a portal."

"Don't even think about it. Let's do this fast and go home." He glanced at Tammy, now watching them avidly. "Although, I'd rather get Tammy home first."

"Torrey." Tammy held out a piece of cracker.

Storey smiled and took it. She munched it carefully, staring at the little girl that had become so much a part of her life. "Stylus, we won't be going back in time, will we? I won't lose my memories of these people – right?"

There was no answer.

In her mind she could hear a weird humming as if the Broken One was considering the issue.

In horror she stared at Eric. He reached out and grasped her hand. "Don't even begin to think that. I was in your life before you twisted time. I'll be in your life afterwards."

She searched his eyes. On impulse, she reached up, captured his face between her hands and kissed him. Pulling back, she whispered, "Just in case."

He smiled, a tender smile that melted her heart. "In that case…" he leaned forward and kissed her. His kiss wasn't smoking hot like when he'd kissed her In-between, or even heated…but it was unbelievably tender. It brought tears to her eyes.

He brushed her hair with his hand. "Hey, none of this. It's going to be fine."

She sniffled the tears back. "Right. Stylus. Please confirm that my memories will remain intact."

"We have discussed this. We are not expecting to affect any of your memories," said the Broken One. "We cannot be sure what might happen unexpectedly."

She crooked her head. "I guess that's the best we can hope for."

With a final glance at Eric, she settled back. "Then let's get this done."

ERIC SAT BACK on the bed, and reached absently for another of the unusual beef jerky strips. He pulled the last one from the bag and it was snatched from his fingers. His gaze widened as he tracked the piece back to Tammy. She popped it into her mouth and laughed silently.

"I would so love to communicate with you, Tammy," he said. Her smile was so infectious and she chewed with such joy that he chuckled. "Minx."

She offered him the last little piece now all gummed up in her fingers. He barely managed to keep from pulling back in horror. He shook his head and pointed at her. She popped the last bite into her mouth and licked her lips. He grinned. At least she was enjoying it.

He turned back to Storey, head bent, she focused on the paper pad in her lap. Her hand was in the start up phase of her drawing process and she covered the page with large, casual strokes. He knew before long he'd barely be able to discern her hand movements as they would speed up faster than his eyes could follow.

Odd to think Paxton had possessed a stylus for over a century now, and never did any type of artwork. Thinking of Paxton, Eric realized it was a good time to let him know what they were doing. He snorted. That's all he ever seemed to do when Storey was out of commission. Ferry information. At least it made him feel useful.

He sent his mentor a message via codex. And received the answer back that Paxton already knew. The styluses had updated him. And that was a good thing. It saved time and energy to have everyone on the same page – to borrow one of Storey's turns of phrase. But, he couldn't say that he was entirely comfortable with this communication system that kept everyone informed – except him.

At one point he'd suggested to Storey that they hide away in her dimension from those of his world looking to kill him. Now he realized that would be harder than ever to do. The styluses could communicate with each other at will. He doubted that they'd listen to Storey's request and not pass on information about their whereabouts. Especially if they considered they had a better way for events to play out.

In fact, other styluses would volunteer the information before being asked.

That meant secrecy was out. In fact, privacy was also out. How did that affect his relationship with Storey? He hadn't had much quality time with her, and he'd been looking forward to a time when it was just the two of them in a time of peace. Sure his job required him to travel often, but it wasn't the same as in her dimension.

He glanced out the window. In the blue sky he saw the scars in the air made by the flying cars. Planes. He'd studied everything about Storey's world that he could. The archives were surprisingly complete. Storey had been a well of information as well.

Nothing he'd learned would convince him to go inside those metal death traps. The ones on the road were bad enough, but to think of trying to lift them into the air and let them fly like her people did…well. He shook his head. Not for him.

Something growled outside the window. He kneeled on the bed and looked out the window. "Shit," he whispered hoarsely. A vehicle was driving up the driveway to Storey's house. "No, no. Not now." He spun around and searched the room. Maybe Storey could stop – they could get the hell away? No, Storey's hand was moving over the sketchbook so fast he could barely see the flesh of her fingers.

Damn. She was in the zone. With the stylus's warnings fresh in his thoughts, Eric realized they couldn't afford to get caught here. He jumped off the bed and ran over to the door. He flicked the lock closed and turned off the light. What were the chances that the family wouldn't come to her room? That they'd stay downstairs until Storey was done and they were gone? He had no explanation for their presence…or Tammy. He also couldn't allow anything to stop Storey. This whole dimension would be shifting soon. After they did a reset – whatever that meant. But they had to get the hell out of here before the changes took effect or the changes would impact them too. That also couldn't be allowed to happen.

Then he heard people downstairs.

"Please don't come upstairs. Stay down there." He closed his eyes and waited.

And sighed with relief when there were no footsteps

on the stairs. He could only hope Storey's parents would stay downstairs a little longer.

He reset his codex for Paxton's lab. If there was no other option he wanted to make sure that he got Tammy away. He could take her back to her dimension, but if her father was there waiting for him, he might not be able to come and help Storey when she needed it, and that came first.

Paxton would not appreciate seeing Tammy again. Eric closed his eyes as he leaned against the locked door. "Hurry up, Storey. Aren't you almost done by now?"

Storey didn't answer.

Head bent over, she was frozen in place while all her energy appeared to keeping her arm moving at an impossible rate. He closed his eyes, his heart pounded and his blood pulsed. *Storey, faster.*

Footsteps sounded on the stairs.

CHAPTER 17

STOREY WAS AWARE of her surroundings. Aware of palpable waves of urgency coming off of Eric. Aware, but not able to speak with Eric, or her stylus. At least she didn't think she could. Just as the Broken One had taken her over her vocal cords at will, it now controlled her arm like she'd never experienced before. When her stylus drew through her, she was still aware on some level what was happening. In this case, it was like there was a wall between her and the understanding of her actions.

She was grateful she hadn't been put to sleep this time. Yet being awake gave her a whole new level of perspective. The Broken One had taken over so quickly, she'd barely understood it was happening at the time. She could only put it down to the fact that she'd been accustomed to her stylus for so long.

And so long only meant what...a little more than a week? She couldn't believe that was all it had been since she'd met Eric and the stylus had come into her world. In her peripheral vision she saw Eric walk over to the door. He stayed at the corner of her vision. She wished she could ask him what was wrong. But she already knew. He was worried about her. About being caught. About how long it would take.

She wished she had answers. She closed her eyes and tried to relax. Inside, her stomach knotted. If this took much longer it would drive her nuts. And Eric. She peered in the direction of Tammy. And inside she smiled. Tammy had curled up into a ball and appeared to be sleeping.

That was good. A quiet Tammy was heaven. If she was startled awake…so not. She tried to relax further, willing the styluses to finish. She had no idea how they could do what they were doing, but she remembered sitting in the dark in her den for hours while she created the first mess that they were now trying to fix.

Please hurry, she whispered.

We are.

She groaned silently. Then stilled. What was that? Oh no. Footsteps in the hallway. They had company. She caught and held her breath.

Please don't come to my room. Please don't.

Had she remembered to lock the door? If they found the door locked, then what?

Please don't come. She chanted silently in a mantra that wouldn't quit, while her hand blurred with speed.

"Storey, are you home?"

Her eyes flew open. And stared into Eric's wide eyed panic. He mouthed silently, "What do we do?"

She couldn't move her head. Eric tapped his codex. She widened her eyes. She blinked several times. He straightened.

"Storey. Are you in there?"

They froze.

Eric tapped several keys on his codex. She held her breath waiting for the musical notes to fill the air and give their presence away. Only they didn't come.

He stepped over to Tammy and struggled to pick her up. Sleeping, she was a dead weight. He managed to straighten, shifted her in his arms, and pressed the final button to go. She watched as he stood in the middle of the smoke. She hated that he was leaving. That she was being left behind. Tears welled up inside as she watched them disappear in front of her.

He mouthed at her, *I'll be back.*

She managed a tiny nod.

As she watched the smoke disappeared.

Her bedroom door rattled as someone grabbed the door knob.

"Honey, what are you doing?" Her father's voice came from down the hallway.

Surprisingly close, Storey heard her mother say, "I wanted to look and see if she was there."

"You know she's not. She's run away. I don't know what happened, but we have to let the police handle it. Like they said they would."

Her mother's voice made her want to cry out. There was so much pain and loss threading through it. She wanted to tell her mother that it would all be okay. But she couldn't. There was no guarantee that it *would* be okay. She didn't know what would happen after this point. Would there be anything left of them? Would her mother be happy to *not* have her father again? Would she have any lingering emotions from this blip on her screen?

Storey hoped not. But she didn't know and she hated the doubts. The fear. Maybe she wasn't doing the right thing.

Was it possible that she should leave well enough alone?

As SOON AS the black smoke blotted Storey and her frantic drawing from his sight, Eric knew he'd done the wrong thing. Hell. His nerves bit at him.

He shouldn't have left her alone.

She was defenseless in this state. It didn't matter that

she was at home. Her parents didn't know her. Not like he did. In fact, these parents didn't know anything about her. They were from another reality.

He shifted his feet wishing the black smoke to disappear. If anything happened to her before he could get back…

"Hurry up. Hurry up."

He glanced down at Tammy, who slept in a deep, relaxed manner. Thankfully. She might not be so impressed with waking up without Storey. If she opened her mouth…Eric shuddered. Tammy's secret weapon was that cry of hers. And he did not want to hear it again.

At least at home, Paxton's stylus should be able to communicate with Tammy. Enough to keep her calm so he could get away. He wanted to return for Storey. Of course that wasn't likely to go so well with Paxton. Neither was it fair on Tammy. She was a sweetheart. She should be home, safe with her family.

The mist dropped low enough Eric could see the familiar white walls of Paxton's lab. Thank you! He strode out of the portal and over to the empty table. Barely holding back a groan, he carefully placed Tammy down. His back screamed as he straightened. Tammy might be young, but she, like the rest of her people, was stocky.

"Eric," Paxton called from the far side of the room. "Is that you? Is it all done?" He rushed over then came to a screeching halt. "Oh no. No. No. No. That's not good."

"No it isn't." Eric gently stroked Tammy's hair. "But I had no options. I have to leave her with you." Not giving Paxton a chance to argue, Eric ran back to the portal crying out, "I have to help Storey."

"No!" Paxton ran toward him, his voice squawking loudly. "Don't leave her here."

"I have to." The black mist rose as the reassuring musical notes floated out. "I have to rescue Storey. I'll get back as soon as I can."

And the black mist rose up to block out everything.

CHAPTER 18

"HONEY, YOU HAVE to stop haunting her room. It's not normal. You have to let it go."

"I can't let it go. I can't let *her* go. She's my daughter. She's my life."

Storey listened to the voices yelling outside her door, then a bang as something hit the other side of her bedroom door. Her mother started weeping. Not a gentle crying, but heart wrenching sobs. Storey would have bawled herself if she could. Instead she was frozen in her own body as her hand whistled across the page.

She hated the pain she'd caused her mother. In either world. How had things gone so wrong? In trying to make things right, she'd ended up making things so much worse.

"Now, come on. Let's go downstairs and get you a cup of tea. That will make you feel better."

The crying jag became muffled. Storey could only hope her father was holding her mother. Comforting her as Storey couldn't. Their voices were barely audible as their footsteps receded down the hallway. Her mother's sobs slowed the further away she went. Much to Storey's relief.

It is well, the Broken One said.

If you say so, Storey muttered restlessly. *Are you almost done?*

Yes.

She shuddered in relief. *Then what?*

We exit this dimension.

Good. Then let's go to the closest or fastest point. She thought about it for a moment. *On second thought, let's go wherever we cause the least amount of damage.*

Paxton's lab.

She closed her eyes. She couldn't remember what they'd said before. *Wasn't it supposed to be the Louers' dimension?*

Tammy is with Paxton.

Right. Tammy needed to go home. To avoid too many cross traffic scenarios, better to go to the Torans' dimension, then back over to the Louers' dimension. Of course Paxton wouldn't think much of that either. He wouldn't want them to go directly to the Louers' as that would make it easier for the Louers to travel to his dimension.

Arrrg. This was getting so confusing. Why couldn't it be easy?

She'd made life complicated by crossing over to the Louers' dimension. And meeting Eric. But that was a good thing. Not a complication. Keeping a relationship going – now that was a complication. How were they going to do that? She wasn't ready to leave her dimension and doubted Paxton would be willing to have her permanently anyway.

She stilled. Something had changed. What? She opened her gaze and studied her bedroom.

Her hand had stopped moving.

She stretched out her arm and gave it a good shake. It throbbed like crazy. Not injured, but bruised and aching as if she'd hung onto a tree branch or something for a long time before dropping to the ground. The elbow joint was especially bad.

Moving stiffly, she struggled to her feet and caught a

glimpse of the top of her bed. Food wrappers and empty boxes, cracker crumbs and napkins littered the crumpled bedding. All she did was clean up behind those two. She smiled. They felt like a family already.

A whisper of sound behind her had her spinning around. She held her hand to her head as the room twisted crazily. Why was she starting to feel faint? Weak.

Black mist filled the room. Eric.

She smiled brightly. "Yes! Perfect timing. We're done."

Eric stared at her through the blackness. But he never said a word. It was as if he couldn't see her.

She waved her arms back and forth in front of him. "Eric? What's wrong? You're scaring me."

The black mist slowed worked its way down his body. He opened his mouth and closed it again. His gaze spanned the room before zooming back to her. "Storey?" he asked hesitantly.

"Uh oh. Do I look different? Sound different? What is it?" She turned to look around her room. It looked as it had before he'd left. A mess. Normal. She, on the other hand, felt sick. Like really sick. Not the upchuck type of sick, but a woozy pass-out-kind-of-sick.

She took a step and wavered. She started to panic. *Stylus. What's wrong here?*

Silence.

Stylus. Talk. To meeeeee. She collapsed to the floor.

But she did hear Eric's voice, calling, "Storeeeey?"

"OH NO. STOREY, where are you?" Eric called out, desperation and panic filling him. He couldn't move yet for the mist, but he couldn't see her anywhere. The door was closed, but he couldn't tell if it was still locked from the inside. She should be there.

As he looked around he caught sight of something faint, like a misty outline of something, but it wasn't clear enough to identify.

"Paxton. Is Storey still in the same location?" His fingers tapped the codex frantically, fumbling to get it right as he stayed…stuck in the portal. And then he realized that's what he was. Stuck. Had he come back during the reset? Whatever that meant. Was *he* now caught between time?

Clearly something odd had happened. He hadn't even questioned the repercussions of his return jump on Storey. He'd acted out of instinct. Fear. The need to save her. He'd presumed she'd still be there.

And she was…or some part of her was.

Or was he going crazy? He was locked into his portal. Outside the black smoke, the room looked the same. And to make matters worse, he could hear someone racing up the stairs in the main house. He couldn't move. And if that wispy image was Storey, it seemed neither could she.

Paxton, he tapped. *We need help and now!*

There was no answer.

"Damn it! I heard someone in there. I heard someone calling." A woman's voice cried out in pain.

That was Storey's mother. She sounded….devastated. Like her only child had died. Which, as he looked around the room yet again, his stomach muscles contracting, Storey might have. It was one thing to end up banished in the Louers' dimension and another to be dumped into In-between, but if that ghost-like essence was Storey — something was even more wrong than before.

And all he wanted was for things to finally go right.

Was nothing ever as it seemed to be? Even his world appeared to be fake. A deceptive face on reality. Paxton a Louer, their supposed enemy. The styluses, alive and also

Louers, had proven to be staunch friends and allies.

His father, a betrayer, instead of his beloved leader.

Storey wasn't even what he'd always believed. In fact, he'd been raised to be afraid of the Humans. They were destroyers, he'd been told. War mongers. Instead, she was the most caring, loving, of all the species he'd met yet. And that didn't say much about his own people.

His own father had attempted to kill her – several times in fact. So who were the war mongers?

In contrast Tammy hadn't been afraid of Storey or Eric. Yet she'd been raised in harsh conditions brought about by Eric's own people. Had she been raised to hate his people? Not according to her behavior. Maybe the adults in her world hated his people, but from what he'd seen so far, the adults were fighting between themselves to try and improve their lot in life. Having seen their home world, Eric was willing to cheer them on.

Maybe Storey was right. Could they help the Louers to have a better life? Give them the tools to build what they'd need in their own world? Would that bring peace to the three worlds? Not that Storey had mentioned bringing her world into an alliance or anything. She didn't appear to be naive about her own society. She'd even mentioned that peace wasn't likely. But that didn't mean he couldn't help fix the problems between the Louers and the Torans.

The Torans had banished the Louers after all. Maybe they could rectify that by giving them assistance right now.

Or maybe he should leave well enough alone.

And then he heard the man outside the door say, "Look, we can check. It's not that big a deal."

The door opened.

Eric stood frozen in place.

CHAPTER 19

STOREY STRUGGLED TO her feet and stared at Eric, finally realizing he couldn't see her. What was going on?

She was supposed to leave and come back so that the changes could take place. Sure, she'd delayed her departure, but just long enough to clean up. It's not like her stylus had said go now. Hell, she didn't even have a portal ready. In fact, she'd half assumed she'd have a portal made for her and she wouldn't even know it. She'd been doing so much that was out of her control. Why not that? But this…this being here, but not being seen…was horrible. And frightening.

What was going on?

She felt normal. At least as normal as she could after having just collapsed to the floor. She had no idea what that had been about either.

She stared at her fingers.

Talk about scary. Her hands appeared normal-shaped, but they were faint, thin. As if she had been half erased or something. As if she were only half here. Her stomach bottomed out. If there was a bottom. She wore the same clothes, but she could see through them. She had shoes on. But she saw the floor underneath them. She'd become transparent.

She spun to look at Eric. Could he see the bit of her that was left?

God, she hoped so.

"Eric?"

He spun around and she gasped. His features seemed almost blurry around the edges.

"Oh thank God. You can hear me?" she asked.

"Storey? Where are you?"

"Eric, I'm right in front of you." She stepped forward again into his line of sight. "Eric, can you hear me?"

His face crinkled up and he tilted his head toward her. As if hearing something. But not her apparently. She heard the same noises he did. To her, the sounds were faint, like coming down a long tunnel. Maybe that's how he heard her, too.

Stylus? What's happening?

Silence.

That worried her more than anything else so far. She needed to connect with the stylus. It had the means to save her.

Wait. The Broken One should be with her. She should be able to communicate with him. And if she couldn't, then she didn't understand anything because he was inside her. One with her and she could talk to herself.

She heard a sound. She spun around and watched her bedroom door crack open slightly. And then it started to fade too.

She shouldn't be here. She knew that deep inside. While whatever was happening was probably good for her world, it was not good for her. She needed to get out of this place. And so did Eric.

How?

"Broken One," she whispered. "Where are you?"

A stuttering whisper slipped through her mind, her thoughts.

Fading, he said. *Quickly.*

"Why? What's happening?" Storey needed answers.

And fast. That was the only way she'd get out of this.

The dimensional change happened more quickly than anticipated. This dimension was already trying to revert back to its natural state, but there were just enough changes that it couldn't. Now that we have unlocked the restraints the dimension is spontaneously swinging back to the way it should be.

"Am I here?"

You are caught in the dimensional shift.

There was a neutral pause, then he said, *As am I.*

"Will we die? Or is there a way to port out of here and save us?"

A weird hum filled the air. Instead of scaring her, it reassured her that the stylus was there, thinking. But she wanted her stylus. She'd connected to it in a different way. She needed it.

"Stylus are you there?" She waited for a long moment, feeling tears welling up at the weird sense of loss. "Stylus," she whispered plaintively. "I need you."

A rumble slipped down her spine. But inside. She shook her head at the weirdness of it all. "Can you help me, stylus?"

Stay calm, the Broken One said. *We will ride through the shift.*

"And where will we come out at the other end?" She spun around, hating the sense of panic happening inside her. The room faded in and out. Falling and then stabilizing as if the earth itself was attempting to reassert some control. Every movement she took sent her off balance. She careened from side to side trying to remain steady in an unsteady world.

At the same time, she felt like the world was tilting. She tried to lean into the curve, sure she'd fall over. Eric stood still in front of her. Frozen. He hadn't moved, but the floor where he stood shifted – with him. His eyes had locked on the door handle and that was it. She hadn't seen him even blink.

She ran a hand through her hair. Oh man, this was beyond nuts. And scary. She hadn't been this scared since she'd dropped into Eric's dimension so long ago.

The floor, the planet, gave a hard shake.

Earthquake?

No. The dimension reasserting itself. God, what had she done?

Her head started to swim. She shook it to clear her mind, and heard the Broken One in the background.

Let go. Let yourself fall. It will be alright.

She didn't know if she could trust him. She wanted to hear her stylus tell her that.

And there, so faint it was only an impression, a whisper slipped into her mind.

All is well. Reset is happening. Go.

She took a deep breath, recognizing her stylus. And stopped resisting.

For the second time she fell, only this time, the floor, as it trembled and shook, gave one last hard ripple and rose up to meet *her*.

WHAT WAS HAPPENING? To his amazement, the view in front of him shifted and wavered like a ripple from underground. As if someone had picked up a corner of the floor like a rug and gave it a hard shake. Even the bed rippled up and down. The few items on the table flipped up into the air, only to land exactly as the item had sat before the flip.

It couldn't be an accident the way everything came back down in precisely the same way. Was this what happened when something moved *through* the shift?

Like he presumed he had when he'd arrived at the start. If Storey had still been there at the time, he figured she'd be like the bed, and land exactly where she'd been at the start of the shift. But the styluses had said she was supposed to leave the dimension and then return.

Had she done that? Had her trip gone wrong – like so many other trips? Was the whispery version of her that stood in front of him residual energy? He closed his eyes on that thought. Please not.

He tried to move again, but his feet were cemented to the floor. He could lean and twist but he couldn't take a step. As everything else rippled around him, he appeared to be caught and held in the eye of the storm. The portal mist swirled in place around his feet. Protecting him? Or unable to complete the port because the conditions were too unstable?

Either was probably in his favor.

Then what about Storey?

Another hard ripple zapped the world. He closed his eyes and rode the wave.

How long could this last?

This ripple wasn't slowing. Fear clutched his heart. Why wasn't it stopping? The mist around his feet snugged up close. Then the tendrils wrapped around his legs as if clutching him tight. He could only think he was being held down.

Pressure built around him, his head started to pound, his chest squeezed tight. He gasped for air. His vision blurred. He tried to focus, but every movement was like plowing through molasses.

Something was wrong. Storey? Paxton? Someone?

He couldn't breathe. His chest clamped and locked with his next breath. Black spots appeared before his eyes and his ears pounded. He felt himself falling, but the portal mist had climbed higher up his legs, as if trying to escape this hell as well.

He couldn't hold on any longer. Pain took out his senses, weakened his resolve. He needed help.

Now.

Then another mighty shove sent the world slamming up against him. A gasp escaped, taking the last of his air with it.

Storey, I'm so sorry.

And he lost consciousness.

Chapter 20

STOREY WOKE TO a hell of a headache. She could barely open her eyes. And wasn't sure she wanted to make the effort. What happened? Then she remembered. Her and her brilliant idea to fix the chaos she'd created messing around with things she shouldn't.

That she'd done it all with the best of intentions didn't matter. Now she had to deal with the results of this latest mess. Had her world reset? Was it back to normal? Or was she not that lucky?

She hadn't been lucky yet.

Even as she thought that, she chastised herself for ignoring all the good things that she'd done. And the people she'd met through her actions. She had to believe it was all for the best and things would work out.

Still, the teen who'd been so despondent over the loss of her boyfriend seemed a long ways away. She'd grown and then some.

Would anyone else notice? School seemed so juvenile. And so…necessary. And didn't that beat all. She'd not had any purpose to going before, except that it gave her a reason to get up and do…something. She hadn't been lost, but neither had she been found. If that made any sense. Not that anything did these days.

She'd been gone from school for so long. Everyone thought she'd been sick to begin with. So now they'd think she'd been *really* sick. She giggled at her earth humor. Not that her black wit was helping her adjust to the current mess.

Her body ached like she'd struggled through a thorny thicket barely ahead of a bear. Her skin had taken on a scraped, raw feeling – from the inside out. She tried to take stock. With her eyes closed, she wiggled fingers, then toes. She rotated her ankles and shifted her legs. Rolling onto her back she stared up at the blue sky. Then closed her eyes again.

And had to wonder. Who's blue sky was it?

Where had she landed? She'd been inside her bedroom before the shift. And if she could move her body, did she have a real body or only that weird, ghostly, half-there-half-dead-and-gone version? To find out would mean opening her eyes again. And that hurt. Like the rest of her. Her neck was stiff. Her throat felt swollen, too large for her mouth.

Kind of a horrible feeling, actually.

She groaned. And at least heard that. So she had a voice, and her ears worked. But that didn't erase the feeling of having survived a bomb blast.

Then she remembered just what that bomb had been.

Her home. Eric. Her mother.

She sat upright, and gasped. Clutching her head, she had to wait for the world around her to stop spinning.

It slowed enough that she could straighten a little more. She dropped her hands and looked around. She was out in the country on a beautiful day. The sun was high, there wasn't a cloud in the sky.

Did that mean she was in Eric's dimension?

Only there was no sign of Eric. Damn. No sign of Tammy, or her home. Moving slowly she stood up and smiled happily. The world no longer rotated. Even her headache was dissipating.

Still, as she looked around she realized there were no

paths in the meadow, no roads, no signs showing which direction she should travel. Neither did she recognize any landmarks.

Hell.

She suddenly remembered her stylus and slapped her hand to her chest where it hung around her neck. It was there. Thankfully. Then she frowned. Even that was different. The connection was different. Disconnected, yet whole for the first time, so maybe the better term was reconnected. Stronger. Some of the rawness had eased and like putting on a new set of clothes, she wiggled to settle in better.

And what was with the Broken One? Was he still with her?

Yes.

She grinned. "Hey you survived. That's great. What about you, stylus, are you in there?"

Fainter, weaker than the Broken One, the answer was audible. *Yes.*

She did a happy jig. "Good. We all made it. That's excellent."

She spun around, feeling stronger and more alive than she'd expected to feel. After what she'd been through…she could have died. But she hadn't. She was here, alive and well and still had both styluses safe and sound.

Life was good.

"So, where are we?"

A noise sounded behind her. She turned slowly to see several Louer warriors coming toward her, each holding long poles like the two warrior women she'd seen on her first visit to their dimension. The air whooshed out of her. *Damn.* She switched to speaking mentally. *Stylus, Broken One. I need a little help here. You need to tell these Louers that I'm not here to hurt anyone.*

We did.

And?

No answer.

Come on guys, they're getting closer. I could use a way out.

They know you have Tammy. They are not happy.

Storey eyed the look on the approaching Louers' faces. Stone-faced as usual. How could anyone tell if those people were happy or mad? Well the damn poles pointing at her gave her some indication.

Did you explain that Tammy leaving with us was a mistake? That I'll happily go and get her?

They don't believe you.

Just then a high pitch sound screamed through her head. She knew what was coming. *Tell Paxton. Eric. Get help.*

And the world around her went black.

She pitched forward to the ground. Out cold. Again.

"Eric?"

His shoulder was shaken, then again harder. "Eric, wake up.

The next shake hurt. He groaned in protest. "Stop. I'm here. I'm here."

"Then sit up. I need to make sure you aren't injured."

"I'm fine." But he rolled onto his back and stared at the white ceiling tiles of Paxton's lab. And then his gaze landed on Paxton. His mentor's face flushed, then grew pale, then flushed again as waves of emotion rolled across his face. His hair, normally slicked back, was standing on end, giving him a frazzled appearance. An appearance that had become much more common these days. He let his eyes close again.

"You don't look fine," Paxton snapped. "You've been unconscious for a long time."

Eric snapped his eyes open. "How long?" He struggled to sit up. "Where's Storey?"

"I don't know. To both questions. I wasn't here when you arrived so I don't know how long you were out. And you arrived alone. I was going to ask *you* about Storey."

Eric tried to remember what had happened. There had been that weird, world-tilting scenario in Storey's room. That had been crazy. But Storey had been there. Or part of her had been. He just didn't know what part, where the rest had been, or where any of her was now.

"Can you talk to your stylus? Contact hers?"

Paxton scurried for his stylus and tablet on his workbench. Eric struggled to his feet. He was so glad to be home. But not if Storey wasn't there with him. Damn that girl. He needed her to stay out of trouble for once.

"Where's Tammy?" He looked around. Where was the little girl? Had Paxton taken her home? "Paxton, what happened to Tammy?"

Paxton spun around, horror on his face. "She should be here. She has to be."

Eric groaned. "Didn't you feed her? Talk to her? Get the stylus to talk to her?"

Paxton's eyes grew round. He became even more flustered. "I never thought to. I couldn't talk to her. She was sleeping. I just left her to sleep. In truth I'd hoped she wouldn't wake up until you returned. I didn't know what else to do with her."

"She's a child Paxton, you can't just forget about her. She's also a Louer. Do you have any idea what kind of trouble she can get into out there?" Eric was almost shouting as he stumbled forward, fear helping to power up his strength as he ran through the lab and conference room, searching under and over all the furniture. "Tammy?"

"Tammy, where are you?" He spun around to the helpless Paxton who stood in the middle of the room wringing his hands. "Ask your stylus where she is."

Paxton's face brightened and he raced back to his stylus.

Eric groaned softly. He had to remember that using the stylus wasn't intuitive for Paxton. For Storey, using her stylus had become instinctive.

"It says she's here," Paxton announced.

"Where?" Eric chomped down on his impatience. "Where is here?"

"In this room apparently." Paxton spun around, staring at the empty lab. "But she's not. Is she?"

"No. She's not."

And that wasn't good.

"What's going on, Paxton?" His voice took on a demanding tone. He hadn't intended that, but worry eclipsed everything, including manners at the moment.

"I don't know," Paxton muttered, shaking his head. "I am trying to find out."

Eric reined in his impatience. Pushing Paxton wasn't going to help. To make sure, he strode across the room and checked the main door to the lab. Locked. Even Tammy couldn't have undone this door. She had to be still here. He glanced at the portal. "Could she have activated the portal in any way?"

"No no. She couldn't." Paxton's terrified gaze zipped from the portal to Eric and back to the portal. He shuddered and bent his head over his stylus and muttered, "Not possible."

"Well something happened to her."

Eric couldn't stand doing nothing so he searched the entire room again. "Where had she been sleeping?"

Paxton waved off in the direction of the far corner. "I

moved her over there."

There was a blanket on the floor.

Eric strode closer then came to a shuddering stop.

The blanket moved – slightly. But it lay on the ground flat. He crouched down to view the surface of the blanket from a different angle. Oh no. He bowed his head. "Paxton," he whispered, "We've got a problem."

"Yes. Yes, I know," Paxton snapped. "I'm trying to get answers."

But Eric already had one answer. He could see the vague outline of some energy. He could only presume it to be Tammy. Probably caught in the same dimensional shift as Storey, Tammy was almost invisible.

So where was the rest of her?

And if that had happened to Storey, where was she?

CHAPTER 21

STOREY WOKE TO the king of all headaches. Why? Then she remembered the Louers and their damn telepathic weapon. Man, if her people could figure out how to do that...

Part of her was getting royally pissed off over getting knocked out so often. With effort, she managed to assess her latest location. She was alone and there appeared to be nothing around her. Dirt walls and, she patted the flooring, dirt floors. And a squared off ceiling. How much had the Louers managed to build in the short time they'd been here? Probably not much.

She stood and walked the room. It reminded her of the room she'd been banished to in their old dimension by Eric's father – just much smaller. With that in mind she said, "Lights on." No lights. "Door open." No grating sound to say that a door had opened. So maybe they hadn't gotten that far yet in their building. "Stylus? Some suggestions for getting out of here would be good."

She turned around and jumped back, her hand slamming to her chest. Two female Louer guards stood in front of her. Damn. They motioned her to the side. She smiled amiably and followed their instructions.

"Ah Stylus. Could you please tell them I mean no harm?"

They don't believe you.

"Is this about Tammy again? If they let me leave I

promise I'll bring her back."

Yes. They believe you are responsible.

"I returned her last time," she protested. "I've never cheated them. Lied to them. Why won't they believe me?"

This isn't the group that loves Tammy. This is the group that captured Tammy and held her hostage. They have reconciled with Tammy's father, but now this has happened and they believe you are responsible. They have Tammy's body. But she is unconscious and they are being blamed. They need you to fix this.

What? Tammy's body? Only her body? Damn. When was she ever going to catch a break? "Did we do this to Tammy?"

Yes. She should have been in her dimension when the shift happened. Everyone needed to be in their own dimension. Or connected to their dimension in some way. Like Eric.

"But I was in my dimension. It didn't help me," she grumbled.

You are the only one that needed to leave your dimension.

Ah shit. Just to clarify, she asked, *So Eric is all right, but he took Tammy to Paxton instead of home, so she wasn't in the right place when this happened?*

Correct.

Storey remembered how odd Eric had looked. So faint, yet so distinct because of that weird shift. She stopped walking. He'd been caught inside the portal. "Is Eric okay?"

Yes. He was locked in the portal. He saw and felt the shift, but was safe inside the tunnel.

She released her pent up breath. "Thank heavens for that."

A pole poked her in the back – hard. She jumped back. With a hand up to say okay silently, she moved in the direction indicated, finding a doorway opening in front of her.

Going back to telepathic communication she asked the stylus to tell Paxton what had happened.

We already have. They have Tammy.

Wait. She came to a dead stop and whispered mentally, *You said Tammy was here. And unconscious.*

Yes.

How can she be unconscious here, but be with Eric and Paxton in the Toran dimension?

She was caught in the dimensional shift. Because she should have been home, part of her went there, but as she was actually in another place, part of her stayed there.

Storey stumbled. *You're saying she's been split into two!*

Her soul, her spirit, is in the Torans' dimension. Her body is here.

How are we supposed to fix that? And fast? Poor Tammy. Storey hated to hear she'd been hurt. And in such a way. Eric was right. She should have turned right around and returned her to her home after the little Louer had snuck into the transfer with them. Her father had to be going nuts right now.

Hence the guards. Damn.

Stylus, do you know how to fix this?

We need to bring Tammy to her body.

Right. That sounds so easy.

And so obviously wasn't. She was nudged from behind again. She closed her eyes briefly then forged ahead. Where were they directing her? *Stylus, talk to them. Explain to them what we need to do.*

We spoke to Tammy's father. He thinks Tammy was deliberately hurt by this group. He insists they fix this or be banished to their old world.

Could this get any worse?

Yes.

I was being sarcastic, she muttered. Then she noticed where she'd been led. In front of Tammy's father. *Uhm, Stylus? I need help. Now. Can you port us out of here? Can Eric come rescue me? Someone?*

A busy hum wafted around her, filling the air. She understood that meant conversations were going on around her. Discussing her, but not including her.

"Stop it," she said crossly out loud. "Stylus. Can't I be included here?"

She glared at the circle of stern faced Louers. Damned if she was going to take the blame for this mess, too. It hadn't been her fault that Tammy had jumped her mid shift. Sure, she should have taken her right back, but she hadn't known that this would happen. Hell, how would anyone? Up until now she hadn't known such a thing as a dimensional shift and a soul split was even possible.

They think I am you.

What! She had to stop and get her mind wrapped around that tidbit. *Because you are the one speaking?*

Yes.

Well, tell them the truth.

I tried. They don't understand.

She dropped her head into her hands. Now what did she do?

They want you to fix Tammy.

She straightened with a small gasp. *That's what I want too, but can we?*

Yes.

Her shoulders sagged with relief. *Thank you. Now…what do I need to do?*

I've contacted Paxton. Eric needs to bring Tammy home. We can't move her body to her spirit so her spirit needs to come here.

Storey struggled with that. *Does he see her? Know where she is?*

Somewhat.

That did not sound good. *Does he understand what he needs to do?*

Yes, we have relayed the message to Paxton.

Nice. And what about Tammy, does she understand?

No.

And an uncooperative Tammy, even if in spirit only, was a bad thing.

ERIC STRAIGHTENED AS he realized how serious an issue this had all of a sudden become. And how unbelievable. "Paxton, she's here, but without her body."

"That's nonsense." Paxton rushed over, his face reddening with irritation. "You've been spending too much time around Storey. Now that girl has an imagination."

"Ask your stylus. I'm right. I know I am. I saw something similar in the dimensional shift. Storey looked something like this, although a little more substantial." He twisted his head to see Tammy from another angle and she did appear slightly more solid. He shook his head. The things he'd seen and experienced lately were crazy.

"Um?"

When more wasn't forthcoming, Eric straightened and turned to look at Paxton. "What?"

Paxton held his stylus and tablet up in front of him. "We've got a problem."

Eric's eyebrows shot straight up. "Really. I hadn't noticed."

Paxton beetled his bushy brows at him. He tapped his stylus against the hard surface in an irritating series of click. "There's more. Storey is now a captive in the Louers' dimension. Apparently Tammy's body is there and is unconscious, and they are blaming Storey."

Oh great. He closed his eyes briefly. Damn the girl could get into trouble. "Don't suppose there is any good news?"

Paxton gasped and stepped closer. "My stylus says Tammy is separated from her body." He glared at Eric as if he had known this all along and was just springing it on him now. "How can this be? Surely, it's not possible?"

Eric shrugged. "I wouldn't have thought so, but…" He motioned to the blanket where Tammy lay, "Look for yourself. The blanket moves with her as she shifts." He stepped back a bit for Paxton to get closer. "The biggest issue is what are we going to do when Tammy wakes up?"

Paxton jumped back several feet at that threat. He glanced wildly from the blanket to Eric and back again as if Tammy were going to explode. "Take her away. Get her back to where she belongs." He waved his hands at Eric, "Now. Before she wakes up."

Eric stared at him in shock. "And how do you expect me to do that."

Paxton shook his head, sending his hair flying in all directions. "I don't care. But this is big trouble. She needs to go home. Now. We can't have them trying to come here after her. You have to fix this."

Eric studied Paxton. He was right. They needed to fix this, but how? He couldn't just pick up a wispy cloud and carry it to the next dimension. Could he?

"You have to fix this." Paxton was almost shrieking at him. His eyes were panicked, his face turned red and puffy. Eric was starting to get more worried about his health than about him waking up Tammy.

Then he changed his mind.

A wail filled the room and damn near killed him. Eric slapped his hands over his ears against the horrible noise. It wasn't the same as before. It was…worse. It had a disembodied sound, almost an echo that made it amplify in layers. He'd barely heard Storey earlier in her room. Tammy appeared to be able to communicate much better. Or much worse. He shuddered as the waves of sounds scraped down his spine.

"Make her stop!" Paxton ran to the far side of the room.

"Paxton? Get the stylus to talk to her," he shouted over the noise. "Fast!"

Paxton's eyes widened. He started writing with the stylus.

Within seconds, the noise stopped.

Eric glanced back down to where Tammy had been lying.

She was gone.

CHAPTER 22

STOREY WAS LED back out of the room. Tammy's father never said a word or motioned to her in any way. The styluses had been doing the communicating. But something had changed. The same two guards were taking her somewhere – but where? *Stylus, what's going on?*

You have been given an ultimatum.

What does that mean?

You have one night's passing to return his daughter to the way she was.

The way she was? Oh great. I sure hope you know how to put a spirit and body back together again.

Great. Not. First things first, she had to get out of here, then travel to the Torans' and find Tammy's spirit to bring it back here.

Got any ideas, Stylus?

You are being taken to Tammy's room now. You will be under guard the whole time.

As she tried to assimilate what the Stylus was saying, Storey was poked – hard – in the back. She spun around. "Hey, be nice." She glared at the woman staring back at her. To Storey's artistic eye, the hard angles of the woman's wide face appeared frozen in clay for the lack of emotion in it. How could they not show anything? She didn't get it.

Storey chained her anger up tighter, knowing she needed to stay calm to get out of this place and help

Tammy. That was the concern right now. Not Storey or Tammy's heavy handed father, but Tammy herself. Somehow she needed to be made whole again.

The trip this time was through a maze of caves and tunnels. She didn't know how these people had managed to dig so much so fast. They must have some advantage that the Toran and her own people didn't know about. If they were in the same cave system that she'd seen on her previous trip, it would have given them a start, but nothing like this. The hallways seemed to go on for miles. And maybe they did.

She was led into another room. And came to a complete stop.

Tammy lay on a raised surface surrounded by several Louers. She didn't know if they were a medical team, family, or more security. Nothing in their demeanor or dress gave her any clues to their association. Why couldn't these people make it easy?

Then, they were a simple folk and probably didn't have all the trappings of her own world. Tammy would be undergoing all kinds of tests back home by now if they were in Storey's dimension. She approached cautiously, afraid she'd be stopped before reaching Tammy's side.

No one moved.

She took a deep breath, then reached out to clasp Tammy's chunky hand. She was so cold. Her hand, normally hot and active, always tugging Storey in one direction or another, or squeezing tight, lay dead in Storey's palm. So not good.

Storey leaned forward to study Tammy's face. The skin hung slack, her mouth slightly open. Air whistled gently with every breath. Definitely alive, but empty. Like no one was home.

Except Tammy's hair moved. Storey's eyes widened as she understood. Skorky lay curled into Tammy's shoulder and nestled protectively into her hair. His beady eyes watched Storey's every move.

She straightened, fighting back the urge to cry. Her hot tears refused to listen, welling up in the corners of her eyes. She stared at the wall straight ahead until she could regain control.

Stylus. What are we going to do?

Wait.

She almost snorted, barely catching back the sound at the last moment. The last thing she wanted to do was give anything away to those watching her so intently. *Wait for what?* Eric wasn't going to be able to sneak in and help her out. He'd end up captive as well. And that was not the answer.

She had to get away.

No. The dimension is still settling. Any more travelling right now could be harmful. You could end up anywhere.

Damn. I thought that problem was done.

Those were big changes. It takes a little time.

I don't have time, she bit off. *Tammy needs me.*

So does Eric. He's lost Tammy.

ERIC WALKED THE room slowly. "Tammy?" He twisted around slightly so he could see Paxton. "What does the stylus say?"

"It says she's trying to go home. She's scared." Paxton's voice rose. "And so am I."

Eric ignored the last part. "Of course, she is. When she went to sleep she was at Storey's house. She doesn't know how she got here. And if she looks weird to us, we probably look weird to her." He paused, searching the room for Tammy's misty outline. "Have you contacted Storey?"

"There is only so much I can do," Paxton snapped. "I'm trying."

"Have the stylus do it." Eric wanted to shake the older man. His way of doing things was slowing the process. The styluses could do dozens of things at one time. "Remember, they can get other styluses to help."

Paxton's gaze lit with understanding and he started scribbling furiously.

"First, someone needs to talk to Tammy. Tell her Storey is with her father and that's where we want to take her."

Eric bowed his head, struggling for calm as he waited for Paxton. He thrust his hands into his pockets. He still wanted to clench them, but it was harder to in the small space.

Then he felt it.

A slight warmth against his bare arm.

"Tammy?"

The heat of his arm deepened.

"Paxton," Eric said, "I think she is standing here beside me."

Paxton looked up over at him, looked at the space beside Eric, shuddered and returned to his tablet.

Eric wasn't sure what that meant, but figured the older man had enough trouble dealing with the current scenario without Eric questioning him on it. "Tammy, it's going to be okay."

He stared down and caught the faint shape of the little girl. She was looking up at him. Like she had so many times before. His heart wrenched. He couldn't see the expression on her face, but she had to be freaking out. "Storey is with your Father. We're trying to get you home too."

Did she understand anything? He hoped Paxton would hurry up. Surely the styluses had spoken to Tammy by now. He wished he could talk to her.

Paxton spun around. "Storey's stylus and the Broken One say you are to go to the Louers' dimension and take Tammy with you."

Eric just stared. "Really? I'm supposed to just take this energy mass to the Louers' dimension? Tammy in a form they can't see and therefore won't recognize that I'm there to deliver?"

Even Paxton looked unsure on that point. Eric sighed and turned to look down at Tammy. The heat in his arm warmed yet again, as if she understood the problem. He felt like he needed to say something to her, but up until now he had to admit it had always been Storey who'd been the one to reassure Tammy.

"It will be fine, Tammy. We've been in worse scenarios before."

He couldn't think of another one quite like this though. And hoped he never would again, but after what had happened with Dillon, he realized how much he still had to learn and experience. He was just a youngster when compared to Paxton. Yet he'd experienced so much in this short time.

And that was, to quote Storey once again, 'way cool.'

He laughed. He loved Storey's attitude. She took on life like it was the greatest of adventures. Facing her troubles instead of running away. She never backed down from a fight, either. If she were in trouble right now, she'd be looking for a way out. And waiting for him to come help her out.

So he needed to find a way to do just that.

CHAPTER 23

STOREY BENT HER head, and tried to get the stylus to help her communicate. She whispered to Tammy, "I'm so sorry, Tammy. We never meant for this to happen. We're working on a solution. Hopefully it won't be much longer."

As she finished, she realized the others were listening. None of the guards stopped her though. They'd surrounded her, but had so far stayed back and allowed her to do her thing.

Now if only she understood what her thing was. Skorky lay curled on Tammy's shoulder. Its eyes locked on Storey as if it knew she was here to help. Too bad she didn't know how.

She could write on Tammy's arm, but she couldn't create a portal on her. Not without destroying her body. She had paper in one of Eric's bags – at least she thought she did, but it's not like she'd be allowed to keep it if she brought it out for long enough to do what she needed to do. Besides, as much as escaping here would be wonderful, it wouldn't help Tammy. And that was paramount.

You don't need paper.

She straightened. The guards straightened. Oh shit. She forced her shoulders to relax and gave the guards a smile. She'd forgotten how intently she was being watched. They could knock her out at the slightest wrong move if they didn't like her actions.

She had to remember that. *Stylus, what do you mean?*

You are developing more skills. Have more abilities. A surface is helpful for some things. And necessary for bigger things. Small things — no longer.

So how do we help her then?

You use your new honor symbols.

Symbols. She was trying to follow her stylus's trail of thoughts. Honestly. But at the moment, it was a leap to think she, herself, could create portals and that was just for starters. *I don't understand. You are the one that creates. Not me.*

No, it was *I — before. Now it is you…and I.*

She shook her head. *Not possible. You are the one that creates. I am just the tool that holds you.*

You have earned your honor marks. They carry abilities with them.

Abilities? She didn't know if she should be excited or terrified. She had yet to question how the stylus might have earned their abilities. She had no idea how the honor marks had come about, they'd simply appeared on her skin. Now she realized that the times her stylus had said they would honor her meant they would give her honor marks.

It had been magical in the beginning, the first mark simply appearing on her after she'd been recognized for a good deed. Now she understood it was so much more than that. They worked on time, energy and even dimensional shifts.

Abilities had to be earned. And learned. Hence the Broken One's higher place in their world. He'd been there the longest, learned the most, earned his position. And had the most to offer. Saving him was important.

She was a novice.

Not as much as you think.

What can I do?

Leave.

Inside she smiled. *Now that's the right answer. What about Tammy? Can I help her get back to here where she belongs?*

Yes. But not without the Broken One, her stylus said. *He must do the transition. Like he performed Dillon's transition.*

Right. So we need Tammy here. Can I leave, go to Tammy's…soul…and then bring her back here? Without the Louers knowing?

Not as you mean.

She almost groaned. Why was nothing ever simple? *How do you mean?*

You can leave your body behind. Go in the same form that Tammy currently exists.

Oh boy. Now that was a mind bender…again. *Really?*

Yes.

And you're saying I can do that without the guards noticing? How hard a process is this?

For you now, with your marks…it is not hard.

She didn't know if she should believe the stylus or not, but had no reason to doubt it after all the other crazy things he'd helped her do. *Is this something Louers can do on their own? Without styluses?*

No.

So it wasn't normal what happened to Tammy?

No.

What about the Torans — can they do that?

No.

So why is this something I can do?

The Broken One thought it would be an ability to help you as you moved through dimensions.

She tilted her head. *The Broken One?*

You earned your first marks after rescuing the Broken One and the others. We are and always have been connected.

He awarded the first honor marks.

And the second?

I did

She brightened. Really? Sweet.

She wanted to ask more. About other abilities, but time was a definite issue. *How do I go to Tammy?*

You need only detach.

Only? She'd have laughed aloud if she could have. But ever mindful of her audience, she managed to hold back. *What about my body? Should I be lying down so I don't fall? Or can I just leave from here as I am now?*

There was a faint hum in the background. She stole a look at her guards to see if they'd notice. But they appeared unaware. Unless they were causing it. She'd thought it was her stylus. Maybe she was wrong.

Use the honor marks as a guide.

That came out of nowhere. Storey stared down at her arm where the marks seemed to glow and twist in place. They were almost alive. Somehow. Maybe not alive, but there was a force in there she didn't recognize. Energy of some kind. The marks, even as she watched, looked brighter, stronger. More powerful. She was drawn into the glow. Feeling the warmth of it surround her. A tingling sensation she'd never experienced before. She didn't understand. She hadn't lifted her arm, yet they seemed closer. Heat soothed her inside and out. How odd was that?

She desperately wanted to stand up. Did she dare? What was the worst the guards could do, but push her down again? She tossed them a defiant look and stood. Skorky's head jerked back, his gaze widening. But he never shifted away from his protective stance at Tammy's shoulder. She took a step.

And left her body behind.

She froze. *Oh God. Oh God, Oh my God.*

Stylus? Have I separated from my body?

You are correct.

Her gaze widened. *How?*

You used the honor markings as a guide.

She stared down at her arm. Her physical arm. The one still resting on the bed, holding Tammy's hand. The honor marks now seemed softer, calmer and no longer moving. She gulped. Then looked down at what passed for an arm on her body now. Wispy smoke in a lovely white, with a tinge of lavender, filled the space she'd expected to have an arm. Her body was no better. Her hair no longer brushed her ears. Her clothes had disappeared, and boy did she gulp at that one. Although technically she wasn't exactly standing there in the buff, either. It was weird. She was there, but wasn't there. There was something representing clothing, but nothing she'd ever seen before. She let her pent up breath out slowly.

Well she'd done it.

Whatever *it* was.

Now what Stylus? How do I help Tammy and get back inside my body?

Think of Tammy as you last saw her. Feel the emotions of having her at your side.

Closing her eyes, she imagined Tammy beside her. Smiling and joyous; so full of life. The last time Storey had seen her, she'd been in Eric's arms. He was carrying her away to safety. Good. She needed to be safe.

And she is safe. Look.

Storey's eyes flew open. She gasped. Oh my God. I'm in Paxton's lab. She spun around; aware she was leaving wispy tendrils as she moved. Like a princess with a long train, Storey was leaving wispy bits of her new material – energy or clouds – wafting out behind her as she spun. *This is amazing. I so don't understand. But it is definitely cool.*

You can travel by thought in this form.

Thought? As in I don't need you, stylus?

She clasped her hand to her chest, afraid she'd lost the stylus, and realized she not only had no stylus, she had no chest! Her breath came out in harsh gasps as she fought to control the panic. This couldn't be, could it?

Yes. Our souls are connected to our bodies, but the physical body is not a prison. You can move freely in and out. We in the stylus no longer have bodies. They do not keep long term. But our souls are forever.

Forever. She repeated the word, really liking the concept. And this whole state of being, for all it was scary and fragile feeling, was also incredibly exhilarating and…liberating. *If only all people could realize they were more than an organic body.*

They can, but few would want the experience.

Are you kidding? This is awesome.

For many, the fear would be overwhelming.

True.

She was so caught up in the sensation and conversation it took a moment for her to hear the other voices. Eric. And Paxton. She laughed, a sound of pure pleasure pealing across the room.

Eric stopped talking, an arrested look on his face.

"Did you hear that?" he asked Paxton.

"Hear what?"

Storey grinned. Good for Eric. He was always so sensitive to her moods and presence. Maybe he couldn't see her in this form, but he was aware of something different. And then she gasped again. Tammy stood beside Eric, her hand nestled in his much bigger one. And she was in the same form as Storey, but in a slightly different color. Tammy appeared as a light blue to white energy swirling in place at Eric's side.

Did he know? Considering he was holding her hand, he must.

"Tammy!" Storey cried out.

The energy beside Eric turned, then shot toward Storey like a bullet fired from a gun. The blue energy surged around Storey, over her and then finally through her.

She'd have gasped in shocked delight if she could have, but the sensation of being one with another soul overwhelmed her into silence. She'd have shed tears if she'd had them; instead it felt like her heart was being squeezed small and so tight. Only it was beating hard and strong, because Tammy was inside, helping her.

"Oh Tammy. I was so afraid for you," she whispered.

"Torrey." Tammy's faint pudgy hand reached up to pat Storey's cheek. "I'm happy you are here."

They could talk like this. Without the trappings and physical limitations that defined their other reality, the two of them could communicate like they'd always wanted to. She wrapped her arms around the little girl and held her tight.

"Paxton. Something just happened," Eric said.

Paxton spun on Eric. "Now what? I can only work on one thing at a time."

"Well for one, Tammy, who'd been holding my hand, isn't any longer. And I think someone else is here now?"

Storey watched at Paxton spun around searching the brightly lit room. "There is no one here."

Yes, there is. Hi Paxton.

He didn't hear her. Holding Tammy close, Storey walked over to Paxton's monitor and hit the keys she needed with a little bump of her non-existent fingers. *Hi, Paxton,* she typed. *I'm here in the same form as Tammy. We're spirits. Storey.*

Both men raced over to the typing keypad.

Paxton grabbed his chest and stared at the place in front of his key panel. "That's not possible.

Eric whispered, "I sure as hell hope it is. Storey," He took a deep breath. "Please tell me you're not dead."

ERIC STUDIED THE space in front of Paxton's desk. There was a shimmer to the air, a motion to it that he didn't understand. And hadn't seen before. He asked, "Is that possible?"

The keys depressed even as Eric watched. Storey typed in the words, *Yes. I am alive. I left my body in the Louers' dimension so I could help Tammy return.*

Eric froze at the part where she'd left her body. What? He wanted to repeat Paxton's horrified rejection about that not being possible. He took a deep breath and let it out shakily. "Storey, how do you propose to take Tammy back?"

The keys tapped faster this time. The words appearing as if by magic. *Easy. The same way I came here. Tammy can travel by holding on to me.*

His mind refused to see how this was possible.

Just then the door to Paxton's lab opened up and his father strode in, two Toran guards trailing behind. "Paxton, I demand a hearing." He glared at his son. "These charges against me are preposterous. I have done nothing wrong."

Eric struggled to shift from one subject to the next. And adjust to his father's presence. He opened his mouth to say something, when his father rounded on him.

"And you, letting your father be treated this way. How dare you?" The pompous man strode across the room as if he still had the right.

Eric's felt his eyebrows shoot straight up. His father

was actually accusing Eric of not standing up for him? Unbelievable. He glanced at Paxton, who appeared to have had one shock too many.

"Why are you not in your chambers under guard?" Paxton's fury was slowly rising as a tidal wave of red filled his face.

The Councilman sniffed. "Why should I be? My people are loyal to me. And not that upstart otherworlder. How dare she accuse me of such things?" He walked over to the workbench, putting his back to the others.

Eric blinked. Was he really that dense? Still, he felt himself looking to Paxton for guidance. Except, Paxton looked like he was about to yell at his father. Eric almost wanted to warn him. He glanced back and his eyes widened in horror. His father's gaze was locked on the monitor. And a fat smile had slipped out. It disappeared as Eric stepped forward and wiped the screen clean with the press of one button.

But somehow, he knew the damage had been done. He didn't need to see his father's beady eyes to know he had seen and processed Storey's explanation. And was even now looking for ways to use it.

"However, I will return to my quarters now. To make sure all is how I left it." He spun on his heels and headed for the door, leaving as abruptly as he'd arrived.

"Paxton, we have to stop him. He saw the monitor. He's going after Storey."

"How? He can't." Paxton ran over to the keyboard.

"He did already. Look at all the trouble he caused with the Louers last time. If he can get the message to them that Storey has left her body, well…" Eric didn't want to finish that thought. The stricken look on Paxton's face said it all. "Why was he walking around as free as you or I? And how is it he is free to go to his quarters? He should be going to the dungeons."

"He was taken for medical testing first. To make sure there was nothing physically wrong that could account for the change in his behavior."

"And now what, he's allowed to walk around – free?" Eric couldn't believe it. An anger like he'd never felt before surged through his veins. His fists clenched. Then opened. Then clenched again.

"No. No. He's not." Paxton ran to his control panel and immediately brought up the guard room. While Eric watched, he ordered guards to watch the Councilman's room. He was not to be allowed to leave without Paxton's permission. Paxton then warned that a full inquiry was in progress as to why his orders to place the Councilman in the dungeon after his medical hadn't been carried out in the first place.

"Do you think that will do anything? Or have we got a dissident force happening within our own people? People as loyal to him as he claims?"

"It's possible. He's ruled here for a long time," Paxton muttered. "There won't be when they find out what he's done."

"Then we need to tell every one of them the truth of his actions. Because I don't trust him even under guard." Eric spun around to look for Storey. He couldn't see her faint energy. He hoped she'd gone back to where she belonged. But just in case, "Storey, we'll stop him. Honest."

There was no answering tap on the keyboard. No answering movement from anywhere around him.

Paxton stared wide eyed. "What about Tammy? Is she here? We can't have her running around loose. Please tell me they are still together. Tammy might have run away after your father's appearance."

Eric would have liked to run away too. He called out, "Storey? Are you still here? Do you have Tammy with you?"

"Storey? Please talk on the monitor if you are here."

Paxton and Eric stared at the keypad. There was no movement. No words appearing anywhere.

"Damn," he whispered. "I think Storey is gone." He could only hope she was okay. Had she been yanked back to her body? Gone back willingly with Tammy at her side?

Or was she still here – somewhere?

CHAPTER 24

STOREY WATCHED ERIC'S father approach. That man gave her the creeps. He was so…so…arrogant, so sure of his power. She hated that about him. And she couldn't believe he was still walking around. Why? How? Hadn't Eric said something about his father being taken care of?

Surely Paxton had followed through?

Surely?

She watched his gaze land on the monitor and realized the moment he understood the message she'd written. And the danger of his understanding.

But it was too late. The energy around her swirled as Tammy snuggled up closer. "It's okay Tammy. He can't hurt us." At least she hoped not. She no longer felt so confident that he'd be punished for his actions. She narrowed her gaze and watched as he bolted to the door. Had he taken something off the bench? Maybe not, but he was up to something. Suspicions raised, she trailed behind him as he walked to the door. Tammy stuck close by.

Storey looked down at her. Should they follow the Councilman? He was one scary dude, even if he was more of a fat merchant to look at him. She couldn't trust him, and she didn't dare let him get up to his old plans again. She had to find out what he had planned.

She knew it couldn't be good. Not for her. Or Tammy, and she highly doubted Eric would come out on top. In fact, if the Councilman found out about Paxton being a Louer…well, he'd twist all this mess up and make it look like Paxton was to blame.

Get himself reinstated at the same time. Next week it would all have been forgotten. The scandal written into the archives for future students to study.

And that couldn't happen. She slipped out the door before it closed. She could probably think herself to the other side, but this way was natural. Tammy refused to stay behind.

Please, Tammy, stay with Eric.

Tammy's face grew mutinous and her shoulders squared. Not that she had much for shoulders. Still, she could understand Tammy not wanting to be separated from her again. Storey didn't want to lose track of Tammy either. And in their current forms, that was all too possible.

Okay, you can come. Just stay close and stay quiet.

With Tammy's nod, Storey picked up speed and raced behind the Councilman.

He swept into his chambers, the guards taking up their position outside the entrance, and headed directly to the big communication center on the far wall. With a furtive glance around he started clicking on the keypad in front of him. Within moments, a picture formed on the monitor above.

She heard Tammy's gasp before the identity of the person on the screen filtered in.

It was Tammy's father. How did they have the technology for this? As much as it surprised her, it also delighted her. They'd do just fine in their new home.

Oh Shit. Tammy tried to pull away from Storey's hand, but Storey held on. *It's not your father here in this room, Tammy. He's still in his home, your home. That's just an image for communication.*

Tammy shook her head. She opened her mouth, and Storey cringed waiting for that horrible sound to come loose. But it didn't happen. Tammy had stopped, an arrested look on her face.

Who are you talking to, Tammy?

She blinked then pointed at the monitor.

Storey glanced at the monitor then back again. *You can talk to your father through the dimension?* Not that Tammy understood the dimension stuff. She rephrased the question, *Tammy, can you talk to your father from here?*

Tammy nodded.

Can you tell him that you are safe?

Tammy nodded again.

Good. Do that. Tell him that you are coming home. And can you also tell him… Storey stopped. Did she dare have Tammy warn her father about the Councilman? Did she have any choice?

Tammy, can you warn your father about this bad man?

Tammy's face turned fearful. She shuddered. The faint ripples of blue ripple outward like a stone thrown into a pond. *I know. I don't like him either. But he's trying to hurt me. And you.*

Tammy's eyes widened. She reached up to pat Storey's cheek. *Torrey.*

Storey leaned into the delicate touch, and smiled. *Yes. He is coming.*

Storey froze. *Who is coming, Tammy?*

The little girl pointed to her father on the monitor.

Storey gasped, her own gaze tracking the Louer that dominated the screen. *Does he know the form you are in?*

Tammy shook her head. "No."

How is he going to come here? That was so not good. He wasn't likely to come alone either. Damn. Storey glanced over at the Councilman, now pacing in front of the monitor and talking in a language she didn't understand. Apparently Tammy's father did, though. His face was getting redder and redder. Whatever the conversation, it wasn't to his liking.

Stylus, can you make it so that this conversation is recorded and a record is sent to the other councilmen and Paxton? Can you translate the conversation as well?

Yes. It is simple.

Then do it. If there are speakers to send this conversation live to all the councilmen, guards, whoever you can reach — do that as well. Broken One, do you agree? Can you do more?

His voice murmured in her mind. *Done. And more. We've taken the message to the people.*

Good. At least whatever the Councilman was up to would be recorded. Someone somewhere would stop him, surely. In the meantime, they were about to have the Louers arrive. And that wasn't good for anyone.

Tammy, tell your father not to come, we're coming home right now.

Tammy's gaze widened. She spun around as if looking for Eric and his portal. *No honey, I can take you home. Jump into my arms.*

Tammy grinned and immediately did just that.

Storey laughed. *Now. Tell your father.* Storey waited a few minutes. *Did you do it?*

Tammy nodded. *Good, then hold on and I'll take you home.*

With her arms wrapped tightly around Storey, Tammy laid her head against her shoulder. Their energy snuggled together. Good.

Stylus, please tell Eric what we are doing.

I have told Paxton.

Good enough. Eric might need to come and rescue me.

She took a deep breath and thought about her body, the beautiful pattern on her arm. She could see the glow on her arm, the warmth of the pattern. Such a weird feeling. But the warmth wasn't painful. In fact, it was invigorating.

Storey leaned her head back and smiled.

And found herself sitting beside Tammy's bed.

Back in her body.

"DAMN IT PAXTON, how does he manage to live so charmed? He should not be walking around free like that." Eric hated the thought. His father still had some supporters obviously.

It was as if Paxton aged before him. He wilted, his shoulders slumping. "I don't know. I don't understand." But he wouldn't look Eric in the eye.

Eric knew he wouldn't like what was to come. "Paxton, you need to tell me the truth, did you let him go?"

"He's not free," Paxton blustered. "But the other council members didn't believe everything I had to say. They want to give him a fair chance to explain." He looked around, a little lost, and added, "I was working on trying to bring Dillon back and didn't attend the last meeting. That's when they loosened the restrictions on him."

Dillon? Eric had forgotten about him. Eric stared at Paxton, seeing for the first time how much Paxton had devoted to helping his people. How much he'd lost personally in his lifetime. Had he ever married? Had children? Eric knew relatively little about his mentor and friend's family history. What he did know was that something was bothering him right now.

He suspected it had to do with Dillon.

He took several steps closer, asking in a quiet voice, "Is there something you want to say to me, Paxton?"

The older man's shoulders shifted as if to straighten, then finding the effort too much, collapsed again. Eric sighed. "And does it have to do with the fact that you are a Louer?"

Paxton gasped, he spun around so fast that Eric was afraid he'd fall over. His eyes took on a glassy look and the color, never much in his face to begin with, drained right away. Concerned, Eric led him to the stool in front of the workbench and pushed him gently into it. "Paxton?"

Paxton clasped his hands to his chest, gasping for air. His skin color faded to gray.

"Oh no. Paxton, hang on. I'm getting you help."

"No, I'm fine." He gasped, "Just give me a moment."

Eric wasn't too sure. Damn. He spun around looking for help. Where was Storey? She was so level headed, he could always count on her to give him a hand. But he knew she wasn't around. He knew because it felt like a part of him was missing. He'd never heard of anyone else having that feeling. He'd never thought something like this was even possible.

And that just made it all the more special.

"Paxton? Are you feeling better?" Eric bent over his friend, hating that he had to get answers from him and stress him out to this extent. But he suspected that it was Paxton's secret that had made him the exemplary mentor and council head that he was. And a potential victim to anything the Councilman wanted. If he knew about Dillon, which was possible given that he had access to his quarters and therefore to the database, he'd have been automatically updated on Dillon's arrival. Whether he knew about Dillon being a Louer or not was another thing…Paxton's life would be ruined if he did.

"Our grandparents had heard rumors about the banishment of the Louers. They were young, too young to get married and too young to be independent...but my grandmother got pregnant. They were owned by your father's family. They couldn't get free. His sires have all been the same."

"When the Louers were banished, my family hid away in the mountains. Trying to live their life alone. But the life was hard. My grandparents kept the secret, and my parents after them. I never knew I was different. Dillon was the younger by several years. My mother perished soon after his birth. My father was a simple man, he tried hard, but couldn't do much without her. He took a chance and moved into town and tried to make a go of it. He told me the whole story and swore me to secrecy. Warned me what could happen if anyone found out. In truth I kind of forgot about it. I was a Toran in every way. And besides, by then, everyone had forgotten about the Louers. My father worked hard and kept a low profile.

But your grandfather knew. He didn't do anything publicly, but one night my father disappeared. Dillon and I were still young. The neighbors took us in. And I never forgot again that what I was had to be hidden. That I couldn't be me. That my family was so bad we had to be banished – or worse."

The look in Paxton's eyes broke Eric's heart. How long did it take for history to be forgotten? One generation or two? Three maybe.

"Why did the Louers get banished?"

"My father once told me that at that time, many of the Toran people were dying. No one knew why. Because my people weren't dying, the Torans blamed them. When my people had no answers to the illness, things went from bad to worse. The Louers were treated horribly. This went on for years, and once everyone had gotten used to the bad behavior, it continued well past the point when the Torans were healthy again. But the damage had been done and the behavior continued. The Louers tried to gather together to fight the problem. They were serfs and not slaves. But the distinction became lost over time as their roles slid further into slave and master.

"When the Louers rose up and started fighting back, the Torans banished my people." The lost look in his eyes made Eric think he was looking back through time. "All those years, I did nothing to help my people and did everything to help your people. I'd hoped there'd be a way to find Dillon, but knew I had no means to help him as a Louer. But as a Toran, so much more was possible." He gave a broken cry. "He was all I had… I tried so hard, but couldn't help him."

He stared glassy eyed at Eric. "Then Storey found Dillon."

And Eric understood. "And you realized that in helping your brother, you were risking your own secret coming to light. Now that Dillon is safe inside a stylus, you are afraid for yourself."

"No," Paxton whispered shaking his head, "I don't care what happens to me anymore. I'm old. My time is done. I stayed around to find an answer for Dillon, now that I've done that, I'm happy to die. But I'd like to die here. Not be banished to that cold dark place. Look what they've done to my people. Look how they've changed as each generation had to deal with the hardships they've endured."

"They can't banish you, Paxton. Look at all you've done for my – our – people."

"They won't care when I'm gone." He looked up. "In fact, they are liable to look at you sideways too. Wonder if you can be trusted."

Eric laughed at that. "No, if they look at me that way, it will be due to my father's actions, not yours."

As if he'd heard his name spoken, the Councilman's

voiced filled the air and his face appeared in each monitor in the room. It was kind of eerie.

"No. You must finish this. Our bargain still stands. You get rid of the girl and then I'll give you the means to travel to my dimension."

An odd-sounding voice answered, and a strong male's face filled the screen. "My daughter says otherwise."

A Louer male. It took a moment for Eric to understand. His heart slammed against his ribs. Tammy's father. The Councilman, Eric's father, was negotiating with the Louers against his own people.

"Your daughter?" blustered the councilman, "What does she have to do with this?"

"She says you tried to get rid of the girl already and now you are no longer in power. That you can't promise anything."

The councilman's face reddened. "That's not true. I have a secret up my sleeve. It will change the game entirely. I have information on the chief person who is against me. He will rue the day he went against me."

The Louer elder's face twisted. It was almost as if he were listening to something – to someone – else. His face cleared. "Ah. You are talking about your great scientist, Paxton."

Paxton gasped. His eyes widened. Eric didn't know how to help him. He could only hope his father would never see power again after this. To have actually guaranteed that he could give the Louers travel back to his dimension – that was beyond anything. The council would be screaming over this. Even as that thought registered, the key pad on Paxton's desk lit up as multiple messages clogged up their communication system.

"Yes, yes, you see, he is not a Toran. He is a Louer. Like you."

Paxton, standing in shock beside Eric, bowed his head in shame.

CHAPTER 25

STOREY RAISED HER head and took a deep breath. *Tammy, time to wake up.*

Tammy shifted on the bed. Immediately the others in the room jumped forward. They surrounded the little girl, watching intently as she started to wake up. Skorky stayed put at her shoulder, but he lifted a tiny paw to bat Tammy's cheek.

Then Tammy's eyes opened. She stared at the Louers gathered around as a hum filled the air. Storey understood they were all conversing. She could probably tune in, but that damn hum hurt.

Use the honor mark.

Storey frowned. *The same one?*

No the newest one.

She reached to touch the new honor marks on her shoulders, instinctively tracing the flowing lines. Immediately the hum muted and words of a bubbling conversation filtered into her mind. The noise was too loud. She continued to trace, finding that as she went lower down her arm, the volume muted. As she traced higher, the sound rose.

She laughed. *It's a communication device.*

It's communication energy, the stylus corrected. Now you can speak with Tammy normally.

Is Tammy going to be okay now?

Yes.

"Torrey!"

Storey smiled down at the little girl. "Hello, Tammy."

Tammy smiled, a look that lit up the room and caused all the other Louers to murmur in shock.

"I guess they don't do much smiling, do they?"

Tammy shook her head. "No. But I will teach them. You showed me. I'll show them." She practically beamed. She sat up and threw herself at Storey. Skorky jumped onto Tammy's back and scurried across to Storey's shoulder, where it chattered happily.

Wrapping her arms tight around the little girl, Storey said, "At least now we can talk to each other. Let's hope we still can after I go home."

"Torrey leaving?"

Storey nodded. "I hope so. I need to go back to see my mother."

At that Tammy held out her hand to one of the Louers at her side. "You can share my mother."

The other Louer stared down at Tammy in obvious alarm.

Storey laughed. "That's okay. I have my own mother. Thank you for the offer though."

Tammy smiled. "But you don't have a father, right? So you can share mine."

The little girl's generous spirit was heartwarming, but there was no way that her stone-faced father would be interested in adopting Storey. And the feeling was mutual. Storey wanted minimal contact with Tammy's family. Still, they had a few issues to be resolved.

The Louers at her side poked her suddenly. Storey sat back and glared at them. "You could just ask me to stand up you know."

They backed up in shock. Tammy giggled. "They didn't know that you could speak"

She looked at Tammy. "But I spoke with you?"

"I didn't let them hear the conversation."

Oh boy. She had a lot to learn. Storey said, "I couldn't speak to them before, but now apparently I can." She motioned to the shimmering marks on her shoulder.

Tammy gasped, she pointed to the marks. Skorky jumped to Tammy's arms. "Mutre, look."

Mutre, which Storey could only surmise meant mother, bent closer. Something shifted in her eyes, but so quickly Tammy didn't recognize the emotions. Shock maybe. Understanding. Definitely something along that line. It wasn't like Storey could speak Louer herself, more along the line of bad translation. Most of the message came through, but some of the finer nuances were lost.

"Tammy, what's going on?"

"Potre wants to speak to you. And to make sure I'm okay." She scrambled off the platform and grabbed Storey's hand. "Come on."

She tugged Storey to her feet and ran down the hall, holding on tight to Skorky. "It will be fine. I promise."

That the little girl was mimicking Storey's own words probably meant she didn't understand their real meaning. Tammy's father wasn't going to like anything about Storey. But she hoped with Tammy's help, they could convince him to let her go. She needed to go back to her own family soon. And somewhere along the line she had to transfer the Broken One to his new home.

And how she was going to do that was still a mystery.

It will happen in time.

Says you, she muttered mentally. *Just help me get out of this mess, first.*

As they walked into the large cave she had to wonder again if the Torans had technology that could help the Louers out as they built their new world. Then again, the Louers obviously had skills that were far more advanced than they'd initially thought. They'd dug this vast network of caves and had the technology to communicate with the Councilman in another dimension. Although he might have had a hand in that.

The damn place bulged with Louers. Oh crap. She really didn't like the look of the room full of strangers, and not friendly ones, either. All those unsmiling faces staring at her gave her a bad case of the willies. Besides, they could knock her out in an instant. She hadn't forgotten the last time.

At that memory her feet slowed, but Tammy would have none of it. Tammy was much heavier than Storey and she giggled as she pulled Storey forward. Before she knew it, she'd reached the front of the cave to face the Louer leader.

"You are Storey?" he asked, the sound reverberating loudly outside and inside her head. For such a huge man, his voice was calm, not aggressive. Still this form of communication was beyond weird. As if they were speaking aloud, but not quite. This was almost a group conversation.

She barely held back her gasp of shock, but managed to say, "Yes."

Tammy bounced between her father and Storey. Her joy at having them both there on a relatively friendly basis was more than evident. Storey took that to mean she wasn't about to be killed.

"Why are you here?"

Her gaze widened. "To help Tammy." Then she realized they'd never actually learned what Tammy's real name was. She quickly added, "To help your daughter."

Potre gazed at Tammy, but there was no easing of the stony look on his face.

"And the Toran with you?"

"Eric?" She frowned. "He's not with me. He's in his dimension."

"Is he? And his father."

She scoffed. "That man should be locked up."

"You are not here as his messenger?"

She reared back. "I am nothing to him. He wants to kill me."

"So I understand."

She frowned. "He wants you to take care of that." She stiffened, remembering the conversation she'd overheard in the Councilman's room. "I suppose he's willing to make a deal to get that job done."

The Louer leader nodded.

"And?" she asked in a cool voice, "What is your decision?"

He tilted his head and she thought she saw something flash in his eyes. She didn't understand, but a weird hum filled the air. Dread filled her stomach; was she about to be knocked out? Quickly, she said to Tammy, "Tammy, stop your father."

"Why?" Tammy bounced in front of her, the short tubby body surprisingly agile. Skorky raced from one shoulder to the other and back again.

"I don't want to be knocked out again." Storey said in a dry voice.

"He won't." She giggled. "It won't work anymore on you now. He already tried."

"He did?"

"Yes." Tammy laughed and danced through the room. None of the other Louers noticed or paid any attention to her. Storey didn't understand the lack of interest. "Tammy, why are there no other children?"

"There are. But not many."

As the adults were looking at her. Storey continued to ask Tammy, "Do you know why there aren't many?"

"No." Tammy danced a little jig that made Storey grin. The humor was out of place, given the silent room and situation, but hard to resist. Tammy had always been a joy.

Crossover influence. She had to stop herself and think about that. She'd definitely been influenced by Tammy. Look where she was. There's no way she'd have come to rescue the little girl – time and time again – if she hadn't been. She'd also been hoping to find a way to improve relations between the Louers and the Torans. They were one and the same, inside.

And maybe so were her people, but they were a long ways away from being ready to have a relationship with other dimensions. She couldn't even imagine trying to explain such a concept to her government. Add in all the other governments of all the other countries…and things would get very icky.

"Storey."

She straightened to face the Louers' leader. He motioned to her to move forward down a corridor. She stepped forward before the guards could prod her.

Tammy grabbed her hand, and tugged her closer. Storey grinned. It was stupid to feel so happy and carefree with her fate yet to be decided, but she'd been through so much. Done so much. How could she not want to enjoy the moment? Knowing her time with this cherub was coming to an end, Storey couldn't help, but open her arms. Tammy launched herself into them. Storey stumbled. She'd forgotten how heavy Tammy was when in her body. She gave her a big hug, the two of them laughing. Finally she put her down and the two ran forward. They ended up in another cave, darker and much smaller than the previous once. On the wall was a large monitor. Filled with the Councilman's face.

For a moment Storey was sidetracked by the apparent lack of power here and the appearance of a big, functioning monitor. Maybe her people could learn more than she thought from the Louers. From the rest of the furnishings in the room, she assumed the Louers had made good use of the doorways she'd made leading back to their old world.

The voices brought her back to her surroundings.

And her lip curled.

"Why did you walk away?" the Councilman growled. "I gave you important information. You can use it to get more of what you want."

"And I wanted to check the information." Tammy's father motioned Storey closer.

"What is she doing there?" The Councilman gasped in horror. "Kill her. She's right there. Do it. Now." His voice rose to a shout as temper and outrage rippled across his face. His color went dark and he appeared to be on the edge of an apoplectic fit.

Storey laughed. "Still trying to get someone else to do your dirty work. Does the Louer leader know that you were cheating him?"

The man at her side straightened. She kept her mocking gaze on Eric's father. "That you promised to give them technology you don't have the power to give?" She snorted. "And of course you haven't told the Council members or Paxton either, of your deal. And what about Eric?"

"Don't you even mention my son's name. You've ruined him." This time the Councilman appeared to be hopping from one foot to the other. His rotund face twisted and reddened with temper. "Kill her."

Storey tried to not to look at Tammy's father's face. She didn't want to know if he was of the same mind as the Councilman. But eventually she had no choice. Shit. She turned to face Tammy's father. "You know...Potre....Paxton *is* a Louer. But he is also a very revered Toran scholar. And he is capable of helping you."

As an afterthought, she added, "If he wanted to, that is."

There was a silent murmur behind her. "As for Eric, yes, it's true he is the Councilman's son. But Eric is not like his father. He is what his father could have been. And never will be."

She didn't know if they could understand that message. She didn't speak Louer properly.

But the stylus did. *Stylus, can you tell them? Can you explain?*

We have.

And?

He isn't sure. He doesn't trust us.

Wait…does he have any relatives who are related to any of the souls in the styluses we have? Are there any Louers today that remember styluses?

The stylus bubbled with the concept. Noise filled the back of her mind. She waited, watching the Councilman and the Louer leader glare at each other. How could she convince Potre? "Tammy, have you told your father about all the adventures we had?"

"Yes!" Tammy shouted at her. "He asked lots of questions."

"Good. Do you understand that Eric's father is asking your father to kill me?"

Tammy gasped. She cried out and her arms wrapped around Storey and squeezed her tight. "Did your father say anything about it?"

Tammy shook her head.

"Has he said anything about the new dimension, problems with the Torans? Anything at all."

This time, Tammy nodded.

"Yes? What part?" Storey bent to look into Tammy's face.

"He asked about how we went from one place to the other. The types of guards you have. Eric's guards."

Storey groaned. All Tammy had seen was her house and Paxton's lab. His father must think the two dimensions were playgrounds. Neither had visible guards and both would appear developed, but empty. Sigh.

She wondered what he had planned. And why?

The Councilman's face swelled in temper as he ranted and raved about the damn people betraying him, about their lack of appreciation and how he was going to get his own back when the traitor Paxton was shown for the liar and fraud he was.

The longer Storey listened to his rants the madder she got. Finally she'd had enough. She stepped back up in front of the monitor. "That Paxton is a Louer doesn't surprise me. And of course he had to hide his identity. When your people became sick and started dying, you blamed the Louers. Your people enslaved them. Turned them into something they weren't supposed to be. When they protested and started to fight back, you banished them. How difficult it must have been then, when so much of your knowledge went with them. The knowledge in the styluses. The styluses couldn't be renewed because that technology was lost. Because it was Louer technology. Paxton's technology created in the Toran dimension."

She gave a hard laugh. "You are such an egotistical bastard. You deserve to spend your lifetime in servitude. In service to others so you can understand an honest day's work. To teach you to give, not just take. Wait until your people find out how you let the Louers back to your world out of revenge. That you were willing to give up their safety out of spite. You never counseled your people. You have been a ruler without compassion. A monarch over serfs. Do your people understand that it was you and the leaders before you who banished the Louers, and turned your own people into their replacements? Instead of all Torans being above the Louers you made yourself above the Torans."

The last words ran through her like lightening, giving her the understanding of their truth. "How many people have you hurt by your greed? Or have you been just a rotund clown at the head of the table, while the worker bees carried on without knowing what you were really like? You couldn't even spend time with your son, could you? Be a part of raising him? You left it to Paxton."

She laughed. "So maybe he was the lucky one after all."

The stylus spoke quietly. *The Broken One remembers the time of the banishment.*

Storey nodded, sorry for the pain the Broken One had been through. "Do you realize that there are still souls that remember all this? Everything that happened when the Louers were banished?"

The Councilman spluttered. "Not possible."

"Yes, it is possible. It's a fact. The styluses carry Louer souls." She shook her head. "I rescued several that had been damaged, forgotten. Lost through time. The Broken One is alive and well. I don't remember his original name…but he is here."

Her stylus spoke. *His name was Barrat.*

Storey repeated the name aloud, "Barrat – the Broken One was once called Barrat."

A shocked hum rose around her. Excited murmurs filled the air. Storey didn't understand what they were saying and she couldn't take the time to work it out as she was trying to keep two conversations together at the same time. The Councilman shrugged. "So. He is nothing to me."

"Maybe, but from the reaction I'm getting here, he means something to the Louers."

Potre leaned forward, his commanding voice breaking through the rest of the noise in her head. And spoke to her directly — for the first time. "What do you know of Barrat?"

She turned to look at him. "Everything. I carry his soul."

ERIC AND PAXTON stood shoulder to shoulder as they watched the byplay between the Councilman and Storey with Tammy's father popping on screen every once in a while. Eric was horrified at his father's machinations.

"Barrat? Barrat," murmured Paxton. "Why do I know that name?" He grabbed up his stylus and asked him for information on Barrat. The stylus started writing, filling the tablet in no time. "Barrat was the leader of the Louers. Enslaved by the Torans and sent to join the stylus when he became too old and broken to work. His knowledge was important, but his physical presence too dangerous." Paxton looked at Eric.

"How is it that Storey is carrying him? She can't have bonded to two styluses."

Eric winced. "I guess you weren't told all the details, huh?" At Paxton's wide eyed stare, Eric nodded. "You know Storey, she can't leave anyone to die. So she is carrying the Broken One inside her until he can be moved to a new stylus. If she dies, so does he."

"That is not good. We need his information." Paxton looked ready to panic. "I understood she was doing something to help him, but not what or how that help would be administered."

"Yeah, that's Storey all over. Now she's trying to fix the Louer and Toran problem."

Paxton looked at him sideways. "What problem?"

"She wants our people to share technology with the Louers. And she wants peace between the dimensions."

"They aren't my people." Paxton stared straight ahead. "I'm a Toran."

Eric sighed. "See that's the problem. There shouldn't be them and us. We were all the same at one time."

"But no longer."

"And that's wrong. We banished them and they suffered. Now they have a chance at a better life thanks to Storey and they need help to get started. They don't even have enough necessary food stores for the coming winter."

Paxton's lips thinned.

Eric grinned. "I'm warning you now, Storey won't let them suffer."

Paxton spun on his heels. "What does she expect us to do?"

"Help."

Paxton gasped. "They attacked us."

"Because they couldn't stay where they were any longer. When they found a way through…"

"That was Storey's fault. She opened a portal. If she hadn't done that…"

"You would never have found your brother, the Councilman would never have been put in a position to show his true colors and I'd have never met Storey." He smiled, a gentle twitch of his lips. "And that is something I wouldn't have wanted to miss."

"You can't keep her. You know that – right?" Paxton said slowly. "We have enough problems with just one dimension. There's no way we can handle dealing with multiple dimensions. That would be a political nightmare."

"I know that. But," he faced Paxton, "I have no intention of breaking off what's happening with her. I've spent all my life watching cold Toran relationships and wondering why none felt right for me. Now I've met Storey, I know. She's different. I saw her as a young girl when I first met her – only she wasn't. I was seeing what I expected to see. Not what she is – what she has become. She's a woman. She's become the star here. Not you or me or even the styluses. It's been her that has risen to the top of each challenge. I'm blessed to know her and I'll be incredibly lucky if she decides that I'm right for her – as I know she's right for me."

Paxton shook his head. "She can't keep going back and forth like this. It's going to cause problems."

"Maybe. But that door has been opened. We can't just ignore that." Eric shrugged. "I'm sure there's a way we can live in both dimensions. No one has to know. Just think of all I can learn. And Tammy is going to want to see Storey, too. And Storey will want to see her. Just think, the three of us can represent our worlds to each other."

Paxton's face puckered as he considered Eric's words. "Would Storey leave her world?"

Eric's eyebrows flew up. "She might. Particularly after her mother is gone. In the meantime, she'd certainly want to come back and forth. She's seen almost nothing of our world."

Just then, Storey's face filled the screen. "Eric? Paxton? Are you there?"

Paxton immediately tapped the keypad. "We are here."

As he tapped, the door opened and Toran council members and many others poured into his lab. Their voices raised in both outraged and terror.

"What has he done?"

"Are the Louers attacking?"

"What can we do?"

"Why has he been allowed to do this?"

Eric rounded on the last councilman who'd spoken, his temper flaring red once again. "He's done this because you people didn't believe Paxton and I. You let him loose. *You* gave him the means and methods to do this."

The group stopped and stared at each other. "We didn't think he'd do something so awful."

And Eric realized another truth. His people were as innocent as newborn babes. They'd handed over control, given complete power to his father and when he'd accepted it and made it his own, they were stunned. Now they felt betrayed. In truth, they should have seen it coming. He had. Storey certainly had.

"And…Paxton, is it true?" the elderly councilman Marxel asked, his voice tremulous. "Are you really a Louer?"

Eric stepped in before his mentor could try and explain. "Paxton's family descended from the Louers." He smiled at them, his face grim, "As did we all. Remember that? Even the Councilman comes from Louers."

They all stared at each other, unsure of what to say. Who to listen to. Who to believe.

Then a woman stepped forward and brought the conversation around to the biggest issue.

"Is he still free?"

Eric didn't recognize the speaker, but the woman was tiny and wedged in-between several other women. He was happy to see them here. To see them sticking together and speaking up. He wouldn't be surprised if they'd been influenced by Storey's behavior to do so. Not that they'd had much of a chance to see her. But they'd have heard of her. And her exploits. These women could do so much more than they did. Storey would be good for them.

It was Storey that had opened his eyes.

"Is the human, Storey, coming back?" asked one of the woman.

"How can she?" said one grim faced male Eric didn't recognize. "The Councilman has ordered her death. Now he is trying to arrange an assassin to kill her."

"Are the Louers going to kill her? Paxton needs to help her."

The mass of questions and cries rose as each person set off another until Eric held up his hands. "Stop!"

Silence. Everyone looked at him, even Paxton, who said, "Eric, what do you suggest?"

"I suggest we take care of my father, and if that means sending him out to the fields as a laborer, then we do so."

"No." Paxton shook his head. "We can't trust him. Even out there he will find followers and rise up again."

Eric nodded, relieved that Paxton's words echoed his own thoughts.

"And he's sent many a prisoner to his death." Paxton added, "Or left them alone to exist in that horrible prison. He needs to experience the same isolation. Maybe after ten years, then he could work in the fields. Not now. He has to learn repentance."

Privately, Eric wasn't sure such a thing was possible. Maybe after a decade. He doubted it though. "And Storey?"

The cries were unanimous. "You have to go rescue her."

Eric waited to hear a dissent amongst them. Nothing. Neither did Paxton's vague origins appear to be more than a news item, quickly discarded as not important.

He smiled. "Good. But there is more to that." Just then Storey's face filled the monitor. Tammy was beside her. "Hi, Tammy," Eric said. He motioned the crowd to look at the monitor.

Several of them gasped and shrank back. Then Tammy smiled. A big toothy grin that made her more adorable than ever. "Everyone, this is Tammy. A Louer child that Storey saved from the old Louer dimension after my father banished Storey there secretly." Storey's face disappeared and then reappeared. This time she had Tammy in her arms.

Eric studied the group of Louer in the room standing behind Storey. He presumed they were looking at the motley group of Torans standing around him. His group showed mixed emotions at the sight of the Louer child in Storey's arms – or maybe it was the sight of all the Louers lined up behind her. Some showed shock, some understanding, some disgust, but there was a softening to their expressions. Enough that he could see, with time, they'd come to understand the Louers were not so different.

Paxton tugged him back away from the crowd staring fascinated at the screen. He whispered beside him, "Do you see how they turn to you?"

He had, but figured it was just the situation.

"You have changed yourself, son. You've gone from a green ranger to a leader. Matured into a good man." He paused a moment, then said, "You should be proud of yourself."

Eric heard the quiet pride in Paxton's voice and smiled. "I guess I am at that."

He had changed. He might not be quite as far along the road as he might want, but he hadn't done anything that made him ashamed of his actions and that had to account for something. At least he knew value when he saw it. And Storey was valuable.

In a quiet voice, he said, "I still want Storey in my life."

"And we'll work on a way to make that happen."

Paxton's hand holding his stylus jerked. He raced over to his tablet where he'd left it on his desk. Immediately the stylus started writing. "They are ready to transfer the Broken One to a new stylus." Paxton read off. "Storey wants Eric there when it happens."

"Is it safe?"

"Yes. Especially now that your father is under guard." Paxton's head bobbed rapidly as he read the answer. He lifted his gaze to Eric. "Which stylus is the Broken One planning on being moved to?"

"To Storey's stylus." Eric smiled. "There really isn't much option at this point."

"Or we could move him to another stylus?" Paxton frowned and raced to his box of styluses. He opened his box of styluses. "Which would be better?"

"I don't think we have a choice. It was done this way on purpose. Without Storey and her stylus, the process won't work. There's already a connection." Eric produced the broken stylus he'd removed from the box and had carried since, and replaced it into the box. "I guess it's a good thing I took that. I wonder if there are other styluses there that need help?"

Paxton's stylus jumped, sending him running back to his tablet. "Yes. They all need souls."

"And how do we do that?"

Paxton's hand once again twitched, the stylus apparently anxious to write the answer. "Once the Broken One is in his stylus he can coordinate the process. But souls are needed."

"Right." They were still at that balking point. They'd need some volunteers, and who would want that? He tabled the thought for the moment. There were other more immediate problems. "I need to go to the Louers' dimension."

"Good. You do that."

Just then the monitors on Paxton's workbench went crazy. Eric raced over and tapped the keypad, but nothing changed. Paxton nudged him gently aside. "Someone has initiated a cross-dimensional travel sequence on a codex." He studied the screen. "Using one of my spare codexes…"

"What? Who?"

Paxton's voice was grim. "I think it is your father. I'm checking the serial number." He clicked again. "It's one you brought back when you brought Tammy here. He must have grabbed it up before going to his chambers."

Unbelievable. Eric hadn't seen him touch anything, but he'd been looking at the monitor, then wiping the screen clean at the time.

Paxton ran to the sideboard where his fingers tapped frantically on the keyboards. The monitor opened up on the Councilman's chambers. He turned back to stare at Eric. "He's knocked out his guards."

"But where can he go?" Eric strode to the monitor, staring at the forms of the two unconscious men. He'd thought he was past being surprised by anything his father did. Apparently not.

Paxton riffled through items on the top of his desk, then raced to his workbench. He turned back to Eric and the others, the color draining from his face. "He's got a pre-coded destination."

Eric stared at him, his mind racing through which of the codexes had been preset.

"Preset? To where?"

CHAPTER 26

S TOREY LAY NERVOUSLY on a raised, flat surface. At least that's what she called it. She had no idea what *ipous* meant, but that's the word Tammy kept repeating as she tried to get Storey to lie down. Skorky's antics hadn't helped.

Potre sat on the side. And that made her feel a little more nervous than she could believe. Apparently the Broken One, Barrat, was a man of great importance to their people. He needed to survive. Hence the process she was about to undergo.

Still, she couldn't help but be a little nervous at the thought of what they might do to her afterwards. She wanted Eric. Someone needed to be on her side. To stand *for* her.

The process will not be difficult.

Broken One, are you sure you should be going into this stylus?

Yes.

My stylus? Are you sure you want Barrat in there with you?

We are honored.

Sure. Everyone was feeling honored…except her. In truth, she'd gotten accustomed to hearing and feeling the Broken One.

And for that we thank you. You have saved us, welcomed us, sheltered us. We are in your debt.

And now you need to move to the stylus. Fine. Let's get this done. She laid her head back down. Then lifted it again. *Are you sure you explained this to the Louers?*

Yes. They know what is going to happen.

Are they going to kill me once you have been saved?

No. They understand that you communicate with us. And with us, to them.

And that's okay? She hated to keep questioning every step, but the doubts kept her prodding. This was a little unnerving. *And they know about Eric coming?*

Eric has arrived.

Oh, thank God. Noises around her said that more people were arriving. In fact, the place had filled up to standing room only. Then she saw Eric. She smiled brightly. And her heart swelled with warmth. She loved that he'd hurried to be beside her.

"Storey." Eric rushed over to her side. "Are you okay?"

She laughed. "Definitely. And getting better now that you're here."

Just then he fell to his knees as Tammy jumped on him from behind. "Ris."

"Ooomph." But he was grinning. He grabbed the little girl, tugged her around to his chest and pulled her into his arms. He hugged her tight. Storey caught sight of Potre's face. The love in his gaze, the surprise and the acceptance. Eric closed his eyes and hugged Tammy tight.

Then she wiggled free and ran back to her father.

The stylus spoke. *It is time.*

Storey took a deep breath. *Then let's do it.*

She reached out, squeezed Eric's hand. And leaned back and closed her eyes.

Not so fast. Eric placed his hands on either side of her face, leaned down and kissed her. A tender, comforting, sample of so much more to come. Storey opened her eyes to see that wonderful gaze staring down at her. She wanted him. In her life, in her heart, in her soul. He was the other half of her. She'd traveled through dimensions to find him, and he'd traveled back the same way to help her.

They were meant to be together, and nothing, not even this, would stop that.

He smiled. "Now get this done so we can go have a cup of tea with your mother."

Storey brightened. "Thank you," she whispered. Then she leaned her head back. *Stylus, let's do this.*

Eric held her one hand and Tammy held her other. She smiled inside. *Thanks, Tammy.*

Torrey. Her name was said with such caring, tears came to Storey's eyes. Eric squeezed her hand – he'd seen her tears and worried. She whispered, "I'm fine."

"Good. Make sure you stay that way. I want lots of years with you."

"So do I."

The stylus spoke. *We need you to leave now.*

She started. *Leave and go where?*

Leave your body so that you aren't tugged into the stylus when we move the Broken One.

Crap that sounded so bad. But she'd forgotten how to do that. Her arm pulsed. Right, the honor marks.

Just think of them.

Ah, okay. In her mind's eye, she traced the marks. Instantly she was outside her body. She turned around to stare at the others. Everyone's eyes were glued to the transfer process in progress. There was an effervescent glow around her body. She didn't know if it was her own energy or that of the Broken One – or a product of the transfer process.

She turned around slowly, taking her time to study the room. Anything to take her mind off what was happening to her body.

The councilman flashed onto the screen, fine lines at the corner of his mouth, a sense of desperation in his eyes. Storey didn't recognize the room he was in. But he held a codex in his hands. As she watched, he clipped the unit on his wrist. She didn't know why he'd have one, but vaguely remembered seeing him snatch something off Paxton's desk. Then with one last hurried look around, he punched the large button. Immediately the black mist started at his feet.

He smiled, satisfaction oozing from his pores. Damn the man was smug. She didn't know if she dared say anything while the transfer was happening, but the stylus could multi-task like no one else. She asked hesitantly, *Stylus?*

Yes.

She watched the smoke rise up the Councilman's face. It was too late to change anything now. *The Louers should be warned that they're about to have company.*

No. They aren't.

They aren't? I don't understand. The Councilman has a codex. He's travelling to one of the dimensions. He must be coming here.

Yes. He has taken one of Eric's codexes. Eric had spares when he came to rescue you In-between. Several were pre-coded to help him find you…just in case of trouble. On his return he gave them back to Paxton, putting them on the workbench. The Councilman slipped one into his pocket while he was looking at your message on the monitor.

She started. *I remember him seeing that message. Where are those preset coordinates going to take him?*

In-between.

She gasped in horror. Then in surprise. And finally at the justice of it all. *Oh my God. That is perfect.*

Dry humor lit the styluses' voice. *We thought so.*

She was still trying to grasp the truth of the Councilman's predicament when something shifted.

And then she was back in her body. She opened her eyes to see Eric's smiling face. She stretched up and kissed him.

Torrey! Tammy reached up and hugged her too.

Eric pulled back. "Are you okay?"

"Yes. I'm fine." And she was. In fact, she felt wonderful. "Stylus, how is the Broken One? Is he okay?"

When the answer didn't come immediately, she asked again. "Did he survive the transfer?" She frowned. Eric leaned closer. Tammy pulled back, her gaze flitting from Storey's face to Eric's. Then she tried to twist her features to match Eric's.

She had to laugh at their identical looks. Tammy was learning quickly.

"Is there still no answer?" Eric asked, his voice tense.

They waited in silence for several long minutes.

We are here.

"Yes." Storey gave a fist bump in the air. Just to confirm, she had to ask, "So the Broken One is fine now?"

He is. Now we are fine.

Perfect.

And it was.

ERIC WATCHED STOREY'S approach to her house. They'd left immediately after the transfer, the Louers giving her a rousing send off. Efforts to create a workable truce between Paxton and Tammy's father were in progress. The Louers were ecstatic that Storey had saved the Broken One. Apparently that, more than any promises made, had convinced them of her sincerity.

That and her new honor marks.

Eric knew they were for saving the stylus, who needed souls, and for saving Barrat, who needed a stylus. There might even be a few extra curls in there for having made peace with the Louers. He didn't know. Tammy had seen them. The other Louers had definitely seen them. They'd spoken amongst each other and pointed at her the whole time. Typical Storey, she'd been oblivious.

Now he wondered how long it would take her to realize the marks traveled up her neck and down her back. If she kept this up, she'd be covered from head to toe.

Considering she wore them so well, he wouldn't mind in the least.

She was such an honorable person. So not like his father. That his father had done himself in was something he couldn't quite get out of his mind.

It was fitting.

Eric didn't know if there was anything they could do to help him. At least at this point. Not that anyone seemed to care. He knew he didn't dare go back In-between to save him.

Storey turned back and motioned at him. "Aren't you coming?"

"I just thought you'd like to see for yourself, first." He smiled down at her.

She turned to stare at her house. "I do. But I'd like you there with me."

Nice. He'd helped her put on a sweater earlier, not wanting the honor marks to show – at least initially. She had enough to deal with without trying to explain the unexplainable right away.

He knew she'd do fine regardless of what they found in her dimension, but he hoped for her sake, her world was back the way it should be.

He held out his hand and together they approached the house they'd raided endless times. "It looks the same."

"Yes," she said, "It does. And that worries me."

"Front door or back?"

"Kitchen door."

They walked around to the back and stepped onto the porch. "I'm so glad to be back."

The door opened in front of them. Storey's mother smiled and opened her arms.

Storey ran into her mother's embrace.

At this point, Eric didn't think she cared which mother it was.

CHAPTER 27

"I WAS SO afraid you'd not have gotten my message." Her mother kissed Storey's cheek. "It was all so crazy with the festivities, the people I met – one in particular – and the wild weather. It seems like every time I managed to call home, you were out." Her mother shook her head and tugged Storey inside. "I'm so glad that's all over and we're back together again." Her mother glanced over at Eric. "How nice to see you again too, Eric." She motioned to the table. "Come. Sit down."

Storey cast a questioning look back at Eric. He shrugged. Storey sat down at the kitchen table. She glanced around. It looked wonderful. It looked like home.

"I'm so sorry. I wasn't supposed to be gone so long. The ceremony lasted all weekend, and…" she blushed, "I met someone there. And given who it was, I needed to stay and work through a few things. And of course with all that weird weather, and highways being closed, well… I stayed. Still, I hadn't expected to be gone so long." She leaned forward earnestly. "I did try to call several times, but the crazy weather had service out all around the country.

Weird weather? Closed highways? No phone service? Storey exchanged a long look with Eric, knowing it was most likely the time twists and portal tears that had caused all the damage. And then she remembered the festival. There'd been special festivities planned that weekend. She was stunned. Everything that had happened to her had taken only a couple of days, even though it seems like weeks or months. If she'd been here, she would hardly have seen her mother anyway.

"And who did you meet at the ceremonies?" Storey asked cautiously, still trying to figure out if her mother had been aware at all of her absence.

Her mother smiled, a little lopsided, a little insecure, but sweet. She glanced between Storey and Eric then back to Storey. She took a deep breath. "I didn't expect this. I'd never imagined…after all this time." She reached out and grabbed Storey's hand and sat down beside her. "I don't know how to tell you this, and with Eric here…but…well…I have to tell you." The words burst out in an excited, girlish torrent. "I met your father."

Storey jerked. Her gaze met Eric's. *Her father?* Her thoughts spun on the possibilities. Time twisting. Dimensions trying to reestablish balance…was this real…?

Her stylus spoke quietly in the back of her mind.

This is real. Balance returning for all.

"And…" she asked cautiously, shocked and yet, intrigued.

Her mother's excited voice bubbled over. "I know this is sudden. Maybe it's good that Eric is here. You can talk with him." She took a deep breath and barreled forward. "He would like to get to know you," her face pleaded for acceptance, "if you're open to the idea. We talked. About our past. The mess we'd made of our lives since. Our relationship. Like really talked. And…" she took another deep breath, as if not believing this herself, "We've started…well, you know…seeing each other."

Her mother sat back, a worried look on her face. "But he's concerned about how you'll feel."

STOREY SHUT DOWN for a moment. Shock was too mild a word to describe what she was feeling. Stupefied might be better. If that was a word. Yet, inside, with all that had happened, she had to wonder. She's been so torn over her father's presence in the other dimension, so confused over her own emotions, this just seemed too bizarre.

Maybe her parents were being offered a second chance.

That, she hadn't expected. When the dimensions shifted, she'd had a pang of regret for what could never be with her father. And now here was the opportunity again.

And this time, her father wanted back in *her* life?

Had she created this? And did it matter?

No and no.

She smiled at her stylus's answer. Eric's silent support made her want to laugh and cry at the same time. She wanted to rage at him and hug him. To laugh and scream a million questions. Yet none would form in her head.

"I don't know what to say." She tried to speak her words carefully, not wanting to upset her mother, but not knowing how she felt herself. She had to find a way forward. Somehow.

"Then don't say anything. We're going to take it slow," her mother promised. "This isn't about him or me. This is about us."

She smiled. "Now, how about a cup of tea."

Tea. Her mother's answer to everything. She watched her mother bustle about the kitchen, putting on the kettle. Probably to give Storey some time to process the huge bombshell she'd just dumped on her.

Eric took the chair her mother had been sitting in. She leaned closer and whispered, "I can't help but think this happened because of us."

"Or maybe we just made it happen faster." He tilted his head to look at her closer. "Is it so bad?"

She frowned, considering it. Then shrugged. "I don't know."

He turned slightly to look at her mother, then glanced back at Storey. "Your mother appears happy. Young almost."

That was true, and after all she'd been through, Storey knew how important happiness was. She studied the dreamy look in her mother's face and smiled.

Storey had found someone, so why shouldn't her mother find someone? And if that someone ended up being her father...maybe that *was* a good thing – for everyone.

It would certainly change things. But then, as she'd found, change could be good – very good.

Just then her mother, from deep inside the fridge, popped her head out and asked, "Storey, do you know what happened to the cheese?"

Storey gasped, looked over at Eric wide eyed and the two broke out laughing.

In fact, the world looked damn bright all over.

Author's Note

Thank you for reading Design Trilogy! If you enjoyed my book, I'd appreciate it if you'd leave a review.

Dear reader,

I love to hear from readers, and you can contact me at my website: www.dalemayer.com or at my Facebook author page. To be informed of new releases and special offers, sign up for my newsletter or follow me on BookBub. And if you are interested in joining Dale Mayer's Reader Group, here is the Facebook sign up page. http://geni.us/DaleMayerFBGroup

Cheers,
Dale Mayer

Gem Stone (A Gemma Stone Mystery)

A juvie kid trying to stay on the right path stumbles into trouble…

Gemma takes her camera everywhere. From juvie hall to a halfway home, the new hobby gives her a focus she'd never had before and… hope in a future. Until she takes pictures of something that could get her killed.

And not just her…after she and another juvie girl are chased by a stranger to the halfway home that same night, the other girl goes missing and Gemma knows she needs help. But who can she trust?

Not the authorities that's for sure. Trusting them is impossible for a girl with her damaged history, and besides, who cares about a troubled kid…especially when trouble just naturally seems to find her.

In Cassie's Corner

Faith and loyalty are tested as a young girl learns what it is to believe – in herself, in her friends, and in life after death.

Cassie's best friend, bad boy Todd, is gone. Gone as in dead. Gone as in he's now a ghost.

But she doesn't realize that when he wakes her in her bedroom and begs her not to believe what they say about him. It's not until the next day when her parents tell her about the accident that she learns the truth…

The police believe Todd was living up to the family name, drinking and driving and coming to a predictable end. It's up to her to find out the truth and clear his name.

Todd is shocked at his sudden change in circumstances…and angry. He struggles with his new ghostly reality, realizing all he's lost as he watches his brother build a relationship with Cassie as the two pair up to find out what really happened to him.

The truth isn't always pretty, and Cassie has to be stronger than ever before. Especially when the whole world seems to be against her.

About the Author

Dale Mayer is a *USA Today* best-selling author, best known for her SEALs military romances, her Psychic Visions series, and her Lovely Lethal Garden cozy series. Her contemporary romances are raw and full of passion and emotion (Broken But ... Mending, Hathaway House series). Her thrillers will keep you guessing (Kate Morgan, By Death series), and her romantic comedies will keep you giggling (*It's a Dog's Life*, a stand-alone novella; and the Broken Protocols series, starring Charming Marvin, the cat).

Dale honors the stories that come to her—and some of them are crazy, break all the rules and cross multiple genres!

To go with her fiction, she also writes nonfiction in many different fields, with books available on résumé writing, companion gardening, and the US mortgage system. All her books are available in print and ebook format.

Connect with Dale Mayer Online

Dale's Website – www.dalemayer.com
Twitter – @DaleMayer
Facebook Page – geni.us/DaleMayerFBFanPage
Facebook Group – geni.us/DaleMayerFBGroup
BookBub – geni.us/DaleMayerBookbub
Instagram – geni.us/DaleMayerInstagram
Goodreads – geni.us/DaleMayerGoodreads
Newsletter – geni.us/DaleNews

Also by Dale Mayer

Published Adult Books:

Psychic Vision Series

Tuesday's Child

Hide'n Go Seek

Maddy's Floor

Garden of Sorrow

Knock, Knock…

Rare Find

Eyes to the Soul

Now You See Her

Psychic Visions 3in1

By Death Series

Touched by Death – Part 1

Touched by Death – Part 2

Touched by Death – Parts 1&2

Haunted by Death

Chilled by Death

Second Chances…at Love Series

Second Chances – Part 1

Second Chances – Part 2

Second Chances – complete book (Parts 1 & 2)

Charmin Marvin Romantic Comedy Series

Broken Protocols

Broken Protocols 2

Broken Protocols 3

Broken Protocols 3.5

Broken Protocols 1-3

Broken and... Mending

Skin

Scars

Scales (of Justice)

Glory

Genesis

Tori

Celeste

Biker Blues

Biker Blues: Morgan, Part 1

Biker Blues: Morgan, Part 2

Biker Blues: Morgan, Part 3

Biker Baby Blues: Morgan, Part 4

Biker Blues: Morgan, Full Set

Biker Blues: Salvation, Part 1

Biker Blues: Salvation, Part 2

Biker Blues: Salvation, Part 3

SEALs of Honor

Mason: SEALs of Honor, Book 1

Hawk: SEALs of Honor, Book 2

Dane: SEALs of Honor, Book 3

Swede: SEALs of Honor, Book 4
Shadow: SEALs of Honor, Book 5
Cooper: SEALs of Honor, Book 6
SEALs of Honor, Books 1–3

Collections

Dare to Be You…
Dare to Love…
Dare to be Strong…
RomanceX3

Standalone Novellas

It's a Dog's Life
Riana's Revenge

Published Young Adult Books:

Family Blood Ties Series

Vampire in Denial
Vampire in Distress
Vampire in Design
Vampire in Deceit
Vampire in Defiance
Vampire in Conflict
Vampire in Chaos
Vampire in Crisis
Vampire in Control
Family Blood Ties 3in1
Family Blood Ties set 4–6
Sian's Solution – A Family Blood Ties Short Story

Design series

Dangerous Designs

Deadly Designs

Darkest Designs

Design Series Trilogy

Standalone

In Cassie's Corner

Gem Stone (a Gemma Stone Mystery)

Time Thieves

Published Non-Fiction Books:

Career Essentials

Career Essentials: The Résumé

Career Essentials: The Cover Letter

Career Essentials: The Interview

Career Essentials: 3 in 1